PÉREZ GALDÓS

MIAU

TRANSLATED WITH AN INTRODUCTION BY

J. M. COHEN

PENGUIN BOOKS

BALTIMORE · MARYLAND

Penguin Books Ltd, Harmondsworth, Middlesex, England
Penguin Books Inc., 3300 Clipper Mill Road, Baltimore 11, Md, U.S.A.
Penguin Books Pty Ltd, Ringwood, Victoria, Australia

—

First published by Methuen 1963
Published in Penguin Books 1966
Copyright © Methuen & Co. Ltd, 1963

—

Made and printed in Great Britain by
Hazell Watson & Viney Ltd
Aylesbury, Bucks
Set in Linotype Pilgrim

INTRODUCTION

THE reputation of Benito Pérez Galdós (1843–1920) stands high in all Spanish-speaking countries, where he is considered the greatest novelist in the language since Cervantes. Abroad, he has been little translated; the great French and Russian novelists of the nineteenth century have crowded him out. But such of his novels as have appeared in English or German have been both praised and read. He is clearly a major figure, even by European standards. For he is one of those rare writers who bring to life a whole world, that of fashionable and shabby-genteel Madrid between the late sixties and early eighties of last century. Galdós' Madrid moreover still survives in the side-streets to this day.

Miau is the story of a *cesante*, a respectable and unoriginal civil-servant who has lost his post on the fall of one government, and expects reinstatement from the next. Señor de Villaamil is a very ordinary old gentleman, saddled with a pack of worthless womenfolk – the *miaus* or pussy-faces of the title – and within a few months of his retiring pension. But circumstances make him into a tragic figure since, though he seems merely the victim of an antiquated system, his troubles arise largely from his own stupidity. All his efforts to wield his non-existent influence not only rob him of his natural dignity but sap his self-respect, which has already been sufficiently damaged by his pretentious family. The old man's one joy in life is his grandson Luisito, whom we meet on his way home from school as the book opens, and who in the end brings him to destruction. The boy's conversations with God, during the black-outs from which he suffers, form a touching and ironic commentary on the action.

Pérez Galdós has frequently been compared to Balzac; and in his social interests he certainly follows the creator of the *Comédie humaine*. Like Balzac he takes a meticulous interest in his urban setting. We know how his characters earn their

5

livings; we know their ambitions and snobberies, the more luxurious life to which they hope to rise, the greater parsimony to which they fear they may descend. We know the streets and shops they frequented, the churches into which they slipped for a moment's prayer, the courtyards they crossed to visit a neighbour. Anyone who knows contemporary Madrid has only to allow for the widening of the Plaza de San Marcial to form the Plaza de España, and the driving through of the Gran Vía, to find his way about Galdós' city, which has of course also been extended by the building of vast new suburbs to the north, where Señor de Villaamil in his last walk saw only vacant lots.

Galdós is, like Balzac, a social novelist; and like Balzac he invents major characters who transcend the urban and particular. But whereas Balzac's creations are monstrous and romantic, his women models of purity or deceit, his men either conquerors or pathetic victims, Galdós' are more carefully observed; their qualities are more faithfully blended. Yet they too, and increasingly in the later novels, become larger than life and their surroundings. For Galdós was greatly interested in psychological abnormality, particularly when it took religious forms. On the whole agnostic in viewpoint, he was nevertheless much concerned with ideas of sanctity and possession. Luisito's visions may be explained as entirely pathological but such later creations as Nazarín, the priest who consorted like his master with whores and beggars, suggest a Dostoyevskian belief in madness as a path to divine inspiration.

In the twenty Novelas españolas contemporáneos of which Miau (1888) is one, many of the characters appear several times. Torquemada, the money-lender, is the central figure of three short novels in the series; and the same Señor de Pez who is so unobliging to Villaamil failed to extricate Rosalía de Bringas from her financial troubles in La de Bringas (1884) (translated as The Spendthrifts). She and her circle belong to the hangers-on of the palace; the characters in Miau, standing one step lower, depend on the Ministries; while the scene of the later novels descends to the world of lodging-houses for beggars and outcasts. Galdós knows his way about all these places. He knows the Ministries as Dickens knew his Circumlocution Office : the gossip of the clerks, the backbiting of the senior officials, the grumbling of the door-keepers. Quickly, one is as familiar with these corridors and staircases of patronage as Villaamil himself.

Galdós was a universal observer, who devoted almost the whole of his long life to writing. He understood women because he had known and kept so many of all classes, but he did not marry. He frequented cafés, where the men met and talked and did their business, but himself engaged in no business. He studied law as a young man, did a little journalism, but after his first publication, at the age of 27, devoted his remaining fifty years to his huge cycle of historical novels, the forty-six volumes of the *Episodios nacionales* (1873–1912), to the novels of contemporary life, and to the theatre, in which he was unsuccessful. His masterpieces, in addition to *Miau*, are *The Spendthrifts*, already mentioned, and its forerunner, *Torment* (1884), the story of a girl unable to escape from a relationship with a dissolute priest. This can be compared with *The Sin of Father Amaro*, a novel on the same subject by Galdós' Portuguese contemporary Eça de Queiroz. Only these three novels have so far been translated. *Fortunata y Jacinta* (1886–7), another masterpiece, in four volumes, still awaits a translator. A superb panorama, whose central character is a weakling pulled in either direction by a childless wife and a full-blooded proletarian mistress, it covers in its subsidiary characters the whole of Galdós' social world. In addition the later novels *Nazarín* (1895) and *Misericordia* (1897) concentrate rather on psychological abnormality and the underworld of morbid religion.

Galdós' speculative secularism has led him into disfavour in Franco's Spain, where cheap editions of his contemporary novels, to be found in every bookshop in Spanish America, are not on sale. Leather-bound collected editions are however available. Thus the well-to-do can read what the régime seems to consider might be harmful to the faith or morals of the young and poor. Such is the power of a great writer, almost fifty years after his death.

J.M.C.

1

AT four in the afternoon the boys of the parish school in the Plazuela del Limón rushed wildly out of class, kicking up the most devilish din. No hymn to freedom composed on earth can compare with that of the slaves of elementary education when they throw off the fetters of school discipline and rush on to the streets, leaping and shouting in their excitement. The wild fury with which they attempt the most perilous acrobatics, the minor injuries they cause to peaceful passers-by, their delirious assertion of personal freedom, which often ends in blows, tears and bruises, are like preliminary rehearsals for those revolutionary triumphs that take place, perforce, in less fortunate epochs. They rushed out, as I have said, in a mob; the last tried to catch up with the first, and the small shouted louder than the big. Among them was a middling-sized boy, who separated himself from the crowd and very quietly started to walk home alone. But when his schoolfellows noticed this boy's departure, which was more like a flight, they pursued him with jokes and unpleasant ribaldry. One of them caught his arm, another rubbed his cheeks with 'innocent' hands that were perfect representations of all the nastiness in the world. But he managed to break free and took to his heels. Then two or three of the most shameless threw stones after him and shouted 'Miau!'; and soon the infernal screeching was taken up by all the rest: 'Miau, Miau, Miau!'

The unfortunate butt of his schoolfellows' mockery was called Luis Cadalso. He was shortish, timid and pale, and looked like eight though he might have been ten. So timid was he that he avoided his classmates' company, being afraid of the jokes that some of them played since he had not the courage to pay them back. He was the least venturesome in mischief, the dullest and slowest in a game, and the best-behaved boy in the class, though he seldom distinguished himself, perhaps because his shyness prevented him from saying what he knew or concealing what he did not. As he turned the corner of the Plaza de las Comendadoras de Santiago on his way home to the Calle de Quiñones – the house faced the women's prison – he was joined by one of his schoolfellows, heavily loaded with books. He had his slate on his back, his trousers bagged at the knees, his shoes were in holes, and a blue beret covered his thin hair. In face he was very like a mouse. His name was Silvestre Murillo, and he was the most hard-working boy in the school, also Cadalso's best friend. His father, the sacristan of the Montserrat church, intended him for the law. For he had got it into his head that the little sniveller was going to be 'somebody' one day, perhaps a famous speaker – and why not a minister of the crown? The future celebrity addressed his companion as follows: 'I say, Ca'arso, I'd give them a good punch on the head, I would, if they played those tricks on me. But you haven't got the pluck. They've got no right to call names after people, that's what I say. And do you know who started it? The Performer did, the one from the pawnshop. He was telling us yesterday how his mum said they call your aunts and your granny the Miaus, because that's what they look like. I mean because they've got faces like cats. He said that's the name they gave them in the gallery at the Real. He said they always sit in the same seats, and when the people in the audience see them come in, they always say, "Here come the Miaus".'

Luis Cadalso went deep red. Indignation, shame and astonishment combined to prevent him from defending his family's outraged dignity.

'The Performer's a cad,' added Silvestre. 'He's common, and his aunts are common. They live by bloodsucking the poor. And I'll tell you something, when a man doesn't redeem his coat then they leave him bare. I mean they sell his coat and leave him to die of cold. My mum calls them the harpies. Haven't you seen them out on their balcony, giving the coats an airing? They're as ugly as sin, and my dad says you could use their long noses as wood to make table-legs, and then you'd have some over. The Performer's like a monkey too, always showing off and behaving like a clown at a circus. It's because he's got a nickname himself. That's why he's trying to get his own back and give you one too. But he couldn't do that to me, blowed if he could! He knows I've got a bad temper, a very bad temper! But you don't matter. I mean you don't get nasty when they shout nasty things after you. So they don't have any respect for you, of course.'

Cadalso stopped at the door of his house, and looked at his friend sadly. Silvestre gave him a jab with his elbow and went on: 'I don't call you Miau, blowed if I do. No need to be afraid I shall call you Miau'; and he ran off in the direction of the Montserrat.

In the porter's lodge of the house where Cadalso lived there was a public scribe's office. A screen or frame thickly covered with papers marbled in various colours and veinings hid the way into the writing-office or agency where affairs of great moment were hourly transacted. The different sorts of trans-actions were inscribed on a handwritten notice which hung in the entrance to the house. It took the form of a list which ran as follows:

Marriages	Banns cheaply and promptly drawn up and presented at any vicarage
Maids	introduced
Waiters	provided
Cooks	procured
Accordeon Teacher	recommended
Note	An office is especially reserved for ladies.

Young Cadalso was just passing the screen, deep in thought, when a voice called from the office behind: 'Luis, you little silly! Here I am.'

The boy went across to be caught in the arms of a very stout woman who came out from behind the screen and gave him a kiss.

'What a simpleton you are! Going by without calling me. I've got your snack for you here. Mendizábal has gone out on business. I'm alone here, looking after the office in case anybody comes. Won't you keep me company?'

Señora Mendizábal was so stout that when she was in the office it was as if a cow had come in, put its haunches on the bench, and occupied all the rest of the space with the abounding flesh of its fore-quarters. Having no children herself, she spoilt all the children in the neighbourhood, especially young Luis, whom she pitied and cosseted because he was so sweet and meek, and also, as she said, because he was always hungry at home. Every day she had some tit-bit ready to give him when he got back from school. Today's was what they call an angel-cake. It stood on the sand-caster, and quite a few grains of sand were sticking to its sugary crust. But young Cadalso was not put off. He bit into it greedily. 'Now go up,' said the wife of the porter and public scribe as he devoured the cake with its dusting of drying sand. 'Go up now, my pet, or your granny'll scold you. Leave your books up there, and come and keep me company, and play with Canelo.'

The boy hurried upstairs; and the door was opened for him by a lady whose face might have occasioned disputes of the sort that rage among numismatists concerning the age of certain coins the inscriptions of which have been rubbed away. Seen in profile and in a certain light, she might have been taken for sixty. But under other conditions even a skilled observer might have put her at no more than forty-eight or fifty – and well preserved at that.

She had small and delicate features, a sort of baby-face, as they say. Her complexion was still pink, and her hair ash-blonde – its colour suggested some alchemy – with the locks around her forehead extravagantly puffed out. Twenty or so years before the time we are speaking of, a journalist, covering the movement of wheat prices and also society gossip, announced this lady's appearance in the drawing-room of the governor of a third-class province in this way : 'Who is this figure out of a Fra Angelico painting, who comes enveloped in filmy clouds and crowned with a golden halo drawn from the iconography of the XIV century?' The filmy clouds were the pretty gauze dress which Señora de Villaamil had recently ordered in Madrid, and the golden halo – believe it or not – was her frizzed hair, which must then have been really fair and quotable at par with the gold of Arabia.

Twenty or twenty-five years after her fashionable success in that provincial city, which there is no point in naming, Doña

Pura – for this was the lady's name – as she opened the door for her little grandson, was wearing a not too clean dressing-jacket over a loose morning gown of green tartan material, and felt slippers that were none too new.

'Oh, it's you, Luis,' she said. 'I thought it was Ponce with the tickets for the Real. He promised to come at two. What manners the young people have today!'

At this point there appeared another lady, very like the first. She too was short, her features were childish also, and her age was equally doubtful. She wore a jacket that had come down in the world, having begun as a man's overcoat, and a long crash apron of the kind worn in every kitchen. She was Doña Pura's sister, and her name was Milagros. In the dining-room, where Luis went to leave his books, a girl was sewing; she sat very close to the window in order to catch the last daylight, for in February the day is short. Except for the difference in age, she was rather like the other two women. This was Abelarda, Doña Pura's daughter, and young Luis Cadalso's aunt. His own mother, Luisa Villaamil, had died when he was a child of two. Of his father, Victor Cadalso, we shall speak later.

Now that the three were together, they discussed the unheard-of situation, that Ponce – who was Abelarda's fiancé and presented the family with tickets for the Teatro Real – had not yet appeared at half-past four in the afternoon, although he usually brought the tickets at two.

'With all this uncertainty, not knowing whether we're going to the theatre or not,' said Doña Pura with marked disdain for her daughter's fiancé, 'we can't decide about anything, or make any plans for tonight. What a dawdler the man is!'

'It's still not late, Mamma,' answered her daughter. 'There's plenty of time. He'll bring the tickets all right, you'll see.'

'Yes, but for a performance like tonight's, when tickets are so short that you have to use influence to get hold of them, it's really very unkind to keep us in this suspense.'

As young Luis looked from his grandmother to his great-aunt, and then to his aunt, comparing their features to those of the cat which was there in the dining-room, sleeping at Abelarda's feet, he found them all exactly alike. His lively imagination then

13

promptly suggested to him that the three women were really cats on legs dressed up as people, like those described in the book *The Animals tell their own Stories*, and this illusion made him wonder whether he wasn't a cat as well, and whether he wouldn't miau when he talked. From here he rapidly went on to observe that the nickname they had given his grandmother and aunt in the gallery of the Real was quite right and suited them exactly. All this arose in his mind quicker than words, in a succession of bright and wavering flashes characteristic of a young brain that is beginning to learn how to observe and reason. He pursued his feline theories no further. For his grandmother put her hand to her head and said: 'But hasn't Paca given you your snack today?'

'Yes, Grandma. I've just eaten it. She told me to come up and leave my books and then go down again and play with Canelo.'

'Very well, darling. Run down quickly then, and stay there as long as you like. I've just thought of something though. You'll have to come up again quite soon because your grandfather wants you to run an errand.'

Just as the old lady was seeing the boy out through the door a deep and sepulchral voice called from a room near the entrance to the apartment: 'Pu-ura! Pu-ura!'

She opened a door on the left of the entrance and entered the so-called office, which was little more than nine foot square and had a window that gave on to a dark courtyard. As the daylight was now dim, scarcely anything could be seen inside the office except the white square of the window. Against it stood out a long lean shape that seemed to be unfolding itself as it got out of its chair. While it was stretching its limbs its frightening and muffled voice complained: 'Didn't it ever occur to you, Pura, that you might bring me the lamp? You knew that I was writing, and that it gets dark in no time. But still you leave me here ruining my eyes over these confounded papers.'

Doña Pura went to the dining-room where her sister was just lighting an oil-lamp, and returned quickly to her husband, bearing the lamp in her hand. The small room and its occupant emerged from the darkness, like something that arises newly created out of nothingness.

'I'm frozen to death,' said Doña Pura's husband, Don Ramón Villaamil, a tall lean man with large frightening eyes and a sallow skin, furrowed all over with deep wrinkles in which the lines of shadow were like stains. His ears were large, transparent and close to his head. His beard with short, thin and bristly, and peppered at random with white hairs, which made snowy streaks among the black. His smooth skull, which was the colour of disinterred bones, might have been picked up in a charnel-house as a covering for his brains. The strength of his jaw, the width of his mouth, the black, white and yellow stripes of his cheeks, and the fierce look of his dark eyes suggested a comparison between his face and that of an old, consumptive tiger, which has once been the chief draw in a travelling fair but now preserves nothing of its former beauty except its bright skin.

'Tell me, who have you written to?' asked the lady, turning down the wick, for a smoking flame was leaping out of the tube.

'To the Chief of Personnel, to Señor de Pez, to Sánchez Botín, and everyone else who might be able to extricate me from my present situation. But to settle our immediate predicament' (heaving a deep sigh) 'I've decided to trouble friend Cucúrbitas once more. He is the only true Christian among all my friends. He's a true gentleman, a splendid man who cares for other people's troubles. How different from the rest! You know the treatment I got yesterday from that wretch Rubín. I described our situation, begged and entreated him till I was red with shame. Nothing. A small loan and God knows the gall I had to swallow while he was making up his mind, and the humiliation. Then that thankless wretch, that ungrateful scoundrel, who was a clerk in my office when I was Financial Inspector, fourth class, that shameless rogue who by sheer audacity has got himself promoted over my head, and become no less than a governor, that man has the indelicacy to hand me two and a half pesetas.'

As Villaamil sat down he thumped the table so hard that all the letters bounced up as if to escape in terror. On hearing his wife sigh, he raised his sallow brow and proceeded in a painful voice: 'There's nothing left in the world but selfishness and ingratitude. The more knavery you see, the more there is to discover. Take that great clodhopper Montes, for example, who owes his career to me, because I proposed his promotion in the Central Auditry. Do you know he doesn't even greet me in the street? He gives himself such airs that not even the Minister . . . And he's going ahead all the time. They've just raised him to fourteen thousand. He gets a rise every year. Nothing stops him. That's what you gain by flattering and crawling. He doesn't understand the least thing about administration. All he can do is talk about shooting with the Director, and about dogs and birds and goodness knows what else. His handwriting's no better than a dog's. He spells "hatchet" without an h and "able" with one. But let's forget all these miseries. I've decided to approach friend Cucúrbitas again, as I told you. It's true that he's responded four or five times already, but now I simply don't know which blessed way to turn. Cucúrbitas understands what trouble is, and he has pity on it because he's been in trouble himself. I've known him with holes in his trousers, and two inches of dirt on his hat. He knows that I'm grateful. Do you think that I've exhausted his kindness? God have mercy on us, for if this friend deserts us we might as well all throw ourselves over the Viaduct.'

Villaamil heaved a deep sigh and fixed his glance on the ceiling. The sickly tiger became transformed. He assumed the sublime expression of an apostle at the moment when he is martyred for his faith; a little like Ribera's Saint Bartholomew when he has been tied to a tree, and those heathen ruffians are skinning him like a goat. Be it remarked that this was the man who had been nicknamed Rameses II by the 'regulars' of certain cafés.

'Very well. Give me the letter for Cucúrbitas,' said Doña Pura, who, being accustomed to these tales of woe, took them in the natural course of things. 'The boy will run and take it. And trust in Providence, man, as I do. You mustn't lose heart.' (She gave an optimistic smile.) 'I've had a presentiment. And you know I'm not often wrong. I've had a presentiment that you'll be back in the service before the end of the month.'

2

'BACK in the service!' exclaimed Villaamil, putting his whole
soul into the phrase. After waving his hands for a second above
his head, he dropped them heavily on the arms of the chair. But
by that time Doña Pura was no longer in the room. She had
gone out with the letter to call downstairs to her grandson, who
was in the porter's lodge.

It was almost six when Luis departed on his errand, having
dropped into the scribe's office for a further brief stay.

'Good-bye, my darling,' said Paca, giving him a kiss. 'Run
quickly and then you'll be back by dinner time;' (reading the
envelope) 'I say, it's quite a long stretch from here to the Calle
del Amor de Dios. Do you know the way all right? You won't
get lost, will you?'

How on earth could he get lost, seeing that he had been more
than twenty times to Señor Cucúrbitas and to the houses of
various other gentlemen with verbal or written messages! It was
he who carried the news of his grandfather's terrible necessities,
depressions and agitations; it was he who bore to one district
and another the petitions of this poor unemployed official,*
asking for a recommendation or assistance. In this pedestrian
employment he had gained such complete topographical knowledge that he could cover every suburb of the city without
getting lost. But although he knew the shortest way to his des-
tination, he invariably took the longest, because he was by vice
or custom a stroller, or by instinct an observer. He loved to look
at shop-windows and to listen without missing a syllable to the
patter of patent-medicine sellers or conjurers. He might meet a
monkey riding a dog or turning the handle of a chocolate
grinder, exactly like a human being; or sometimes it was a poor
thin bear on a chain, or men dressed up as Italians or Turks or

---

* *Cesante.* He has in fact been suspended on the resignation of a
government, and is awaiting reappointment by the next administration.

17

Moors who did tricks and begged for money. Grand funerals also pleased him, and the watering of the streets, and soldiers marching with a band, and the sight of stone blocks being hoisted on to a building in construction, and the Viaticum followed by many candles, and the extra horses waiting to haul the trams, and the planting of trees, and any other happening that could be watched in the public streets.

'Keep yourself wrapped up,' said Paca, kissing him again and twisting the muffler round his neck. 'They might have bought you some woollen gloves. Your hands are ice-cold and covered with chilblains. You'd be a lot better off with your Aunt Quintina! Give Mendizábal a kiss, and off you go. Canelo will go with you.'

From beneath the table emerged a biscuit-coloured dog with a fine head, short legs and a curly tail, who leapt joyfully ahead of Luis. Paca followed them out of the door and watched them depart. Then she returned to the little office, and said to her husband as she picked up her knitting: 'Poor child! All the blessed day they're sending him out on these postman's errands. It's the same man again tonight, the one they've been sponging on every day lately. What that good fellow has to put up with! These Villaamils are a real blight, and worse than that. And tonight, let me tell you, those three fine ladies will be gadding off to the theatre as usual and coming back at any old hour.'

'There's no Christian virtue in families nowadays,' said Mendizábal gravely and sententiously. 'Everything's just pretentiousness.'

'And they're up to the neck in debts' (waggling her needles furiously). 'The butcher says he'll be hanged if he gives them any more credit. The fruiterer has cut them off and so has the baker. If those dressed-up dummies could just pull themselves together and make do on a dish of potatoes when they can get one. But God forbid! Potatoes for them, poor dears! The day they get a penny, even out of charity, off they go leading the grand life and spending what they haven't got. Yes, and they furbish up their clothes so as to look like the height of fashion. Doña Pura has spent the whole blessed morning crimping her kiss-curls, and Doña Milagros has been turning the material of that ancient dress that's the colour of a mustard-plaster. And that hateful girl of theirs isn't satisfied with just mending her hat. She has to trim it up with old ribbons, or a hen's feather, or one of those gilt-headed nails they hang pictures with.'

'All pretentiousness. The unhappy consequences of materialism,' said Mendizábal, who was in the habit of repeating phrases from the newspaper to which he subscribed. 'There's no modesty today, no simplicity of living. What's become of the honest poverty of our fathers, of that' (failing to remember the rest) . . . 'of that, well . . . I mean to say . . .?'

'Now when poor Don Ramón closes his eyes, poor man, he'll go straight to heaven. He's a saint and a martyr. Believe me, if I could get him a post, I certainly would do so. The way he looks at you, you'd think he was going to eat you, poor man! And he might eat somebody too, one day, not out of wickedness but from pure hunger' (sticking her fourth needle in her hair). 'It frightens you to look at him. I don't know why the Minister isn't scared to death when he sees him come into the office. I don't know why he doesn't give him a post so as to get him out of his sight.'

'Villaamil,' said Mendizábal with conviction, 'is an honourable man, and today the government's full of rogues. Today there's no honour, no religion and no justice. And what is there instead? Thieving, unbelief, shamelessness. That's why they don't give him a post, and they won't until the one man comes in who will bring justice. I tell him this every time he goes by and stops at the door to have a chat. "There's nothing you can do about it, Don Ramón," I say, "There's nothing you can do about it. It's this freedom of worship that's to blame. For so long as we've got rationalism, Don Ramón, for so long as we haven't scotched the head of the serpent, sir, and" (losing the thread of his sentence and not knowing what he was going to say) . . . "and until the time comes when . . . stands to reason . . . I mean to say . . " (cutting the matter short). "There's no Christianity today!"' '

Meanwhile young Luis and Canelo walked down part of the Calle Ancha and turned into the Calle del Pez, in pursuit of their itinerary. When the dog got too far ahead, he would stop

19

and look back, with his tongue hanging out. Luis paused to inspect the shop-windows, and from time to time would make some such remark to his companion as: 'Look, Canelo, what lovely trumpets!' The animal would then get on his hind legs and lean his fore-paws on the frame of the window. But these trumpets could not have interested him much, because very soon he would be on his way again. Finally they reached the Calle del Amor de Dios. Ever since a certain occasion on which Canelo had exchanged barks with another dog who inhabited Cucúrbitas' house, he had adopted the prudent course of not coming up, but waiting for his friend in the street. Young Luis climbed to the second floor, on which his grandfather's unfailing protector lived. The manservant who opened the door made him a very ugly face that night. 'The master isn't at home.' But, having been prepared by his grandfather for the eventuality that his victim might be out, young Luis said that he would wait. He knew that Don Francisco Cucúrbitas would come into supper at seven o'clock without fail. The boy sat down on the hall bench. His feet did not reach the floor, and he swung them, as if to relieve the boredom of his long spell of guard duty. In the past he had greatly admired the hall-stand, which was made of pine polished to look like antique oak, and had gilt hooks for hats, a mirror, and holes for umbrellas. But today it left him unmoved. He was more concerned with the cat, which generally came out from the interior of the apartment to have a game with him. But that night puss must have been busy, for he did not appear in the hall. But instead Luis saw Cucúrbitas' young daughters, who were pretty and attractive. Generally they would come up to him with pitying or scornful looks, but they had never thrown him a pleasant word. Señora Cucúrbitas, who was so round and fat that she seemed to Luis a human imitation of the elephant Pizarro – much beloved at that time by Madrid children – came down the passage on the right, and from the point where it led into the hall viewed the messenger suspiciously. She then turned back without a word. When the boy heard her coming, he jumped up stiffly like a jack-in-the-box, remembering the lessons in good manners his grandfather had given him. 'How are you? I hope you are well.' But that corpulent mass, only comparable for bulk with Paca the scribe's wife, did not deign to answer him but departed, making the floor tremble like the steamroller that Luis had seen in the Madrid streets.

The excellent Cucúrbitas came in very late to dinner that night. Villaamil's grandson noticed that the girls were impatient. This was because they were going to the theatre and wanted to eat punctually. Finally the door-bell rang, and the manservant hastened to open the door, while the girls, who knew their papa's step and his way of ringing, ran down the passage to call out that dinner could be served. When the master came in and saw Luis he expressed his displeasure by a slight grimace. The boy got up, firing his 'good evening' like a shot point-blank, and Cucúrbitas shut himself in his study without answering him. As he waited for the master to invite him in as on previous occasions, the boy saw the daughters go in to hurry their father, and heard him say : 'Just coming. Tell them to bring in the soup,' and he could not help thinking how rich that soup must be that was just going to be served. Such were his thoughts when one of the young ladies emerged from the study and said : 'Go in, you.' As he entered, cap in hand, Luis repeated his 'good evening', which Don Francisco finally deigned to answer in a paternal voice. He was a very good man, so Luis thought; and having failed to understand the slightly grim expression on the shining face of the provident official, he expected him to do the same thing that night that he had done before. Luis remembered very well the way it went. Having read Villaamil's letter, Señor Cucúrbitas would either write one in reply, or without writing would take from his wallet a small green or red note, put it in an envelope and say as he handed it to him : 'Off you go, son. Your errand is done.' Alternatively, he was liable to take some pesetas out of his pocket, wrap them in paper, and hand them to the boy, still with the same words, but adding in this case : 'Be careful you don't lose this or let anybody snatch it. Put it in your trouser pocket. Like that. Clever boy, God bless you.'

That night, alas, standing in front of the great man's desk, Luis watched Don Francisco penning with thick and knitted brow a letter which he sealed without enclosing either a bank-note or coins. The boy observed also that as that excellent person signed the letter he heaved a deep sigh and afterwards gave him a look of the most profound compassion.

'Good night, sir,' said young Cadalso on taking the letter, and the good man laid a hand on his head. As he wished him good-bye, he gave him two ten-céntimo pieces and supplemented his generous action with these great-hearted words: 'Buy some cakes with these.' The boy departed, full of gratitude. But on the way downstairs a sad thought struck him: Today there's noth-ing in the letter. It was, in fact, the first time he had left that apartment with an empty envelope. It was the first time that Don Francisco had given him a tip for his private pocket, and to foster his addiction to angel-cakes. The boy realized all this with a discernment gained by his precocious experience of these errands. But who knows, he afterwards reflected, following an idea that arose in his innocent mind, he may be telling him that they're going to give him a post tomorrow.

Canelo, who was waiting impatiently, joined him at the door and they started back together. In a cake shop in the Calle de las Huertas Luis bought two ten-céntimo angel-cakes. The dog ate one and the boy the other. Then, licking their lips, they hurried on, seeking the shortest way through the labyrinth of streets and squares, some well and some ill lit, some full of people and some deserted. Here there were many gas-lamps, there darkness. Here many people, and there solitude with a few wandering figures. They went down streets which could scarcely contain the surging crowd; and others in which they saw more women than lights; and yet others in which there were more dogs than people.

3

WHEN they came to the Calle de la Puebla young Luis was so tired that he sat down to recover his strength on the step of one of the three grilled doors of the convent of Don Juan de Alarcón, which is in this street. And the moment he sat down on the cold stone, he fell into a deep sleep. It was really more like one of the fainting attacks, with which the boy was not unacquainted, but which never came on him without his first feeling its strange precursory symptoms. Gracious, he thought in great surprise, it's one of those things coming on. It's coming on. It's coming. . . . In fact from time to time a very strange disorder did 'come on' young Cadalso. It began with a heavy head, a sleepy feeling and shivers down the spine, and ended with a total loss of sensation and consciousness. That night, in the brief interval between the moment that he felt himself fainting and that in which his senses were blotted out he remembered a poor man who used to beg for alms on that same step on which he was sitting. He was very old and blind, with a long yellowish-white beard, and was swathed in a patched and filthy brown cloak that fell in long folds. His head was white and bare, and he held out his hat, begging only by gesture and never moving his lips. The venerable figure of this beggar aroused Luis' respect, and he would throw a céntimo into his hat when he had one to spare, which was very seldom.

Now when, as I was saying, the boy fell into this stupor, with his head bowed on his chest, he found that he was not alone. A grown-up person was sitting beside him. Was it the blind man? For an instant Luis believed it was, because he had a thick white beard and his body was wrapped in a mantle or cloak. Then the boy began to notice the differences and similarities between the poor man and this grown-up person. For the person looked and could see, and his eyes were like stars. His nose, eyes and forehead, on the other hand, were exactly like the beggar's, and his beard was just as large but whiter, a great deal whiter. Then the cloak was the same and yet different; the wide folds were the same, and so was the way he was wrapped in it; but the colour was different and the boy could not give it a name. Was it white, or blue, or what the devil was its colour? It had very soft shadows in which there were luminous reflections like the light that filters through the rifts in clouds. Luis thought he had never seen a material so pretty. From out of the folds the person extended a white hand which was very lovely. Luis had never seen a hand like that. It was strong, and muscular like a man's, and

23

fine like a lady's. The person gazed at him with fatherly affection and said: 'Don't you know me? Don't you know who I am?'

Young Luis looked hard at him. Shyness prevented him from answering. Then the mysterious gentleman, smiling like a bishop conferring a blessing, said: 'I am God. Didn't you recognize me?'

The boy now felt not only shy but afraid, and could hardly breathe. He summoned up the courage to show his incredulity, and after a great effort was able to say: 'You God? You? If only you were!'

And the apparition, for such he should be called, treating the boy's incredulity with indulgence, deepened his affectionate smile and repeated what he had said: 'I am God. You seem to be surprised. Don't be frightened of me. I love you, yes, I love you very much.'

Luis began to lose his fear. He felt moved and wanted to cry.

'I know where you've come from,' continued the apparition. 'Señor de Cucúrbitas didn't give you anything tonight. He can't always, son. As he says himself, there are so many poor people to help.'

The boy heaved a deep sigh to recover his breath, and looked at the handsome old man, who sat with one elbow propped on his knee and one hand on his shining beard. The apparition turned his head to one side to look at the child, attaching great importance, apparently, to the conversation they were having: 'You and your family will have to be very patient, Cadalso my young friend, very patient.'

Luis sighed more deeply. Finding his mind free of fear and at the same time full of initiative, he pulled himself together and asked: 'And when will they give my grandfather a post?'

The exalted person addressed by young Luis ceased for a moment to look at the boy and, fixing his eyes on the ground, appeared to meditate. Then he turned his face to the boy once more and with a sigh – for he sighed too! – pronounced these grave words: 'Consider how things are. For every vacant post there are two hundred applicants. The ministers are driven off their heads, and don't know whom to please. They have so many obligations that I've no idea how they keep alive, poor devils.

Patience, my son, patience. You'll get a nomination when a favourable opportunity occurs. For my part, I'd like to do something for your grandfather too. How sad he'll be tonight when he gets this letter! Be careful you don't lose it. You're a good lad. But you must study harder. You didn't know your grammar-lesson today. You made so many silly mistakes that the whole class started laughing, and I'm not surprised. What made you say that the participle expresses the idea of the verb in the abstract? You were confusing it with the gerund, and then you got the moods and the tenses all mixed up. It's because you don't concentrate, your mind's always wandering when you're doing your lessons.'

Young Cadalso went very red and, putting his two hands between his knees, pressed them hard.

'It's not enough to be good in class. You've got to study, you've got to concentrate on what you read and remember it. You and I will never get on unless you do. I shall be very cross with you in fact, and it'll be no good your coming to me then and asking why they don't give your grandfather a post. And while I'm talking to you there's something else I'd like to tell you. You're quite right to complain about the Performer. He's common, and if he says Miau to you again I'll rub a red pepper into his tongue. But people have got to be patient when they're called nicknames. When they shout Miau, just keep quiet and put up with it. They might say things that were much worse.'

The boy was most grateful and, although he knew that God is everywhere, surprised also that he should be so well informed about what went on at school. After a while he ventured to say: 'Blow me! If I catch him!'

'Look here, friend Cadalso,' said his companion with paternal severity. 'Don't set yourself up as a bruiser. You're not strong enough to fight your schoolmates. They're very rough. Shall I tell you what to do? When they call you Miau, you tell the master, and he'll make the Performer kneel for half an hour with his arms out, you'll see.'

'I wish he would. For a whole hour.'

'That nickname now. They gave it to your granny and your

aunts in the Real gallery, because they do look like three pussies, you know. They're so well licked. It's quite a funny joke.'

Luis felt his dignity hurt, but said nothing.

'I know they're going to the Real tonight again,' added the apparition. 'That fellow Ponce brought them the tickets a little while ago. Why don't you ask them to take you too? You'd enjoy the opera very much. I wish you could see how nice it is!'

'They won't take me. Bah!' (very disconsolate). 'You tell them to.'

Even if you address God as Thou in your prayers, it seemed irreverent to Luis to address him so familiarly face to face.

'Me? I don't want to be mixed up in this. Anyhow, they'll be in a very bad mood tonight. Your poor dear grandpa! When he opens that letter ... You haven't lost it, have you?'

'No, sir, I've got it here,' said Cadalso, fetching it out. 'Would you like to read it?'

'No, silly. I know what it says. Your grandfather is going to have a bad spell. But he must put up with it. Times are very bad, very bad.'

The exalted apparition repeated 'very bad, very bad' two or three times, nodding his head with a sad expression. Then, dissolving in a moment, he vanished completely. Luis rubbed his eyes, found that he was awake and recognized the street. He saw in front of him the basket-maker's shop, above the door of which were two bull's heads with wicker snouts and horns, a favourite toy of Madrid children. He also recognized the wine-shop with bottles in the window. He saw that the passers-by were 'real people'. He saw Canelo who was still beside him and realized that he was a real dog. He looked away once more, seeking some remnant of his marvellous vision, but there was nothing. It was that 'thing' coming on, thought young Cadalso, not knowing how to define what it was. But it came on in a different way. When he got up his legs were so weak that they hardly supported him. He felt his coat, afraid that he had lost the letter, but the letter was still in its place. 'Blow me!' This fainting-attack had come on him before, but he had never seen personages so ... so ... He did not know how to put it. But that he had seen him and talked to him, he had no doubt. What a marvellous 'gentleman' he was! Supposing he was the heavenly Father really and truly! Or had it been the old blind-man trying to play a trick on him?

Thinking these thoughts, Luis made for home as quickly as his weak legs allowed. His head was going round, and the shivers down his spine did not stop while he was walking. Canelo seemed much preoccupied. Suppose he had seen something too. What a pity he couldn't talk and bear witness to that marvellous vision! For Luis remembered that two or three times during the conversation God had patted Canelo's head, and Canelo had looked up at him, sticking his tongue right out. So Canelo could have borne witness.

Finally he arrived home and, since they had heard him coming upstairs, Abelarda opened the door before he could ring. His grandfather came out anxiously to meet him, and the child silently put the letter into his hand. Feeling it before he opened it, Don Ramón went off to his study, and at the same moment Pura called Luis to come in and eat his dinner, since the family was just finishing. They had not waited for him because he had been so long, and the ladies had to go to the theatre in a great hurry, so as to get good seats in the gallery before the crowd arrived. They had kept their grandson's soup and boiled meat on two covered plates, one on top of the other, but they were already cold by the time he took the first spoonful. As he was so hungry, however, he did not worry about their temperature.

Doña Pura was tying the three-weeks-old napkin round her grandson's neck when Villaamil came in to eat his fruit. On distressing occasions his face wore an expression of blood-thirsty ferocity. When embittered by affliction, that blessed angel who could not kill a fly seemed to be gnawing at raw human flesh seasoned with aloes instead of salt. By merely looking at him, Doña Pura realized that the letter had contained nothing. The unhappy man began mechanically to shell the two dried-up nuts on his plate. His sister-in-law and his daughter looked at him also, and read on his worn and ancient tiger's face the grief that devoured him within. To contribute a cheerful note to this sad scene, Abelarda threw in the remark: 'Ponce says that the Pellegrini will get all the applause tonight.'

'It seems quite wrong to me,' said Doña Pura feelingly, 'that they should want to humiliate Scolpi Rolla. She gives a most finished performance in her part as Amneris. Of course she owes most of her success to her face and the way she shows her legs. But the Pellegrini, with all her airs, isn't anything out of the ordinary.'

'Don't be ridiculous,' said Milagros portentously. 'The other night she did the "Fuggi, fuggi, tu sei perduto" as we haven't heard it sung since Rossina Penco's time. There's only one thing wrong with her. She gesticulates too much. And honestly, the point about opera is to sing well, not to make faces.'

'But don't let's dawdle,' said Pura. 'On these sort of nights, you get left on the stairs if you dawdle.'

'Come now! Don't you think that Guillén or the medical boys will keep seats for us?'

'There's no counting on it. Hurry up, or it will be like the other night. Goodness me, if it hadn't been for those very nice boys, the pharmacy students you know, we should have been left like dummies at the door.'

Villaamil, who heard none of this, ate a dried fig, swallowing it whole, I think, and went off to his study with a resolute step, like a man about to commit a crime. His wife followed him and asked him affectionately: 'What's the matter? Hasn't that nincompoop sent you anything?'

'Nothing,' answered Villaamil in a voice that seemed to issue from the centre of the earth. 'Just as I told you, he's had enough. You can't abuse a man's kindness day after day. He's done me so many favours, so many that it's foolish to beg for any more. I'm very sorry that I wrote to him today.'

'The scoundrel!' exclaimed his wife angrily. She was in the habit of applying this and worse names to friends who parried his demands.

'Scoundrel no,' declared Villaamil, who not even in moments of greatest embarrassment allowed 'contributors' to be abused. 'A man's not always in the position to help his neighbour. He's not a scoundrel. He hasn't an idea in his head, and never has had. But all the same he's one of the most honourable men in the service.'

28

'There's nothing marvellous about him' (peevishly and angrily) 'even though he has all the virtues. Do you remember when he was your colleague in Central Accounts? He was the stupidest man in the department. Everyone knew it. Whenever there was a blunder they all said, "Cucúrbitas!" But he's never been out of a post for a day, and he's always had promotion. What's that mean? He may be stupid, but he knows better than you how to push himself. And don't you think people grease his palm for settling their accounts?'

'Be quiet, woman!'

'How innocent you are! That's why you are where you are, that's why you're poor and they pass you over. Because you haven't a grain of foresight, and because you've been so careful about your blessed scruples. That isn't honesty, let me tell you, it's just obtuseness and stupidity. Compare yourself to Cucúrbitas. He can be as much of a dunderhead as he likes, but you'll see, he'll end up as a director, perhaps as a minister. And you'll never be anything. If they do give you a post, it'll be a bread and butter one, and we'll always be as we are' (warming to it). 'And all because of your priggishness, because you don't make the most of yourself, because Brother Modesty never becomes Prior. If I were in your shoes, I'd go to a newspaper and cough up all the scandal you know about the administration, and the dirty work that many of them have been up to who are now in high places. Yes, I'd bring it all out, never mind who got hurt. Unmask all those scamps. That'd touch the spot. It wouldn't take them long to find you a post then, you'd see. You'd have the Director himself come here, hat in hand, to beg you to accept a nomination.'

'It's getting late, Mamma,' said Abelarda from the door, putting on her veil.

'I'm coming. All your finicking and politeness, calling everybody "Respected sir" the way you do, and all your squeamishness and correctness, as if butter wouldn't melt in your mouth, what's it all lead to? They just reckon you're a nobody. But' (raising her voice) 'as sure as this light shines you ought to be a director by now. And why aren't you? Because you've got no drive and no spirit, because you don't count for anything, because you don't know the way to go about things. Sighing and complaining won't make them give you what you want. Nominations go to men who know how to show their teeth. You're harmless, you don't bite, you don't even bark, and they all laugh at you. "Ah, Villaamil," they say, "what an honest man he is! The upright official." When they show me a man that's "upright", I look to see if he's out-at-elbow. It's this honesty of yours that's your undoing. Honesty is sometimes taken as just another word for foolishness. But that's not right, it's not right. A man can preserve all the integrity in the world and still take care of himself and his family.'

'Leave me in peace,' muttered Villaamil faintly, straining the joints of his chair as he sat down.

'Mamma,' repeated the young lady impatiently.

'I'm just coming. I'm just coming.'

'I can't be any different from the way God made me,' said the unhappy official without a post. 'But now it's not a question of what I am or I'm not. It's a question of our daily bread, our bread for tomorrow. We're in a fine pickle, yes. There's no prospect in any direction. Tomorrow. . . .'

'God won't forsake us,' said Pura, trying to strengthen her spirits with a forced effort of hope that was like the struggles of a drowning man. 'I'm so used to shortages that to have plenty would be a surprise, or even a shock. Tomorrow . . .'

She did not complete the sentence or even the thought. Her daughter and sister were urging her so hard that she hastily put on her things. As she wound her blue veil round her head, she gave her husband his orders: 'Put the boy to bed. If he doesn't want to do his lessons, tell him to leave them. He has enough to do, poor soul. I expect he'll be going out to deliver a ton of letters tomorrow.'

The good Villaamil felt a great lightening of the heart as he saw them depart. His sorrow kept him better company than his family. It gave him more relief and comfort than his wife's words. For though it oppressed his heart it did not scratch his face, and when Doña Pura discussed matters with him she was all beak and claw.

4

YOUNG Cadalso was in the dining-room, sitting with his el-
bows propped on the table and his books in front of him. He
had so many that he was quite proud when he put them in a
row. He felt like a general reviewing his tactical units. But they
were as tattered, poor things, as if they had served as projectiles
in a furious battle; their pages were dog-eared, the corners of
their bindings bent or broken, their covers sticky with dirt.
But each one bore on its first page an inscription in wavering
letters which declared it the property of its owner. For it would
truly have been most lamentable had anyone failed to know
that they belonged exclusively to Luis Cadalso y Villaamil. This
personage picked one of them up at random, and looked to see
which it was. Blowed if it wasn't that beastly grammar every
time! He opened it gingerly and watched the letters swarming
over the page, which was lit by the hanging lamp. They looked
like gnats dancing in a sunbeam. The boy read a few lines.
'What is an adverb?' The letters of the answer were the ones
that had decided not to let him read them. They ran and leapt
from one side of the page to the other. On the whole, an adverb
must be a very good thing, but the boy could not get a clear
idea of what it was. After this he read whole pages without
their meaning penetrating his mind, which was still taken up
with that surprising vision. His physical malaise had not left
him, even though he had eaten his dinner with such appetite.
And when he discovered that fixing his attention on the book
made him feel worse, he thought the best cure was to turn
down the corners of every page in the grammar till the book
bristled like an endive.

He was doing this when he heard his grandfather coming out
of the study. His lamp had gone out through lack of oil, and
although he was not writing the darkness drove him out of his
den into the dining-room. For a while the unfortunate man
paced excitedly about that room and the passage, talking to him-

self and sometimes stumbling. For the uneven matting, which at some places was in holes, impeded his free passage through this territory.

On other nights, when grandfather and grandson were left together, the old man would take the boy's lessons and repeat them to him till they stuck in his memory. That night, however, Villaamil was in no mood for lessons, for which the boy was most thankful. For appearance' sake he began to uncurl the leaves of the tortured text-book and flatten them with the palm of his hand. A little later the book made a soft cushion for his head. Tired out by lessons and visions, he let it fall on the definition of the adverb and went off to sleep.

Villaamil was saying: 'Almighty God, this is truly more than I can bear. What have I done that you should treat me like this? Why do they not give me a post? Why do even the friends I trusted most abandon me?' The spirits of this poor, out-of-work official were as easily depressed as excited. Now he believed himself to be persecuted by secret enemies who had sworn eternal hatred against him. 'Who can it be? Who can be the rogue that is pursuing a campaign against me? Some ungrateful fellow, perhaps, who owes his career to me.' To console himself he called up the whole of his life as an official, a slow and honourable career at home and overseas which had begun when he entered to serve abroad in the year '41, at the age of twenty-four (when Señor Surrá was Finance Minister). He had seldom been out of employment before the crisis in which we meet him: for four months in the time of Bertrán de Lis, for eleven during the two years of progressive government, and for three and a half in Salaverria's time. After the revolution he transferred to Cuba and then to the Philippines, which he left after an attack of dysentery. In short, he was now sixty, and had spent a total of thirty-four years and ten months in the service. He was now only two months short of retirement on four-fifths of his statutory salary, which was that of the highest post he had occupied: Chief of Department, third class, 'What a world it is! So full of injustice! And they hope to escape without revolutions. All I ask is those two months, so that I can retire with my four-fifths, that's all, O Lord. . . .' At the height of his soliloquy, he swayed and bumped against the door, rebounding immediately against the edge of the table, which shook with the impact of his body. Waking with a start, Luis heard his grandfather clearly pronouncing these words as he pulled himself up : 'In conformity with the Budgetary law of '35, revised in '65 and '68.' They seemed the most terrifying words he had ever heard.

'What, Grandpapa?' he exclaimed in alarm.

'Nothing, my boy. Nothing that concerns you. Go off to sleep. Don't you feel like doing your lessons? Quite right. What's the good of studying? The more of an ass a man is, and the more of a knave, the better his career. Come on, to bed with you. It's late.'

Villaamil looked for and found a candle-stick, but it was not so easy for him to find a candle to put in it. Finally, after much searching, he discovered some ends on Pura's night-table and, having lit one of them, prepared to put the boy to bed. Luis slept in Milagros' bedroom, which was part of the dining-room. Here stood a dressing-table, which was about seventy years old, a commode with four-fifths of its drawers out of action, various trunks and the two beds. The whole house, except for the drawing-room, which was furnished with relative elegance, revealed poverty, neglect and that slow decay which comes of not repairing the tarnishings and ravages of time.

As the grandfather began to undress his grandson, he said : 'Yes, my boy, blessed are the stupid, for theirs is the kingdom . . . of the service.' He unbuttoned his jacket and pulled it so hard by the sleeves that the boy almost fell over.

'Set about learning, son, set about learning for when you're a man. Nobody remembers you if you've fallen; all they do is tread on you and smash you so that you will never get up again. Think now, I ought to be a Departmental Chief, second class because I am due for promotion by Cánovas' law of '76. But here I am starving to death. Letters of recommendation pour in to the Minister, but nothing happens. They say, "Look at his previous service", but nothing happens. Do you think he troubles to examine my previous service? If only he would! All I get is promises and postponements, that he is waiting for a favourable opportunity, that he has noted my case and will give it precedence. In fact, all the dodges they use when they want to get out of something. I've always given them loyal service. I've worked like a black, I've never caused my chiefs the slightest trouble. When I was in the Secretariat, in about '52, Don Juan Bravo was particularly pleased with me. He called me into his office one day, and told me . . . what modesty prevents me from repeating. Oh, if that great man were to lift his head now and see me out of employment! Me, who in '55 drew up a budgetary plan that earned the praises of Don Pascual Madoz and Don Juan Bruil, a plan that I have improved after twenty years of reflection, and that I explain in four memoranda which I have here! And it's not been a light task. Suppression of all indirect taxation, which is replaced by an income tax. . . . Ah, the income tax! It's the dream of my whole life, the object of my innumerable researches, and the outcome of my long experience. They refuse to understand it, and that's why our country is . . . closer to ruin and poorer every day. It's painful to watch all the sources of wealth dry up. I still believe in it. A single tax based on the good faith, competitive spirit and pride of the tax-payer, is the best remedy for the poverty of the state. In addition, the proceeds from customs, which will be considerably raised in order to protect national industries. And finally, the unification of the national debt, which will be limited to one form of issue and one rate of interest.'

On reaching this point, Villaamil tugged so hard at his grandson's trousers that the boy shouted: 'Oh, Grandpapa, you're pulling my legs off!' To which the angry old man replied morosely: 'Certainly there must be some secret enemy, some scoundrel who has made up his mind to ruin and dishonour me.'

In the end Luis got to bed. He did not have the light put out until long after he was asleep because he suffered from nightmares and if he woke up suddenly was frightened by the dark. Therefore when the first candle-end went out his grandfather lit another and, sitting down beside the commode, began to read *La Correspondencia*, which had just been pushed under the door. In his feverish confusion, the unhappy man anxiously looked for Appointments of Personnel and with fatal perspicacity immediately discovered bad news. ' "To first officer in the

34

Department for Indirect Taxation, Señor Montes . . . Royal decree conferring on Don Basilio Andrés de la Cana the rank of First Ministerial Secretary." This is scandalous! This is protectionism gone mad! Not even among the Berbers of Africa do things like this take place. Poor Spain, my poor country! My hair stands on end at the thought of what this administrative madness will lead to. Basilio is a good fellow. But I had him under me only yesterday, so to speak, as a clerk, fourth class!' After grief came hope. ' "Appointments of personnel for the new establishment of the Taxation Department will be made shortly. It is rumoured that several intelligent officials at present out of employment will receive posts." '

Villaamil's glances danced for a moment over the paper, from letter to letter. His eyes moistened. Would he be included in that list? The friends who were recommending him to the Minister in this weary campaign had proposed him, in so many words, for the next batch. 'Oh God, if only I could be in that blessed list. And when will the choice be made? In the next three or four days, Pantoja told me.'

As hope revived his whole being, it gave him a restless itch and he rushed out into the dark maze of passages. 'The list. The new establishment. Posts for intelligent officials, and more than intelligent, I say, identified with . . . O Lord, whisper in their ears, pour all your light into those brains. So that they may see clearly. So that they may pick on me. So that they may make inquiries into my previous service. If they do, they'll certainly appoint me. Will they appoint me? Some secret voice within me says they will. I have hopes. No, I won't allow them, I won't get excited. It's better to be pessimistic, very pessimistic. Then events prove the opposite of what you fear. I've noticed that when you feel quite certain, then your hopes come crashing to the ground. The fact is we're always mistaken. The best thing is to have no hopes, to see everything black, black as the wolf's maw, and then suddenly, hey presto! It's light. Yes, Ramón, imagine that you won't get anything, that there's no hope for you. Then you'll see. If you accept that, what happens will prove just the opposite. But in the meantime I'll muster all my resources tomorrow. I'll write to some of my friends and see others . . . and the Minister! In face of all these recommendations. . . . My God, that's an idea! Wouldn't it be a good thing if I were to write to the Minister myself?'

As he spoke, he turned automatically towards the sleeping boy, and while gazing at him thought of all the traipsing about he would have to do next day to distribute the correspondence. How all this connected with the pictures which arose in the boy's dream it is impossible to say. But the fact is that as his grandfather looked at him, Luis in deep sleep saw the personage with the white beard once more; and the strange thing was that he saw him seated at a desk, on which there were so many, so very many letters, that by young Cadalso's reckoning they must have added up to at least two quadrillions. The Lord's handwriting was so beautiful that Luis thought it the most perfect script in the world. Not even Don Celedonio, the writing master at school, could write better. As he finished each letter, the Eternal Father placed it in an envelope that was whiter than snow, lifted it to his mouth, and put out quite a bit of his delicate, pink tongue, which he ran quickly over the gum to moisten it. Having stuck it down, he picked up his pen again. And the extraordinary thing was that it was Mendizábal's pen, and, moreover, it was dipped in Mendizábal's inkwell. Then he started to write the address. Looking over his shoulder, Luis believed he saw that immortal hand tracing the following address on the paper.

B. L. M.
To His Excellency the Minister of Finance,
whoever he may be,
His humble servant
God.

5

T H A T night Villaamil did not sleep for a quarter of an hour on end. He would doze off for a moment. But the thought of the coming appointments, and the pessimistic viewpoint that he had forced himself to adopt, by which he put his money on disaster and expected the worst in order that the best should turn up, sowed thorns in his bed and awoke him the moment he closed his eyes. When his wife returned from the theatre, he had a brief and depressing conversation with her on the subject of the difficulty of getting food for the next day, since there was not a peseta in the house, and the generosity and patience of their friends was exhausted.

Although she pretended to be calm and hopeful, Doña Pura was greatly disturbed, and she too passed a sleepless night, making plans for the following day, which promised to be so gloomy and fearful. She no longer dared to send to any shop for goods on credit; everywhere she met with gloomy faces, rudeness and contempt, and not a day passed without some insolent and demanding tradesman raising Cain at the door of their second-floor apartment itself. Pawn something! Mentally the lady made a rapid survey of the useful articles that had been sent into banishment: household utensils, cloaks, women's mantles, overcoats. Exports of this kind had already, so to speak, reached their maximum, and it was impossible for the family to be any further despoiled in this respect than it had been already. Pawning on a great scale had taken place in the previous month (January '78) on the very day of Don Alfonso's marriage to Queen Mercedes. Nevertheless the three Miaus had not missed any of the celebrations that had taken place in Madrid in honour of that event. Illuminations, military parades, the procession of the royal suite to the Atocha station; they had seen them all perfectly, and enjoyed them all from the best positions by dint of simply elbowing their way through the crowds.

The drawing-room. To pawn something from the drawing-room! This idea always sent a shiver of fear down Doña Pura's spine. For the drawing-room was the part of the apartment dearest to her heart, the true symbol for her of the domestic hearth. Its furniture, which was pretty though rather old-fashioned, bore witness to the past splendour of the Villaamil family. It comprised two small black commodes picked out in gold and red lacquer, with marble tops, which stood between the windows; damask-covered sofas and easy chairs, a moquette

37

carpet, and silk curtains that they had bought from the president of the court at Cáceres when he had been transferred and moved house. Doña Pura was as fond of those curtains as of the keys to her own heart. And when the spectre of poverty appeared to her, whispering the fearful sum in her ear which would meet the next day's needs, the lady exclaimed with a shiver of fear: 'No, no. Rather our shifts than the curtains!' To strip their bodies seemed to her a bearable sacrifice but to strip the drawing-room – never! Although her husband was out of employment, and their social standing thereby considerably diminished, the Villaamils had quite a few visitors. What would they say if they saw that the silk curtains, admired and envied by everyone who saw them, were missing! Doña Pura closed her eyes, wishing to dismiss the baleful idea and go to sleep. But the drawing-room had got into her brain, and it remained before her eyes all night in its spotlessness and its elegance. None of her friends had a drawing-room like it. The carpet was so well preserved that it seemed never to have been trodden by human foot. They kept it under dust-sheets all day long, and carefully cleaned it very often. The upright piano, which was out-of-tune – yes, very much out-of-tune – was of brightly shining rosewood. There was not a speck to be seen on the upholstery. The commodes gleamed, and the objects upon them – the gilt clock which had stopped, the candelabra under glass, all were exquisitely kept. Then the countless trifles that completed the decoration, photographs in stitched paper frames, boxes that had once contained sweets, little china dogs, and a bottle-rack of imitation Bohemian glass, also shone without a speck of dust. Abelarda spent her spare time dusting these trifles, and others not so far mentioned. There were delicate pierced wooden objects, of the kind that amuse amateurs of domestic marquetry. A neighbour possessed a borer with which he made countless masterpieces that he presented to his friends. There were baskets, little stands, miniature furniture, Gothic chapels and Chinese pagodas, all very pretty and very fragile, of the 'look and don't touch' variety, which were very difficult to clean.

Doña Pura turned in her bed, in the hope of changing her

mournful ideas by a change of position. But then she had an even clearer vision of those sumptuous purple curtains, made of richest silk, of that silk 'that you don't see anywhere any more'. All the ladies who visited her handled and felt that matchless material, and rubbed it between their fingers to appreciate its quality. You had only to feel its weight to know what marvellous stuff it was! In fact, Doña Pura considered that to send those curtains to the pawnbroker's or moneylender's would be as painful as to see a son off to America.

Whilst that Fra Angelico figure was turning on her narrow couch (she slept in a little alcove of the drawing-room, and her husband, since his return from the Philippines, slept alone in the study) it struck her that she might distract or while away her sorrow by remembering the emotions of the opera, and the baritone's magnificent singing of 'Rivedrai le foreste imbalsamate'.

Villaamil, alone, sleepless and feverish, tossed in the ugly double bed, the sprung mattress of which was in a lamentable state, some of its springs having collapsed and broken, while others had come adrift and now stuck out. The woollen mattress which lay on top was in no better condition, since it was all lumpy in some places and hollow in others. The whole bed, in fact, might fittingly have stood in the dungeons of the Inquisition as an instrument of torture for heretics. The poor official without a post lay in a bed that was the external expression or symbol of his inward tortures. So then the itch of insomnia caused him to turn, he fell into a deep pit, from the centre of which projected like a devil's goad a giant spur which stuck into his back; and when he climbed out of the pit, a lump of wool, hard and strong as a fist, stuck into his ribs.

Sometimes he slept quite well despite these conditions; but that night the excitement of his brain exaggerated, in the darkness, the unevenness of the terrain. At one moment he seemed to be falling head foremost down a precipice, at another he was balancing on the top of a hill or sailing to the Philippines in a hellish typhoon. 'Let's be pessimistic,' was his theme. 'Let us think as determinedly as we can that I shan't be included in the list, and then we'll see if I don't get a lucky surprise and find myself nominated. I won't expect to be lucky. No, I won't expect it, and that will do the trick. It's always the thing you don't expect that happens. I'll put my money on misfortune. They won't give you a post. Poor Ramón, they won't give you a post. They'll fool you again this time, you'll see. But although I'm convinced that I shan't get anything, absolutely convinced, and there's nobody can help me here, although I know that my enemies won't take pity on me, I will bring my influence into play and make everyone to the last man speak on my behalf to the Minister. But of course, friend Ramón, it will be no use. You'll be passed over just the same, you'll see. I'm as sure of that as of the darkness in this room. You might as well give up your last crumb of illusion. None of your silly hopes. None of this "Maybe yes, maybe no". No more feeble optimism. Do what you will, things will turn out ill.'

6

DOÑA Pura went to sleep in the end, and slept well into the morning. Villaamil got up at eight without having closed his eyes. When he came out of the bedroom, having first rubbed a little cold water on his face and passed a comb through his hair, no one had yet got up. Their present poverty did not allow them to have a maid, and the three women divided the duties of the untidy household between them. As Milagros did the cooking, she was in the habit of getting up before the other two; but as she had gone to bed late on the previous night, there was no cook in the kitchen when Villaamil left his own room and went there. He looked at the unlighted stove and the empty coal-scuttle, and found in the cupboard which served as a larder some crusts of bread, a greasy paper bag which must once have contained some remains of ham, cold meat or something of the sort, a few chick-peas on a dish, a piece of sausage, an egg and half a lemon. The tiger heaved a sigh, and went into the dining-room to investigate the sideboard cupboard, in which there were some more bits of hard bread among the knives and table-napkins. At this point he heard a gurgling, followed by the sound of water, and Milagros appeared with her feline face washed clean, her dressing-gown flapping, her hair in curl-papers and a white kerchief on her head.

'Is there any chocolate?' he asked his sister-in-law without further greeting.

'Half an ounce. That's all,' answered the lady, hurriedly opening the drawer of the kitchen table in which it was kept. 'I'll make you a cup right away.'

'No, not for me. Make it for the boy. I don't need chocolate. I don't fancy it. I'll have a bit of dry bread and a glass of water.'

'All right. You'll find it in here. We're not short of bread. There's a slice of ham too in the cupboard. This egg is for my sister, if you don't mind. I'm just going to light the stove. Chop me a few sticks please, while I go and see if I can't find some matches.'

After chewing his bread, Don Ramón picked up the chopper and began to split the wood, which was the leg of an old chair. He heaved a sigh at each stroke. The cracks of the splitting wood seemed to emanate from Villaamil's own person. It was as if he were rending quivering particles of his own withered flesh and splinters of his own poor bones. Meanwhile Milagros was filling the bucket with coals and lumps of wood.

'Shall we get a stew today?' she asked her brother-in-law somewhat mysteriously.

Vilaamil meditated on this problem so brutally presented to him.

'Perhaps. Who can tell!' he answered, launching his imagination into the unknown.

'Let's wait until Pura gets up.'

It was she who resolved all arguments. Being a person with initiative, she was given to unexpected actions and swift decisions. Milagros was all passivity, modesty and obedience. She never raised her voice or commented on her sister's orders. Impelled by her humble conscience and the habit of subordination, she worked for the others. Fatally linked throughout her life to the miserable fate of this family whose vicissitudes she

41

shared, she never complained, and was never heard to protest against her unfortunate fate. She thought of herself as a great artist destroyed, cut off in full flower by lack of environment; and when she thought of herself as lost to art, sorrow for this condition drowned all her other sorrows. It must be mentioned that Milagros had been splendidly endowed at birth for an opera singer. At twenty-five she had a most beautiful voice and a fair training, and was crazy about music. But fate never permitted her to embark on a true artiste's career. Unfortunate love-affairs and family difficulties postponed from day to day the public début that she longed for. And when these obstacles vanished, Milagros was past it; she had lost her voice. She had not even herself noticed the gradual decline by which her hopes as a singer had brought her to the precarious situation in which we now find her; by which her dreams of the stage and of triumphs as an artiste had ended in the Villaamils' foodless kitchen. When she thought of the cruel contrast between her hopes and her fate, she was unable to measure the steps of that slow descent from the heights of poetry to the cellars of vulgarity.

Milagros had a fine, slender figure suitable for the roles of Margarita, Dinorah, Gilda, and La Traviata. Her voice was a high soprano. But all this vanished in smoke, for she never won public applause. Only once did she sing the part of Adalgisa at the Real, by favour of the management, when she was a pupil at the conservatoire. She was delighted and the papers promised her a brilliant future. In the Liceo Jover, before an invited and not very exacting audience, she sang in *Sappho** and *The Capulets* of Bellini, together with Act Three of something by Vacai.†
Then she intended to go to Italy, but was prevented by a passionate love-affair and the hopes of a fine marriage. But the young man and her family got across one another very badly. Time passed, and things went badly for the singer; she neither visited Italy nor got an engagement at the Real, nor married.

Doña Pura and Milagros were daughters of a military doctor called Escobios, and nieces of the bandmaster of the Royal and Ancient Regiment of Infantry. Her mother was born a Muñoz,

* Gounod's *Sappho* (1851), perhaps.
† A singing master who composed sixteen forgotten operas.

and claimed relationship with the Marqués of Casa-Muñoz. They decided therefore, when it was a question of Milagros becoming an opera singer, to italianize their name and call her Escobini; but as her artistic career dissolved in smoke, the Italian name was never seen on the play-bills.

Before Señorita Escobios' career was cut short, she enjoyed a period of transitory success and renown in a provincial capital of the third class, where she went with her sister, Villaamil's wife. Here he was Chief of the Finance Department, and his family was, of course, intimate with those of the civil and military governors, who gave parties to which the pick of the town were invited. Singing at the concerts of the brigadier's wife, Milagros fascinated and stunned. Young men pursued her in dozens, as did also the envy of the women, which disturbed her in the midst of her triumphs. A local young man, a poet and journalist, fell madly in love with her. He was the one who in a criticism of a musical evening called Doña Pura, in grandiose style, a figure out of a Fra Angelico painting. He praised Milagros in such ecstatic terms that everyone laughed. The local inhabitants still remember some sentences describing the young lady at the moment when she entered the hall, went across to the piano to sing, and eventually sang. 'She is the modest Ophelia bewailing her faded love, and with heavenly trills singing an elegy to death.' And, strange though it may seem, the man who wrote this on page two of the paper was entrusted with the task, for which he received his pay, of writing the commercial report on page one. He was therefore responsible for this elegy as well: '*Wheat*. The whole week has seen a marked quietness in this commodity. Only two hundred sacks, selling at twenty-two and three-quarters, have been loaded on the canal, and yesterday two thousand sacks were offered at twenty-two and a half without attracting a bid.' On the following day he returned to the subject of 'the modest Ophelia or angel who brings the harmonies of heaven down to earth.' Indeed, the young man grew most passionate, and wilder every day since his love was not returned. Finally he became so ill, so very ill, that one day he jumped head first into a mill-race; and though they rushed out of the flour-mill to help him, he was a corpse when they brought him out. A little after this unfortunate occurrence, which made a great impression on Milagros, she returned to Madrid. It was then that her début at the Real took place, and was followed by the performance in the Liceo Jover, and all the other events to which I have briefly referred. Let us pile a heap of sad years, of rapid ageing and of decay over these events, and we meet the 'Modest Ophelia' in the Villaamils' kitchen, where the stove is lit and she does not know what to put on it.

From a dark little room on the inner corridor came Abelarda rubbing her eyes, and with her hair in disorder. She was dragging behind her the dirty train of a dressing-gown which was too big for her, and which had been used by her mother in happier times. She too went to the kitchen where she appeared at the moment when Villaamil emerged to go and wake and dress his grandson. Abelarda asked if the baker would come: a question to which Milagros did not know the reply, being unable to form a judgement on so serious a problem before she had heard her sister's opinion.

'See that your mother gets up quickly,' she said in some dismay, 'and let her decide.' A little later a great clearing of the throat was heard from the alcove in the drawing-room where Doña Pura slept. Through the door which led from this alcove into the hall opposite the study door appeared the lady of the house, radiating displeasure, with her body swathed in a coat of Villaamil's, her hair in curl-papers, and her little face purple from the cold water with which she had just washed it. A torn shawl was tied across her breast, and she wore voluminous slippers on her feet.

'What! Can't you get along without me? What a couple of ninnies you are. The thing's not worth talking about. Have you made the boy his chocolate?'

Milagros came out of the kitchen with the jug, while Abelarda sat the boy down at the table and put his napkin round his neck. Villaamil went to his study, from which he returned shortly afterwards, carrying his inkwell and saying: 'There's no ink and I've got forty letters to write today. When you've finished, Luis, you might go down and ask friend Mendizábal to oblige me with a little ink.'

44

'I'll go,' said Abelarda, picking up the inkwell and going downstairs just as she was.

The two sisters meanwhile were whispering in the kitchen. What about? Presumably about the impossibility of feeding the family on one egg, some stale bread, and some remains of meat which were not enough for the cat. Pura frowned and pouted so strangely that her lips met her nose, which seemed to grow longer. The modest Ophelia imitated this sign of puzzlement, which made the two look so alike that they might have been one woman. Villaamil interrupted their reflections by entering the kitchen to say that he had to go to the Ministry and needed a clean shirt.

'Oh, my goodness!' exclaimed Pura dispiritedly. 'The only clean one he's got is in such a state that it needs a general overhaul.' But Abelarda promised to have it ready by midday, and ironed as well, provided she had a fire in the stove. Don Ramón also made sundry observations to his daughter concerning certain frayings and tears which were to be seen on the lapel of his overcoat and asked her to employ her cunning needle upon them. The young woman pacified him, and the good man shut himself in his study. The conference which the Miaus were holding in the kitchen ended with a sudden movement by Doña Pura, who ran to her bedroom to dress and depart for the street. A marvellous idea had exploded in the gunpowder of her brain, which seemed to have caught fire from the flames that burned in her eyes.

'Make a blaze in the stove, and fill all the pots with water,' she said to her sister as she went out, slipping away as eagerly and rapidly as a weasel. Seeing her determination, Abelarda and Milagros, who knew the head of the household well, worried no more about the problem of provisions for that day, and started to sing, one from the kitchen and one from her own room, the duet from *Norma*, 'In mia mano al fin tu sei.'

7

I T was almost eleven when Doña Pura returned, somewhat out of breath and followed by an errand-boy from the Plazuela de los Mostenses, who was groaning under the weight of a basket full of provisions. Milagros, who had come to the door, crossed herself repeatedly from shoulder to shoulder and forehead to waist. She had seen her sister sail out with forceful initiative on many very difficult occasions; but that morning's master-stroke seemed to her superior to anything that could be expected even of so masterful a woman. Rapidly examining the basket she saw various kinds of food, animal and vegetable, all of the best quality and more suitable for the table of a Director General than for that of a poor office-seeker. But this was Doña Pura's way: either the whole hog or nothing at all. But to her even greater astonishment Milagros saw the purse in her sister's hand, which was almost bursting with money.

'Darling,' said the lady of the house, drawing her sister after her into the hall, 'I could only think of one thing to do. I went to Carolina Lantigua, who married Pez, you know. It was a dreadful humiliation. I had to close my eyes and rush in. It was like jumping into the water. I swallowed hard. But I gave her such a picture of our situation that the tears came into her eyes. She's very kind. She gave me fifty pesetas, and I promised to pay her back soon. I will too, I will, because in this next list they will give him a post. They're bound to put him back on the establishment. I'm absolutely convinced. Anyhow, take this in. I'm just coming. Is the water on the boil?'

She went into the study to tell her husband that for that day the tremendous crisis was over. She added no details. They must have talked also about the likelihood of his appointment, because from the passage Villaamil's angry voice could be heard shouting: 'Don't bring me any more of your false optimism. I tell you once more that I shan't be included in the list. I've no hopes, absolutely none, believe me. You only upset me with your silly illusions, and your mania for seeing everything in such a rosy light. All I get is a knock on the head from reality, and everything goes dark.'

The blessed man was so steeped in his pessimistic objections that when they called him into the dining-room and put a splendid lunch in front of him, it did not occur to him to inquire or even to think where this abundance, so out of keeping with his economic situation, could have come from. Having eaten it rapidly, he dressed to go out. Abelarda had darned the lapels of his overcoat with incredible perfection, imitating the weave of the torn material. She had also cleaned the collar with petrol, so that the coat now looked five years younger. Before he went out he entrusted Luis with the delivery of the letters he had written, giving him topographical instructions so as to ensure their methodical distribution in the shortest possible time. He could not have given the boy a job more to his taste since it excused him from attendance at school, and enabled him to spend the whole blessed afternoon like a gentleman, walking the streets with his friend Canelo. The dog was very quick to know when things were good. He seldom came up to the second floor, perhaps because he did not relish the poverty that generally reigned there. But with the finest instinct he recognized the rare abundance of the present moment, which was all the more splendid for the contrast with the scarcity of ordinary days. Whether the dog was keeping guard in the porter's lodge or inside the house, or sleeping under the scribe's table, it never escaped his notice that provisions had been brought in for the Villaamil family. How he discovered this no one knew. But the most astute excise officer could have taught him nothing. Turning his knowledge to practical advantage, he would of course go up to the house of abundance where he would spend the whole day and sometimes the next. But once the smell of burning came to his nostrils he would say, 'See you later,' and put in no further appearance. That day he arrived a little after seeing Doña Pura come in with the errand boy; and as the Miaus always spoilt him and gave him tit-bits it was quite hard for young Cadalso to get him out for his walk through the streets. Canelo departed very unwillingly to fulfil his social duty; he did not want to make a scandal.

The three Miaus were very lively that afternoon. They had the very happy gift of always living in the present, and never thinking of the morrow. This is a mental characteristic like any other, and a practical philosophy which, whatever you may say, has never been discredited though many have fulminated against it. Pura and Milagros were in the kitchen preparing the evening meal, which would have to be good, plentiful and rich in all its ingredients to act as a relief for unhappy stomachs. Without interrupting their work – one of them was skimming pots or preparing the meat, the other pounding in a mortar to the rhythm of an *andante con espressione* or *allegro con brio* – they chatted about the probable, or rather certain, appointment of the head of the household. Pura talked of paying all their debts, and bringing home the various useful objects which were wandering the weary world in the hands of usurers.

Abelarda was in the dining-room with her sewing-box open, pinning a little purple dress on to a dressmaker's dummy. She did not strike one as either pretty or plain; in a competition for unnoticeable faces she would have won first prize. Her skin was bad, her eyes were dark, and her features much like her mother's and aunt's. Indeed it was this general harmony that had given them their nickname of the three Miaus. I mean that, considered apart, the resemblance of the young woman's face to a cat's was not very pronounced, but put beside those of the other two it seemed to derive from them certain physiognomical characteristics that amounted to a racial or family stamp. Taken in a group, their three mouths looked small and prim, their mouths and the tips of their noses seemed to be joined by an indefinable line, their eyes were round and bright, and their hair characteristically tousled, as if they had been rolling on the floor after a ball of paper or tangle of wool.

Everything was marvellous that afternoon, for to Pura's great delight visitors called. She quickly abandoned her culinary tasks to put on a wrap and tidy her hair, and complacently walked into the drawing-room. The callers were Federico Ruiz and his wife Pepita Ballester. The famous 'Thinker' was also out of employment and passing through a terrible crisis, of which there were more signs in his clothing than in his wife's. But he took his lack of post calmly or, to be more correct, so optimistic was his nature that he took it with a certain pleasure. He was still unchanged, the same tireless jack-of-all-trades, devising plans for literary or scientific revolutions, or arranging soirées or centenary celebrations in honour of celebrities, or inventing some kind of occupation that would never have occurred to any other mortal. A sight of this dear fellow made one wonder whether there was not a sort of second-line army of learning.

He wrote articles on what should be done to make agriculture prosperous, and on the advantages of cremation of the dead, or gave a careful outline of life in the Stone Age, as if it was only a matter of yesterday. His economic position was pretty precarious, for he lived by his pen. Every now and then he managed to get the Ministry of Public Works to take a certain number of copies of old publications and of such rubbishy works as *Communism in the Light of Reason*, or *Fire Prevention in all the Countries of Europe*, or *A Picturesque Tour of the Castles*. But there was such a rich fount of comfort in his soul that he had no need of Christian resignation to reconcile him with his misfortunes. To be happy had come to be a matter of pride with him. In order not to be humiliated, he managed by force of imagination to love the idea of poverty, and to reach the absurdity of thinking that the greatest pleasure in the world is not to have a farthing or anywhere to look for one. To search for a livelihood, to go out in the morning wondering to what editor of a sickly review or dying periodical he should take the article he had written the night before, provided him with a series of emotions which the rich can never enjoy. He worked like a black and, compared with him, the veriest hack was an infant-in-arms in the art of pen-pushing. This way of earning his meat gave him a great and even licentious joy. And his meat never failed. His wife was a treasure, and helped him to cope with the situation. But even more efficacious was his own nature, his optimistic disposition, his ideal method of converting evil into good, and harsh scarcity into smiling abundance. Resignation removes grief. Poverty is the root of wisdom, and you will not

find happiness in the privileged classes. The 'Thinker' remembered Eguílaz' play in which, to show how amusing it is to be
poor, the hero says impassionedly :

> *I had five duros in my purse*
> *Upon my wedding day.*

And he also remembered that the whole gallery burst into a
thunder of applause and enthusiastic stamping : a proof that
shortage of money is very popular among our people. Ruiz too
had written a play in his time in which he had proved that to be
honest and just it is necessary to be out-at-elbow, and that rich
men always come to a bad end. However, despite this idealism
with which he gilded the copper of his economic crisis passing
base metal off as gold, Ruiz did not abandon hope of reinstatement in the service. He ceaselessly haunted the Ministry of Public Works, and the Boards of Public Education and Agriculture began to tremble as soon as he came round the screen. If he
could not have a post he asked for some small commission to
study something. It might be the law of literary copyright in all
countries or state granaries in Spain.

8

THE first subject of conversation with the visitors was the
opera, which Ruiz frequented like the Miaus, receiving a free
seat as one of the *claque*. 'They won't keep Don Ramón waiting
much longer,' said Ruiz.

'He'll be included in the list that is to be published in a day or
two,' said Pura, beaming. 'He's been left out so far because he
wouldn't accept a post out of Madrid. The Minister was very
anxious for him to go to one of the provinces that is very short
of men like my husband. But Ramón's not the man to go on his
travels now. To be frank with you, I very much want him to
have a post to keep him occupied, merely to keep him occupied.
You can't imagine, Federico, how upsetting it is to my husband
to be idle. It's a living death to him. What else would you expect

seeing that he's been accustomed to work ever since he was a boy? And would you believe it, Don Ramón has only another two months to do before he retires on four-fifths of his salary. If it wasn't for that, he'd be better off at home. "Don't you worry, my boy," I tell him, "we've got enough, thank God, to live on in a modest way." But he won't give up. He loves the bustle of the office. Even his cigar doesn't taste so good to him if he isn't smoking it between dealing with one file and the next.'

'I believe you. What a fine man he is, God bless him! And how is he in health?'

'His digestion is a bit delicate. I have to think out something new every day to tempt his appetite. My sister and I are doing the cooking ourselves at present, so as not to be bothered by maids. They're a perfect calamity! We make him a different little dish every day. Dainties and tasty morsels, you know. I have to go to the Plazuela del Carmen sometimes, for things you don't get in the Mostenses.'

'Well, that's a trouble I don't have,' said Señora de Ruiz; 'this man has a stomach that doesn't require it. His appetite is far too hearty to need tempting with tit-bits.'

'Yes, thank God!' said the Publicist jovially. 'I owe my happy disposition and the confidence I feel in my future to a sound digestion. Believe me, Doña Pura, there's nothing like a sound digestion. So here I am, as equable as ever. If they give me a post, splendid. If they don't, splendid just the same. To tell you the truth, I don't like working in an office. I'd rather have the job that the Minister offered me yesterday. A commission to study the pawnshops of Germany. A very important subject.'

'Very important of course. I should just think it is,' exclaimed Señora de Villaamil, raising her eyebrows.

At this point another visitor entered, a man called Guillén, who was a friend of Villaamil's and lived in the Calle del Acuerdo. He was lame in one leg and had a post in the Taxation department. Once greetings had been exchanged this man announced that a colleague of his in Personnel had assured him that very afternoon that Villaamil would be in the next list of appointments. Doña Pura accepted this as a certainty, and Ruiz and his wife supported the flattering belief. Congratulations mingled so freely in their talk that Doña Pura finally forced herself to offer her good friends some cakes and wine. Among the provisions collected on that happy day was a three-peseta bottle of muscatel, a liquor which Doña Pura was in the habit of offering her husband with his fruit. Ruiz and Guillén chinked glasses, and expressed with equal warmth their affection for this charming family. The 'Thinker's' sobriety contrasted strangely with the somewhat coarse appetite of the lame official, who begged Doña Pura not to take away the bottle. After he had filled his glass once or twice, it was seen that rather less than half the liquid was left.

When the lamps were lit and the visitors had departed Villaamil appeared. Pura ran to meet him, and saw with satisfaction that the fierce countenance of the tiger showed a slight tinge of pleasure.

'Well, what's the news? What have they told you?'

'Nothing, my dear,' said Villaamil, who was entrenched in his pessimism and could not be got out. 'Still nothing, still the same empty phrases.'

'And the Minister? Did you see him?'

'Yes, he gave me such a reception,' Villaamil allowed himself to say, committing heedless disloyalty to his affected misanthropy, 'he gave me such a good reception that...I don't know. It looks as if God has moved his heart, and spoken to him in my favour. He was most charming. Delighted to see me there. Very sorry not to have me beside him. Determined to bring me . . .'

'Come, you won't say that you've got no hopes now.'

'None, woman, absolutely none' – resuming his role. 'They're just leading me up the garden, as you'll see. As if I didn't know it! They won't give me a post till Judgement Day, and late in the evening at that.'

'Oh, what a man! This is flying in the face of Providence. The Lord might be angry with you, and he'd have good reason.'

'Stop talking nonsense. If you indulge in hopes you'll be bitterly disappointed. I don't want to be disappointed. So I indulge in no hopes, d'you see? I shall be perfectly calm when the blow falls.'

Just as his grandfather and grandmother were discussing whether or not they should indulge in hopes, young Luis arrived and announced that he had duly delivered all the letters. He was cold and hungry, and had a slight headache. On the way back from his expedition he had sat down in the portico of the Alarconas. But 'the thing' didn't come to him, nor did the vision think fit to appear in any form. Canelo refused to leave Doña Pura, and followed her from the larder to the kitchen, and from there into the dining-room. When they called the master of the house to his dinner and he did not come immediately, the knowing dog was sent to find him. By the wagging of his tail Canelo appeared to be saying, 'If you're not hungry say so. But don't keep us so long on tenterhooks.'

They ate with a fine appetite and very fair spirits, and afterwards over table Villaamil smoked with great enjoyment a Havana that Señor de Pez had given him that afternoon. It was very big, and when he took it the official without a post had told his friend that he would keep it for afterwards. That cigar reminded him of his prosperous days. Was it perhaps an omen that these days would return? It almost looked as if Villaamil were reading good fortune in the spirals of blue smoke, for he watched them in a daze as they ascended towards the dining-room ceiling and lightly veiled the lamp.

Later in the evening they had visitors (Ruiz, Guillén, Ponce, Cuevas and his wife, and Pantoja and his family – we shall speak of Pantoja later). A plan was then worked out for a project which had been mooted a month before: the production of a short play. Several friends of the Villaamils had uncommon theatrical talents, particularly for comedy. Federico Ruiz undertook to choose the piece, to cast it, and to direct the rehearsals. It was agreed that Abelarda should play one of the chief roles, and Ponce another. But Ponce admitted with praiseworthy modesty that he had not a spot of comedy in him and that even in the most humorous part he would reduce the audience to tears. He reserved for himself, therefore, the role of 'father' if there was one in the play.

Tired of all this nonsense, Don Ramón fled from the room to seek in the dark interior of the house the shadows that suited his pessimism. Automatically he went into Milagros' room, where she was undressing Luis to put him to bed. The poor boy had made some attempt to do his lessons but it had been completely useless. His head ached and he felt a sort of frightened premonition of an approaching vision. For his visions frightened him a little, since although he enjoyed them they also caused him some distress. He went to bed with the idea that an attack was coming, and that he would see some very strange things. He was already in bed when his grandfather came in, and his aunt was making him say his usual prayers, 'God guard me in my sleep, God guard me when I wake', etc., which he repeated by heart. Breaking off abruptly, the boy turned to ask Villaamil : 'Grandpa, is it true that the Minister received you very kindly?'

'Yes, my boy,' replied the old man, stunned by the question and the tone in which it was asked. 'But how did you know?'

'Me? Oh, I know.'

Young Cadalso gave his grandfather such a strange look that he did not know what to think. His expression was like that of the Infant Jesus, in which the seriousness of a man and the charm of a child are mingled.

'I know. I know,' repeated Luis unsmilingly and fixed his grandfather with a look that reduced him to immobility. 'And the Minister likes you very much. Because they wrote to him.'

'Who wrote to him?' asked the official without a post anxiously, taking a step towards the bed, and his eyes were bright.

'They wrote to him about you,' repeated young Cadalso; feeling the fear come on him and prevent him from continuing.

At that same moment it struck Villaamil that this was all nonsense. Half turning away, he lifted his hand to his head and said : 'But what ideas this child does get into his head!'

9

STRANGELY enough, nothing happened to Luis Cadalso that night. He did not feel or see anything, but shortly after going to bed fell into a very deep sleep. Next day he found it difficult to get up. He felt exhausted, as if he had taken a long journey through an unknown and distant country that he could not remember. He went to school and did not know his lessons. In fact he was so sluggish that day that the master made fun of him and hurt his pride in front of the whole class. Seldom in the school had anyone had to run the gauntlet as young Cadalso had to after being sent to the bottom of the class for ignorance and inattention. At eleven, when the writing lesson began, he had been sitting next to the famous Performer, a mischievous and very comical boy who wriggled like a worm and was so restless that where he was there could never be any peace. His name was Paquito Ramos y Guillén, and his parents were the owners of the pawnshop in the Calle del Acuerdo. Guillén, the lame official whom we have met at the Villaamils' celebrating his friend's coming appointment with copious libations of muscatel, was the Performer's maternal uncle. The boy owed his nickname to the mouselike liveliness of his movements, and the skill with which he mimicked the attitudes and gestures of the clowns and acrobats in the circus. Everything that he did ended with a grimace; he would put out his tongue, turn up his eyes, and when possible put his finger in an ink-pot and draw stripes on his face.

That morning, when the master was not looking, the Performer opened his satchel, and he and his friend Cadalso stuck their heads in to examine its various contents. The most remarkable was a collection of rings which shone with gold and rubies. Of course they were not made of metal but of paper. They were the rings that manufacturers put on middling cigars to make them pass for good ones. This treasure had come into Paquito Ramos' hands by a swap. The collection had belonged to another boy called Polidura, whose father, a waiter in a restaurant or café, was in the habit of picking up the cigar-bands that smokers dropped on the floor and giving them to his son for lack of better playthings. Polidura had succeeded in collecting more than fifty rings of different calibre. Some were inscribed *Flor fina*, others *Selectos de Julián Alvarez*. Finally tiring of his collection he had exchanged it with the Performer for a top in good condition, by means of a solemn contract before witnesses. Cadalso presented the new owner with the band of the 'stinker' which Pez had given to his grandfather, and which Señor Villaamil had smoked majestically after his dinner.

The Performer's trick, faithfully imitated by his friend Cadalso, was to load two or three of these dazzling jewels on each of his fingers and, raising his arm when the master was not looking, to display them to all the other urchins. If the master came round, however, they took them off very quickly and went on writing as if nothing was wrong. But by a sudden turn the master surprised young Cadalso with his hand up, disturbing the whole class. Immediately he became a raging lion. It was soon evident that the Performer was the chief culprit since he had a stock of paper rings in his satchel. In a twinkling the master pulled the load of jewels from their fingers, seized the whole stock and destroyed it, and finally gave both boys a good slap on the head. Ramos then complained, breaking into tears: 'It wasn't me. It was Miau's fault.'

And Miau, as much insulted by this calumny as by the nickname, protested with grave dignity: 'It was he who had them. I only put on one.'

'That's not true.'

'He's a liar, not me.'

'Miau's a hypocrite,' said the master. And when Cadalso heard the insulting nickname on Don Celedonio's lips he could not restrain his tears. He broke into bitter sobs, which were mimicked by the whole class, who cried 'Miau! Miau!' until the master slapped them all round, striking out at shoulders and faces, striding like a cruel galley-master between his lines of oarsmen, and flogging them all without mercy.

'I shall tell my grandfather,' exclaimed Cadalso with a burst of dignity, 'and I shan't come to this school any more.'

'Silence! Silence, everybody,' cried the executioner, threatening them with a ruler which had sides as sharp as knife-edges. 'Get on with your writing, you scoundrels. If anyone plays me up again I'll cut his head open.'

When school came out Cadalso was still angry with his friend the Performer, who was as bumptious as ever. With brazen impudence he gave Luis a shove, and said to him: 'It was your fault, idiot. Softy! Puss-face! If I catch you . . .'

Cadalso was furious again. His cheeks went white with nervous rage. His eyes flashed.

'Do you know what I say to you? You've got no business to call me nicknames. Blow me if you have. You're common, you are. You've got no manners. You're no class!'

'Miau!' mewed the Performer contemptuously, sticking out his tongue and clenching his fists.

'Go it, puss! Miau, Miau! Foo, foo, foo!'

For the first time in his life Luis found a situation that made him brave. Blind with anger, he rushed at his enemy and would have done so just as wildly if the Performer had been a man. A shriek of savage and childish joy rose from the whole band at the unaccustomed sight of young Cadalso fighting. Many of them shouted: 'Go at him! Go at him!'

A fight between Miau and the Performer was a rare spectacle, which roused dramatic and hitherto unknown excitement. It was like a hare turning on a ferret, or a partridge pecking at a dog. The Performer's calmness on receiving the first blow was a splendid sight. He spread his feet to keep his balance, and dropped his books and slate to have his arms free. And all the time he muttered in his crazy self-confidence: 'You'll see, you'll see. Blowed if I don't show you, blowed to hell if I don't. . . .'

Then one of those primitive Homeric fights broke out, man against man, which are all the more thrilling because neither party has weapons. They seize each other's arms, and push and shove and butt one another like rams, each trying to throw his opponent down. The Performer was strong, but so was Cadalso. Little Murillo, Polidura and the rest watched and cheered, dancing round them with the fierce excitement of savages thirsting for blood. But just at that moment the master's daughter, a rather mannish young woman, happened to come out of the house. Separating them with a couple of slaps, she said: 'Go home, you little brutes, or I'll call the police to put you in the cells.'

Both boys were red in the face, and panting like bellows, and

57

shouting tavern oaths, especially Paco Ramos, who was a past master of draymen's language.

'Come on, you fellows,' said young Murillo, the son of the sacristan of the Montserrat, in his most conciliatory tone. 'It's not as bad as all that. Come on. Come on, let go. Or else I shall . . . That's enough now.'

The peacemaker showed his determination to give a good hiding to either of them who tried to resume the fight. A policeman who was passing dispersed them, and they went off shouting and running, and some of them praising young Cadalso for his pluck. He made his way home in silence. His anger was quietly subsiding, though he would never forgive the Performer for using his nickname. He felt in his soul the first bubblings of heroic pride, and a knowledge that he was equal to life, or rather that he was capable of attacking an opponent, as his attempt on that day had proved.

There was no school in the afternoon, because it was Thursday. Luis went home, and none of the family noticed during lunch how hot he was. Afterwards he went down to spend a little time with his friends the scribes, who had no doubt kept a tit-bit or two for him.

'You seem to be having a very gay time upstairs,' said Paca. 'Tell me, have they given your grandfather a post? I should think they must have made him a minister, or an ambassador at least. That was a fine basket of provisions they brought in yesterday! And bottles of muscatel, as if they were given away free. Well, well, what goings on! But we are as God made us. There's been no getting Canelo down from your place.'

Luis said that they had not given his grandfather a post yet, but he would get it any moment now. It was a very fine day, and Paca suggested to her young friend that they should go and sit in the sun on the Conde Duque terrace, a stone's throw from the Calle de Quiñones. The scribe's huge wife put on her shawl while Luis went up to ask for permission, and they set out. It was three o'clock. The vast area between the Paseo de Areneros and the guards' barracks was bathed in sun, and full of local people who had come out to stretch themselves. A large part of this area was then, and still is, occupied by stone blocks, tiles, paving stones and such like, left over from, or lying in readiness for, some municipal building works; and between these piles of stones the housewives of the district hung the lines on which they dried their washing. The part that was free from obstruction was used by the soldiers for their drill, and that afternoon young Luis saw some cavalry recruits learning to march in step. The officer who was instructing them carried a bare sabre, and shouted his words of command. It amused the boy to watch their evolutions and to listen to the regular shouts of 'One, two, three, four', to which the recruits kept step. It was a dull rumble that got mixed up with the vibration of the ground, on which they stamped to time, like an immense drum beaten by a giant. Among the company that had gathered there to enjoy the sun sellers of pea-nuts and walnuts circulated, lazily crying their merchandise. Paca bought young Luis some of these good things, and sat down on a block of stone to gossip with various of her friends. The boy then ran behind the recruits, imitating their movements. He went up and down for more than an hour, playing at soldiers, and shouting 'One, two, three, four' with them, at the end of which time, feeling tired, he sat down on a pile of paving-stones. Then his head began to swim. He saw that the heavy mass of the barracks ran from right to left, and that the Liria palace lay in the same direction, deep among the boughs of its garden, the trees of which appeared to stretch out of the immense tomb in which they had been planted, in order to breathe more freely. Young Cadalso began to feel the familiar discomfort; his consciousness of the objects before him swam and vanished, and he was overtaken by a mysterious terror, which was in reality a fear of the unknown. Then, resting his head on a huge stone beside him, he slept like an angel. At the first moment the vision of the convent steps appeared, clear and palpable, like a living being, seated opposite him, though he could not say where. This fantastic picture had no background and nothing round it; it consisted of this splendid figure alone. It was the same person with the long, white beard, dressed in undefinable clothes, his left hand hidden in the folds of his mantle and his right outside it, the hand of one who is about to speak. But the surprising thing was that before uttering the first word, the Lord stretched his right hand out to him, and when young Cadalso gazed at it he saw that its fingers were loaded with those very rings of the Performer's rich collection. Only on those almighty fingers that had created the world in seven days they shone as if they were really gold and precious stones. Young Cadalso listened spell-bound, as the Lord said to him: 'Look, Luis, at what the master took away from you. Look at these pretty rings. I picked them up off the ground, and quickly put them together again. It was no trouble. The master's a brute, and I'll teach him not to slap you like that. As for the Peformer, of course he's a scamp, but he doesn't mean badly. He's just badly brought up. Nice children don't call nicknames. You were quite right to be cross with him, and you behaved very well. I can see you're a brave boy and know how to stand up for your honour.'

Luis was very pleased to hear himself called brave by a person of such authority. He felt too much respect to be able to thank him. But he was on the point of saying something when the Lord raised his bejewelled hand in a threatening manner and observed severely: 'But, my boy, though in this respect I am pleased with you, in another I have reason to scold you. You did not know your lesson today. You were never right once, even by accident. It was quite obvious that you had not opened the book all the blessed day.' (Luis, in great grief, moved his lips to utter an excuse.) 'Yes, I know what you're going to say to me. You were out till very late delivering letters. You did not get home till night. But you could have studied a bit then. Don't tell me fibs. And this morning, why didn't you look over the geography lesson this morning? What a lot of silly mistakes you made. Why did you imagine that France is bounded on the north by the Danube, and that the Po passes through Pau? What a lot of nonsense! Do you think that's what I made the world for, to have you and your snivelling friends turning it upside down every few minutes?'

The exalted person ceased, but kept his eyes fixed on young Cadalso, who changed colour and was too overwhelmed to speak. He could not look at his interlocutor, nor could he look away from him.

'You really must see how things are,' added the Father at length, making a gesture with his bejewelled hand. 'How can you expect me to find your grandfather a post if you don't do your lessons? You can see how depressed the poor man is, waiting for his appointment as if it were the blessed wafer. A breath would blow him away. And it's all your fault, because if you did your lessons . . .'

Young Cadalso was so grieved when he heard this that he felt as if he had a noose round his neck and was choking to death. He tried to breathe a sigh and could not.

'You'll understand this,' added God, 'because you're not a fool. Put yourself in my position. Put yourself in my position, and you'll see that I'm right.'

Luis reflected on this. His reason had to accept the argument, for he saw that its logic was irrefutable. It was as clear as daylight. So long as he did not work, how on earth could they find his grandfather an appointment? It seemed absolutely true, and the tears sprang to his eyes. He was about to speak, perhaps to make a solemn promise that he would do his lessons, that he would work like a fiend, when he felt himself seized by the collar.

'Don't go to sleep here, boy,' said Paca, giving him a shake, 'or you'll catch a cold.'

Luis looked at her thunderstruck, and for a moment the outlines of the vision were confused with those of the real world. Soon his eyesight cleared, though not his thoughts. He saw the barracks of the Conde Duque, and heard the 'One, two, three, four' sound as if from underground. His vision, nevertheless, remained indelibly stamped on his mind. When he remembered the bejewelled hand and the ineffable voice of the Father and Creator of all things, he could not doubt it. Paca made him get up, and led him away. Then, taking the pea-nuts out of her pocket, she said before she gave them to him : 'Don't eat too many of these or they'll clog your stomach. I'll keep them for you. Let's go now. It's beginning to get chilly.'

But he wanted to go on sleeping. His brain was dull, as if he had just been drinking. His legs trembled and he felt an intense cold down his back. As he walked home, he was struck by doubts concerning the reality and divine nature of the apparition. Was it God, or wasn't it? he reflected. Seems that it was because he knew absolutely everything. Seems that it wasn't because he had no angels with him.

After his walk he kept his good friends company. Mendizábal, his day's work concluded, gathered together his papers, cleaned his busy pens, and set about lighting the staircase. Paca polished the glass of the lamp, and lit the oil-burner inside. The 'Public Secretary' then took it, and with an air of solemnity, as if escorting the Viaticum, went and hung it in its place between the first and the second floor. Villaamil then came upstairs, and stopped as usual to have a chat with the scribe.

'Good luck to you, Don Ramón!' he remarked.

'Hush, my dear fellow,' answered Villaamil, putting on the expression of a man with terrible toothache. 'If there hasn't been anything till now, there never will be.'

'Oh, but I thought . . . They're a pig-headed lot, Don Ramón. These ministers are just a farce! What I say is, until we have a clean sweep . . .'

'Oh, my friend,' exclaimed Villaamil with a slight air of governmental moderation, 'you know I don't like exaggerations. I don't share your ideas. What is it you ask for? More religion? Very well, let's have more religion, but not obscurantism. Let us clear our minds. What we want in Spain is administration, morality. . . .'

'That's the trouble. That's the trouble' (with a triumphant expression). 'That's just what we shan't get until we have faith. The first thing is faith. Am I right or am I not?'

'Quite right, but . . . No, friend Mendizábal, don't let's exaggerate.'

'And societies that lose their faith' (with triumph in his voice) 'fall straight, as you might say, into the abyss.'

'That's all very well, but . . . There is such a thing as morality, morality. As a man sows so shall he reap. Leave matters of conscience to the clergy. Don't confuse one power with another.'

'I'm not confusing anything, but you'll see' (going down a stair as Villaamil went up one). 'So long as there's freedom of conscience, you'll still be without a post. Seeing that there's no

62

justice nowadays and no one pays any attention to merit. . . .
Good night.'

This very ugly man disappeared downstairs. The strangeness
of his expression was due to the closeness of his eyes which
seemed to run together. When he looked at you fixedly they
appeared like a single eye. His nose continued from his forehead, descending, straight and flat, to end in two broad nostrils
just above his upper lip. His lips were wide and thick, and
stretched so far in all directions that they filled almost half his
face. His mouth was big and ended in two creases, which
divided his thin grey beard into three limp sections. His hands
were large and hairy, his neck was strong, and his short body
tilted forward as if he belonged to a race which until not long
ago had walked on four legs. As he went down the staircase he
seemed to swing on his hands, which gripped the banisters.
Despite his likeness to a gorilla, Mendizábal was a good man,
with no other defect but his furious aversion to free-thought.
He had traded in flints during the first civil war, had spied for
the rebels and been cook to Father Cirulo. 'Ah,' he would say
times out of number, 'if I were to write my story!' One final
biographical detail. He had repaired a wheel of the famous
coach of San Carlos de la Rápita.*

10

A s he climbed the stairs to go home at nightfall, little Cadalso
heard steps behind him, but did not turn round. But when he
was a couple of steps from the second floor, unknown hands
caught his head and clasped it to prevent him from looking
back. Thinking himself in the power of some ugly bearded thief,
who was going to rob the house and was making sure of him for
a start, the boy was afraid. But before he had time to cry out,
the stranger lifted him up and gave him a kiss. Luis could then
see his face, but he felt no calmer when he recognized him. He

* The pretender Don Carlos, who had landed at this port, travelled
by coach to meet his supporters. His coup, however, failed.

had last seen that face some time ago, though he could not quite say when, on an evening when there was trouble and strife, and everyone in the house was shouting. Abelarda had fallen in a faint, and his grandma had called to the neighbours for help. This dramatic domestic scene had left an indelible impression on Luis, who did not know why his aunts and his grandmother had been so furious.

At that time his grandpa had been in Cuba, and the family had not lived in the Calle de Quiñones. He remembered that the Miaus' rage had fallen on a person who had then disappeared from the house, never to return till the occasion now described. That man was his father. Luis did not dare to utter this affectionate title. He said peevishly, 'Let me go!' And this person rang.

When Doña Pura opened the door and saw the person who had rung in the company of his son, for a moment she could not believe her eyes. Surprise and terror were painted on her face. And then anger. Finally she muttered: 'Victor! You?'

As he entered he greeted his mother-in-law with some feeling. His manner was polite and affectionate. Villaamil, who had a very sensitive ear, shuddered as he recognized that voice from his study. 'Victor here. Victor in the house again. The man always brings us bad luck.' And when his son-in-law came in to greet him, Don Ramón's tigerish face became frightening, his carnivorous jaw trembled, as if he longed to plunge it into the first creature that came into his sight. 'But how did you get here? Have you got leave?' was all that he said.

Victor Cadalso sat down opposite his father-in-law. The lamp, which stood between them, lit their two faces and threw up the contrast between them. Victor was a perfect example of masculine good-looks, a type of those who appear destined to preserve and transmit comeliness of shape throughout the human race, which has grown ugly by crossbreeding and yet by an endless succession of crossbreedings every now and then succeeds in producing a splendid model: a model in which to contemplate itself with delight as in its own mirror, thus convincing itself that despite the countless progeny of ugliness the archetypes of beauty are permanent. The half-light shed by the lamp outlined

64

the handsome young man's features. His nose was perfectly curved, his eyes were black with large pupils, the expression of which varied at will from the tenderest to the most serious gaze. His pale forehead had the form and polish that is used by sculptors to express nobility. (This nobility arises from a balanced relationship between the bones of the skull and a harmony in their outline.) A strong neck, jet-black, rather untidy hair and a short beard which was dark also completed that finely modelled bust, which was Italian rather than Spanish. He was of middling size, and his body was as proud and well-proportioned as his head; his age must have been between thirty-two and thirty-five. Being unable to answer his father-in-law's question exactly, he hesitated for a moment, then pulled himself together and said: 'Leave, no. That's to say . . . I've had an argument with the chief. I came away without telling anybody. You know the sort of man I am. I don't like people playing the fool with me. I'll tell you later. I've something else to say now. I arrived this morning on the eight o'clock train, and took a room in a guest-house in the Calle del Fucar. I was thinking of staying there. But things are so bad with me that if the two of you don't mind' (Doña Pura had been present all the time) 'I'll come here for a few days, only for a few days.'

Doña Pura began to tremble, and ran to carry the fatal news to her sister and her daughter. 'He's coming to stay here, the horror! Now we're in for it!'

'We're very tight for space here,' protested Villaamil, his face becoming fiercer and more baleful every minute. 'Why don't you go to your sister Quintina's?'

'You know,' he answered, 'that my brother-in-law Ildefonso and I are, so to speak, on rather strained terms. I get on better with you. I promise you I'll be quiet and reasonable, and some little things I'll forget.'

'But, tell me briefly, are you still in your job in Valencia or not?'

'I'll tell you' (swallowing his first words, but finally thinking out an answer that would conceal his embarrassment). 'That Chief of the Finance Department is a twister . . . He has done his best to throw me out. He's been trying to lodge a complaint against me. He won't have any success, of course; I've got more brains than he has.'

Villaamil sighed, and tried to read from his son-in-law's face the mystery of his untimely arrival. But he knew from experience that Victor's features were impenetrable, and that, being a consummate actor, he suited his expression to whatever at the moment were his ends.

'And what do you think of your son?' he asked, seeing Pura return with Luis. 'He's grown, and we're taking care of his health. He's always been a bit delicate, and so we don't like to force him to do his lessons.'

'He's got plenty of time,' said Cadalso, putting his arms round the boy and giving him a kiss. 'He gets more like his mother every day, more like my poor Luisa. Doesn't he?'

The old man's eyes grew moist. That daughter who had perished in the flower of her youth had been his only love. On the day of her premature death Villaamil had suddenly grown ten years older. Every time someone in the house mentioned her name, the poor man felt his immense suffering return; and when that someone was Victor, his sorrow was mixed with the hatred one feels for a murderer who mourns his victim after he has killed her. Doña Pura's heart sank also at the sight and the voice of the man who had been her beloved daughter's husband. Luis grew sad, but rather out of habit, because he had noticed that whenever anyone in the house pronounced his mamma's name everyone sighed and put on a very serious face.

Victor took his son and went to greet Milagros and Abelarda. The former loathed him with all her heart, and replied to his greeting with cold scorn. His young sister-in-law had shut herself in her room when she heard him and when she came out her colour, which was always bad, was like that of a corpse. Her voice quavered; she wanted to express the same contempt for Victor as her aunt. Victor clasped her hand. 'So you're back again, you good-for-nothing?' she mumbled and, not knowing what to do, shut herself up once more in her room.

Meanwhile Villaamil, shocked and apprehensive, despaired, sitting there in his chair as if about to be crucified, and said to

66

his wife: 'This man will bring misfortune to our house today, as he has brought it before. You can be sure of that. When I heard his voice, I thought that hell itself was entering at the door. I curse the hour' (getting excited and letting the palms of his hands fall with noisy weight on the table top) – 'I curse the hour when our beloved daughter fell in love with him, and I curse the day on which we let them marry. There was nothing else we could do. If only I had my daughter alive again! Alive even if dishonoured! It was stupid of us to let her marry in such a hurry, without our knowing to whom. You take good care with this dodger, Pura. Don't you trust him. He has a way of covering up his wickedness with words that suddenly charm and seduce you. He doesn't take me in. No, he only deceived me once. I saw through him pretty quickly, and now I keep on my guard, because he is the wickedest man God has ever put into the world.'

'But didn't he tell you why he has come? Have they taken away his job? I'm sure he's done something sharp, and has come here for you to hide him.'

'Me?' (scared and with his eyes starting out of his head). 'No one on the face of the earth would hide him! He's come to the wrong place.'

When dinnertime came Victor sat down at table with the greatest effrontery, and allowed himself some sprightly flourishes of conversation. Everyone looked at him with enmity, and avoided the jovial themes that he brought into play. Occasionally his brow clouded with resentment. But like an actor who after a brief lapse remembers his part, he assumed a studied pose of good nature and good cheer. Then the great difficulty reappeared. Where would they put him? And Doña Pura, at a loss for anywhere to lodge the intruder, angrily dug her heels in and said: 'No, it's impossible, Victor. You can see there's no way of having you in the house.'

'Don't get upset, Mamma,' he answered, affectionately stressing his address. 'I'll sleep here on the dining-room sofa. Give me a blanket, and I'll sleep the sleep of the just.'

Doña Pura and the other Miaus could find no objection to this considerate proposal. When the guests began to arrive for the evening party, Victor said to his mother-in-law: 'Look, Mamma, I won't come in. I haven't the slightest wish to meet people, at least for a day or two. I think I heard Pantoja's voice. Don't tell him I'm here.'

'What's the reason for this strange behaviour?' asked his mother-in-law angrily. 'Are you going to stay like a dummy in the dining-room? You know I shall put the glasses out on the table here in case anyone's thirsty and wants some water. And I warn you that Pantoja comes out and drinks half a bucket every night.'

'Then I'll go into Luis' room, unless you'll put the water somewhere else tonight.'

'But where?'

'Nowhere. It doesn't matter, Mamma. Don't change your habits on my account. You go into the drawing-room, where all the *crème* are now assembled. Don't forget to put the blanket out for me. Tomorrow morning early I'll bring my luggage.'

When Doña Pura conveyed to her husband the reluctance to be seen that she had noticed in Cadalso, the good gentleman became more uneasy, and cursed the intruder once again. After the tray with the glasses of water, which were the only refreshment that the Villaamils could offer their friends, had been laid on the dining-room table, Cadalso stayed for a while alone with his son, who that night displayed unusual application. 'Do you study much?' asked his father, fondling him. And the boy nodded a shy, reluctant assent, as if studying were a crime. His father was like a stranger to him, and when he tried to talk to him he was tongue-tied with shyness. The feelings which that man aroused in the poor boy were a very strange mixture of respect and fear. He respected him because he was his father, and the word Father had its natural value for his tender soul; and he feared him because he had heard him referred to countless times in the house in fairly unfavourable terms. Cadalso was the wicked father as Villaamil was the good father.

When Victor heard the steps of some thirsty visitor approaching the watering-place, he slipped into Milagros' room. He recognized the voice of Ponce, who in addition to being a theatre critic was Abelarda's fiancé. He also recognized Pantoja, an

68

employee in the Taxation office, and a friend of Villaamil's, also of his own, whom he considered the most sly and useless human machine to be found in any office. I cannot pass over the fact that one of the thirstiest persons that night was Abelarda herself, who came out for water two or three times, and also volunteered to put the little boy to bed instead of Milagros. While she was doing so, Victor entered the bedroom to take refuge from another dry-throated guest who had come out for refreshment.

'Papa is very disturbed at your turning up again like this,' said Abelarda, when she saw him. 'You came into the house like Mephistopheles through the trap-door, and we're all very upset at seeing you.'

'Do I eat people?' asked Victor, sitting down on Luis' bed. 'Besides, there's nothing mysterious about my coming. There is something of course that your father and mother won't understand. But you'll understand, Abelarda, when I explain it to you, because you're always kind to me. You don't loathe me like the others. You know about my misfortunes, you recognize my faults and feel pity for me.'

He said this very sweetly, with his eyes on his son, who was now half-undressed. Abelarda avoided looking at him. But not so Luis, who had fixed his gaze on his father, as if trying to make out the meaning of his words.

'We pity you?' the little nobody finally answered in a trembling voice. 'How do you make that out? Do you really suppose I believe a word you say? You may take some women in, but not my mother's daughter!'

And as Victor began to reply somewhat vehemently, Abelarda silenced him with an expressive gesture. She was afraid that someone might come in, or that Luis might understand. And this gesture marked a fresh stage in their conversation.

'I don't want to know anything,' she said, finally making up her mind to look him in the face.

'But whom am I to confide in if I don't confide in you, the only person who understands me?'

'Go to church, and kneel in the confessional.'

'The light of faith was extinguished in me a long time ago.

I'm in the dark,' declared Victor, looking at the child whose hands were already clasped to begin his prayers.

And when the boy had finished, Abelarda turned to his father and said with feeling: 'You are very wicked, very wicked. Turn towards God, and invoke his help, and . . .'

'I don't believe in God,' answered Victor dryly. 'God appears in dreams, and I woke up long ago.'

Young Luis hid his face in the pillows. He felt frightfully cold and most uneasy: all the precursory symptoms, in fact, of that state in which his mysterious friend appeared to him.

11

AT twelve o'clock, when the guests had departed, Cadalso made himself comfortable on the dining-room sofa, and covered himself with the blanket that Abelarda had given him. He did not know that his sister-in-law would have to sleep in her clothes that night since she had nothing to put on her bed. Everyone retired except Villaamil, who would not do so till he had had an explanation from his son-in-law. The dining-room lamp was still alight, and when the old man came in he saw Victor sitting up on his hard couch, wrapped in the blanket from the waist downwards. Cadalso immediately realized that his father-in-law wanted to talk, and prepared himself, which he did not find difficult, for he was a man with a ready imagination, a free flow of words. He could always find swift and well-timed answers, being of pure southern blood, for he was born on the coast of the province of Granada which has the Alpujarra behind it and faces towards Morocco. The old boy's coming in to attack, he thought. Well, let him attack and welcome. Let the fight begin. We'll play him deftly with the cloak.

'Now that we're alone,' said Villaamil with a gravity that had once inspired fear, 'make up your mind to be frank with me. You've done something stupid, Victor. I can see it in your face, although your face very seldom expresses what is in your mind. Tell me the truth, and don't try to confuse me with your verbal fencing, or with those odd ideas of yours that you find so useful.'

'I have no odd ideas, my dear Don Ramón. It's my dear father-in-law that has the odd ideas. We must judge a man's ideas by the profit he gets from them. Have they given you a post yet? I imagine not. And yet you're still cheerfully hoping that justice will give you your reward. You might just as well expect it to fall from the moon. As I've told you a thousand times, the state itself teaches us that we have a right to a living. If the state never dies, administratively speaking a government servant should not perish either. But I'd like to tell you something else. Unless you change your tactics, they won't give you a post. You'll spend months and years living on illusions, and trusting the flattering promises and deceptive smiles of men who swell out their chests when they see a fool, and pretend they mean to assist him.'

'But you're a fool,' said Villaamil in a great fury. 'What makes you think that I have any hopes? Why do you imagine, blockhead, that I've fostered even the thousandth part of blessed illusion? Find a post for me! Why, the idea of such a thing has never crossed my mind. I have no hopes, absolutely none, and I'll say more, I am insulted that anyone should think I listen to polite protestations and empty words.'

'You are just as you have always been, so confident, so optimistic.'

'Optimistic? Me?' (much annoyed). 'Don't laugh at an old man, Victor. And what's more, don't avoid the question. We are not talking about me now, but about you. I ask you once more, what have you done? Why are you here, and why are you hiding yourself from people?'

'Evening parties in this house bore me. You know that I am very strong in my antipathies. I'm not hiding myself. I just don't want to see Ponce's bleary-eyed face, or to be talked to by Pantoja. His breath stinks from a mile off.'

'We're not talking about Pantoja's breath, but your leaving your post, which you didn't do with a clean conscience.'

'My conscience is so clean that if my chief were to make any complaint, I should be in the position to get him a jail-sentence' (getting warmer). 'I have done such good service, let me tell you, that if the state had any gratitude I should be chief of a department. But the state is notoriously ungrateful, as well you know, and doesn't reward merit. If an intelligent official doesn't look after himself he's lost. Let me make myself clear. When I went to Valencia to take over State Monopolies and Excise, the whole department was in chaos. My predecessor was an actor who had lost his voice, and had been given the job on his retirement from the stage. The poor man didn't know what he was doing. Then I turned up, and, hey presto, things began to move! What a stir! They hadn't been able to get personal contributions in for love or money. There were terrible deficits in the Excise. I called the mayors together, I put pressure on them, I put the fear of God into them. To cut a long story short, I got a vast sum in for the Treasury, which would have been lost to them but for me. Then I reflected and said to myself: What is the natural consequence of this service I have done to the nation? The natural, logical and inevitable consequence of defending the state against the tax-payer is the state's ingratitude. Let us provide ourselves with an umbrella, therefore, to protect ourselves from this ingratitude, which is certain to bring us misery.'

'You could not say more clearly that your hands are none too clean.'

'Not at all. No, sir' (sitting up and gesticulating with great energy). 'Because, as mediator between the tax-payer and the state, I have to prevent them both from devouring one another. If I didn't make peace between them, there'd be nothing left but the tips of their tails. I am part of the tax-paying community, which is the Nation; and as an official I am part of the state. In this dual capacity I, as mediator, have to preserve my own life, in order to continue to prevent the mortal clash between the tax-payer and the state.'

'I don't understand you, and nobody else would' (with an angry and contemptuous gesture). 'It's always the same. With all this mental ingenuity you are trying to cover up your cheating. Well, do you know what I have to say? You cannot stay in my house.'

'Don't get heated, my dear father-in-law. Let me say in passing that I never supposed you would keep me here for my good looks. I'll pay for my keep. It will only be for a few days, because when they promote me . . .'

'Promote you? What do you mean?' (as if a scorpion had stung him).

'Oh dear! But what did you suppose? What an innocent you are! Always the same Don Ramón, the pure virgin! You should be drinking lime-flower tea. Now. . . . But what did you expect? Am I not God and shall I not rise? Am I not God's child, and should I not get promotion? Do you know that I've already been a first-class official for two years, and that by Cánovas' law I'm due for promotion to departmental chief, third class? And you, who are so optimistic about your own affairs and so pessimistic about other people's, believe that I'm going to spend my life writing letters, and watching for a Director General to smile, or brushing the dust off Cucúrbitas' coat? No sir, I'm not going for the red rag but for the figure behind it.'

'Yes, yes, there's no beating you for bare-faced effrontery. Because you've got no shame' (livid with fury and swallowing his bitterness) 'you get everything you want. The world is at your feet. Promotion at all costs, and devil take the hindmost!'

'Whereas you' (with cruel sarcasm) 'continue to rock yourself in the sweetest of dreams, and continue to believe that the angels will bring you your appointment, and wake up every day saying, "Today, today it will come," and you read the *Correspondencia* every evening in the hope of seeing your name printed there.'

'Once and for all, I repeat' (wishing he had a bottle or an inkwell or a candlestick to throw at his head) 'that I haven't the least hope they'll ever give me a post. I don't even think of it. But I'm quite convinced that you've been defrauding the Treasury this time, and that your tricks will bring you a reward. For that's the way things happen. That's how this swinish government . . . My God, that ever I should live to see such things!' (getting up and clutching his hands to his head).

'What you should do' (in a somewhat conceited tone) 'is to take a lesson from me.'

'A fine model! I don't wish to hear you or to see you, not

73

even your picture. Good-bye' (departing, but turning back at the door). 'And get this into your head. I don't hope for anything, I'm quite content. I bear my misfortunes patiently, and it never even occurs to me that they will give me a post today, tomorrow or any time this century, however badly we need it. But . . .'

'But what?' (he begins to laugh maliciously). 'Tell me, what post am I to get for you if I go and worry them?'

'You . . . you! I be beholden to you!'

And his indignation was such that through fear of saying something stupid he was reduced to silence. Giving the door a bang which shook the house, he fled to his bedroom and threw himself on the rucked cover of his martyr's bed like a despairing man plunging into the sea.

Victor wound himself in his blanket and tried to sleep. But he was too excited, not so much because of his argument with his father-in-law, but because the memory of some recent events was still vivid in his mind. The hardness of the couch on which he lay, however, also contributed something to his sleepless state. The light became so dim after midnight that its uncertain rays hardly lit the room; and in Victor's sleepless and feverish brain, this half-light and the smell of cold meat which hung on the air mingled to form a single disagreeable impression. He examined the dining-room detail by detail, and its walls on which the paper was torn in some places and dirty in others. In some spots, especially beside the doors, the filth was caused by human contact; in others he could see the traces of Luis' fingers and even the marks of his artistic pencil. The ceiling, which was smoke-stained above the lamp, had two or three cracks, which formed a huge M and perhaps some other letters that were not so clear. On the wall were holes left by the nails on which prints had once hung. Victor remembered having seen a clock there which had never struck the hour, and the hands of which had always indicated some unlikely time. There had also been coloured still-lifes, showing different kinds of melons sliced open. Pictures and clock had disappeared, like a cargo thrown overboard to save the ship. The sideboard remained. But how old and worn it looked with the paint flaking from the blackened edges of its shelves, with the glass of one door broken and no finial at the top! Inside could be seen some glasses upside down, cruets with bottles that did not match, a very shrunken lemon, a coffee-grinder, some grimy tins and a few pieces of earthenware. The door leading into the passage to the kitchen was covered with a heavy Manila hemp curtain, filthy on the edge by which it was handled, and with a hole in the middle that could have served for a hatch.

Tired of shifting his position, Victor sat up in his bed, that was like a rack, and his restlessness now took the form of rambling thoughts. He felt a desire to come to an explanation with himself, and to still his bad conscience by putting the blame elsewhere. He began therefore to speak in a low but audible voice: 'I've a right to it, you idiots! You're just a pack of office-rats who gnaw at the files. I'm worth more than the lot of you put together. I can get through a whole month of the Department's work in a single day.'

Shocked by the sound of his own voice, he now threw himself down on the couch. Then, a little later, with eyes closed and furrowed brow, like a sort of somnambulist, he mentally reviewed the whole business, which he could not get out of his thoughts.

Excise. . . . Ah, the excise! It's the most ingenious of inventions. Those rogues in the towns! They'd sell themselves to the devil if they could avoid paying it. The demand-notes stink in their nostrils when we send them in. But I don't let them worry me. If they try to put me off with excuses, I burn them alive. Interest on arrears, that's the trick! And since like calls to like, there's nothing easier than to find an accountant with whom you can come to an agreement on the subject of these demands for interest. A town's very lucky if it can slide out interest-free when it's maybe two years in arrears. Señor Alcalde, let's come to an understanding. You want a breathing-space? Well, I need oxygen too. We're all God's children. And why should the Treasury complain? Haven't I saved six millions for it, that my predecessor gave up for lost? So why should it whimper like a fallen woman? When a man's rendered such great services, doesn't he deserve a reward? Haven't we got to protect ourselves from the state's ingratitude, and reward ourselves for our own loyal services? Recompense is the first moral law, the application of justice, right and the *jus* to public affairs. A state without gratitude, that has no regard for merit, is a barbarous state. What I say is that where a service is rendered, there a commission is owed. Debit and credit, that's elementary. With one hand I give the state six millions that had disappeared, and so I stretch out the other to receive my commission. What does the confounded thieving, cheating state expect? That I shall get in the millions and come off empty-handed? Yes, that's how it would have been, you wretches, if I hadn't looked after myself. But clever though you may be, I'm cleverer, I promise you. The state's a sly one, and so am I. And as for you who pay the taxes, what have you got to complain of? Can't you see that I'm defending you? If you want a breathing-space, I must have air too. If I choke, someone else'll come who'll flay you alive.

And that fool of a chief! That idiot! That bandit who ate up the collection for the shipwrecked sailors in Pontevedra, and at Cáceres left the widows of the dead miners without a farthing. A man capable of swallowing a whole cemetery with all its dead! How could he start proceedings against me? But proof's a very difficult matter, you rogue. And if you attack me, I'll denounce you, I'll expose you in the streets complete with facts, dates and figures. I have good friends, and men with clean reputations to defend me. That's what you can't forgive. You're eaten up with envy. That's why you're attacking me now, you thief. Because you weren't fit to wind up the clocks, and you entered the public service.

At the end of a quarter of an hour, when he seemed to have dozed off, he exclaimed with a sudden laugh, 'They can't prove anything against me. But even if they could . . .' Finally he went off to sleep, and had one of those nightmares that always troubled his rest at moments of moral agitation. He dreamt that he was walking down an endlessly long gallery with mirrored walls that reflected his elegant person to infinity. He was walking down this huge street in pursuit of a woman, a smart woman in a silk dress which rustled with the quick movements of her running feet. Cadalso saw the heels of her boots which were . . . large egg-shells! He did not know who the lady could be. She was the same one that he had dreamt of before, and as he followed her he told himself that this was all a dream. He was surprised to find himself pursuing a phantom, but he went on running. Finally he touched her, and the lady stopped, turned round, and said to him in a very hoarse voice: 'Why do you insist on taking this commode away from me?' In fact the lady was carrying a commode of natural size, and she was carrying it as easily as if it had been a purse. Then Victor woke up, feeling himself oppressed by a weight too heavy for him to move, and by a superstitious terror that he could not relate either to the commode or the lady or the mirrors. It was all stupid and quite meaningless.

If he had been truly awake, Cadalso's dreams would have had more meaning for him. For all his life he had been thinking of riches that he did not possess, of honours and power that he desired, of beautiful women whose charms were not unknown to him, of elegant ladies of the most exalted blood, whom he longed with the most ardent curiosity to know and possess; and this aspiration for the supreme pleasures of life always kept him restless, sleepless and on the watch. Devoured by a yearning to get into the upper classes of society, he believed that he held one end and the first knot of the rope by which others less bold than he had climbed there. What was the first knot? This was a secret that Cadalso would not reveal for anything in the world to his very vulgar and limited relatives the Villaamils.

12

THE figure that had stepped out of Fra Angelico, in other words Doña Pura, appeared very early and greeted him with the cutting edge of her displeasure, which was aggravated by a slight toothache that had given her a bad night. 'Now, get out of the dining-room, and go and wash yourself in my room. We've got to sweep up in here. And be quick about it too, unless you want to be covered with dust.' The second Miau seconded this proposal in a very persuasive manner by entering, broom in hand.

'Don't upset yourself, Mamma' (Doña Pura was always very cross when her son-in-law called her Mamma). 'Since you became a great lady, there's no managing you. What a way to treat your unfortunate son-in-law!'

'That's right. Make fun of me. You only have to do that to conquer us entirely. You've a real talent for coming at the right moment! You always turn up here when we're up to our necks in trouble.'

'What if I were to say that I think I've come at a very opportune moment? What would you answer to that now? Because you mustn't despise anybody, dear Mamma, and there are times when the unwelcome guest proves to be the messenger of Providence overnight.'

'A fine Providence!' (following Victor to the room in which he was to wash). 'What is it you mean? That you're going to tighten the rope that's choking us?'

'As sure as you're shouting at me here' (wheedlingly) 'I'm the man who can invite you to a seat in the stalls.'

'We've no need of your stalls. And how can you invite us? You've been as broke as the government as long as I've known you.'

'Mamma, Mamma, please don't insult me like this. Besides, the fact that I'm poor shouldn't make you doubt my kindness of heart.'

'That's enough. I'll leave you in here. Be as quick as you can.'

'I'd rather face a murderer's knife than these black looks' (holding her by the arm). 'Would you like me to pay for my lodging?'

At this moment he took out his wallet. Her eyes lit up when she saw that it was stuffed, and that the stuffing consisted of a great wad of banknotes.

'I don't want to be a burden' (giving her a hundred-peseta note). 'Take this, dear Mamma, and don't judge my will by the insufficiency of my means.'

'Don't imagine' (snatching at the note as if it were a rat) – 'don't imagine that I shall carry my scruples to an incredible extreme, and refuse your money with theatrical scorn. At present we can't afford either scruples or vulgar indignation. I accept it. Yes, I accept it, and when I've paid one sacred debt the rest will come in useful for . . .'

'For what?'

'That's my business. Is there anyone who doesn't have some little secrets?'

'But doesn't a son, an affectionate son, deserve to be admitted to those secrets? You give me the confidence I deserve. But I thought I was better appreciated. Although you don't consider me one of the family, dearest Mamma, I can't become indifferent to it. Tell me to cease loving you all, and I shall not obey you. I can enter other houses with indifference, but not this one. And when I notice signs of poverty here, even though you forbid me I can't help being sad' (putting his hand affectionately on her shoulder). 'My darling mother-in-law, I don't like to see Papa going about without a cloak.'

'Poor dear! But what can we do? He's been in a sad state for some time now. He's been without a job for longer than we expected. Only God and we know what hardships that entails.'

'It's not so bad when help comes in the end, even from someone whom you don't think highly of' (giving Doña Pura another note of the same value, which she hurriedly snatched).

'Thank you. It's not that we don't think highly of you. It's that you . . .'

'I have been wicked, I confess it' (pathetically). 'To acknowledge it is a sign that I'm not so wicked now. I have my faults, like everyone else. But I'm not hardened, my heart isn't closed to all feeling, nor my mind to experience. I may be as wicked as you suppose. But for all my bad qualities I have one fixed idea, you know. I will not allow this family to which I owe so much to suffer hardships. Yes, a fixed idea. Call it a weakness or what you like' (giving her a third note with a courtly gesture, and not looking at the hand which gave it). 'So long as I'm making a penny I will not allow my poor Luisa's father to be poorly dressed, or my son to run about naked.'

'Thank you, Victor, thank you' (half moved and half suspicious).

'You've no reason to thank me. There's no merit in fulfilling a sacred debt. You could make use of let's say five hundred pesetas, I suppose, because you must have taken quite a number of things to the pawn-shop.'

'You're rich' (with a suspicion that the notes are forged).

'Rich, no. A little savings. You don't spend much in Valencia. You can practise economies there without noticing them. But let me say once more, you mustn't speak to me of gratitude, or you'll make me uncomfortable. That's the sort of man I am. I've changed a great deal. Nobody knows how sad I feel when I think of the trouble I've caused you all, and my poor Luisa even more' (with emotion which, whether true or false, brought tears to Doña Pura's eyes). 'My poor darling! Alas, I can never atone for the many wrongs that poor saint suffered at my hands! Alas that I cannot call her back to life so that she can see how my heart has changed, even if we were both to die immediately after' (heaving a deep sigh). 'When death comes between guilt and repentance, one doesn't even have the bitter consolation of begging the person one has injured to forgive one.'

'Life is like that! But don't think sad thoughts now. Would you like another towel? Wait a minute. And if you need hot water I can bring it right away.'

'No, you needn't worry about me. I'll be finished in a moment, and then I'll go and fetch my luggage.'

'Very well, if you think of anything, call me. You can't get a tinkle out of the bell. But put your head round the door, and call out.'

That man, who was capable of displaying such resources of words and wit when he wanted to humiliate anybody, sometimes resorting to fierce sarcasm, and sometimes wounding the most sensitive fibres of the heart with delicate cruelty, marvellously understood the art of pleasing when it suited his purpose. Doña Pura was not unacquainted with her son-in-law's insinuating manners. But this time, perhaps because they were accompanied by a gift in cash, perhaps because Victor exaggerated his flatteries, the poor woman believed that he was morally reformed, or at least on the way to reformation. After a few hours had passed, the Miau could no longer conceal from her spouse the fact that she had money, for the concealment of riches was something completely foreign to Doña Pura's character and habits. Villaamil asked her where what he modestly called her 'resources' had come from, and she confessed that Victor had given them to her, which very much alarmed Don Ramón. The old man began to grind his teeth with fury, and to utter from his fierce mouth words which would have astounded anyone who did not know him.

'But how simple you are! He's only given me a trifle. Would you expect me to keep him here for nothing? We're in a fine state to do that. I gave him a bit of a talking to, of course. Naturally, I did. I said if he insisted on staying he'd have to contribute to the household expenses. Bah, what things you do say! You say he's defrauded the Treasury. There's no proof of that. It's all your imagination. How can you know? And suppose he has, is that any reason why he should live at our expense?'

Villaamil said no more. He had long been content to let his wife wear the trousers. For a very long time he had been used to lowering his head when Doña Pura raised hers; their matrimonial harmony depended on his keeping quiet. This method was recommended to him when he married, and it admirably suited his benevolent and pacific character. In the afternoon Doña Pura returned to the subject and said: 'We must stop up a few holes with that little bit of clay. I'll see about getting you some clothes. You can't possibly do yourself any good when you call at the Ministries looking like a beggar, with your heels trodden down and a hat of the year dot, and your overcoat all dirty and frayed. Get this clear in your mind. Nobody takes any notice of a man who looks shabby. The best he can hope for is a place in the poor-house. Besides, as they're bound to give you an appointment now, you'll also need clothes to go to the office in.'

'Don't make me cross, woman. You don't know how you hurt me with this confidence that I don't share. Quite the contrary, I have no hopes at all.'

'Well, whichever way things turn out, whether they give you a post or not, you still need clothes. Clothes are almost the man. If you don't appear decently dressed they'll despise you, and you're lost. I'll call on the tailor this very morning and tell him

81

he must make you an overcoat. And a new overcoat calls for a new hat, and a new hat for a new pair of boots.'

Villaamil was shocked by so much luxury. But when Pura spoke with governmental emphasis there was no way of contradicting her. He did not fail to realize that her arguments were well-founded, and that these new clothes would have social and political value. He knew very well that a well-dressed applicant has already won half the game. The tailor came, therefore, in answer to an urgent summons, and Villaamil had his measurements taken, but with a taciturn and gloomy expression as if he were being measured for a shroud rather than an overcoat.

The arrival of the tailor gave Paca and her husband enough interest to last them for the rest of the day and a part of the night.

'Didn't you notice, Mendizábal? They brought him a new hat as well. So long as we've been in this house – and that must be fifteen years – I've only seen two top-hats come in, this one today and the one Don Basilio Andrés de la Caña put on for the first time a few days after Alfonso's accession. Do you think there's going to be a revolution?'

'I shouldn't be surprised,' said Mendizábal. 'This man Cánovas has lost his grip. The papers say there's a crisis.'

'Yes, there must be, and Don Ramón and his lot are coming into power. But which lot does Señor de Villaamil belong to?'

'The blessed innocents, that's the lot Señor de Villaamil belongs to' (beginning to laugh). 'But what's the point of this new rig-out, and these grand clothes? But look here, Paca, in view of this . . . er . . . Asiatic luxury I'm going up this very minute with the overdue account, to see if they'll pay what they owe, or at least a part of it. You've got to watch this kind of people, and catch them at the economic moment, if you understand me. I mean at the juncture, the unseen and unheard-of juncture, as you might say, when they have some money.'

The scribe looked at his dog, who seemed to say with his expressive snout: 'Up you go, master. They've got some cash now. So don't miss the chance. I've just come down, and everything's humming. To be more precise, they've brought in an Italian sausage as thick as my head. It smells divine.'

82

Mendizábal went up therefore, preceded by his dog. Whenever the porter appeared with those fatal papers in his hand, Villaamil trembled, feeling his dignity wounded in its tenderest spot, and Doña Pura detected a bitter taste in her mouth. Her lips went white, and her heart overflowed with wrath and dismay. Each in the form appropriate to his or her character, they endeavoured to persuade Mendizábal with infinite arguments that it would be a good thing if he would wait till the following month. Luckily for them, the gorilla, that monster whose hands would touch the ground if he made the slightest bow, that demonstration of zoological evolution whose cranium seemed to offer a proof of Darwin's most audacious theories, did not exercise the powers conferred on him by the owner of the house in a cruel way. Though his ugliness would have earned him a place in the glass case of any anthropological museum, Mendizábal was, in fact, a kindly, indulgent, compassionate man, who took circumstances into consideration. He was sorry for the family, and had a real affection for Villaamil. He only made his demands in the politest and most friendly way; and when he presented his accounts to the landlord, he would plead pitifully through those horrific lips, on behalf of this tenant whose arrears were due to his lack of employment; and as he did so he would scratch his little, flat ear. Thanks to his intercession, the owner, who was no great tyrant, would wait with sad and philosophical resignation.

When Villaamil and Doña Pura were not in a position to pay, they not only excused themselves but chatted politely with the scribe, flattering him and pandering to his prejudices. 'But how much you must have seen of this world, my friend, Mendizábal. How many tragic and interesting events you must have witnessed, how many . . .!' And the gorilla would answer, as he folded up the bills: 'The history of Spain hasn't been written yet, Don Ramón. If I were to pen my memories, my friend, you would see.' Doña Pura laid the flattery on somewhat thicker: 'The world is going to ruin. Mendizábal is right. So long as there is religious liberty and what they call rationalism . . .!' The result was that the porter kept the bills, and the lady's anger evaporated. They had another month's breathing-space.

83

But that day on which, by the mercy of Providence, the pair were able to pay two out of the three months which they owed they somewhat arrogantly changed their tone of agreement. Villaamil spoke with modest authority about modern ideals, and Doña Pura said, as she watched him pocket the banknotes: 'But tell me, Mendizábal, how do you get these ideas? Do you honestly believe that Don Carlos will come in with the Inquisition and all the other horrors? Really, a man must be crazy' (pointing to her temples) 'to believe a thing like that.'

Mendizábal answered them in clipped phrases, imperfectly learnt from the newspaper he read, and departed snorting. An incredible paradox: whenever he received money he went off in a bad temper.

13

BEFORE we continue, let us call up the sorrowful picture of Luisa Villaamil, dead but not forgotten at the time of this human chronicle. But let us go back a few years and catch her in her lifetime. Let us go back to the year '68, the year of Spain's greatest political upheaval of the present century, which also saw great events in the unlucky annals of the Villaamil family.

Luisa was four years older than her sister Abelarda, and somewhat less of a nobody. Neither of the two could call herself pretty; but the elder had something angelic in her eyes, a little more charm, more colour in her lips, and a fuller neck and shoulders. Moreover her voice, her manner of speech and her choice of words were slightly superior to her sister's. The scanty attractions of the pair were not increased by a choice education. They had been to schools in three or four different provinces, and had been repeatedly moved from one to another. Their knowledge, therefore, even of the most elementary subjects, was extremely imperfect. Luisa finally achieved some halting French, which barely allowed her to read, with copious use of the dictionary, the first page of *Télémaque*, and Abelarda succeeded in strumming two or three polkas by torturing the keys of the piano. Of the four girls and one boy whom Doña Pura bore only these two survived; the others died shortly after birth. At the beginning of 1868 Villaamil was chief treasury official in the capital of a third-class province, a city of archaeological interest with a small and not very sparkling population, famous for its cathedral and for the crop of broken-necked jars and unhewn Roman masonry that could be brought out of the ground with a single blow of the pick. In this sleepy little town the Villaamil family spent the most triumphal years of their lives, for here Doña Pura and her sister provided the model of elegance and played a most brilliant role, standing as they did in the front rank of its fashionable society. Here there arrived in Villaamil's office a young and handsome clerk, in the class of *aspirant* with a salary of one thousand two hundred and fifty pesetas, who had just obtained the post by influence. How Victor Cadalso had managed to get here we have no need to know. He was an Andalusian, had partially studied for the service in Granada, had come to Madrid without a bean, and after countless ups-and-downs had acquired a free patronage, which had launched him like a pelota ball into bureaucratic life with a single blow. Shortly after entering the offices of this province, he made a considerable mark for himself, and as he had an attractive personality and was a lively and witty conversationalist, as he knew how to dress and had easy social manners, he was not slow in gaining the interest and hospitality of his chief's family. In their drawing-room – it would be too much to say *salon* – which was well attended on Sundays and public holidays, he was from the first evening a shining star. He was unequalled in the generally equivocal wit of his conversation, in improvising amusing entertainments, in giving displays of hypnotism, conjuring or table-turning. He recited verses in the manner of the most famous actors, he danced well, and he told all the classic Andalusian stories. No one was his equal at amusing the ladies and fascinating the girls. He was the lion of the city, the leader of its smart young men, and their pattern for fine manners, carriage and dress. High society gathered by turns at the Villaamils', at the house of the Brigadier, who was Military Governor and whose wife was a distinguished, middle-aged personage, and in that of a certain individual who was the political boss, the election manager and the autocrat of the district. But the house of the greatest social refinement was the Villaamils', and the Villaamil ladies were the most proud and pretentious. The boss's wife had marriageable daughters, the Brigadier's wife none at all, and the Civil Governor was a bachelor; so the chief treasury official's ladies, the boss's ladies, the Military Governor's wife, and the wife of the mayor, who kept a chemist's shop, formed the whole female élite of the town. They were the mistresses of the 'haute monde', they received the flattery of the young and elegant males in their morning-coats and bowler-hats, they stunned the people by appearing at the bullfight (twice a year) in white mantillas, and they collected for the poor in the cathedral on Maundy Thursday, and visited the Bishop, and set the tone, and constantly received the silent homage of imitation. At that time Milagros still preserved some relics of her beautiful voice; she still had a very fair pitch and a full range. When she had been sufficiently forced by repeated requests, she would still allow herself to go up to the piano and, summoning all that was left of her talent, would sing a couple of cavatinas, which aroused wild applause. The clapping could be heard in the nearby Plaza de la Constitución, and her praise was sung all night, as an accompaniment to the dancing and the games of forfeits.

Victor Cadalso became an ornament of this society as soon as he entered it. As a social entertainer, he deserved a better stage, for his powers, unlike the fading talents of Milagros, were in the fullness of their prime. Therefore the inevitable happened. Luisa suddenly fell madly in love with the aspirant on the first night they met. Hers was an explosive passion, as of a heart filled with gunpowder that is suddenly struck by a flaming dart. This is a usual occurrence among the lower classes and in primitive societies; and it happens from time to time among guileless and infatuated people when there appears among them, like a spark fallen from heaven, a man who seems like a higher being. Luisa Villaamil's passion was so like Juliet's that on the day after she had spoken to him for the first time she would not have hesitated to elope with Victor from her father's house, if

86

he had suggested it. This first infatuation was followed by a frenzy of love-making. Luisa lost her sleep and appetite. They exchanged letters two or three times a day, and telegrams at all hours. In the evenings, they watched out for opportunities of meeting alone even for brief moments. The love-sick girl recounted her joys and sorrows to the moon, the stars, the cat and the linnet, to God and the Virgin. She was ready, if the law of love required it, for any kind of heroism or martyrdom. Doña Pura was not slow to oppose this love-affair, for she dreamt of the Brigadier's adjutant as a son-in-law; and Villaamil, who was beginning to perceive something displeasing in Victor's character, felt compelled to approach the boss with a view to having him transferred to another province. The lovers, warned by that defensive perspicacity which love, like every other great passion, carries with it, scented the danger, and swore an eternal pact against the enemy. They resolved to be united, and to die rather than part, and everything else that is usual in these critical situations. Their frenzied passion drove them to extremes, and opposition compelled them to tie the knot so tight that no one had the power to undo it. As usual, love ended by having its way. The Villaamils were furious. But when they thought it over, what alternative was there but to stomach this aberration as best they could?

Luisa was all sensibility, passion and tenderness; an unbalanced creature, incapable of any intelligent appreciation of reality. Pain and joy throbbed within her with a sickly intensity. She considered Victor the most perfect of men. She raved about his looks, and was completely blind to the defects in his character. Beings and actions took the shape of her own imagination, and in consequence she was credited with little perspicacity or knowledge of the world. The boss was groomsman at the wedding, and as a wedding-present he got Victor's salary increased to twenty-four thousand pesetas, which greatly pleased Don Ramón and his wife, since once Cadalso was a member of their family there was nothing for it but to back him and make a real man of him. Shortly afterwards the revolution broke out, and Villaamil, who owed his position to a friend of González Bravo, found himself without employment. Victor got protection and was promoted to a post in Madrid. The whole family moved there, and their hardships began again. For Doña Pura had always had a way of not saving a céntimo, and a special talent for emptying her purse completely by the first of the month, when Don Ramón received his pay.

To return to Luisa, let me say that after the wedding-feast she remained infatuated with Victor, who was no model husband. The unfortunate girl lived an anxious life and subtly increased the causes of her fear; she watched him continuously, fearing that he would divide his affection or take it away from her entirely. Then disagreements began between her parents and their son-in-law, which were embittered by tiresome questions of money. Luisa spent her days consumed by endless worries and alarms, spying on her husband, and at night followed him in her thoughts, wondering where he could be. And the villain, with his inborn gift of the gab, knew how to disarm her by a single honeyed word. One smile was enough to make his wife think herself happy, and one rough monosyllable sufficed for her to feel inconsolably sad. In March '69 little Luis came into the world, which left his mother so weak and poorly that those who often saw her recognized that her end was near. The child was born with rickets, a living embodiment of his mother's anxieties and prostration. They gave him a nurse, without any hope that he would live, and he wavered between death and survival all through his first year. But he certainly brought the family luck, for six days after his birth his grandfather received a post with promotion in Madrid, and thus Doña Pura was able to plunge into a sea of debts, improvidence and squandering. Victor somewhat mended his ways. Once his wife was past hope, he showed both affection and solicitude. The poor woman had spells of anguished grief and febrile happiness, all of which ended in attacks of blood-spitting. In the last stages of her illness her affection for her husband became so intense that she seemed to be out of her mind. When he was not with her, she would shout for him. By one of those perversions of feeling that can only be attributed to mental disorder, she now lost all interest in her child and treated her parents and her sister with cold asperity. Her whole attention was devoted to

88

her ungrateful husband; all her words of affection were for him. She had lost sight of all the moral and physical beauties of the world; her eyes saw only the imaginary virtues with which her crazy passion had endowed him.

Knowing the viciousness of Victor's life outside the house, Villaamil began to loathe his son-in-law. Pura, who was more conciliatory, let herself be taken in by his lying statements, and so long as he treated his sick wife with kindness and consideration declared herself satisfied and forgave the rest. Finally poor Luisa's madness – for it deserves no other name – came to an end on St John's Eve. She died weeping with gratitude because her husband had given her a warm kiss and was speaking to her affectionately. That morning she had had an attack of insanity more violent than any before, and had jumped out of bed to demand a knife with which to kill Luis. She swore that he was not her son, and that Victor had brought him to the house in a basket, covered over with a cloak. This was a day of most bitter grief for the whole family, especially for the good Villaamil who gave no signs of outward sorrow, but silently, and almost dry-eyed, suffered an inward collapse which left him a pitiable wreck, hopeless and without any illusions in life. From that day his body shrivelled till he became like a mummy, and his face took on the look of ravenous ferocity that gave him the appearance of an ancient and helpless tiger.

The need for a salary which would allow him to save drove him to take a colonial posting. He obtained a modest position that brought him good perquisites, and returned after two years with some savings, which quickly dissolved like grains of salt in the bottomless sea of Doña Pura's housekeeping. He then went abroad for a second time to a better position, but had some difference of opinion with the Treasurer, and returned to Spain in the wretched days of the Federalist revolts. The administration, which after the third of January 1874 was headed by Serrano, sent him to the Philippines, where things promised very well for him; but a bad attack of dysentery obliged him to return to Spain without savings, firmly resolved to take the post of porter at a Ministry rather than cross the ditch again. He did not find it difficult to get back to the Treasury, and lived quietly for three years on a small salary, being left in peace at the Restoration until the unfortunate hour when the blow struck and he was suspended. This disaster befell him when he was only two months from retirement on four-fifths of his basic pay, which was that of a Departmental Chief, third class. He went to the Minister, he knocked on various doors; all the different influences he brought to bear were unavailing. Little by little tiresome stringency yielded to naked and dreadful want; all resources came to an end, and all extraordinary methods and contrivances for supporting a family were exhausted too.

Finally he reached the most painful stage for a man of feeling like Villaamil, of having to knock on the doors of his friends and beg for help or a loan. In his happier days he had performed services of this nature for some who had been grateful and some who had not. Why should he not resort to the same system? In any case, he could not ask himself whether this behaviour was decorous or not. A man who is burnt does not argue whether it is proper or not to shake his fingers. Decorum was now a meaningless word, like the printed name on the label of an empty bottle. Gradually shame wears away like the edge of a file, and the cheeks lose their habit of blushing. The unemployed wretch came to acquire a terrible mastery in the art of writing letters invoking the name of friendship. He embellished them with touching elaborations, and in a style that had an official look, a little like that of the preamble to those decrees which inform the country of an increase in taxation in such phrases as : 'It is the Government's painful duty to demand further sacrifices from the taxpayer.' This was the model, though the text was different.

14

To complete the biographical information about Victor, it must be added that he had a sister called Quintina, the wife of a certain Ildefonso Cabrera who worked for the Northern railways; both of them good people, though rather eccentric. Since they had no children, Quintina wanted her brother to let them bring Luis up, and she would probably have had her way if Victor and his brother-in-law had not come to a serious disagreement about the inheritance of the Cadalso estate. It consisted of a ruined and roofless house in the worst quarter of Vélez Málaga, and the question whether it belonged to Quintina or Victor led to the stormiest of quarrels. The case was clear, according to Cabrera, and to prove that it was as pellucid as water, he put his case in the hands of the lawyers, who in a short time covered it with a sizeable pile of stamped papers. The purpose of all this was to prove that Victor was a rogue, who had unjustly taken this splendid property for himself and, having sold it, had kept the money. Victor, treating the whole thing as a joke, had answered that the proceeds of his crime had not amounted to the price of a pair of boots. Ildefonso had replied that this was a matter of right, not of money, and that what he minded was not the material loss but his brother-in-law's shameful behaviour. For this reason among others, he conceived so deep a hatred for Victor that Quintina trembled for her brother every time he came to the house. Such was Ildefonso's fury that one day he was on the point of firing all six bullets from his revolver at him. Quintina wanted the case to be settled, and these violent arguments to end. So when her brother, taking advantage of the angry Ildefonso's departure to inspect the stretch of line for which he was responsible, came to see her a few days after his arrival from Valencia, she made him the following proposition : 'Look here. If you give Luis to me I promise to pacify my husband. He's as keen as I am to have the boy with us.'

Victor found the offer unacceptable because, hard-hearted though he was, he dared not drag the child from his grand-parents' care and protection. Firm in her resolve, Quintina argued: 'Can't you see how badly they'll bring him up? It's not only that he'll get into bad habits, that's the least of it. But they'll starve the little darling to death. Those women don't know how to look after a child. They haven't the ghost of an idea. All they can do is play-act and paint their faces. All that interests them is whether some singer or other sang his part well or badly, and their house is like a pig-sty.'

Although the Miaus and Quintina were on visiting terms they could not bear one another at any price, because Señora Cabrera, though a good woman – by which it must be understood that she was not like her brother – had a fault : she was extremely meddlesome and curious, a real interferer and pryer. When she paid a call on the Villaamils she did not go straight into the drawing-room but made a detour through the dining-room, and more than once she managed to slip into the kitchen and raise the lids of the pots to see what was cooking. This drove Milagros wild. Quintina inquired about everything, wanted to investigate everything, and to stick her prying nose into everything. She gave advice that was not asked for, inspected Abelarda's dress-making, asked awkward questions, and then broke off in the midst of her impertinent chatter, leaving a sentence half finished on a mocking but would-be innocent note.

She loved young Luis passionately. She never left the house without seeing him, and always brought him some little gift or toy or something to wear. Sometimes she turned up at his school and pestered the master with questions about the boy's progress. 'Don't work so hard, darling,' she would say to him. 'They'll only tire your brains out. Don't take any notice of them. You've plenty of time to develop your intellect. You must eat now, eat a lot and get fat. Play and run about and amuse yourself just as much as you like.' On one occasion, when she saw that the Miaus were in real difficulties, she suggested that they should let her have the boy. But Doña Pura was so furious at the proposal that she could never make it again except as a joke. On concluding her visit, she always stopped for a chat with the Mendizábals, to gather from them every possible detail about the inhabitants of the second floor : whether they were paying their rent or not, whether they owed much at the shop – though she generally drew this information from a more direct source – if they came in late from the theatre, whether that 'silly girl' would in the end marry the ridiculous Ponce, whether the shoe-maker had brought them new shoes. In short she was an insufferable leech, a persistent pryer, and an ever vigilant spy.

Her habits were completely different from those of her victims. She never went to the theatre, she lived a most orderly life, and her house in the Calle de los Reyes was as neat as a new pin. She was not as handsome as her brother, who had all the family's good looks. She was attractive but not beautiful. She had a squint in one eye, and her mouth was both large and ugly, thought it was adorned by perfect teeth. The two Cabreras lived quietly and comfortably, because in addition to his inspector's salary Ildefonso enjoyed the profits from a somewhat clandestine business of bringing in church ornaments from France and selling them in Madrid to the priests of the near-by villages, or even to the clergy of the Capital itself. The stuff was cheap and trashy, the product of modern industry which lets nothing go to waste and knows how to exploit the Church's poverty in these present difficult times. Cabrera had associates in Hendaye, and brought them by arrangement tapestries, wall-lights, articles of real silver, and occasionally pictures or other antiquities taken from the walls of Castilian churches, which were once wealthy and are today so poor. According to malicious gossip, the charm of this business was that on his journeys backwards and forwards he brought these objects over the frontier duty-free. But this is unproved. Generally the ecclesiastical junk that Cabrera brought in – objects of gilded brass, poor, brittle imitations in the worst of taste – was so cheap at the source of production and sold so well in Spain that it could easily have borne the added cost of duty. In earlier times, when he was beginning the business, Quintina would go into the sacristy of a parish church with a parcel under her cloak, as if she were carrying contraband, and would whisper into the sacristan's ear: 'Would you like to see a really splendid chalice? You'll be surprised at the price. It's half what the church-furnishers ask.' But soon the lady gave up hawking her wares, and received visits from the clergy of Madrid and the near-by villages at her own house. Later on, Cabrera imported vast consignments of holy pictures for prizes or first communions, great chromolithographs of the two Sacred Hearts; and finally, enlarging and extending his business, imported stocks of the most vulgar images, St Josephs in bulk, and the Infant Jesus and Mater Dolorosa wholesale and in various sizes. All these were in the French devotional style, very smooth and shiny, with their

93

robes gilt in the Byzantine manner and their cheeks daubed with pink, as if it were the custom to rouge in heaven. I don't know whether it was habitually dealing with sacred objects or her natural disposition that had made Quintina a profound sceptic. Of course she did her Christian duty, and attended mass on all the festivals, and said a few prayers from ancient custom when she went to bed. But no hand-kissing of priests, except perhaps when she was pressing some 'article' on one, or extracting an old brocade cassock which was all tatters.

Young Luis went to the Cabreras every now and then, and was charmed by the sight of their coloured prints. One day he saw a God the Father with a long white beard, holding a blue globe, and the picture made a great impression on him. Does this explain the extraordinary nature of his visions? No one knows, and probably no one will ever know. But, in any case, his grandmother forbade him to go to that saint-filled house again. 'Quintina is a wicked woman,' she said to him. 'She wants to steal you from us and sell you to the French.' Little Luis took fright, and never again visited the Calle de los Reyes.

Villaamil could not stand Ildefonso either. For the inspector was appallingly downright in the expression of his opinions, and not only inconsiderate but sometimes rude. Formerly they had belonged to the same café circle. But ever since Cabrera had said that the introduction of income tax into Spain would be crazy, and that the idea would never have occurred to anyone in his senses, Villaamil had felt a grudge against him. When they met, they raised their hats and passed on. Doña Pura nourished more serious grounds of complaint against Cabrera than this scornful remark about the income tax. Never, absolutely never had that 'fellow' presented them with half-price railway tickets for a little summer excursion. Victor said foul things about his brother-in-law, to avenge himself for the troubles Cabrera caused him with his writs, affidavits and court-summonses. But it seemed quite natural to him that he should cheat the severity of the customs when importing his church ornaments and exporting his artistic rags and tatters. And Cabrera robbed the railway as well as the state. When his business began he used to entrust his parcels to the guard; and when he was sending not parcels but large crates and was afraid of being blown up by his chiefs, he registered them, it is true, but dispatched his luxury merchandise at the rate for returned empties or constructional timber. There were some very comic things in his customs declarations. 'How do you think he entered a crateful of St Josephs?' Victor would ask. 'He called them flints for kindling.' But as he did favours for the customs officials, they passed his improbable declarations; and bronze thuribles went as 'Common ironware', and cheap cloth vestments as 'Umbrellas in parts' and 'Half-manufactured corsets'.

15

IN the next few days Pura paid some of the most pressing bills, brought home various of their most indispensable articles of clothing, and restored the fare of happier times to their table. The modest Ophelia spent her hours of idleness in the kitchen. For imperceptibly she was coming to love the art of Vatel* – so different, heaven knows, from that of Rossini – and she felt a real spiritual delight as she perfected herself in it by launching into the invention or concoction of a dish. When she had provisions or, if you prefer it, an artist's materials, inspiration kindled in her and she cooked with fervour, humming under her breath, out of old custom and in perfect tune, some such tender fragment from an opera as *Moriamo insieme, ah! Si, moriamo*.

Every night that the Miaus were not at the opera, the room was crowded with people. On occasions the generous Doña Pura entertained the cast to sweets and cakes; which made the visitors believe that Villaamil had already received an appointment, or at least had one foot inside the office door. The new list of appointments, however, was not issued, because the Minister, sick of recommendations and interviews, could not make up his mind to give it the finishing touches. Uncertainty increased in

* Famous cook of the age of Louis XIV.

the family, therefore, and Villaamil sank deeper and deeper into his deliberate pessimism. In the end he went so far as to say: 'The sun will rise in the west before we shall ever see men in the service again.'

Two days after his arrival Victor had given up worrying about anybody. He went in and out freely and entered the drawing-room when the visitors were there. But he never settled down there, because he heartily loathed this sort of society. Disarmed by her son-in-law's generosity, Doña Pura was sorry that he had to sleep on the hard dining-room sofa, and finally the three Miaus agreed to put him in Abelarda's room, she having been previously transferred to her aunt Milagros' room, which was Luis'. The bashful Ophelia went to sleep with her sister, on a miserable camp-bed which was put up in her bedroom. Don Ramón was not very pleased with these arrangements because he would have liked to see Victor thrown out neck and crop. In the Taxation Department his friend Pantoja had told him that his son-in-law was trying for promotion, and that there was a complaint against him, the outcome of which might be unfortunate if he did not get some patron to support him. It was something to do with the Board of Excise, some irregularities that had been discovered in the cash account which Cadalso kept with the provincial towns. It appeared that some of the towns that were most in arrears did not figure in the list of interest payments, and it was believed that Cadalso was working in league with the defaulting mayors. Villaamil was also told that the assessment of the taxes which Victor had levied in the last quarter had been done in such a way that the swindle was obvious, and that the chief had refused to confirm it.

Villaamil did not say a word about these matters to his son-in-law. At table he was always silent, and Cadalso was very talkative, though he did not succeed in getting anyone very interested in what he said. He had long conversations with Abelarda if they happened to be alone or engaged in the interesting task of putting Luis to bed. The father enjoyed observing the child's development and watching over his delicate health, and one of his principal cares was that the child should be well covered up at night and decently dressed. He ordered clothes to be made for him, and bought him a very neat little cloak and a complete blue suit with stockings of the same colour. Since he was rather vain, young Luis could not help being grateful to his Papa for making him so smart. But in the matter of new clothes, there was nothing to touch the luxury that this same Victor displayed in his own person within a short time of coming to Madrid. Every day the tailor brought him some brand-new article of clothing; and his tailor certainly was not like Villaamil's, a middling sort of artist not far from the bottom of his class, but one of the most famous in Madrid. And what a handsome fellow Victor looked in his correct and well-cut suits, which were a little on the severe side! For severity is the keynote of true elegance, which must never call attention to itself either by colour or cut. Abelarda observed him slyly and secretly, admiring and recognizing in him that same exceptional person who some years before had turned the head of her unfortunate sister, and she felt in her heart a vast store of indulgence for this young man about whom the whole family spoke so nastily. True, this store appeared small so long as one saw no more than its ill-explored surface. But when one dug and dug one found it was inexhaustible, perhaps infinite, like a great quarry of rich stone! And what purple seams lay there, what gleaming ores! It was as if veins swelled with blood or the stuff of precious stones had been spilt in the bosom of the earth and hardened by the centuries. This indulgence mounted from her heart into her thoughts in this form: 'No, he can't be as bad as they say. It's because they don't understand him, they don't understand him.'

Victor had very often spoken of being misunderstood, not only at this period but at another earlier time, some two years before, when he had spent some months with the family. How could these nobodies understand a man who belonged to another caste, another sphere, in his appearance, his manners, his ideas, his aspirations and his defects as well? Abelarda went back in her imagination to those earlier times and, examining her feelings towards Victor, recognized that she had had them already when poor Luisa was alive. When everyone in the house was abusing him, Abelarda would comfort her sister with specious defences of the traitor, or would excuse him for his faults.

97

'Victor isn't to blame if all the women run after him,' she used to say.

After her sister's death, Abelarda continued to admire the widower in silence. Certainly he had given the dead woman endless trouble and heartache; but the cause of it all was his fatal good-looks. Unwittingly, sometimes out of mere consideration, he would get himself caught in a love-affair or a trap that some immoral woman had prepared for him. But he was good at heart; and he would become more sensible as he got older. All he needed was a woman of heart and character to control him with a combination of affection and severity. The unfortunate Luisa was incapable of that. How could this difficult task be performed by a woman who burst into tears on the slightest provocation, a woman who on one occasion fainted because her husband returned home with his tie differently knotted from when he went out?

At the time of this story, the little nobody found it very hard to conceal the perturbation she felt whenever her brother-in-law addressed her. Sometimes it was a secret and restless joy that frisked and leapt in her heart as if some parasitical insect had nested there and was bringing up its young. But at other times she was weighed down by a heavy pain. Her replies were always hesitant, toneless and awkward.

'Are you really going to marry that half-baked creature Ponce?' he asked her one night as they were putting the boy to bed. 'A fine match, my dear! How your friends must envy you. Not everyone has that sort of luck.'

'Oh, be quiet, you fool. Don't be so wicked.'

Another night, displaying a lively interest in the family, Victor informed her: 'Look here, Abelarda, it's no good expecting that they'll be giving your father an appointment. The selection has been made, although it's not published yet. He's not on the list. They told me so, as a secret. I don't have to tell you how sorry I am. Poor old man, so full of illusions! Because although he says he has no expectations, unfortunately he's living on them. The news will give him a tremendous blow. But don't you worry. My promotion's certain. I've got better backing than your father, and as I shall be staying in Madrid I shan't desert you. You can count on that. I've caused you all a lot of trouble, and now I must relieve my conscience. There'll still be a heavy weight on it however much I do for you.'

No, he's not a wicked man, Abelarda thought, returning to her internal conversation. All that he says about not believing in God is just words, just nonsense that he talks to fool me and make me angry. Because he often says some very strange things, he really does, things nobody else would ever think of. No, he's not a wicked man. He's mischievous, and he's very clever, very clever indeed. Only we don't understand him.

Whenever there was any argument Victor always insisted that he was misunderstood. 'Look, Abelarda, you'd no business to take what I said as rude, because you do understand me a little. You aren't just ordinary, or at least you're not entirely ordinary. You're getting less ordinary, let's say.'

When she was alone, the poor girl lost heart and with remorseless modesty reduced herself to nothing: Yes, I am ordinary, whatever he says. And, my God, how ordinary! My face . . . psh, no one would notice me. My figure . . . let's not think about it! And even if I had good looks, how could I show them off in these miserable clothes? Why, they're just rags, cut up and adapted and turned inside out. Then I'm completely ignorant. I don't know anything. What I say is just silly rubbish. I've got no intelligence. I'm nothing but a cabbage with a mouth and eyes and hands. Gracious me, how stupid I am and what a bore! Why was I born like this?

16

EACH time Victor entered the house, Abelarda looked at him as if he came from a higher social sphere. In his walk and in his manners, in his clothes and in the way he wore his hair, Victor had some quality that stood out in the poor dwelling of the Miaus, something that quarrelled with their ordinary and ill-furnished home. And Cadalso's entries and departures were very irregular. He often dined in restaurants with his friends. He would go to the theatre on two successive evenings; and occasionally he would spend the whole night out. He was not always in a good humour. He had bouts of depression, during which you could not get a word out of him all day. But at other times he was very talkative and, as his parents-in-law had no use for him, he would then resort to his sister-in-law. Their opportunities for private conversation were not many. But conscious of his personal dynamism and the effect of his conversation on the perturbed mind of the little nobody, he was able to make good use of them.

Little Luis was not well. In fact he was so ill that he had to go to bed. Doña Pura and Milagros were at the Real that night, Villaamil was at the café searching for news of the appointments, and Abelarda had stayed behind to look after the boy. Unexpectedly there was a ring at the door. It was Victor coming home very cheerful, and humming a tango from a musical comedy. On being told that his son was not well, he listened to the boy's breathing, and recognized that if he had a temperature it was a very slight one. He then sat down to write letters at the dining-room table. His sister-in-law watched him stealthily; she passed behind him two or three times, pretending that she wanted something from the sideboard, and casting furtive glances at what he was writing. To judge by its length and spacing, and by the feverish facility with which Victor wielded his pen, it was a love-letter. But she could not make out a sentence or even a syllable. Having completed his letter, Cadalso started a conversation with the young woman who brought her sewing into the dining-room.

'I've got something to tell you,' he began, propping one elbow on the table and cupping his face in his hand; 'I saw your Ponce today. D'you know I've changed my mind about him? He suits you. He's a good lad, and when his uncle the lawyer dies he'll be rich. They say he'll be the sole heir. Because we mustn't accept your friend Ruiz' opinion, that you can't be happy unless you're penniless. If Federico were right and I felt convinced by him, then I'd say that Ponce doesn't suit you, and that someone else would, I for example.'

Abelarda turned pale. She was so put out that her attempt to laugh was completely unsuccessful.

'What nonsense you talk! You must always be having your joke!'

'You know very well I'm not joking' (taking a very serious tone). 'One night, two years ago, when you were living in Chamberí, I said to you: "Abelarda, my dear, I'm fond of you. Every time I see you my heart gives a start." I bet you've forgotten. You answered that . . . I don't remember what you answered. But what it amounted to was that if I loved you, you . . . loved me.'

'Oh, what a lie! Stop it now! I never said any such thing.'

'Did I dream it then? Anyhow, the next thing you did was to fall madly in love with your precious Ponce.'

'I . . . fall in love . . . You're being nasty. But all right, let's say I fell in love. What's it got to do with you?'

'A great deal. Because when I learnt I had a rival, I turned my heart in another direction. That's the way with human beings, you see. Two years ago we were on the point of coming to an understanding. Now we are far apart. You went away, I went away, we both went away. And when we meet again, what happens? I'm in a very strange situation with regard to you. My heart says: "Make her love you," and at the same moment a voice comes from I don't know where, and cries: "Look at her but do not touch".'

'What has this got to do with me' (choking herself back), 'seeing that I don't love you a bit, and never could love you?'

'I know, I know. You don't have to be so emphatic. We agree that I can go to the devil for all you care. As is logical and natural, you loathe me. But let me tell you how it is with me. When people loathe me, I always feel forced to love them. And I love you, because I feel forced to, and that's my concern. So, on with the dance, as your Papa says.'

'What ideas you do have. And how silly you are!' (endeavouring to be grave and bursting into a laugh).

'No, I'm not fooling you and I never shall. Believe it or not, this is the truth, I love you and I shouldn't love you, for you're too angelic for me. You can only be mine on terms of marriage, and marriage, an absurd arrangement that only works for common people, is no good to us at a moment like this. For good or for ill, whatever you think of me, immodest though it may sound, I have a mission to fulfil. I have a dangerous and difficult task to accomplish, for which I need, above all, liberty. I am running swiftly towards a goal, which I can only reach alone. With a companion, I should only come half way. Forward, ever forward' (in a theatrical tone). 'What impulse drives me on? Fate, a stronger force than my desires. Better destruction than retreat. I cannot go back or take you with me. I am afraid I might drag you down. And if you were so immeasurably unfortunate as to be the wife of this miserable man . . .' (closing his eyes and stretching out one hand as if to ward off a ghost). 'No, let us strenuously reject such an idea. I love you too much ever to have you beside me. If one day . . .' (in a declamatory singsong) 'if one day I were to lose my head and commit the supreme stupidity of telling you I love you, then despise me. Do not let your very kind heart carry you away, for it would be better for you to die than to be mine.

'Tell me, are you trying to drive me mad?' (trembling and concealing her distress by a vain attempt to thread a needle). 'What is all this nonsense you're talking? I don't . . . I really can't take you seriously. Much you would care if I were to kill myself, or die, or go to the devil.'

'Oh, I know you don't love me. I beg only one thing of you, and I beg it as a very great favour. I beg you to pity me and not to loathe me. Let me, for I know what I'm doing . . . let me preserve my own thoughts and comfort myself with them. In the midst of my misfortunes, of which you know nothing, I have one consolation. I can live by my ideal, and so find strength for my soul. Your fate is very different from mine, Abelarda. Follow your path and I will follow mine. For my fever drives me on and lends me speed. Let us not oppose the fate that rules all things. Perhaps we shall never meet again. But let me give you one piece of advice before we part. If you do not find Ponce repulsive, marry him. It's enough if you don't find him repulsive. If he doesn't please you and if you find no one less damp-eyed, then renounce marriage altogether. This is the advice of a man who loves you more than you believe. Forsake the world, enter a nunnery, devote yourself to an ideal, to the contemplative life. I don't possess the virtue of resignation. If I don't succeed in reaching my desired goal, if my dream dissolves in smoke, I shall shoot myself.'

He spoke with such energy and with such conviction that this nonsense made more impression on Abelarda than anything else he had said.

'But you won't do that. You won't kill yourself. That'd be a fine kettle of fish' (seizing the first idea that came to her). 'But this is ridiculous. All this stuff about despair and killing yourself is just because you're having an unhappy love-affair. There must be some woman who's torturing you. Well, serve you right and I'm very glad of it.'

'Now look, my dear' (trying another tack), 'you only said that as a joke. But perhaps, perhaps you're right . . .'

'You've got a girl-friend?' (feigning indifference).

'Girl-friend, what you'd call a girl-friend . . . no.'

'Well, a love-affair.'

'Call it fatality, martyrdom.'

'Stop talking about fatality and just say you're in love.'

'I don't know how to answer' (feigning a nice and very proper confusion). 'If I say yes, I'm telling a lie; and if I say no, that's a lie too. Seeing that I've sworn to you that I love you, is it conceivable that I could be interested in anyone else? The whole thing can be explained by distinguishing between different kinds of love. There is a holy, pure and tranquil affection which springs from the heart, which takes possession of the soul, and in the end becomes the soul itself. Let us not confuse this feeling with the sickly emanations of the imagination, the pagan cult of beauty, the desire of the senses, in which vanity counts for something too if we are loved by someone of a higher class. What has this unrest, this passing incident, this mere diversion in common with the ineffable tenderness that arouses the soul to long for union with another soul, and the will to strive for self-sacrifice?'

He broke off, for by a subtle instinct he realized that his excessive subtlety was leading him into absurdity. For poor Abelarda these ardent words, pronounced with a certain elegant mimicry by this most handsome man, whose dark eyes expressed such sweetness and pathos as he spoke, were the most eloquent she had ever heard, and her heart was torn as she listened. Conscious of the effect he was making, Victor racked his ready mind for some new method by which to drive the girl still further out of her senses. Here he dropped a few more passionate and paradoxical phrases which contradicted those he had just uttered. But Abelarda did not detect the contradiction. The deep impression made by these last utterances blotted the effect of his earlier words from her mind, and she allowed herself to be torn by the whirlwind into a vortex of contradictory feelings: curiosity, love, joy and fury. Victor embellished his lies with the metaphors and antitheses of a gloomy romanticism now out of fashion. But for Señorita Villaamil this tarnished and valueless metal was true gold. For her lack of education prevented her from identifying the forgotten texts from which Victor took all this rigmarole about fatality. He returned to the charge, and said in somewhat lugubrious tones:

'I mustn't go on talking about this. What must not be, does not exist. I know that it would be better for me to entrust myself to you. Perhaps you would save me. But no, I do not wish to be saved. I must destroy myself and take with me this feeling that I have never deserved, this celestial ray that I preserve in fear as if I had stolen it. You see in me a reflection of the Prometheus of mythology. I have stolen the fire from heaven, and as my punishment a vulture gnaws at my entrails.'

Abelarda, who knew nothing about Prometheus, was frightened by his mention of the vulture; and Victor, delighted at his triumph, went on: 'I am damned, I am a reprobate. I cannot ask you to save me, for fatality would prevent it. Therefore if ever I come to you and tell you that I love you, do not believe me. It's a lie, it's an infamous trap that I've prepared for you. Despise me, fling me from your side. I do not deserve your affection, or even your compassion.'

With great pain and self-disgust, the little nobody reflected: What an idiot I am, and how ordinary, not to be able to think of any answer to all these exalted and emotional things he's saying to me! She heaved a deep sigh and longed to throw her arms round his neck and exclaim: 'I love you more than you can guess. But don't bother about me, I deserve nothing, and I'm worth much less than you.'

Supporting his head with both hands, Victor let his eyes wander restlessly over the oilcloth of the table. He frowned and sighed repeatedly, playing the part of the romantic and mis-understood, a sort of Manfred, or at least a chemist's assistant's or young clerk's version of that hero. He then gave her a look of extraordinary sweetness and said, touching her arm: 'Oh, how I must hurt you with my horrible misanthropy, which cannot interest you at all. Forgive me. I beg you to forgive me. I shall have no rest unless you say you will. You are an angel, and I am not worthy of you, I admit it. I do not even try to be worthy of you. It would be a senseless presumption. All I want now is that you shall understand me. Will you understand me?'

Abelarda had almost exhausted her power of concealing her distress and perturbation. But her sense of honour was still powerful. She would not surrender her soul's secret without defending it to the death. Finally with supreme heroism she gave a laugh which sounded like the hysterical outburst that precedes a nervous collapse.

'I'm sure I don't understand you,' she said. 'You're pretending to be a scoundrel, you're pretending to be a villain though you aren't, just to deceive me. But you won't take me in. You're crazy. I'm cleverer than you. I can see through you. What's the point of trying to make everyone hate you, if you can't bring it off?'

17

LITTLE Luis got worse. It was a gastric attack of the kind that are common in childhood, and that would have no evil results if it were dealt with in time. Victor was worried and brought in the doctor; and although his precautions were unnecessary since the three Miaus tended the little invalid most affectionately, even denying themselves for some nights their visit to the opera, he kept on telling them not to leave the bedside, and himself looked in on his son at all hours, when he would pull up the bedclothes to prevent him from catching cold and feel his pulse for fever. To amuse the boy and cheer him up, a very necessary thing in childish complaints, Victor brought him toys, and his aunt Quintina came too with her hands full of coloured pictures and pictures of saints, Luis' favourite playthings. He had already collected a heap of knick-knacks and trifles under his pillow, which he brought out for inspection at certain hours. During his nights of fever, when he could not sleep, the boy had imagined himself sitting under the convent arch, or on the Conde-Duque terrace. But he did not see God, or rather he only half saw him. He caught a glimpse of his body, of his flowing robes and their matchless whiteness. Sometimes he vaguely made out his hands, but his face never. Why did he not show his face? Little Luis began to feel very distressed. He suspected that the Lord was offended with him. And what was the reason? On one of the prints that his father had brought him God was represented in the act of creating the world. What could be easier! He just raised his finger, and the sky, sea and mountains appeared. He raised his finger again and lions, crocodiles, coiling snakes, and the darting mouse . . . But this picture did not satisfy the boy. Of course the Lord was beautifully drawn, but he certainly was not as handsome or as venerable as his friend.

One morning, when Luis had no more fever, his grandfather came in to see him. It seemed to the boy that Villaamil was silently suffering from a great grief. Already before the old man came in Luis had heard the Miaus whispering together, and this seemed to him a bad augury. They were whispering that he had not got an appointment in the new list. How did they know? The boy remembered that early in the morning, just as he had woken up, he had heard Doña Pura say to her sister: 'Nothing again. They've let us down properly. There's no doubt at all now. Victor told me, and he made certain of it last night at the Ministry.'

These words had stuck in the boy's mind, and he now related them to his grandfather's condemned expression on entering the room. Being a child, Luis only associated ideas imperfectly, but he associated them nevertheless, for his innocent mind was always discovering strange affinities between them. If he had not known his grandfather well, he would have been afraid of him that morning, for really he looked like one of those ogres that gobble little children up. They haven't given him a post, thought young Luis, and as he said this he joined two other ideas in his mind, which was still disturbed by the scarcely departed fever. A child's reasoning is sometimes dreadfully precise, as his thoughts on this occasion prove: Well, if God won't give him a post I don't know why he should be so cross with me and not show his face. I've got a better right to be cross with him.

Villaamil started walking up and down the room with his hands in his pockets. No one dared to speak to him. Luis felt a pang of grief that took away his spirits. They don't give him a post, he thought, because I blooming well don't work, because I don't know my confounded lessons. But at this point his childish reasoning reasserted itself, coming to the defence of his pride: But how can I work if I'm ill? Let him make me better and then see if I don't work!

Victor came in from the street and went straight to embrace Villaamil, cutting short his caged beast's prowl. Doña Pura and Abelarda had also entered the room.

'One mustn't let misfortune get one down,' said Victor, whose show of affection Villaamil received with a very bad grace. 'Men of courage, men of true moral fibre have strength enough in themselves to face adversity. The Minister has broken his word again, and so have all the rest who promised to support you. God forgive them, and may their black consciences torture them for the wrong they have done.'

'Leave me alone, leave me alone,' replied Villaamil, who looked as if he were choking to death.

'I know very well that a strong man has no need of comfort from an ordinary person like myself. What is it we have seen? A natural and logical happening in a society which like ours is corrupted by favouritism. What has occurred? An upright man, the father of a family, a deserving official grown old in the public service, a loyal servant of the state who could have shown the Minister a means of remedying the finances, has been passed over, has been ignored, has been swept like dust through the office door. But this does not surprise me. I should have been surprised if it had been otherwise. Yet there's more to it than this. While this injustice is committed, the brazen and incapable, men without claims or conscience, seize the post as a reward for their ineptitude. In face of this there is nothing to be done but to retire to the sanctuary of one's own conscience and say: Very well. My own approbation is enough for me.'

As Victor spoke this deep philosophy, he looked at Doña Pura and Abelarda, who were so deeply moved that they were within an inch of tears. Villaamil said nothing. With pale face and trembling jaw, he was once more pacing the room.

'Nothing surprises me,' added Victor, overflowing with sanctimonious indignation. 'The world is so rotten today that something even more shocking is about to take place. While this man, who deserves to be a Director General at least, is ignored and thrown on the scrapheap, I who am worthless, who am nothing, and have only a short record of service, I, believe it or not, when I least expect it, shall no doubt get the promotion I put in for. Such is the world, such is Spain. This is why we all grow to despise the state, and to cherish in our thoughts the embers of past revolutions. Merit is met with disappointment and demerit with the sweets of office. This is Spanish logic. Everything upside down. The land of contraries. And I who am calm and unperturbed, who have hardly any needs, who despise office and the man who offers it to me, will receive an appointment, while the father of a family, weighed down with obligations, a man whose worth and services gave him such well-founded expectations of . . .'

'I had no expectations. You're quite wrong there,' said Don Ramón sharply in a burst of anger, raising his arms to just short of the ceiling. 'I never had any hopes. I didn't think they would appoint me, and I never shall, never. That's the game these people play. But I never expected anything. How can I get that into your heads? It really looks as if you're all conspiring to drive me mad.'

'Anyone would think it was a crime to hope for anything,

my dear,' observed Doña Pura. 'But I have hopes, more now than ever. There will be another list. They've promised you a post, and they'll have to keep their promise.'

'Of course,' said Victor, giving Villaamil a glance of filial affection. 'And what's more, it doesn't do to worry. Let things take their course. There's no reason or justice in it. But if they give me my promotion, and I expect they will, my luck will repair the family's misfortunes. The family has been very kind, and I am in their debt. I can never repay them whatever I do. I have been wicked. But now I intend – I will not say to be a good man, because I know that would be difficult, but at least to act in such a way that the family will forget my faults. They will lack for nothing while I have so much as a crust of bread.'

Villaamil was crushed by humiliation. It was as if the roof had collapsed and fallen on his soul. With a deep sigh, he departed from the room, followed by his wife, and Abelarda, actuated by very different feelings from her father's, turned back to Luis' bed. To conceal her emotion, she made a show of pulling up his bed-clothes. No, he's not a wicked man, she reasoned; I'll never believe that whoever says so.

'Abelarda,' Victor began sweetly a few minutes after they had been left alone with the child, 'I know very well that I haven't to repeat to you what I have just said to your parents. You know me a little and you understand me a little. You know that so long as I have a crust of bread none of you will go short of food. But I have to say this to your parents and even to prove it to them before they'll believe me. They have a very poor idea of me. It's true one doesn't get rid of a bad reputation in a couple of days. And how could I help coming to your assistance unless I were a monster? If I did nothing for the rest I should have to do something for my son who has been brought up in this house, for this little angel who loves you all better than he loves me. And he has good reason.'

Abelarda caressed Luis in an endeavour to conceal the tears that were starting to her eyes, and the child, responding to this caress and to the words his father had been saying, which sounded to him like a sermon or a passage from a devotional book, was so moved that he began to weep like a Magdalen.

The pair of them endeavoured to revive his spirits by laughing and telling him jokes and making up stories for him.

In the afternoon the boy asked for his books, which surprised everybody. For they did not understand why, since he did no lessons when he was well, he wanted to study in bed. But he was so insistent that they gave him his grammar and his arithmetic, which he thumbed through, muttering as he did so: 'Not now, because my eyes are swimming. But as soon as I can, blowed if I don't learn them from cover to cover. And then we'll see. We'll see then!'

18

POOR Abelarda fell into such low spirits that her mother and aunt thought she was ill and talked of calling the doctor. Nevertheless she went on with her ordinary life, working for most of the day on alterations and repairs to her clothes. She used a cane dummy, which had migrated from the dining-room cabinet and which in the evening looked like a person, the fourth Miau, or the ghost of one of the family that had come from the other world to visit her descendants. The little nobody tried on this dummy the things she had cut out and was making, which were rather pretty. At this epoch she was making a dress from some pieces of cashmere which had already been used twice, and had been turned inside out and upside down. She was now piecing them together with some poor stuff at a peseta a yard. These piecings together were a habit of Pura's. If a material could not be washed or turned she would send it to be dyed and . . . it came back looking as if it were new. By this system she would produce a dress for as little as six pesetas. But Abelarda showed her greatest talents in the transformation of hats. Doña Pura's bonnet had passed through a series of different existences which, like reincarnations, made it always new and always old. For winter they lined it with velvet, and for summer covered it with lace from an old curtain. The flowers or other decorations were the gift of their neighbours on the first floor. The tortured shape of Abelarda's hat had already, during Don Ramón's unemployment, taken on different forms and styles according to the dictates of fashion. But thanks to Doña Pura's exquisite art of disguising their poverty the Villaamils walked out into the street as smart as could be.

On the nights when the Miaus did not go to render homage to Euterpe, Abelarda had to listen for two or three hours to Ponce's chatter, or to teach him his part in the play. It annoyed Doña Pura very much that she still had to give a dramatic performance now that her hopes of a post for her husband had come to nothing. But as it had been announced with a flourish of trumpets, and the parts had been assigned, and the rehearsals had advanced so far there was nothing for it but to sacrifice herself on the altars of tyrannical society. Abelarda had deliberately chosen an unimportant part, that of the maid who when the curtain rises comes forward dusting-brush in hand to complain that her employers do not pay her wages and to reveal to the public that the house in which she works is the 'stoniest' in Madrid. The play was of the kind most favoured by the wits of the capital. All it did was to present a commomplace family with more pride than money; a wife who wore the trousers and her downtrodden husband, a betrothal, an intrigue arising from a confusion of names, and a sequence of entrances and exits which culminated in a moment when, just as the whole place seemed a madhouse, the fool of a father entered and said, 'Now I understand everything.' The farce ended with a wedding and an epilogue in which the audience was asked to applaud. Ponce was taking the part of the foolish father; and the rakish and headstrong young man who caused all the confusion and provided the wit and spice for the play was to be played by a certain Cuevas, a son of the first-floor tenant, Don Isidoro Cuevas, a widower with a large family who worked in the governor's office of the near-by women's jail and was generally known in the neighbourhood as the ladies' prison keeper. Young Cuevas was witty and popular, and told stories about drunkards so pleasingly that he made you die of laughter. He imitated vulgar speech, sang flamenco very well, and had many other attainments all of which made him a great favourite at evening parties like those given by the Villaamils. The part of the daughter of the house fell to the Pantoja girl (her father, Don Buenaventura Pantoja, a Treasury official, was an intimate friend of Villaamil's); and that of the ill-mannered, common, loud-mouthed sergeant-major of a mother was taken by one of the Cuevas girls – there were four of them and they helped themselves out by making hats, which they did very well. Other parts, a man-servant, an old money-lender, a bankrupt who pretended to be a marquis and proved to be a first-class swindler, were divided among different youngsters of the circle. The lame Guillén acted as prompter. Federico Ruiz functioned as stage-manager, and would have liked the performances to be advertised on the street-corners so that he could put on the placards in large letters: Under the direction of the well-known publicist, etc. etc.

Abelarda had an excellent memory and learnt her part very quickly. She performed like an automaton at the rehearsals, lending herself meekly to the life of this world, that was for her secondary and artificial. It was as if the house, her family, the evening party and Ponce were really the play, a play with easy and commonplace parts. Her mind remained detached, absorbed in her inner life, the true and real one, in a drama that palpitated with interest and was exclusively hers, a drama with only one actor, herself, and only one spectator, God.

A disorderly and endless monologue. One morning while the girl was combing her hair, an eavesdropper might have heard the following: 'How plain I am! Goodness me, I look like nothing at all. But I'm worse than plain. I'm stupid, a nobody. I haven't a spark of intelligence. If at least I had some talent; but not even that. How can he possibly love me when there are so many beautiful women in the world, and he a man of special merits, a man with a future, handsome, smart and with a great deal of intelligence, let them say what they like?' (Pause.) 'Last night Bibiana Cuevas told me that they've given us a nickname in the gallery of the Real. They call us the Miau women or the Miaus, because they say we look like three little cats – yes, little china cats, the sort people buy for ornaments on corner-tables. And Bibiana thought I should be annoyed by the nickname.

How silly she is! I don't get annoyed by anything now. Do we look like cats? Perhaps we do. All right. Does everyone laugh at us? All right again. What do I care? We're just poor pretentious people. But people are born like that, and no power on earth can make them anything else. I was born like that, and I shall die like that. I shall marry another pretentious person and have pretentious children, and everyone will call them the kittens.' (Pause.) 'And when will they give Papa an appointment? Now I come to think of it, I don't care. It's all the same to me. With a post or without a post we're always just the same. Our house has been more or less just like this all my life. Mamma is a bad housekeeper, and so is my aunt, and so am I. If they give Papa a post I shall be glad for him, because then he'll have something to amuse him and occupy his mind. But as for the question of being well-off, I reckon we shall never be free from penury and shams and rags and patches. Poor Miaus! It's an amusing name. Mamma will be furious if she knows, but it doesn't annoy me, I've got no pride left. Everything's used up, like the family money, if the family ever had any money. I shall tell Ponce all this about the Miaus, to see if he laughs or makes a fuss. I hope he loses his temper one day so that I can lose my temper too. Really I should like to give him a slap or something. . . .' (Pause.) 'How stupid and unattractive I am! My sister Luisa was better, although, really and truly, there was nothing very special about her. My eyes have got no expression. The most they do is to show that I'm sad, but not what I'm sad about. No one would ever believe that behind these pupils there is . . . what there is. No one would ever believe that this narrow forehead and this frown conceal what they do conceal. How difficult it is for me to conceive what heaven looks like. I can't manage it. I see nothing. And how easy for me to imagine hell! I conjure it up as if I had been there. Yes, they're quite right. The likeness to a cat's face is quite striking. The mouth's the worst thing, the mouth that turns down in a point. We all three have it. Yes, but it's most striking in Mamma. My mouth, on the whole, isn't too bad, especially when I'm smiling. But there's one thing I wonder. Would it be a bit better if I were to paint my lips? No, no! Victor would laugh at me. He might despise me. But he doesn't find me absurd and repulsive. Heavens, can I be repulsive? That's a thought I really can't bear. My God no, not repulsive. Once I believed I was repulsive, I should kill myself.' (Pause.) 'Last night he came in and went straight to his room without saying a word. It's better like that. When he speaks to me my heart sticks in my throat. I would be capable of committing a crime to make him love me. What crime? Any crime. All crimes. But he'll never love me, and I shall stay with my crime planned, unhappy for ever.'

'Abelarda,' called Doña Pura and suddenly started her out of her abstraction. 'Tell Ponce when he comes that we'll kill him if he doesn't bring us tickets for Madame Pellegrini's benefit. If he hasn't got any, let him go and get some. She must give tickets to the newspapers and the grand people in the claque. If Ponce goes and asks her, believe me she won't refuse him. We shall be really furious if he doesn't bring us some.'

'He'll bring them,' said Aberlarda, who had now finished putting up her bun. 'I'll never speak to him again if he doesn't.'

Ponce made himself at home in the house and went straight to the dining-room, where he generally found his fiancée. That afternoon he arrived at about four, hung up his cloak and bowler-hat on the hooks in the hall, and entered, smoothing his hair. He was a feeble, lymphatic young man, of the sort who have a fiancée as they might have an umbrella. A bit of a writer, an unpaid critic, he was always busy, and always complaining because nobody read him (nobody reads in this country). He was a minor lawyer, a good enough fellow with large ears and pince-nez and a slight squint in both eyes. His trousers were very baggy at the knees, he had very little grey matter, and about a peseta and a half in his pocket at the most. He had a small post in the government of the province, which brought in six thousand, and he was straining after the eight he had been promised the year before. It might come today, it might come tomorrow, and they'd have the wedding the moment it did. These prospects had not sufficed to make the Villaamils accept him as a son-in-law. But he had a rich and childless uncle, a notary, who suffered from cancer and was sure to die within a year, perhaps within a month, and Ponce was his heir. So the

Miau family regarded this suitor as a lucky draw. According to Pantoja, who was his friend and executor, the unfortunate uncle would leave two houses, some thousands of pesetas, and his practice.

The moment Ponce entered the dining-room, Abelarda gave him this broad hint: 'If you don't bring us tickets for Pellegrini's benefit, never set foot in this house again.'

'Gently, gently, my girl. Let me sit down and get my breath. I've been running. Things are happening, big things are happening to me.'

'What things are happening, for goodness' sake?' asked Doña Pura, who was in the habit of scolding him like a son. 'You're always producing these excitements, and when it comes to it there's nothing in them.'

'Listen to me, Doña Pura, and you, Abelarda, listen to me too. My uncle's very ill, very ill indeed.'

'Oh, gracious heavens,' exclaimed Doña Pura, feeling her heart give a bound. And like a young deer, she leapt into the kitchen to give the news to her sister.

'He's dying.'

'Who?'

'His uncle, woman, the uncle. Don't you understand? But tell me, Ponce' (she had darted back like a cat into the dining-room), 'is he really going? You must be very pleased, very . . . sorry, I mean.'

'You must understand that I can't go to the theatre, or pay a call on Madame Pellegrini. As you know . . . Very bad, in a very bad way. The doctors say he won't last two days.'

'Poor man! And why aren't you sitting on the dead man's – I mean the sick man's doorstep?'

'I've just come away . . . At seven tonight they're taking him the Sacrament.' Doña Pura ran to the study where Villaamil had gone.

'The Sacrament, do you hear?'

'What? . . . Who?'

'The uncle, man, Ponce's uncle. He's at his last gasp' (slipping away again towards the dining-room). 'Ponce, dear boy, won't you have a glass of wine and a biscuit? You must be very upset.

Of course you can't think of going to the theatre. It's out of the question. We shan't go either. Out of mourning, naturally. We shall observe strict mourning. Are you sure you won't have a glass of wine and a biscuit? Oh, I've got a head like a sieve. Of course the wine's finished. But we'll send for some. Really, wouldn't you like some?'

'No thank you, you know that wine always goes to my head.'

Abelarda and Ponce began a conversation of which Luis was the only witness. He was wandering perplexedly about the dining-room, and stopped at times in front of the lovers to gaze at them with childish wonder. They were talking softly. What were they saying? The usual trivialities. Abelarda played her part with the same heavy passivity that she displayed in her everyday life. It was a matter of routine to chatter with this fool, to tell him she loved him, and discuss some detail about their wedding. She had acquired the habit of saying yes to Ponce's questions, which were always proper and restrained. Her own will played no part in these confidences. The external and visible woman performed a series of unconscious acts, like a sleep-walker, while the inner woman remained detached, pursuing her own more human feelings. Before Victor's sudden appearance in the house, Abelarda considered Ponce as a possible support, and marriage as a resource against the ups-and-downs of fortune. She would marry him to establish herself, and to have a name and position, and to escape the unbearable poverty of her home. Since 'the other man' had come she still allowed herself to be guided by the same thoughts, but like a skater who, once launched, continues to turn and glide without ever tumbling on the ice. It never occurred to the girl to change her mind and break her engagement with Ponce; because to have him for a husband was like having a fan, a safety-pin, or another of those objects that are so usual one takes no notice of them. That day the tiresome critic felt himself obliged to display more tenderness than usual. He was so bold as to fix the day of the nuptials and, concealing his timidity, to propound some plans for their future married life. The little nobody heard him as she might the rain, and in view of its enhanced proximity testified agreement with his plans, accepting them in cold and colourless tones like someone yawning through the paternosters and ave marias of a rosary, and repeating them without the least feeling of devotion.

The doorbell rang and Abelarda's heart gave a bound, though her manner remained as cold as before. She recognized him by his way of ringing, she knew his tread as he came upstairs, and if between the door of the apartment and the dining-room he exchanged any conversation with Doña Pura or Villaamil, she knew by the distant inflexion of his voice whether he had arrived in a good or bad humour. As Doña Pura opened the door to Victor she immediately gave him the news of the imminent death of Ponce's uncle. The good lady was incapable of restraint, and took everyone into her confidence down to the *dancing-master* (in vulgar language the water-carrier). Victor came in smiling, and by mistake or malice went and congratulated Ponce, who was struck speechless.

19

'OH, no . . . excuse me. I made a mistake. It was because of the light in my mother-in-law's eyes when she told me the news. It must be the affection she feels for you, my excellent Ponce. Affection blinds people's eyes. You're a member of the family now. We're very fond of you, and seeing that we haven't the pleasure of knowing your good uncle even by sight . . .'

He caressed Luis, rubbing his face and pinching his cheeks to kiss them. Then he showed him the present he had brought him. It was a stamp-album, which he had promised the boy the day that he took his purgative, and with it he gave him a collection of different coloured stamps, some of them foreign, but most of them Spanish, so that he could amuse himself by sticking them on the proper pages. Young Luis' gratitude for this gift was immeasurable. He was at an age in which the sense for classification begins to develop, and in which we relate our playthings to our serious knowledge of life. Victor explained to him the arrangement of pages in the album, and showed him how to identify the nationality of the stamps. 'Look, this bold-looking young woman is the French republic. That lady with the crown and ribbons in her hair is the queen of England, and this eagle with two heads is Germany. Now you must put them in their right places, and the next thing to do is to collect a lot more to fill the vacant spaces.' The little boy was delighted. He was only sorry that there were not sufficient stamps to cover the whole table. He quickly understood the process, and swore in his heart to keep the album and look after it for as long as he lived.

Victor meanwhile broke into the intimate conversation between Abelarda and Ponce. They were almost nose to nose, sharing a secret, an interchange of nonsense in his case amorous, in hers indifferent and wearisome. Victor thrust himself between them, and said: 'My friends, this is really too much, I protest. Couldn't you wait for your honeymoon before playing at turtle-doves? Frankly it rubs salt in a man's wounds. Happiness should be concealed from the unhappy, like riches from the poor. Charity demands it.'

'But what's it got to do with you whether we're in love or out of love,' asked Abelarda, 'and whether we get married or call it off? Whether we shall be happy or not depends on us. It's our business, and has nothing to do with you.'

'Don Victor,' protested Ponce in his usual feeble fashion, 'if you're envious you can put it in your pipe and smoke it.'

'Envious? I won't deny that I am. It wouldn't be true to say I'm not.'

'Very well then, rage and swear.'

'Papa, Papa,' piped little Luis, and to force his father to look in his direction put his hands on his face and made him turn round. 'Where's this one from, that has a man with very big moustaches?'

'Can't you see, boy. It's Italian . . . Yes, of course I'm envious. This girl tells me to rage, and I can't see why I shouldn't rage, or bite either. Because when I see two people who are fond of one another, two who have solved the problem of love, and smoothed out every difficulty, and little by little, treading the road of good-fortune, are approaching the goal of matrimony, it makes me die of envy. As I see it, believe it or not, you have solved the problem. In this charming couple I see what I have never been able to attain. You have no ambitions, you are satisfied with a peaceful and modest existence. You respect and love one another with none of the fever and madness that . . . You won't have much cash, but you won't be short of meat in the pot. Without being saint-like, you have enough goodness between you to give one another pleasure. What more could a man desire? Oh, excellent Ponce, you have been clever enough to understand her, you have been clever enough to choose her. And she too, the sly girl who looks as if she couldn't say boo to a goose, she's put her hand in the basket and taken the best fruit. I congratulate you. For why shouldn't I congratulate you? But that doesn't prevent me from having my grumble, like anyone else, because I find myself in a very different situation. Oh, very different. I would give all I have, all I hope to have, for one thing. Can't you guess what it is?'

With sudden intuition, Abelarda saw what was coming and trembled. 'I would give all I've got to be the excellent Ponce. That's the truth, whether you believe me or not. Would you like to change places with me, Ponce, my friend?'

'Frankly, so long as I keep the lady I can see nothing against the change.'

'Oh no, no. You've missed the whole point. I would give the blood of my veins if I could throw my hook into the sea of life, baited with a declaration of love, and fish out an Abelarda. That's an ambition that would cure me of all others.'

'Papa, Papa' (pulling his nose in order to make him look round). 'And this one with a parrot on it?'

'Guatemala. Leave me alone, my boy . . . That's all I ask. A little Abelarda to spoil me, and in her company I'd face anything. I'd marry a girl like her if she hadn't a penny, if she were poor as a church-mouse. One could always live on pea-soup. I'd prefer a crust of bread with her to all the riches in the world without her. For where would you find a character as sweet, so tender a heart, so good a housekeeper, so . . .'

'You're piling it on very thick, Don Victor' (with a completely unsuccessful attempt at humour). 'She's my fiancée, and all these compliments will make me jealous.'

'It's not a matter for jealousy. You're on to a good thing. This girl, this girl of yours . . . She's safe, my friend. She loves you heart and soul. All the kings and princes in the world wouldn't be able to part her from her beloved Ponce. Do you suppose that if I hadn't known this I shouldn't have glanced in her direction myself? Charity begins at home. If I'd had so much as a glimmer of hope, do you think I shouldn't have made off with her myself? But that's quite out of the question. I tell you that if anyone talked to her about changing her little Ponce for another man she'd throw the furniture at his head. Look at her now, with her enigmatic expression, and that little smile that looks as if she has put it on. Tell me, would anyone have the courage to make a proposal?'

'Come, Don Victor,' protested Ponce with his mouth full of spittle, 'all this talk means that you've had pretensions yourself, and that you didn't learn your lesson.'

'Don't listen to him, silly,' said Abelarda, much disturbed, and forced a smile, though she felt more like tears than joking. 'Can't you see that he's agreeing with you really?'

'Let him agree. The point is that Abelarda is a sensible woman, and once she's given her word no one can shift her. We were of one mind the first time we talked. Our natures are in perfect harmony. I'm cut out for her, she's cut out exactly for me.'

'Gently, gently, my noble Ponce' (assuming a very serious expression as he always did when he raised his cruel jokes to the heroic scale). 'You may be cut out for whoever you like; that's no concern of mine. But as for Abelarda, as for Abelarda . . .'

Ponce gazed at him, serious also, awaiting the end of his sentence, and the little nobody looked down at her sewing.

'What I say is that she is not cut out for you. And I'll defend that statement against anyone who contradicts it. Truth before all things. She loves you, that I'll agree. But as for being cut out, she's cut out on a large scale. I'm speaking of the moral scale, but of the physical as well. Yes, sir, of the physical as well. Do you want me to be quite frank? Do you know whom she's cut out for? She's cut out for me. For me, and I mean no offence to you. For me, although this may seem nonsense to you. You're not in the same position to judge her as I am. I've known her since she was a child. Moreover you haven't had enough to do with me to know if she and I are suited or not. I know that I'm talking about an impossibility. I know that I've committed the sin of arriving too late. I know that you've got in before me, and we won't quarrel. But as for recognizing merit when I see it, as for regretting that all these gifts are not for me, as for that' (pronouncing the sentence with the greatest seriousness and in a rhetorical voice) – 'oh, as for that, I do not yield, and I cannot yield.'

'Don't take any notice of him, let him alone,' said Abelarda to her fiancé, who was beginning to lose his temper.

'My dear Don Victor, all this may be true, but it's not much to the point.'

'You seem to be getting nettled, excellent Ponce. But let me tell you I'm a very honourable man. I acknowledge that you have won the prize which in my opinion should have been mine' (with pathos). 'It was a fair victory, in honest battle. What I lost I lost through my own fault. I don't complain. We shall be friends, friends for ever. Let's shake hands on it.'

'Oh this man Don Victor, what ideas he does have!' (letting his hand be shaken).

Cadalso would have taken good care not to use such insolent language with anyone else; but he knew very well with whom he was dealing. Abelarda's fiancé was nettled; and she did not know what to think. It seemed to her too cruel to be a joke, and somewhat outspoken if it were serious. Ponce was very sorry that he had to go. He supposed that Victor would go on talking to the girl in the same tone; and frankly, Abelarda was his fiancée, his future wife, and this fine brother-in-law who lived under the same roof was beginning to worry him. Conscious of the disturbance in the critic's mind, the wicked Cadalso shook his hand long and warmly as he took his leave, and repeated : 'I'm an honourable man, a very honourable man. You've nothing to fear from me.'

And when he returned to the girl who gazed at him with alarm : 'I'm sorry, my dear, the thought slipped out although I wanted to conceal it from everybody. One's sometimes spontaneous when one least expects to be. However skilful one is at concealment, sometimes one can't control oneself. I didn't want to talk about that. I don't know what came over me. I felt so envious when I saw you like a couple of turtle-doves. I was so shocked to discover how lonely I am, because I arrived too late, only because I arrived too late! Forgive me. I won't say another word. I know that this subject bores and annoys you. I will be sensible.'

Abelarda could not restrain herself. She got up, terrified and longing to run away and hide. For she could not conceal the colour which was rising impetuously to her pale cheeks.

'Victor,' she exclaimed unnerved and trembling, 'if you aren't the wickedest man on earth, I don't know what you are.'

She ran into her room and burst into tears, hiding her face in the pillows of her bed. Victor stayed in the dining-room; and Luis, who understood in his innocence that something strange was happening, did not dare for some time to worry his father with the complicated business of the stamps. It was his father who then affected interest in this intellectual pastime, and began to explain to his son the national symbols that he did not understand : 'This king with a beard is Belgium, and this cross is the Helvetic Republic, that is to say Switzerland.'

Doña Pura came in from the street and, not finding her daughter in the dining-room or the kitchen, went to look for her in the bedroom. Abelarda was just coming out with very red eyes. But she gave her mother no satisfactory explanation of these signs of grief. When Doña Pura asked Victor for the reason, he answered slyly : 'How silly you are, Mamma. She's crying about Ponce's uncle.'

20

THEY put Luis to bed early, and he took the stamp-album with him, holding it very tight as he went to sleep. That night he did not have one of those convulsive attacks that preceded his visions of the celestial old man. But he dreamt that he had one, and that he was therefore eagerly awaiting the fantastic vision. The mysterious person played truant. At least, that is how the disconsolate little boy thought of it, for he wanted to show him his stamp-album. He waited for a very long time, unable to decide where he was, for the place might equally well have been school, or the dining-room at home, or the scribe's office. In the course of his dream, which was all illogical nonsense, the boy was struck by a piece of admirable sense. How silly I am, he thought. How could he come if tonight they've taken him to Ponce's uncle's?

Next day they said he was well, but it was decided that he should not go to school for the rest of the week, for which he was very grateful. He made up his mind to do some work in the evenings, but only a little. He reserved his great efforts at application for the time when he had homework to do again. They let him go down to the porter's lodge, and he took the album with him, to show it to Paca and Canelo. He would have liked to take it to his aunt Quintina's, but he could not get permission. He stayed in the porter's lodge till nightfall, when they called him back, afraid that he might get chilled by the air in the doorway. When he came up he brought with him an idea derived from his conversations with Mendizábal and Paca, an idea which at first seemed to him rather strange, but which he afterwards accepted as the most natural thing in the world. Finding himself alone with Abelarda, for Milagros and his grandmother were gossiping in the kitchen, the boy decided to tell his aunt his famous idea. She was caressing him with great fervour, kissing him again and again and promising to give him a bigger album, when Luis, returning all these caresses with others no less affectionate, said to her: 'Aunty, why don't you marry my Papa?'

The young woman was left speechless, half inclined to laugh and half to be annoyed: 'Wherever did you get that idea, Luis?' she said, frightening him by the fierceness of her expression. 'You never made it up for yourself. Someone must have said that to you.'

'Paca said it,' answered Luis, not wanting to take a responsibility that was not his. 'She says that Ponce is ever so silly, and doesn't suit you, and that my father's handsome and clever and will make a very great career, a very great career.'

'Tell Paca not to meddle in other people's business. But what else, what else did she tell you?'

'Well . . .' (scratching around in his memory). 'Oh, that my papa's a very proper gentleman. Because he always gives Paca money whenever she does an errand for him. And that you ought to marry my Papa, so that everything should stay in the house.'

'Does she do errands for him? Take letters? Whom does she take them to? Do you know?'

'It must be to the Minister. They're great friends.'

'Everything that Paca's told you about poor Ponce is just nonsense,' stated Abelarda with a smile. 'You like Ponce, don't you? Tell me the truth, tell me what you think.'

Luis hesitated a moment before answering. The presents he had received and the polite way in which he had seen his father treat the whole family had removed his former attitude of fear. As for Ponce, one could say that young Cadalso had not formed any opinion about him. Therefore he accepted Paca's views on the subject unquestioningly: 'Ponce's no good at all. Don't you imagine he is. When he walks down the street he looks as if his trousers are coming down. And as for brains, even Cuevas has got more brains. Don't you think so too?'

Abelarda laughed at these ideas, and would have gone on discussing the subject with Luis if her father had not called her to sew some buttons on his jacket, which kept her busy till suppertime. Doña Pura announced that Victor was not eating at home, but with a friend, who was a deputy and leader of a small parliamentary group. On this Villamil made some bitter comments which were very painful to Abelarda, who did not answer them. There was a discussion as to whether they should go to the theatre that night, and it was decided that they should since Luis was now better. Abelarda asked to stay behind, and when they were alone her mother attacked her vigorously with a fusillade of questions: 'Why don't you eat? What's the matter with you? Why do you put on a face like a dying cow? Why won't you come to the theatre? Don't aggravate me now, but get dressed, because we're just going.'

And the three Miaus went out, leaving Villaamil with his grandson and his funereal reflections. After putting the boy to bed, he sat down to read *La Correspondencia*, which spoke of a new list of appointments.

When the Miaus came back, Victor was already there writing letters at the dining-room table. Don Ramón was still glued to his newspaper; father-in-law and son-in-law did not exchange a word. They all went to bed except Abelarda, who had to wash some clothes which must be ironed next day. Seeing her thus occupied, Victor spoke to her without putting down his pen: 'I've been thinking of you all day. I was afraid I'd annoyed you by what I said yesterday. I had made up my mind never to reveal my feelings to you. I still haven't told you the whole truth, nor will I, please God. When one arrives too late one must resign oneself and keep silent. But aren't you going to say anything? Aren't you even going to scold me?'

The little nobody kept her eyes fixed on the table, and her mouth quivered as if words were rising to her lips. But in the end she said nothing.

'I'll speak to you as a brother' (with that kindly gravity that he knew so well how to assume) 'since I have no right to speak to you in any other way. I am in a very unhappy state. You will not understand it. You see me here caught in a web of wild passion. You see me here, oppressed by a relationship on which I embarked thoughtlessly, which I have kept up out of laziness and habit, and which I now want to break. For this I counted on the help of an angelic being, whose interest I wished to arouse, and to whom I then meant to entrust myself body and soul. But now this cannot be. What am I to do in this situation? To sink deeper and deeper in the mire and to lose myself more and more irretrievably in a maze from which there is no way out. Fate drags me on. You cannot understand this, Abelarda. But who knows? Perhaps you do understand, for you have very great insight. Oh, if I had only found you free! So often I have told myself that I must say nothing. Only the words slip from my mouth. But that's enough, enough. Take no notice of me. I said all this to you at the beginning. Take no notice of this unfortunate man. Despise me. I am unworthy of you. I am expiating the wild follies I committed when I lost my poor Luisa, that angel. A heavenly angel, but not equal to you. So little your equal that there is no point of comparison between you. To be frank' (rising in exaltation) 'when I see a treasure like you about to belong to a Ponce, when I think that such a combination of qualities will fall into the hands of . . .'

Abelarda gasped for breath. She was so overcome by her feelings that she would have choked if she had not given herself the relief of a word.

'But if I were to tell you . . . I mean' (turning pale) 'what if I were to tell you that I don't love Ponce?'

'You don't? Is this true?'

'What if I were to tell you that I never have loved him and never shall? What then?'

Victor had not reckoned on this outburst and lost his head.

'Well, that's something. I mean' (stammering) 'something that absolutely stuns me. But is it the truth? If you say it, it must be the truth. Abelarda, Abelarda, Abelarda, don't play with me. Don't play with fire. Jokes like this, if they are jokes, inevitably lead to catastrophe. Because when a person loathes someone as you loathe me (confused and not knowing which way to turn), then a person doesn't say something to him that may drive him wild, something about . . . I mean something about the feelings of the person who loathes him, because it might happen that the person who is loathed . . . No, I can't get it right. I can't explain what I feel. If you don't love Ponce, it's because you love someone else. But you mustn't tell me that. What would be the effect? Why, you would drive me more distracted

126

than I am at present' (spying a way of escape and using all his wits to slip out through it). 'But I don't want to question you about that, because it might drive me mad. Keep your secret and respect my situation. If I inspire you only with dislike, if you do not feel a positive repugnance for me, leave me to myself, I beg of you. Go away now and say not one word more. I do not offer you my advice, for you would not accept it. But if ever you find yourself in a difficult situation and my advice could be any good to you, you know that I will be to you whatever you wish, a brother if you treat me as a brother . . .'

'And if I should need it, if I should need your advice?' put in Abelarda, who was looking not for a way of escape, but for an approach if she could find one.

'Then dispose of me' (disconcerted once more). 'If you love some man and are afraid of your parents' opposition, if you find it difficult to break with Ponce and need help, here I am ready to help you, however painful it may be for me' (coming closer to her). 'Tell me, tell me, don't be afraid. Do you love some other man, some other man than Ponce?'

'It's asking a great deal that I should confess . . . like this . . . straight out' (resorting to coquetry to get out of her fix). 'Who invited you to poke your nose in?'

'I'm one of the family. I'm your friend, and I could be something more if you wished. But I arrived too late. I mustn't speak about myself. I am out of court. If you won't confide your secret to me, all the better for me. I shan't suffer so badly. But answer me one question. Does this man whom you love love you also?'

'I haven't said I loved anybody. I don't think I ever said that. But supposing I did. That's no affair of yours. You're very inquisitive. Of course I shouldn't love anybody who didn't love me back. That'd be a fine look out!'

'So there's love on both sides' (with a pretence of anger). 'And you tell me a thing like that to my face!'

'Tell you? I never told you a thing.'

'But you gave me to understand it. Come, I don't want to be your confidant. So this other man loves you, does he?'

'I don't know' (allowing herself to be carried away by her

spontaneity, which was now irresistible). 'That's what I haven't been able to find out yet.'

'And you've come to me no doubt to ask me to find out for you' (sarcastically). 'Abelarda, that's the kind of job I don't do. No, don't tell me who he is. I don't have to know. Is he perhaps someone I know? But don't mention his name. Don't mention it unless you want us no longer to be friends. I speak to you as one who feels an affection for you . . . but an affection that now I do not wish to define. A man who lives under the weight of his fatal destiny' (these philosophical statements and others of the same kind Cadalso took from certain novels that he had read). 'A man who is prevented from telling you of his sufferings. And since I may not love you, and I cannot be yours, nor can you be mine, I must not torture myself or allow you to torture me. Keep your secret, and I will keep that part of it that I have guessed. If fate had not sundered us, I would still try to cure you of this love by plucking that man's image from your thoughts and substituting my own. But I am not the master of my will. This feeling of mine' (striking his chest) 'will never leave my heart; it will never come into the light of day. Why do you incite me to reveal it? Let it rest within me, buried but living still. Do not tempt me, do not provoke me. Do you love another? Do not tell me then. Why inflame an incurable wound? And to avoid greater conflicts, tomorrow I will leave this house never to enter it again.'

Abelarda was so upset by this resolve that she could not hide her distress. Her poor brain contained no arms with which to fight this monster of infinite resources and inexhaustible invention, who was used to trifling with deep and serious feelings. Stunned and bewildered, she was about to surrender her secret and offer herself as an absurd and defenceless butt for Victor's brutal sarcasm, when she managed to gain some control over herself, to recover some equilibrium, and to say to him with a pretence of calm : 'No, no, there's no reason for you to go. Have you made peace with Quintina?'

'What? Don't be ridiculous. Yesterday Cabrera almost knocked me down. He's a barbarian. No, but I'll go and live somewhere or other.'

'No, don't do that. You can stay here.'

'Then promise not to speak one word about this again.'

'But I didn't speak about it. It was you who said all that was said. That you love me, that you cannot love me. What am I to think?'

'I'll give you the final proof that I love you and that I must not love you' (with subtlety), 'I'll give it to you now with this piece of advice. Turn your eyes towards Ponce . . .'

'Thank you very much.'

'Turn your eyes towards the excellent Ponce. Marry him. Take a practical view. You don't love him? That doesn't matter.'

'You're mad' (completely bewildered). 'Did I by any chance tell you that I don't love him?'

'Yes, you did indeed.'

'Then I take it back. What absolute nonsense! If I said it, it was a joke, just to keep you talking.'

'You're wicked, very wicked. I didn't think you were like that.'

'Do you know what I think?' (getting up in a sudden access of scorn and anger). 'I think you're an insufferable bore with all these riddles . . . and I can't bear you, I can't bear you. But it's all my fault for listening to your rubbish. Good night. I'm going to bed. And I shall sleep like a log, I promise you that.'

'Great hate, like great love, keeps people awake.'

'Not me . . . You beast, you stupid beast!'

'You'll sleep and I shall lie awake thinking of you. Good night Abelarda. I'll see you tomorrow.'

And the minute after the disappearance of his victim, who rushed into her room and banged the door as if fleeing from a murderer, the wretch went to bed. There, with a diabolical little smile on his lips, he indulged in the following bitter and cruel monologue: She'll quite unashamedly make me a declaration of love if I'm not careful. But what an unattractive girl she is! Utterly brainless and ordinary to the last degree. I could forgive her everything if she were pretty. Oh Ponce, what a windfall you've got! A rotten apple, only fit to be thrown on the refuse heap.

21

ALTHOUGH the Villaamils' hopes, cut down in full flower, sprouted again in new luxuriance, that much tried and officeless official, true to his policy of hopeless hope, pronounced them definitely dead. His pessimism, however, was contradicted by his passion for writing letters and pulling every wire that might convey some vibration to the Minister's failing will. 'The idea of waiting for a vacancy is just madness,' he would say. 'I know very well that when they want to get something done they don't bother about vacancies, or even about the law itself. I'm not quite an imbecile. I've seen it happen a thousand times. A party boss comes into the Ministry, knife in hand, and demands a really fat post. Quick as a flash the Minister sends for the Chief of Personnel . . . "There's no vacancy" . . . "Then make one". No sooner said than done. Never mind who suffers, there it is . . . But where's my great patron? Where's the personage with a breast full of ribbons who enters the office with a fierce scowl and says: "I don't move from here until you give me . . . that"? But alas for me, I'm still left in balk. With this confounded Restoration, following on the damned revolution, so many new people have come up that you don't know where to look for a familiar face. When a Don Claudio Moyana, a Don Antonio Benavides, or a Marqués de Novaliches turns to you and says: "Villaamil, my friend, we've been put on the retired list," then the world's really coming to an end. Mendizábal is quite right when he says that politics have fallen into the hands of nobodies.'

To relieve his sorrow and review some other appointments, now that he affected not to believe or had actually given up belief in his own, he went in the afternoons to the Treasury, where many of his friends filled different posts in different offices. He spent long hours there, chatting and informing himself about what was going on. He would smoke a cigarette and act as adviser to the new or inexperienced clerks, who would consult him on some obscure point in the complicated procedure of the office.

Villaamil felt a profound affection for the colossal pile of the Ministry. He loved it as the loyal servant loves the house and family whose bread he has eaten for so many years; and in that sad period of his unemployment he visited it with the respect and sadness of a servant who hangs around the place from which he has been dismissed, and dreams of being received back again. He crossed the entrance hall, went down the great passage that divides the two courtyards, and slowly climbed the monumental staircase, which is flanked by two massive walls and seems to belong either to a castle or a prison. Almost always he met some old colleague going up or coming down those steps.

'Hallo, Villaamil. How are you?'

'Struggling along.'

When he reached the first floor he hesitated before deciding whether to go into Customs or the Treasury, because he had a host of acquaintances in both departments. But on the second floor he always preferred Taxation to Estates. The porters saluted Villaamil and, being an affable man, he always stopped for a word with them. If it was late he always met them carrying a shovelful of coals from the office grates, the last embers of which serve to feed the braziers in the porters' lodges. If it was early, on the other hand, they would be carrying papers from one office to another, or trays with glasses of water and lumps of sugar.

'Hullo, Bermejo, how are you?'

'So-so, Don Ramón, sorry not to see you here in the mornings.'

'Tell me, how's Ceferino?'

'He's been transferred to Taxation. Poor old Cruz has snuffed it.'

'Gracious me! Why, man, I saw him only the other day, looking ever so hale and hearty. What a world! There aren't many of us left of the old brigade. When I first came, in Don Juan Bravo Murillo's time, Cruz was in "the House" already. But you no sooner turn round . . . Poor old Cruz, I'm very sorry.'

The best of all Villaamil's many good friends in that place was

Don Buenaventura Pantoja, whom we already know a little about as the father of Virginia Pantoja, one of the actresses in the Miaus' private company. The office of this excellent and ancient colleague (in Taxation) whose chief he had once been was Villaamil's favourite visiting-place. Sitting down in the chair nearest to the table, he would turn over the papers if Pantoja was not there, and if he was there would start a delightful chat, all office tittle-tattle.

'Have you heard?' Pantoja would ask. 'We've got two new first officers today and a new chief of department, fresh out of the oven. That clown' (here followed the name of some famous politician) 'was here yesterday, and of course it was like greased lightning. When they want things done, let me tell you, they go over everyone's heads.'

'Good gracious me!' Villaamil would answer, heaving a grievous sigh which fluttered the papers nearest to him.

That day the good man was very late in arriving before Pantoja's table. He met acquaintances at every step. Somebody came out of an office here grasping a bundle of papers tied up with office tape. Somebody else came into another, late and in fear of a wigging from the chief.

'How are things? How are you, Villaamil?'

'Rubbing along, old boy.'

Pantoja's office formed part of an enormous hall, divided by partitions which were about twelve feet high. The ceiling was common to the various departments, and in the vast upper space could be seen the long black pipes of the stoves, which turned at right angles to run out horizontally through the walls. The whole hall was loud with the ringing of bells, and the distant voice of chiefs ceaselessly calling their subordinates. As this was the time when the late-comers arrive and early arrivals take their lunch, and others drink coffee for which they have sent out, silence which is so propitious for brainwork did not reign. Instead, there was nothing but a banging of doors, a chinking of cups and coffee-pots, shouts and impatient exclamations.

Villaamil came into the sub-department, exchanging greetings to right and left. Here the third officer was the lame Guillén, a great friend of the Villaamil family, a constant guest at their evenings, and prompter in the play that they were going to present. He was moreover the uncle of the famous Performer, Luis Cadalso's friend and rival, and lived with his sisters who owned the pawnshop. Guillén had the reputation for biting malice, and was said to be capable of demolishing anything. In the office he wrote crude, comical and obscene sketches, and an occasional hair-raising melodrama, which never reached the footlights. He drew caricatures too, and wrote verse satires on the many ridiculous characters in the Ministry. Also in this office was a junior, son of the director of the Treasury, who was hardly sixteen but had a salary of something like twelve fifty. He was very quick on the uptake, and good at carrying messages from one office to another. The second officer was a certain Espinosa, an elegant young man with an amateurish manner and neatly parted hair, somewhat ornamental in his dress and defective in his spelling. He was a good-natured lad, and never took offence at Guillén's tiresome jokes. But the most remarkable character of all was one Argüelles y Mora, a second officer who was a perfect parody of a gentleman of the time of Philip IV; small, a genuine Madrid type, with a lean pale face, dyed black moustaches and pointed beard, and long and well-combed hair. And to complete the resemblance, he carried a short black cloak, that looked as if it were a relic of the poet Quevedo's wardrobe. He wore a low bowler hat with a broad brim, which was thick with grease. It was a pity he did not wear a ruff. But even without one, he was the perfect image of an old-type village magistrate. In his time he had had pretensions to good looks, originality and elegance. But now he had begun to be round-shouldered, and his face with his dyed hair, gave the pitiful impression that he practised enforced vigils. He played the trumpet in a theatre orchestra. His colleagues called him The Head of the Household, because during all office conversations, in and out of season, he quoted the number of mouths he had to feed on his miserable net salary of three thousand pesetas. There were three or four more clerks who sat, taciturn and devoted to their tasks, at several tables placed at a respectful distance from the chief's, which was near the window that gave on to the courtyard.

Beside the tables were the stands on which the officials hung their hats and cloaks. Guillén had his crutches beside him. Between the tables were racks and waste-paper baskets, of a shape and appearance that is only to be seen in government offices, many of them old, with something about their smell and faded colour that was reminiscent of the store-rooms from which they no doubt came, and others new but unlike any object used outside the world of bureaucracy. On all the desks lay innumerable bundles of documents tied with red tape, some of them yellowing and dusty with a funereal tinge about their paper in which lay buried the hopes of several generations; others, by contrast, consisting of brand-new sheets with fresh writing, marginal notes and indecipherable signatures. These were the most recent documents in the endless case of the Revenue v. the People.

Pantoja was not there; the chief had sent for him.

'Take a seat, Don Ramón. Would you like a cigarette?'

'And what have you got on hand?' (going up to the lame man's table and seizing a piece of paper). 'Let's see, let's see . . . *Original drama in verse*. Title? *The Stepdaughter of Her Stepsister*. Splendid. So that's how you idlers waste your time!'

'Don Ramón, Don Ramón,' said the elegant second officer, who had just finished sipping his coffee. 'Have you heard the news? You remember Canizares, who used to be in Estates, the one we called Simple Simon, do you know they've just given him three thousand? Did you ever hear of such favouritism?'

'I had him in my office fourteen years ago, when he had twelve fifty,' said the Head of the Household, waving his clenched fist and expressing all the sorrow in the world in his village magistrate's face. 'He was such an ass that we used to bring in wood for the stove. He wasn't even good for that. Damn me if I've ever known an idiot like him! I was getting three thousand then, the same as I am now. Tell me, is that justice? Am I right or wrong when I say that it's better to scrape up dung in the streets than to serve this stinking state? Don't you agree that there's no shame left today?'

'My dear Argüelles,' sighed Villaamil with stoical sadness 'there's nothing for it but to swallow your gall. You're speaking to a man, remember, who has had the Director of the department himself under him, in the provinces, on fifteen hundred . . . the fellow was in Monopolies . . . and he wasn't good enough to stick tax-stamps on the cigar-boxes.'

'How right you are! Damn it all, when I remember that my father wanted to put me as a shop-boy in a shop, and I refused because I thought it wasn't good enough for me – when I think of that now, it makes me want to tear all the hair I've still got on my head, to tear it out in handfuls. That was back in '51. Not only did I refuse to hear of the shop-counter, I became a civil-servant because I wanted to be a gentleman, and to crown everything I got married. If I'd had any sense . . . After that, bit by bit, nine in family, mother-in-law and two orphan nephews. Think of having all that crowd to feed. But thank God my trumpet helps me, gentlemen. In '64 I touched three thousand, and there I've stopped. Do you know who got me my three thousand? Julián Romea. I shall never get any further. I've been fourteen years in this job. Now I don't even ask for promotion. What would be the good? Unless you demand it pistol in hand . . .'

The lamentations of the trumpet-playing Head of the Household were always heard with delight. At that point Pantoja entered, and all fell silent. The chief of the department wore a little scarlet cap fringed with what looked like golden artichokes. He wore a very shabby brown coat, and trousers that bagged at the knees and were so short in the leg that they showed the tops of his brand-new boots which had not yet been polished. After greeting his friend, he sat down in his chair. Villaamil came over to him and they chatted. Nevertheless Pantoja did not forget his duties, and was all the time giving orders to his troop.

'Just a moment, Argüelles. Please be so kind as to make me out an order to the Provincial Finance office, requesting such-and-such . . . You, Espinosa, let me have the figures for the deficit on excise.' And with expert hand he untied the string of a bundle, in order to pick out a document and gut it. He was also very adroit in tying them up again, and he seemed to caress the papers as he moved them about on the table and put them in the rack.

The man's appearance expressed a kind of spiritual inertia

135

which was reflected in all his features. His brow was broad and smooth and as expressionless as one of those ruled account books on which no label has been stuck. His nose was broad at the base and, as a result, his eyes were so far apart that they seemed to have quarrelled, each looking independently in its own direction without bothering about the other. No one could tell where his mouth ended, though his ears must have known. His pursed lips seemed to do violence to themselves when opened to speak, for they might have been created solely for purposes of discretion.

Morally, Pantoja was the prototype of official integrity. The title of 'the upright official' was as proper to him as his baptismal name. He was proverbially quoted, in and out of season; to mention Pantoja was to evoke the very image of moral rectitude. A man of few needs, he lived in obscurity and without ambition, satisfied with a promotion every six or seven years, not greedy for preference or afraid of being out of office. For he was one of those few who, on account of their minute, practical and meticulous knowledge of office routine, can never find their larder empty. He had come to consider his permanence in office as a tribute to his uprightness, and this idea had developed into a feeling of superiority or a superstition. He was a naturally honourable soul and his vision was so narrow that he was appalled to hear of the many millions who did not belong to the Treasury. Very high sums, other than those in the state budget, set him trembling convulsively; and if any project were being prepared in which the Ministry was to collaborate with some large industrial or banking organization the word chicanery would rise automatically to his lips. He never went to the Central Treasury without a feeling of dread, as if he were in the presence of a fearful chasm or abyss in which lay peril and death; and when he saw high officials of the Bank enter the head office of the Treasury or the Secretariat he would tremble for the riches in the Exchequer, of which he believed himself to be the watchdog. According to Pantoja, no one had the right to be really rich except the state. All other fortunes were gained by bribery and fraud. He had always served in Taxation, and all through his long and hard-working career he had harboured in his soul an insane delight in persecuting the unwilling or recalcitrant payer, a delight that is something like the cruel pleasure of the chase. For him it was an ineffable delight to see great and small enterprises defending themselves with tooth and claw against the onslaughts of the Tax Office, and succumbing every time to the superior power of the hunter. In every conflict between the Treasury and the taxpayer, the Treasury was invariably right, according to Pantoja's inflexible judgement; and this point-of-view was expressed in his minutes which never recognized the rights of any private person against the state. For him Property, Industry, and the consumer himself were organs or instruments of fraud, subversive and revolutionary entities whose purpose was to dispute the immortal rights of the unique owner and proprietor of all things, the Nation. Pantoja had never owned more than his clothes and furniture. He was the son of an usher in the Royal Court of Appeal, and had been brought up in a garret of the Courts, without ever leaving Madrid. He knew no more of the world than the public offices, and life for him was a continuous succession of small services to the state, from which he received as reward his daily crusty loaf and chick-peas.

22

GOODNESS me, what would the world be like without the homely stew? And where would poor man be without a salary? A salary is the only form of earthly goods that conforms to moral principles, since for every other class of commodity Pantoja preserved on the files of his soul a haughty contempt. He scarcely admitted that any rich man could be really honest, and he looked on large undertakings and bold public contractors with religious horror. To build up a fat fortune in a few years, to pass from poverty to opulence . . . was impossible by lawful means. To bring such a thing off one was bound 'to soil one's hands', by robbing the eternal victim, the primal possessor of all things, the state of its rightful property. The excellent Pantoja forgave the millionaire who had inherited his fortune and now merely consumed it; but even so he did not hold him in the odour of sanctity. If he had not stolen, this honest servant would say, his ancestors had; and the responsibility, like the money, was handed on from generation to generation.

When he saw the representative of Rothschild's or of some other wealthy Spanish or foreign house enter the Ministry and go straight to the Minister's office, he thought how good it would be to hang all these gentlemen who only came there in pursuance of some scheme. Pantoja expressed these ideas and others like them among the habitués of the café that he frequented, and was cruelly chaffed for his narrow-mindedness. But he never admitted defeat. Whenever finance was mentioned he would immediately raise his banner with its simple and convincing device: *A strong administration, and little or no politics.* War on the great businesses, war on the bill-brokers, and war also on the foreigner, who only came here to exploit us and make off with the cash, leaving us poorer than church-mice. Pantoja did not hide his sympathy with high tariffs either, for free trade is merely a protection for foreign industry.

At the same time he maintained that property owners only complained out of habit, for nowhere were the taxes lower than in Spain, which is the true homeland of fraud. For politics is merely the art of putting an honest face on fraud, and plundering the Treasury, silently and violently by turns. To be brief, Pantoja had only three or four ideas, which were however as deeply encrusted in his brain as if they had been incised with mallet and chisel. His conversation in the circle of his friends lacked bite, for he never spoke ill of his chiefs, or criticized the plans of the Ministry. He never got into deep water, or revealed any official secrets. At the back of his mind there lay a certain communism of which he was unaware. There still remain a few, though very few, examples of this kind of official, though the crazy politics of recent years have done their best to extirpate them.

In his duties, Pantoja was most punctilious, zealous and incorruptible, and a remorseless enemy of what he called 'the private individual'. He never gave a decision against the Treasury. The Treasury paid him, the Treasury was his master, and he was not there to serve the enemies of 'the House'. When dealing with doubtful cases, cobwebby with antiquity and difficult to decide, his system was that they must never be decided, and when he unavoidably reached the last stage of delay permitted by the law, he sought in the law itself some subterfuge that would enable him to confuse the issue afresh. To write the word Finis to one of these disputes was from the administrative point of view a confession of weakness, an admission of defeat, almost a loss of honour. As for his own honesty, it must be stated that he gave a savage reception to agents who came to offer him inducements for concluding promptly or advantageously this or that matter of business. They all knew him, and dared not approach this porcupine who bristled with all his quills when he heard the approach of the 'private individual', that is to say of the tax-payer.

In his private life Pantoja was a model of all models. No house was more methodical than his, no ant could compare with his wife. They were the contrary of the Villaamils, who spent their whole income in prosperous times and then were left starving. Pantoja's wife had not Doña Pura's fatal weakness for playing a big role, those airs of a person superior to her means and her social position. Pantoja's wife had been a domestic servant (I think she worked for Don Claudio Antón de Luzuriaga, to whom Pantoja owed his first appointment), and the humbleness of her origins inclined her to a modest, retired and self-effacing manner of life. They never spent more than two-thirds of his pay, and their children were trained to love God and fear all worldly pomp and expense. Despite the close friendship between the two men, Villaamil never dared to approach Pantoja in his frequent crises. He knew him through and through. He was perfectly aware that the 'upright man' neither asked nor gave, that importunity and generosity were equally foreign to his character, a safe whose doors never opened either to give out or to receive.

When the two men were seated, one at his desk, and the other on a chair beside him, Pantoja pushed back his skull-cap, which slid about his shiny head at the slightest touch of his hand, and said to his friend: 'I'm glad you've come today. The papers in your son-in-law's case have just come in. I haven't been able to look through them. It doesn't appear too good, though. He omitted certain towns in his demand for interest on arrears, and his assessments for the last quarter smell extremely queer.'

'My son-in-law is a rascal, Ventura, as you very well know. He'll have been up to some mischief or other.'

'And the Director informed me yesterday that he goes about leading the gay life, entertaining all his friends and spending on a wildly luxurious scale. His collection of hats and ties would horrify you. He's a regular fashion-plate, the dirty swine! Tell me one thing. Does he live at your place?'

'Yes,' answered Villaamil curtly, feeling his cheeks flush with shame when he reflected that his clothes too, thanks to Pura's weakness, had been paid for with Cadalso's money. 'But I do wish he would get out. I'd rather die than receive anything from him.'

'Because . . . well, I'm glad to have this opportunity of telling you . . . because this counts against you. Merely because he's your son-in-law and lives under your roof, some people believe that you and he work together.'

'I . . . work with him!' (in horror). 'Ventura, don't say such a thing.'

'It's not I that say it. Such an idea never entered my head. But people here in "the House". There are so many scoundrels here. And once they start to have evil thoughts, the worst of them would flay the innocent.'

'But even though Victor is my son-in-law, I have so little liking for his swindles that if I had the power to save him from prison I shouldn't do it. That's how things are.'

'Oh, he won't go to prison, indeed he won't. Don't worry about that. He won't go although he deserves to. He's got protectors and backers. Things are getting so corrupt today that these rogues like your son-in-law are the ones that are in control. You'll see them bury the complaint in oblivion. They'll approve his conduct and he'll get his confounded promotion. He's one of the most bare-faced rascals I know, no doubt about that. He was here yesterday. Then he went down to see the Under Secretary, and thanks to that gift of the gab of his and his handsome looks, the Under Secretary – I heard this from someone who was there at the time – welcomed him with open arms, and the two were gossiping there for more than half an hour.'

'And did he see the Minister as well?' (in very mournful tones).

'I can't tell you that. But I know for certain that a deputy from the province in which your treasure of a son-in-law served recommended him to the Minister. The more he gets the more he wants, that's the kind of man that deputy is. He never leaves this place until he's pinched two or three fat appointments, really fat ones. He's one of the minority. It's because he's in opposition, you see, that they pay such attention to him.'

'Do you think they'll give Victor his promotion?' (with deep anxiety).

'I can't promise you anything.'

'And about mine, what do you know?' (with even greater anxiety).

'The Chief of Personnel won't give anything away. When I mention you to him, he just says, "We shall see", or "I'll do what I can"; which is as good as saying nothing at all. Oh, by the way, yesterday, after seeing the Under Secretary, Victor dropped into the Personnel office. Espinosa's brother came and told me. The Chief showed him the vacancies in the provinces, and your charming son-in-law haughtily remarked that wild horses wouldn't drag him into the provinces.'

'Ventura, my dear friend,' observed Villaamil in fear and amazement. 'Remember those words of mine. You'll live to see it, and if you don't believe me we'll have a bet on it. I bet you that Victor will be promoted and I shan't get an appointment. Justice and reason would demand the very opposite, but reason and justice have departed for the skies.'

Pantoja shifted his cap on his head once more. It was his particular way of scratching his head. Heaving a deep sigh which hardly escaped through his lips, for he never opened them except with due solemnity, he attempted to console his friend with these words: 'We don't know whether they'll be able to pass over these complaints against Victor despite the partiality that his backers seem to feel for him. As for your case, if I were you, though I wouldn't give up pressing the Director, the Under Secretary and the Minister, I should look for some good wires to pull right at the top.'

'But I do pull and pull, and . . . it doesn't help.'

'Well, go on pulling, man, till they bring something into your hands. Hang on to the fat birds, whether they're on the government side or the other. Go and see Sagasta, Cánovas, Don Venancio, Castelar, the Silvelas. Never mind whether they're whites or blacks or yellows, because by the way you're going about it, and as things are at present, you won't get anything at all. Neither Pez nor Cucúrbitas will help you. They're loaded with obligations, and they only find places for their own gang, their own cronies, their own valets, and even the barbers that shave them. These people who first served the Glorious Revolution, and then the Restoration, are up to their necks in trouble because they have to look after the present lot without abandoning the last lot, who are thieving from sheer hunger. Pez has put one man in here who took part in the uprising and some others who flirted with the Federalists. How can Pez forget that the Republicans left him as Director of the Taxation department, and the Amadeists very nearly made him a Minister, and that the moderates in Sor Patrocinio's time gave him the Grand Cross?'

Villaamil listened to this wise counsel with downcast eyes and a lugubrious expression. He knew how right it was. Whilst the two friends were talking in this way, totally oblivious of all that was happening in the office, the wretched Salvador Guillén was drawing on a sheet of paper, with numerous flourishes of the pen, a caricature of Villaamil. When it was finished and he saw that it was good, he wrote beneath it : 'Señor Miau meditating on his financial reforms.' Having first passed the paper to his colleagues to raise a laugh, the limping ape then went from desk to desk, consoling the unhappy wretches condemned to the perpetual slavery of office life for their boredom.

When Pantoja and Villaamil discussed generalities about the service their voices did not sound in harmonious accord. They

differed appallingly in their ideas, for the 'upright man's' judgement was narrow and exclusive while Villaamil had wider
views and believed in a systematic plan, the outcome of his
studies and experience. What drove Pantoja wild was that his
friend was an enthusiast for income tax, and wanted to do
away with taxes on land, manufactures and consumption. A tax
on income based on a declaration depending on a man's pride
and honesty seemed to him preposterous here where one has to
face the tax-payer with the gallows before he will fork out.
Simplification, in general, was foreign to the spirit of the 'upright official', who got pleasure from a large staff, a great deal
of detail and a tremendous circulation of documents. And in the
last resort there was some personal suspicion in his mind. This
mania for abolishing taxes seemed to him like an attempt to
abolish Pantoja himself. They would discuss the subject heatedly
until both their mouths were dry. And when Pantoja had to
depart because the Director had called for him, and Villaamil
was left alone with the subordinates, they entertained themselves a little at his expense, the lame Guillén distinguishing
himself by his deliberate malice.

'Tell me, Don Ramón, why don't you publish your plan, to
let the country know about it?'

'Don't talk to me about the publication of plans' (walking
agitatedly up and down the office). 'This swinish country would
never listen to me. The Minister has read them and the Director
of Taxes has taken a glance at them. But nothing came of it.
It's not because they're difficult to understand right away, because in the memorandum I've written I have paid especial
attention, first to simplicity, secondly to clarity, and thirdly to
brevity.'

'I imagined they were very long, very long indeed,' said
Espinosa gravely, 'seeing that they cover so many points . . .'

'Whoever told you such a thing?' (taking offence). 'Each
memorandum covers one point, and there are four of them.
That's enough and to spare. I wish I'd never bothered to write
them. Blessed are the stupid . . .'

'For they are on the pay-roll of heaven. You're right, my dear
sir,' observed Argüelles, glancing spitefully at Guillén, whom

he loathed. 'I have thought of a plan also, but I've never cared to talk about it. It would have been better for me if I'd composed a trumpet solo.'

'Play your trumpet then, and stop trying to put the Finances in order. At the rate things are going they'll soon be completely dry. See here, my dear Argüelles' (stopping in front of the table of this gentleman of Philip IV's time, he slings his cloak across his shoulder and throws out his right hand in an expressive gesture). 'I have devoted my experience of many years to this subject. Perhaps I've hit the mark, perhaps I haven't. But there's something in it, there's an idea here, no doubt about that.' (They all listen to him most attentively.) 'My work consists of four memoranda or treatises, each with a title to aid the understanding. Point one: Morality.'

'Very good. Make way for Morality. Morality comes first.'

'It is the basis of administrative order. Morality first and last, and left and right. Second point: Income tax.'

'Which is at the bottom of it all.'

'Abolish taxes on property, industry and consumption. I substitute a tax on income, with a small surcharge for municipal purposes, all very simple, very practical and very clear; and I expound my ideas on methods of collection, compulsion, and investigation, and on penalties, etc. Third point: Additional tariffs. Because tariffs, mark you, are not merely a type of taxation, they are a means of protecting the national industry. I establish pretty high duties, so that the factories shall prosper and we shall all wear Spanish cloth.'

'Far better than Dutch. Bravo Murillo was an infant at the breast, Don Ramón. . . . Go on . . .'

'Fourth point: Unification of the National Debt. I call in all the bonds that are now circulating under various names: Three per cent consolidated, Deferred Bonds, Bank and Treasury bills, mortgage loans, and I exchange them for a four-per cent security, issued in due form. No more headaches . . .'

'You know more than the damned Jew who first invented the Treasury, Don Ramón.' (Chorus of congratulations; the only one who remained silent was Argüelles, who did not like to laugh too much at Guillén's jokes.)

'It isn't that I know a great deal' (modestly). 'It's because I view the affairs of the House as my own. I should like to see this country enter fully on the path of order. It isn't a question of knowledge, but of good will, application, hard work. Now you've listened to me carefully, haven't you? But they don't. Well, so much the worse for them. The day will come when Spain will have to walk barefoot and the richest will be begging for a crust. They won't be begging for alms, let me tell you, for no one will have any to give them. That's the way things are going. Now I ask you, gentlemen, would there be anything out-of-the-way in my being reappointed to my post of administrative chief? Absolutely nothing, would there? You'll see all their whims and fancies though, but that you'll never see. Good-bye.'

He departed with bowed shoulders as if unable to bear the weight of his own head. They all pitied him except the merciless Guillén, who always devised some dart to throw after him the moment his back was turned.

'Look, I've copied out the four points he gave us. All pure gold, gentlemen. Come and see. God, what a good joke! Look, here they are, written one beneath the other.

> Morality
> Income tax
> Additional duties
> Unification of the debt

Put the four initials together, and you get the word Miau.'

A burst of laughter echoed through the office, which now became as gay as a theatre.

23

ABELARDA was upset for several days after her long conversation with Victor. But the poor girl was at such pains to prevent her mother and aunt from realizing her state of mind that in the end she succeeded. On the day after Victor's enigmatic declaration, she was aware of his silence. He avoided meeting his sister-in-law alone. He scarcely looked at her, and did not even throw her a casual word. One would have thought that he was brooding on some delicate personal matter. But after a little while Abelarda noticed that he was in a better mood and was casting her loving and languishing glances, which she could not help returning with the warmest and briefest of looks. Victor spoke to her in front of the family, but not a word alone. They were like two lovers who have not the courage to declare their feelings. But she was waiting for the moment. Suddenly, explosive and unannounced, it is bound to come. It is as if the laws of time and space have marked the point at which the orbits of two beings will meet under the necessity of the supreme will. At this time the little nobody felt the need to go very often to church. The Villaamils' religious observances were confined to a Sunday mass at the Comendadoras, at which their attendance was not invariable. Don Ramón was seldom missing, but Doña Pura and her sister, either because they had not the clothes, or had something to do, or for some other reason, broke their rule on some Sundays. Abelarda was anxious to fortify her spirit by religion and to think her thoughts in church. She comforted herself by looking at the altars, and the ciborium in which God himself was kept, by listening devotedly to the mass, and gazing at the saints and virgins in their spreading robes. These innocent comforts quickly raised in her the idea of another consolation sweeter and more efficacious, that of confession. For she felt an imperious and urgent necessity to confide in someone a secret that she could not contain in her own heart. She was afraid that if she did not confide it, it would probably 'slip out' with indiscreet spontaneity in front of her parents, and this terrified her, for her parents would certainly be furious if they heard of such a thing. In whom could she confide? In Luis? He was too young. The silly idea even passed through her mind of revealing her secret to that kindly idiot Ponce. Finally this same religious feeling that was taking possession of her soul suggested the solution. The morning after it occurred to her she went to the confessional and told the priest what was happening to her, adding some details which the priest had no need to know. After her confession the little nobody was much relieved, and prepared in spirit for any unexpected occurrence.

As it was Lent, there were services every evening in the Comendadoras, and on Fridays in the churches of Montserrat and the Salesas Nuevas. The family were rather shocked by Abelarda's assiduous churchgoing, and Doña Pura could not suppress the following ill-timed remark: 'Come now, there's a place and time for all things, my girl.'

The fact that Ponce was very pleased, even somewhat enthusiastic, about his fiancée's devotions, since he was one of the most religious young men of the present generation (though more in words than in deeds, as is frequently the case), soothed Doña Pura's susceptibilities. On some afternoons the excellent youth accompanied his fiancée to church, despite her repeated entreaties to let her go alone. Generally he waited for her when she came out, and they walked home together discussing the preacher, just as the night before, at the evening party, they had discussed the singers at the Real. If Abelarda went to church early she was accompanied by Luis, who, after giving these expeditions a short trial, became very fond of them. The good child was piously attentive for a while. But he seemed tired and began to walk about the church, looking at the standards of the Order of St James which hang in the Comendadoras, going up to the great grille to peer at the nuns, and inspecting the altars with their loads of wax ex-votos. In the Montserrat, a church belonging to the ancient convent that is today the women's prison, Luis was not as happy as in the Comendadoras, which is one of the gayest and prettiest churches in Madrid. He found the Montserrat cold and bare. The saints were badly dressed, the services seemed to him poor, and besides, in the chapel on the right as you came in, there was a great dark Christ, covered with gouts of blood and with a cloth round his loins, who had real hair as long as a woman's. This image frightened him so much that he never dared to look at it except from a distance, and he would not have entered that chapel for anything on earth.

More than once it happened that during his restless wandering around the church, little Luis would feel that sickness coming on him which was the precursor of his strange vision. He would then sit down on a bench. More than once he told himself that in this place, once he dozed off he would surely see the Man with the white beard, for this was one of his houses. He would close his eyes and, in a way, call up before his mind his strange visitor, but his visitor did not appear. On one occasion, all the same, he thought he saw the venerable old man emerge through the sacristy door and disappear into the altar, as if into an invisible hole. He also believed that it was this same man who came out dressed in the priestly alb and embroidered dalmatic to say mass, *to say a mass to himself*, which seemed a most extraordinary thing to young Cadalso. But he was not very certain that this was really so. He might very well have made a mistake. At least he had great doubts about this incident. One evening in the Montserrat, as he was listening to the priest reciting the rosary, and some two dozen women giving the responses in the church, also the prisoners in the choir, of whom there must have been more than a hundred, to judge from the strength of their mumbling voices, little Luis felt the symptoms of sleepiness coming on him. There was very little light in the church. Everything in it was a mystery, and a shadow that was rendered thicker and more frightening by the gloomy rhythm of the prayer. From the place where he knelt the boy could see one arm of that Christ and the little lamp that hung from the ceiling beside it; and he was seized with such a panic that he would have gone out into the street if he had been able. But he could not get up. He tried to master his drowsiness and pinched his arms, saying: 'Oh dear! If I go to sleep and that Christ with the long hair comes over to me, blowed if I shan't drop dead with fright.' And this fear and his efforts to rouse himself finally conquered his sickly stupor.

As well as these bad moments the Montserrat gave him some good ones when his friend and schoolfellow Silvestre Murillo, the sacristan's son, appeared. Silvestre initiated Luis into some of the church mysteries, explaining to him very many things that he did not know before; for instance what Reservation of the Holy Sacrament was, and the difference between a Gospel and an Epistle, and why San Roque has a dog, and St Peter has keys. His friend displayed a liturgical knowledge that was a wonder to hear. The host, for example, has God inside it, and that is why priests wash their hands before they pick it up, so as not to dirty it. And *dominus vobisco* means : *mind out that you're good*. When the two were shut in the sacristy, Silvestre showed him the robes, the unconsecrated host, which young Cadalso looked at with supersititious awe, the parts of the platform that was soon to be erected at Easter, the canopy and the drapings of the cross, revealing in the off-hand manner of his pointing and explanations a certain scepticism which his friend did not share. But little Murillo could not make Luis enter the chapel of the long-haired Christ, even by assuring him that he had held the tresses in his hand while his mother was combing them, and that this Lord was very good and performed vast numbers of miracles.

As children's minds are impressed by everything, and the nascent will quickly and energetically moulds itself to these impressions, his visits to church awoke in young Cadalso the desire and intention to be a priest. He mentioned this intention several times to his grandparents, and everyone laughed at his premature sense of vocation. Even Victor was greatly amused. But the boy insisted that he would either sing mass or be nothing at all, because he was enthusiastic about all the priestly offices, including preaching and sitting in the confessional 'to listen to the women's sins'. He said this with such charming naivety that they all burst out laughing, and Victor seized this opportunity to talk to the little nobody alone for the first time since their conversation of some days before. No other grownup was present, and the only person who might have heard them was Luis. He, however, was deep in his stamp-album.

'I won't say like my son that I should like to enter holy orders. But I've certainly felt for some time now a burning need to believe. Whatever you may think of it, Abelarda, this feeling has come to me from you' (with a long, sustained glance of great tenderness) – 'from you and from the influence that your soul has over mine.'

'Well, believe then. Who's stopping you?' replied the girl,

who felt it easier to speak to him that evening, and expected great clarity from him.

'Old habits of thought prevent me, false ideas acquired in social life. They make a barrier that is hard to overcome. I should need an angelic teacher, someone who would mould me and be concerned for my salvation. But where is this angel? If one exists, it is not for me. I am a very unfortunate person. I see the good very close to me, and cannot come near it. If you don't understand this you are lucky indeed.'

Señorita Villaamil felt strong enough to speak of this subject. She could even have confessed her secret to this man who ought never to hear it from her lips.

'I wished to believe and I believed,' she said. 'I sought consolation in God and I found it. Would you like me to tell you how?'

Victor had been sitting at the table with his head in his hands. He got up suddenly, saying with the tone and gestures of a consummate actor: 'Do not speak. You will torture me but not console me. I am a wicked man, I am damned . . .'

These tinsel phrases, gleaned at random from various books, were stored ready-made in his mind, to be brought out on the first suitable occasion. No sooner were they said than he remembered that he had an appointment with some friends at a café, and sought for a means of breaking off this conversation in which his sister-in-law was entangling him.

'Abelarda, I must go. Because if I stay here a minute longer . . . I know myself. I shall say something that I should not say . . . at least yet. I am going for a walk, to nowhere in particular. I shall wander feverishly thinking of what cannot be mine . . . at least yet.'

He gave a sigh and departed, leaving the little nobody perplexed and a little taken aback, to try to disentangle the significance of his 'At least yet', which opened up attractive horizons.

Before dinner that night Victor entered the apartment very cheerful, and embraced his father-in-law, who did not care for such demonstrations of affection. In fact he was on the point of saying: 'And what makes you so beastly familiar this evening?' But Victor was quick to explain to him the reasons for his demonstration. He had been at the Ministry that afternoon, and the Chief of Personnel had told him that Villaamil was in the first list.

'Don't tell me that old story!' exclaimed Villaamil furiously. 'When did I give you permission to make fun of me?'

'He's not making fun of you, dear,' put in Doña Pura, inspired by sweet hopes. 'If he tells you this, it's because he knows.'

'Whether you believe it or not, it's the truth.'

'Well, I don't believe it, I don't believe it,' declared Villaamil, wagging the first finger of his right hand. 'And nobody is allowed to make fun of me. D'you understand? When and where have you been concerning yourself about me at the Ministry? You go there on your own business, to get yourself that promotion, which they'll give you. Oh yes, I'm quite sure they'll give it to you. I'd be very surprised if they didn't.'

'Well, let me tell you' (with great emphasis) 'that I may have gone for that purpose on other occasions, but I certainly did not today. Today I took two very influential deputies with me, solely to make representations in your case, and to speak flatly to the Chief of Personnel. I had already prepared the ground with the Minister. I'm not telling you this to earn your thanks. There's no merit in what I did. But as sure as the sun shines in the sky' (with great solemnity) 'this is what I said to the friends who supported me: "Gentlemen, before you think of my promotion please see that my father-in-law is reinstated." I repeat that I'm not telling you this to earn gratitude. It's the very least I could have done . . .'

Doña Pura was radiant, and Villaamil, whose pessimism had received a jolt, was like a soldier whose defences are suddenly destroyed, leaving him disarmed and naked before the enemy's fire. He made an effort to recover his pessimistic self-possession.

'Nonsense. Even if it were true that Juan, Pedro and Diego all recommended me, does it follow that they will give me a post? Leave me in peace, and look after your own affairs. You'll get your promotion even if you don't open your mouth. But as for me, I can pester the whole human race to death, and still I shan't get anything.'

Although she did not open her lips, Abelarda felt her heart

flooded with gratitude to Victor. She was glad that she loved him, and told herself that there could be no possible doubt of his good feeling. It was impossible that his noble and beautiful utterance should not be the utterance of truth. Over dinner they continued their discussion, Villaamil protesting stoutly that the ministerial world would never take pity on him, and the whole family boldly maintaining the contrary. Then it was that little Luis uttered the sentence which was famous in the family for a week and was repeated and commented on to satiety. It was greeted as a priceless joke and as one of those flashes of wisdom which sometimes descend from the mind of God into that of those beings whose state of grace puts them in direct contact with it. Young Cadalso said with enchanting naivety and a sort of cheeky certainty which increased the charm of his words: 'But, Grandfather darling, you must be crazy. Why do you go on begging and begging those beastly Ministers? They're a lot of old so-and-so's, and they never take any notice of you. Beg God to help you, and go to church. Pray a lot and you'll see if God doesn't get you your appointment.'

They all burst out laughing. But the inspired child's outburst had a very different effect on Villaamil's mind. The tears almost started to the good old man's eyes. Striking the table hard with the handle of his fork, he said: 'This little devil knows more than all of us. He knows more than the whole world put together.'

24

IMMEDIATELY after eating his sweet (honey from Alcarria) Victor went off, and when the meal was over Doña Pura scolded her husband for the incredulity and rudeness with which he had greeted his son-in-law's statement.

'Why shouldn't it be true that he's trying to help you? We mustn't always think the worst. What's more, if he didn't do what he says he did, it was his duty to do it at least.'

'That's right,' observed Abelarda, prepared to launch into glowing praise of her brother-in-law. Although she did not understand him on the subject of love, she considered his much vaunted wickedness a libel.

'You,' exclaimed Villaamil, losing his temper, 'you're so simple you believe everything that loud-mouthed liar tells you. I'll bet you anything you like that instead of recommending me what he did was to tell the Chief of Personnel some story that took away such little desire as he had to help me . . .'

'Come now, Ramón!'

'Papa, for goodness' sake! Really, you do imagine . . .'

'I can't believe that in all these years you haven't learnt to know that man' (getting excited). 'He's the wickedest man and the worst traitor under the sun. God created some wild animals beautiful so as to make them more dangerous. That's why he gave Victor that gentle expression, that tender smile, and that gift of the gab that deceives those who don't know him, so that he can befool and fascinate them and then gobble them up. He's the most monstrous . . .'

Villaamil stopped, noticing the presence of little Luis, for whose ears this apologia was not fit. After all, Victor was his father. And indeed the poor child was staring at his grandfather with a terrified expression. Abelarda, whose heart was torn as if by hot pincers, first felt like bursting into tears and then like making a brutal onslaught on her father. She wanted to contradict him, to make him be quiet, and to throw some insult at his venerable head. She got up and went to her room on the pretence of going to find something, and listened to the murmur of the conversation from there. Doña Pura timidly contradicted what her husband had said, and, once Luis had left the table, called to the kitchen by Milagros to wash his face and hands, Don Ramón repeated his savage, implacable and bloodthirsty anathema against Victor, adding that he would not even pick up five-peseta pieces in his company. The good Villaamil's tone was so emphatic, and so full of sincerity and conviction that Abelarda thought she would go mad on the spot. She thought that there could be only one solution for her boundless grief: to rush out of the house, run to the viaduct in the Calle de Segovia and throw herself over. She imagined the brief moment of falling into the abyss, with her skirts over her head, and the crack of

153

her skull on the pavement below. What a joy! Then the feeling of being squashed into a pancake, and nothing more. All her troubles would be over.

A little later the choice company that frequented this elegant dwelling on certain nights began to arrive. Having completed her duties in the kitchen, Milagros prepared the oil lamp that was to light the drawing-room. She tidied herself, leaving in the kitchen the old woman who came to wash up. For though the modest Ophelia devoted herself with pleasure to every branch of cookery she did not undertake the dirty job of washing-up. After a little she came into their *salon*, so nicely smartened up that she was a real joy to see. Abelarda did not make an appearance for some time, and when she finally did her face was so heavily powdered that she looked like a flour-mill. But even this was not enough to conceal the deathly whiteness of her features or the violet rings under her eyes. Virginia Pantoja, her mother and some other ladies noticed her and said nothing, reserving their comments for the aftermath of the party. None of the women friends refrained from saying to herself: 'She's beginning to look old.' That night Salvador Guillén was there also, to present his office colleague, the elegant Espinosa. As soon as the company began to arrive Villaamil went out, cursing this wretched party, and spent a couple of hours in the café listening to talk about the crisis, or proving that, as two and three make five, it had been bound to come. He was generally accompanied by Pantoja, who would come back with him afterwards to fetch his family; and on the way they would go on developing the eternal theme, never exhausting it and never reaching the final variation. Wise in his knowledge of bureaucratic life, and of the mysterious psychological forces that determine the rise and fall of functionaries, Pantoja outlined to his friend a new plan of campaign. First, without ceasing to search among people of political influence for some patron who would back him, he must never leave the Minister or the Chief of Personnel alone; he must act as their shadow, spying on their entrances and departures, approach them when they were off their guard, and confront them with the terrible alternative of an 'appointment or your life'. He must make himself felt by terror. This was the way by which fat jobs were always attained, for after all Ministers, under-secretaries and chiefs of personnel were men; and so to purchase life and breath they would give a pesterer what he wanted, in order to get rid of him, to get the weight of him off their minds and have him out of sight. Recognizing the deep human and political sense of this advice, Villaamil genuinely deplored having himself finally become what he had so often censured in others, a tiresome persecutor and tireless beggar.

Victor did not attend the evening parties. But that evening he came back earlier than usual, and went into the drawing-room where he attracted the admiration of Virginia Pantoja and the Cuevas girls. He was so superior in every way to the types that usually appeared there! Guillén could not stand him, and as Victor returned the compliment, they fired remarks with double meanings which made everyone laugh.

Before lunch next day, when Victor, his mother-in-law, Abelarda and young Luis, who had just come back from school, were in the dining-room, Cadalso said to Doña Pura: 'Why do you invite that lame horror to the house? Don't you realize that he only comes to amuse himself by watching and then telling stories in the office about what he sees?'

'Do we look like such a set of monkeys,' said Doña Pura, offended, 'that this cripple should come here just to laugh at us?'

'He's a poisonous toad. Whenever he sees anything that isn't as dirty as himself, he gets furious and drops his spittle. What do you think he does when Papa goes to see Pantoja in his office? He draws caricatures of him. He's got a whole collection that he hands round among all those idlers. Only yesterday I saw one with an inscription he's written underneath: Señor de Miau contemplating his financial reforms. It had been passed all round the office until in the end Urbanito Cucúrbitas took it to Personnel where that dummy Espinosa, the brother of the pretentious idiot who was here last night, stuck it up on the wall with four wafers to give a laugh to everyone who came in. I was furious when I saw it, and we almost had a battle.'

Doña Pura was so indignant that she could hardly breathe or speak.

'I'll tell that nasty hypocrite never to show his face in my house again. What do you say they call my husband? They ought to be ashamed. . . .'

'They've started calling him by the nickname they gave the family in the Real,' said Victor, sweetening his cruelty with a smile. 'It's a very silly nickname.'

'A nickname for us! For us!' exclaimed the two sisters together, flushing with anger.

'Don't let's take it seriously. It isn't worth it. It's common knowledge, though, that when you take your seats in the gallery all the people say, "Here come the Miaus". It's quite absurd.'

'And the ugly scarecrow finds that joke funny!' exclaimed Doña Pura, picking up the first thing that came to hand, which was a loaf, and pointing it at her son-in-law's head.

'Don't lay the blame on me, Doña Pura. I didn't invent the nickname. If ever I were with you, and one of these vulgar fellows dared to mew it in front of me, I'd knock all his teeth out at one blow.'

'You haven't half got a conceit of yourself' (swallowing her anger). 'That's nothing but talk. If we had no one but you to defend us . . .'

The two sisters' anger was nothing compared with the rage that seized little Luis Cadalso when he heard that the lame Guillén made fun of his grandfather and called him by a nickname. This is all the Performer's fault, he said to himself, and I shall have to give him what for. Because it was his common mother who made up that nickname. She's Guillén's sister. And blowed if she didn't tell it to that cripple, and he must have passed it on to everyone in the office, the horrid creature.

He got so angry that he clenched his fists and ground his teeth as he went to school. If he had met the little Performer in the road he would certainly have gone for him, and given him a good punch 'right in his face'. A little later, when he was sitting next to him in class, he jabbed him with his elbow.

'Don't want anything to do with you, you mean pig. You're not a gentleman, and your family aren't gentlemen either.'

The Performer did not answer, but let his head fall on his arm

156

and closed his eyes, as if overcome by a deep sleep. Young Cadalso could not help noticing that his friend's face was very flushed, that his eyelids were swollen, and that his mouth was open. He was breathing through it, and snorting fiercely every now and then, as if to clear his nose. Fresh and stronger prods with Luis' elbow did not arouse him from his heavy stupor.

'What's the matter with you, blow you? Are you ill?'

The little Performer's face was fiery red. The master went across to him, saw how he was, and found that it was impossible to pull him upright. He looked at him carefully, felt his pulse, and put his hand on his face.

'You must be ill, my boy. Run off home and tell them to put you to bed, and cover you up well to make you sweat.'

Then the boy staggered up, and walked across the classroom looking as if he were in a very bad temper. Some of his colleagues eyed him enviously because he was going home before the others. Others, little Cadalso among them, thought that his illness was a farce, put on so that he could go and lark about for the whole afternoon in the Retiro with all the riff-raff in Madrid. Because he was a great rogue and trickster, and no one could beat him as an inventor and performer of practical jokes.

Next day Murillo brought the news that Paco Ramos had got scarlet fever, and that he'd got it so badly, so very badly, that if his temperature did not come down that night he'd die. There was a discussion as they left school as to whether they should go and see him or not.

'It's catching, man.'

'It's not catching . . . sucks to you!'

'Idiot!'

'He's an idiot.'

In the end young Murillo, another boy whom they called Pando, and Cadalso went to see him. The house, which was only two steps from the school, had a lamp and a money-lender's sign. The three of them went very boldly up the stairs, arguing whether 'scarlet typhoid' was catching or not, and Murillo, the greatest babbler of the party, cheered them all with his bragging.

'Don't be a lot of old hens. If you think you'll both die because you go in . . .' They rang the bell, and a woman opened the door.

157

But when she saw the size and weight of the visitors she ignored them and left them standing. She did not even deign to answer the question young Murillo asked her. Another woman passed through the hall, and said : 'What do these young monkeys want here? Oh! You've come to inquire about little Paco? He's a bit better this evening.'

'Let them come in, let them come in,' cried another woman's voice from inside, 'we'll see if my boy recognizes them.'

When they went in they saw the money-lender's office, in which there was a gentleman in a cap and glasses who looked like a Minister (so young Cadalso thought), and then they crossed a large room where there were clothes, heaps of clothes, oceans of clothes. Finally, in a room that was chock-full of folded cloaks, each with a numbered card on it, lay the sick boy, with two nurses beside him, one sitting on the floor, the other standing by the bed. The little Performer had been dreadfully delirious all night and part of the morning. At that moment he was quieter, because his temperature had not yet begun to go up again.

'Darling,' said the woman or lady standing beside the bed, who must have been his mother, 'here are three of your little friends who have come to ask after you. Would you like to see them?'

The poor child gave a groan as if about to burst into tears; which in the language of sick children indicates that they don't like something, or that it worries them – and the thing may be anything on earth.

'Give them a look, give them a look. They're very fond of you.'

Paco turned over in bed and, propping himself on one elbow, gave his friends a surprised and glassy stare. His eyes were swollen and dull; his lips were so blue that they looked black, and there were wine-coloured blotches on his cheeks. Luis felt sorry for him, but he also felt an instinctive terror that kept him away from the bed. His school-friend's fixed and dull gaze made him tremble. Paco Ramos could have recognized only him of the three; for all he said was 'Miau, Miau', after which his head collapsed on the pillow. His mother signalled to the three boys that they must go; and they obeyed her meekly. In the next room they bumped into the Performer's two smaller brothers. Their faces were dirty and their trousers torn, and their overalls were full of stains. One of them was pulling a rag doll by a string tied round its neck; and the other was shouting like mad, 'Gee up! Gee up!' to a legless horse. On seeing the three boys they ran after them to make friends; but young Murillo, putting on grown-up airs, scolded them for kicking up such a noise when their brother was ill. The children looked at one another in surprise; they did not understand a word. The younger of them took a piece of bread out of his overall pocket, a much-licked piece of bread all covered with spittle, and bit into it hopefully. As the three friends passed through the living-room the gentleman who looked like a Minister was examining two Manila shawls that a woman was offering him. The boys said good-bye to him with exquisite courtesy, but he did not answer them.

25

YOUNG Cadalso returned home very thoughtful that afternoon. His feeling of pity for his school-friend was not as deep as it should have been, because that dolt Ramos had insulted him by casting that opprobrious nickname in his face in front of everybody. Children are implacable in their resentments, and friendship has no roots in them. Nevertheless, while still not forgiving his ill-mannered friend, he decided to pray for him in these words: 'Make the little Performer better. You won't find it difficult. You've only got to say "Performer, get up!" and it's done.' But remembering afterwards that his friend's mamma, that same lady who had been standing in such distress beside the bed, had been the inventor of that ridiculous joke, his hatred for her was born afresh. But she isn't a lady, he thought, she's only a woman, and now God is punishing her properly for calling people nicknames.

That night he was very restless. He slept badly and was continually waking up, for his mind was contending anxiously with a very strange situation. He had gone to bed with the wish to see his kind friend with the white beard; and the precursory symptoms had occurred, but not the vision. What made young Luis sad was that he dreamt he saw him; which was not the same thing as seeing him. At least he was not satisfied, and his mind struggled with this painful and absurd reasoning: It's not right, no, it's not right. Because I don't see him but dream I'm seeing him. He doesn't talk to me but I dream he's talking to me. From this feverish argument he went on to another: And he can't say now that I don't do any work, because today I really knew my lesson, blowed if I didn't. The master said: 'Good, Cadalso, very good.' And the whole class was astonished. I went straight through all that stuff about the adverb and only fluffed one word. And when he asked me about the manna in the wilderness I knew that too. I only made a mistake afterwards about the Commandments when I said he brought them down on a slate and it was on a stone. Luis was exaggerating the success of his performance that day. He had repeated his lesson better than on previous days, but he had no real reason to boast.

It was a bad night for both occupants of that little room. For Abelarda kept tossing and turning on her camp-bed. Sleep kept away, or if she caught it for a few moments a sudden trembling overcame her, and she found herself muttering a sentence the sound of which appalled her: 'I'll run away with him.' Then suddenly she was answered by another whisper: 'With the man who had the cigar-bands.' At the sound of these words she started up in terror. Who had answered her? The bedroom was completely silent. But after a little the voice began again. 'He's punishing you because you're wicked, because you called people nicknames.' At last Abelarda's mind grew clear. She realized what it was and recognized her little nephew's voice. Then turning on her other side, she went off to sleep. Luis made a groaning sound, as if he wanted to cry but could not.

'But I did know my lesson. I did.'

And then, a little later: 'Don't wet my stamp with your black mouth. That's because you're wicked, see? Your mamma's not a lady, she's a woman.'

And Abelarda said in answer: 'That dolled-up creature who

writes you letters isn't a lady but an ugly vulgar baggage. And you're silly enough to prefer her to me, me who would sacrifice my life for you. Mamma, Mamma, I want to be a nun.'

'No,' said Luis, 'I know now that you didn't give Lord Moses the Commandments on a slate, but on a table. . . . Yes, on two tables of stone. The Performer's going to die. His father will wrap him up in that Manila shawl. You're not God because you haven't got angels. Where are your angels then?'

And Abelarda: 'I've pinched the door-key. I'm going to run away. Waiting for me in the street, in all this cold! Lord, how it's pouring!'

Luis: 'There's a mouse coming out of the Performer's mouth, a black mouse with a very long tail. I shall hide under the table. Papa!'

Abelarda, aloud: 'What is it? What's the matter, Luis? What's the matter? Poor boy! Such dreadful nightmares. Wake up, darling, you're talking rubbish. What are you calling your papa for?'

Luis had woken up, but his thoughts were not very clear: 'I'm not asleep, Aunty. It's . . . it's a mouse. But my papa has caught it. Can't you see my papa?'

'Your papa's not here, silly. Go to sleep.'

'Oh, but he is. Look at him, look at him. I'm awake, Aunty. Are you?'

'Rub your eyes, darling. Would you like me to put on the light?'

'No, I'm sleepy. Only everything's very big, things are all very big, and my papa was in the bed with you, and when I called him he came and picked me up.'

'Lie on your side, darling, and you won't have bad dreams. Which side were you sleeping on?'

'On my left-hand side. Why's everything so big, so enormously big?'

'Lie on your right side, treasure.'

'I'm on the side of my left hand and my right foot. Look, this is my right foot, isn't it? It's so big! . . . That's why the Performer's mamma isn't a lady. Aunty . . .!'

'What?'

'Are you asleep? I'm asleep now. Are you sure the Performer isn't going to die?'

'Why should he die, dearest? Don't think of such a thing.'

'Tell me something else. Is my papa going to marry you?' In the mental turmoil produced by darkness and insomnia Abelarda could not reply as she would have done in daylight and with a clear head. The words that escaped her therefore were: 'I don't know yet. Really I don't know at all. Possibly.' A little later Luis murmured 'Good' in a contented voice and went off to sleep. Abelarda did not close her eyes for the rest of the night. The next day she got up very early with a heavy head and swollen eyelids. She was in a very bad temper, and longed to do something strange and new: to quarrel with someone, even with the priest himself whom she was just about to hear saying the mass, or with the server who was to assist him. She went to church, and there some ugly thoughts came to her; either to leave home for no exact reason, or to marry Ponce and betray him afterwards, or to become a nun and make a revolution in the convent, or to make a pretence declaration of love to the limping Guillén, or to begin acting in the play and walk out half-way through, leaving them all standing; or to poison Federico Ruiz, or to throw herself down from the gallery of the Real into the stalls at the climax of the opera, and other crazy ideas of this sort. But remaining in the quiet and peaceful church and listening to three masses in succession gradually calmed her nerves and brought normal ideas back to her brain. When she left she was astounded at all the senseless nonsense she had thought. It even made her laugh. Poison poor Federico Ruiz? Why, in heaven's name?

When she returned home the first thing she did, as usual, was to inquire whether Victor had gone out. It appeared that he had, for Doña Pura answered with unsimulated joy that her son-in-law was lunching somewhere. That lady's resources had been dissolving with the rapidity of salt thrown into water. Her money was like salt. It was a strange thing that she no sooner changed a five-peseta piece than she had spent all five pesetas. And now she saw herself approaching that terrifying frontier that separates short commons from absolute penury.

Beyond that frontier loomed the familiar spectres, who gazed and grimaced at Doña Pura. They were her terrible lifelong companions, debts, begging and pledging, that were determined to accompany her to the grave. Now she was speculating whether Victor would give her the means to escape from these unbearable associates. But Victor had turned a deaf ear to her first indirect approaches : a sign that his wallet did not now contain the treasure of his better days. Moreover, Doña Pura had not failed to observe that shoemakers' and tailors' bills had been presented to her son-in-law two or three times for payment, and that Victor had not paid them, but had told the bearers to come back or that he would be passing the shop in a day or two. This smell of burning made the lady go hot all over.

That afternoon Doña Pura and her sister went to visit some friends. Milagros instructed her niece to keep an eye on the kitchen. But once the overwrought young lady was alone, Villaamil having gone to the Ministry and Luis to school, she lost all thoughts of pots and pans, and went into Victor's room, with the idea of searching and examining, and handling with an intimate touch his clothes and the objects of his use. This forbidden exercise stimulated the little nobody's curiosity, and gave her the most profound spiritual pleasure. To examine his clothing, to explore all his pockets though she found no object of real interest in them, was a pleasure that she would not have exchanged for others more positive and indisputable. As she touched his shirts, she conjured up at moments an intimacy between them to which her lively imagination gave the appearance of reality. She dreamt of the most noble actions, like looking after her man's clothing whether he were her husband or not, and longed to have something to repair : a loose button or an unstitched lining. Meanwhile her sense of smell called up the person, who was so clean and smart, and she enjoyed feeling him a little nearer to her than when they were in public or with the family. On the few occasions when Abelarda had been able to indulge in this surfeit of imagination and subtle sensation her examination of his pockets had thown no light on the mystery which in her opinion surrounded Cadalso's existence. Sometimes she found in his trouser pockets ten- and five-céntimo pieces, tram tickets and theatre seats; and in those of his jacket or morning-coat a note from the Ministry or some quite unimportant letter. When she had finished, she carefully restored everything to its place so that prying should not be noticed and sat down on a trunk to think. It had been impossible to put a wardrobe or chest-of-drawers in Victor's room. So he kept his possessions in his trunk, as if he were staying a few days in an inn. It upset the little nobody always to find this trunk locked. She would have liked to peer in and handle the contents. What secrets could that mysterious interior contain? Several times she had tried to open it with different keys, but in vain.

But gracious! That day when she sat down on the trunk there was a strange clinking of metal. She looked . . . and the keys were hanging there. Forgetful of his usual caution and foresight, Victor had failed to take them out. The moment she saw the keys, she opened the lock and lifted the lid. The upper layers of its contents were in great disorder. There was a crushed felt hat with a soft brim, single collars and cuffs, cigars, a box of writing paper and envelopes, white and spotted shirts, folded newspapers, crumpled ties and others that were quite new. Abelarda looked at these things for some time without touching them, taking good note, as is the habit of pryers and thieves, of how the objects were arranged so as to be able to put them back in the same way. Then she slid her hand down one side, to explore the second layer. She did not know where to begin. At the same time the theory that Victor was conducting an affair with some very swell lady, someone out of the very top drawer, impressed itself on her mind and stood out from all her other thoughts. Soon everything would be revealed; the incontrovertible proof was certainly in the trunk. This expectancy so dominated Abelarda's mind that before discovering the criminal evidence she seemed to smell it, for smell was perhaps her liveliest sense in these investigations. Ah, didn't I tell you? What's this? A bunch of violets. Sure enough, on carefully lifting an article of clothing, she discovered the crushed and scented flowers. She went on exploring. Her instinct, intuition or presentiment, which had the force of a warning light or mysterious guide, led her through the confused depths of the trunk. She

164

took out various articles carefully, put them on the floor and went on. Searching in this direction and that, her feverish hand struck a bundle of letters. Oh, at last the key to the secret had appeared. It was bound to be there. She grasped the packet, and as she felt it between her fingers she was overcome by fear at her own discovery.

She could read something even before taking off the rubber band, for the letters were not wrapped up. The first thing that leapt to view was a coronet stamped at the head of the top letter. But as she was not good at heraldry she did not know if it was a marquesa's or a countess's crown. The little nobody reflected on her great wisdom and perspicacity. No, she could not possible have been wrong in supposing that the mysterious person with whom 'he' was having an affair was a great swell. Victor had been born for the higher spheres of society, as the eagle was born for the heights of air. Absurd to imagine that a man of such a nature would descend to the spheres of ordinariness and poverty in which she lived! And reasoning thus, she convinced herself that if much of Victor's behaviour and talk was dark and incomprehensible, the fault was not his but hers, for not understanding, with her little brain and commonplace attitude to life, the great superiority of a man like him.

The hour had come. Now was her chance to read. The girl did not know where to begin. She would have liked to devour all the letters in a flash from beginning to end. Time pressed; her mother and aunt would soon be in. She read one through rapidly, and each sentence was a knife-thrust to the reader. The writer was refusing to break off the relationship, was offering excuses as if in reply to some jealous accusation. There was a plethora of sugary language such as Abelarda had never read except in novels. All was tenderness, protestations of undying love, plans for happiness to come, arrangements for future meetings and sweet memories of past ones, refined precautions to avoid suspicion, and finally floods of endearment in more or less disguised forms. But however eagerly the reader searched for this shameless hussy's name it was nowhere to be found. Her signature did not break her anonymity. Sometimes it was a conventional 'Your darling' or 'Your poppet', sometimes a mere scrawl. But as for a name, there was no sign of one. By reading everything through carefully, she would have been able to discover by references who this 'poppet' was. But Abelarda could not continue. Time was short already, the doorbell was ringing. Everything must be put back in place so as to leave no sign of her prying hand. She did this quickly, and went to open the door. Not that day or for many days afterwards could she get out of her mind her imagined picture of that hateful lady. Who could she be? The little nobody imagined her immensely beautiful and chic, a bold and wilful woman like all women of the upper class, according to her picture. How pretty she must be! What lovely perfumes she must use, she would say to herself continuously, in words of fire that sprang from her brain and stamped themselves on her heart. And what a lot of clothes she must have, what a lot of hats, and what a lot of carriages!

26

Now once more our friend Don Ramón is visiting Pantoja's office. He does not wish to speak of his plight, of his vast and consuming cares, but he does so involuntarily; and whatever he says always returns without his noticing it to the eternal theme. He is like a man head over heels in love, for whom everything he says or writes has love for its subject. That day he found in his friend's office a person who was arguing heatedly. He was a provincial gentleman, one of those enemies of the administration to whom the 'upright official' referred under the contemptuous title of 'private individuals'. He was a wholesale dealer in wines who had also a retail shop, and the Treasury had caught him by the throat, making him pay a licence for two businesses. The man was protesting that he was giving up retailing and would now confine his trade to his cellars. The matter had come to Pantoja for decision. The private individual complained that he had been made to pay for two concerns. And what does Pantoja go and do? Decide that he must pay for three. The result was that the man was breathing fire and abusing the administration so foully that they almost had to throw him out into the street. Villaamil realized that the man was right. He had never been the executioner of the 'private individual' like his friend Pantoja; but he did not dare to join in the argument for fear of displeasing the 'upright official'. In his weakness, he even went so far as to support the measures of the administrative dragon and declare: 'Of course, he must pay three licences: as a retailer, as a wholesaler and as a cellarman.'

Finally the unfortunate 'private individual' departed, bawling like a nightingale in the mating-season, and when Villaamil and Pantoja were left alone, the old man could not ask quickly enough: 'Has Victor been back here? How is the complaint against him going?'

Pantoja did not reply for some time; he pursed his lips as if they were sewn together. He was busy opening bundles, inside which the sand sticking to the dry ink tinkled as he undid them. The 'upright official' never let this sand fall on the floor, which would have been a shocking waste, but painstakingly tipped it into the caster. It was a matter of ancient custom to save the sand that had been used by other offices, and he did it with excessive zeal, as if guarding the interests of his mistress, the Treasury.

'Believe me,' he finally replied, breaking his silence and putting his hand in front of his mouth to prevent his clerks from overhearing him, 'they won't do anything to your son-in-law. The complaint is just moonshine. Believe me, I know the ropes.'

'Influence can do anything, Ventura,' observed Villaamil in great grief; 'it can acquit wrongdoers, and reward them too, while upright men perish.'

'And the influences that turn the world upside down and make a mockery of justice are not the political ones. I mean that those influences don't cause so much disorder as some others.'

'Which others?' asked Villaamil.

'Petticoats,' answered Pantoja in such a whisper that Villaamil did not hear him and had to make him repeat his remark.

'Oh! That's no news. But tell me, d'you think this is something that Victor . . .'

'I can smell it' (maliciously tapping the tip of his nose). 'I can't swear to it, but with my experience of this house I can certainly smell it. The reek comes to my nose. I don't know. I may be wrong. We shall see in due course. But last night in the café Ildefonso Cabrera, your Victor's brother-in-law, told us some stories about him.'

'God, what things a man sees!' said Villaamil, lifting his hands to his head. And in the midst of his Catonian indignation, as he thought of the shames of petticoat corruption, he wondered why there were not beneficent petticoats who by favouring good men like himself would serve the administration and the country.

'That rogue knows what he's about. You mark my words, the grass will grow on that complaint.'

'On with the promotion! Promotion never mind how!'

The bell rang and Pantoja went to the Director's office. As soon as he had left the room his subordinates addressed the out-of-work official.

'Things won't go right for you or me, friend Villaamil, till our lot get into power, and the boys with the petrol are our lot.'

'I wish they could get power tomorrow,' said Don Ramón, with quivering jaws and all the fierceness of the carnivore flashing from his eyes.

'Don't say that lightly, for things look very bad. There's a crisis.'

'What do you mean by lightly? This is no time for joking. I wish the whole district of Madrid would rise up tonight, and we could have the Paris commune over again, with the bells ringing a tocsin. I tell you friend Job was a spoilt child, and merely complained out of habit. Let's have the petrol, let's have a blessed blaze. They can't take more away from us than they've taken already. Nobody can be worse than this lot.'

'Do you know the rumour that's been going about today? That they're going to cede the Balearics to Germany. And that they're going to lease the Customs to some Belgian concern and the first returns they'll get on them will be some ancient bridges for the railways.'

'I can almost see it, man, I can almost see it. A thing that might be a joke anywhere else is sober reality here. Frankly, Don Antonio may have plenty of shrewdness, but you'd never know it. Mark my words, anyone else they put into his post would do things better.'

'Of course,' said the gentleman of Philip IV's time, twirling his waxed moustaches. 'Just imagine that we in this office were to form a Ministry. Villaamil, first minister. Espinosa being the height of fashion would go to the foreign office to deal with the diplomats' wives.'

'Some of them are first class. And we'll give Guillén the War Office.'

'God almighty! A cripple at the War Office. Better at the Admiralty.'

'Yes, then he could row with his crutches.'

'Or because he's like a turtle,' said Argüelles who never lost an opportunity of throwing a stone at the lame man. 'And for me, let me have the Home Office.'

'Agreed. Then you can put all your string of children on the temporary staff, those at the breast included.'

'And he can issue a royal proclamation ordering that the trumpet be played at all funerals. And the Treasury, gentlemen.'

'The Treasury for Villaamil, with the premiership.'

'And what shall we give the highly respected Pantoja?'

'The Treasury, Ventura, beyond all doubt,' put in Villaamil, who did not take all this seriously, but let the joke run on in order to give a little relief to his anguished spirit.

'That would be a fine catastrophe! What about the income tax?'

'The income tax,' observed Villaamil with a sad and depressed smile, 'I never thought of that.'

'No. Out with Pantoja! He's capable of putting a tax on the fleas on every Tom, Dick or Harry's back. Long live the income tax, foundation stone of the new cabinet, also the unification of the debt.'

'That' (with a yawn and a serious look) 'is something Ventura might very well allow me. . . . But come, gentlemen' (as if returning to his senses, and rising with a lively gesture). 'You have your work to do and so have I. To work, to work!'

And he passed on into Estates (to the right on the same floor), where he was once second-in-command with Francisco Cucúrbitas, and from there down, to descend like a bomb into Personnel, where he had several acquaintances, among them a certain Sevillano, who sometimes told him of actual or presumed vacancies. After this down again to the Treasury, taking a stroll through Credit and Exchange, and in each case he had his usual confidential chat with the porter before entering the office. In some places he was received with a somewhat chilly politeness; in others his repeated visits were beginning to become a bore. They did not know what to tell him now to encourage his hopes, and those who had advised him to be ceaselessly persistent now began to repent, seeing that the tactics they had counselled were in practice used on them. It was in Personnel that Villaamil showed himself most tenacious and tiresome. The head of that department, a nephew of Pez against whom many people had a grudge, knew Villaamil, though not well enough to appreciate his excellent qualities and distinguish the real man from the tiresome beggar. So, when his visits became more frequent, the chief did not conceal his displeasure or his reluctance to enter into conversation. Villaamil was sensitive, and these slights gave him indescribable pain. But imperious necessity compelled him to draw strength from weakness and assume an impassive face. Nevertheless, he sometimes retired in disorder, saying to himself: 'I can't do it, Lord, I can't. The role of persistent beggar is not for me.' And the result of this defeat was that he did not appear in Personnel for some days. Soon, however, the brutal law of necessity began to assert itself again. Pride rose against the thought of being forgotten, and like the starving wolf that, heedless of the danger of death, breaks into the fields and boldly approaches a farm in search of a beast or a man, so Don Ramón made his way once more, hungry for justice, into the Personnel office, to face slights, black looks and even blacker answers. The man who gave him the best reception and the most encouragement was Don Basilio Andrés de la Caña (Indirect

Taxation), who warmly offered him his help. His expedition concluded, Villaamil returned home exhausted in body and spirit. His wife interrogated him skilfully. But he, firm in his studied dignity, maintained that he had only gone to the Ministry to smoke a cigar with his friends; that since he expected nothing he had asked for nothing, and that the family must not build castles in the air but make their preparations for a holiday trip to the poor-house. Doña Pura replied that if he did nothing to get himself an appointment she would take the matter in hand herself and request the intervention of Pez's wife, Carolina de Lantigua, since any fool knew that where political recommendations failed to be effective, petticoat influence generally succeeded.

'No, it isn't that kind of petticoat influence that makes and unmakes careers,' replied Villaamil with a profound scepticism born of his knowledge of the bureaucratic world. 'Carolina Pez is an honest woman, and therefore quite useless in this business. Besides, you've got to realize that Pez and his kind don't count any more; they keep their end up and that's all. Men are saying now that soon they'll be left on the shelf. They've been drinking from every flask, that lot. They were all right in the Revolution and they're still all right under Alfonso. But the sweets they're eating rightfully belong to us loyal servants who are left waiting on providence. Now people are beginning to say things against them. What's more, the administration's in need of loyal servants, identified, mark you, identified with the policy of the monarchy. They mustn't be allowed to occupy these posts in perpetuity. We must have a change. Or else where shall we end up? A fine situation! There you've got the Chief of Personnel, Pez's nephew, selling his protection to men who sacrificed their jobs rather than serve under the confounded republic. It's unheard of. It's a crying scandal. Under these conditions, what can you expect but trouble? The country's bound to go to the devil. That's clear enough, isn't it? So you can't expect much from the Pezes, in petticoats or trousers. But anyhow' (returning to his theme, which he had forgotten in the heat of his discourse), 'with or without the Pez clan there'll be nothing for me. La Caña's the only one who cares about me now, and he'd do something if he could. But I have secret enemies working in the dark to destroy me. Someone has sworn war to the death against me. I've no idea who the scoundrel is. But he exists all right, have no doubt of that.'

About this time, the early days of March, the unfortunate family began to note once more the first symptoms of penury. They had a week of horrible stringency, badly concealed from their intimates, which was borne by Villaamil with stoical integrity and by Doña Pura with the valiant equanimity that always saved her from despair. But the remedy cáme unexpectedly, and from the same source as on another no less painful occasion; Victor was afloat once more. His mother-in-law was surprised by another, unlooked-for offer of cash, which she did not hesitate to accept without undertaking any philosophical inquiry into its source. She did not even think it wise to tell her husband that she had seen Victor's wallet stuffed with banknotes. Her eyes had almost started out of her head. She pocketed the cash that was offered her, and did not express the thoughts that arose in her mind. Where did he get so much money if they hadn't given him a post yet? And even if they had. . . . There must be some hidden agency. But why pry into this dangerous secret? It was no pleasure to her to investigate other people's lives.

Victor was going about in great style again. He had ordered more clothes, and sat in the stalls on various nights in different theatres, including the Real itself. He made frequent little presents to the family, and even carried his liberality so far as to invite the three Miaus to the opera, actually to seats in the stalls.

This made Villaamil really furious, for it was a slight on his poverty and an insult to public morals. Pura and her sister laughed at the invitation because, although they longed to go, they had not the necessary finery for such an appearance. Abelarda resolutely refused. There was a great argument, and her mamma suggested some means of obviating the great practical difficulties presented by her son-in-law's invitation. This was the solution propounded by the scheming acumen of the figure out of Fra Angelico. Her friends and neighbours the Cuevas helped themselves out, as has been said, by making up hats. On a certain occasion when the Miaus had landed three free stalls for the Español, Abelarda, Doña Pura and Bibiana Cuevas had worn the best models that these friends had in their workshop, having first adapted them each to her own taste. Why not do the same thing on the present occasion? Bibiana would not object. And at present she had certainly got three or four beauties in the shop, one for the Marquesa A, another for the Countess B, that couldn't have been prettier or smarter. They could be disguised, for there were plenty of pins and buckles and ribbons and feathers in the shop, and even if their owners happened to be in the theatre they would never recognize them once they were altered. As for dresses, they would manage them with the aid of their friends, and would get themselves cloaks by ordering them from some shop to try on, and as Victor himself had promised to give them the gloves, to sit in the stalls was not an absolute impossibility. How many women there would be just as stony who would disguise it less elegantly!

27

ABELARDA objected to this scheme, insisting that wild horses would not drag her to sit in the stalls under such circumstances, and so the question was dropped. They contented themselves with going in the front of the gallery on a night when they were playing *L'Africaine*; and just as the three were taking their seats there arose from the company on the more remote heights a fitting comment on this rare event: 'Look, the Miaus up in front!' No such event had been seen for ten years. The vast tiers of the centre and sides were chock-full. The Miaus were known to all that concourse as constant fixtures in the gallery, always in the last row on the right beside the exit. If they were missing one night, their absence was noted; it was as if the frescoes had vanished from the ceiling. They were not the only 'gallery regulars', for countless persons, indeed whole families, were eternal occupants of the benches, which they had inherited from generation to generation. These deserving and hardy amateurs constituted the mass of the enlightened public that grants or withholds a musical success, and has been the arch-critic of all the operas sung in the last thirty years and all the singers who have followed one another on that glorious stage. Among them were more or less intimate circles, cliques and café groups. Here acquaintanceships were made and cemented. Here countless marriages were hatched, and here, between romanza and duet, was the chance and the atmosphere for cooings and signallings. From their front seats the Miaus smiled at their friends in the right and centre tiers; and from both directions looks were darted at them, and remarks to the following effect: 'What a sylph Doña Pura is! She's got the whole powder-box on her face.'

'But what about her sister with that velvet band round her neck? If those three wore black neckbands they'd only need the bell to be in character.'

'Look with your glasses at the little Miau. What a sight! That coffee-coloured dress of hers is the one her mother wore last year. Those red ribbons she's put on it look as if she found them in a cigar-box.'

'Yes, yes, they've come off cigar bundles.'

'And the other one, who tried to be a singer, that must be the dress she wore in the Liceo Jover when she sang the part of Adalgisa.'

'Yes, do look. It's a Roman tunic with a Greek key border and all. She's really classical.'

'Tell me, Guillén,' they were whispering in another party of which that confounded cripple set the tone. 'Have they found a post for poor old Miau, the father of those friends of yours? To judge by the oriental luxury of front seats our lot must have come up.'

'Not unless they've found him a place in the madhouse. At present they're living on credit. The good man knows a trick or two.'

Abelarda paid more attention to the audience than to the opera which she had seen a hundred times. She cast anxious glances at the boxes and the stalls, paying particular attention to all the ladies who came up the central gangway in luxurious cloaks, dragging their trains, and slipped with all their finery into the rows which were now filling up. The boxes did not fill up, however, till the end of the first act, when Vasco sings his song to those great gawks of councillors who keep getting in his way. Queen Mercedes appeared in the royal box, followed by Don Alfonso. The inevitable ladies, well-known to the public, appeared during the second act, kept their cloaks on till the third, and applauded mechanically on every fitting occasion. The Miaus, who knew the whole of elegant society – who were subscribers also – remarked on them as they had themselves been remarked on when they took their seats. Having seen them on countless evenings, they had become so familiar with them that anyone would have thought they were on personal terms with these ladies and gentlemen.

'Ah, here's the Duchess. But Rosario hasn't come yet. María Buschental won't be long. Her friends will be driving up in their bus. Look, look, María Heredia's coming in. But how pale Mercedes is! She's dreadfully pale. Here we have Don Antonio in the ministerial box, and that fellow Cos-Gayón . . . I wish they'd shoot him dead.'

After a great deal of searching the little nobody discovered her dear brother-in-law in the second row of the stalls. He was wearing tails and was as smart as the best of them. How strange life is! Who would have said that this man who looked like a duke, this well-dressed young man who was carelessly chatting to the man in the next seat – the Italian Minister – was an obsure and out-of-work civil servant who lodged in a poverty-stricken house, in a bare, humble room, and kept his clothes in a trunk?

'Isn't that Victor?' asked Pura, turning her glasses on him. 'He's putting on fine airs. If they knew who he is! He looks like a prince. How many of his sort there must be in Madrid! I don't know how he brings it off. Fine clothes, stalls in every theatre, and magnificent cigars! Just look at his bounce, the way he talks to that gentleman. He'll be stuffing him full of lies, poor man. Those foreigners are so innocent they'll believe anything.'

Abelarda did not take her eyes off him, and when she saw him glance at any of the boxes she followed the direction of his gaze, thinking that it would betray the secret of his love. Which

175

of these ladies in the theatre can it be? thought the little no-body. Because it must be one of them. Can it be the one in white? Yes, it might be. She seems to be looking at him. But it isn't. He's looking in the other direction. Can it be one of the singers? No, of course not, not a singer, oh dear no! It must be one of those very smart ladies in the boxes, and I shall find out which. She stared at one of them without knowing why, merely out of instinctive curiosity, but immediately abandoned her hypothesis and stared at another, and then at another and another, and finally concluded that it was none of the ladies in the audience. Victor showed no preferences in his glances at the stalls and boxes. Perhaps they had agreed not to look at one another boldly and so betray their secret. The young man also cast a glance at the front of the gallery and gave the family a brief salutation. Doña Pura went on nodding for a quarter of an hour in acknowledgement of this greeting from the swell part of the theatre to the poor Miaus up aloft.

In the intervals, some friends who subscribed like them to ordinary seats in the gallery forced their way through the dense crowd and came up to greet them. Federico Ruiz was one of them, and he like all the rest wanted to hear Milagros' expert opinion on the soprano who was appearing for the first time that night in the part of Selika. Not until she had breathed her last under the poison-tree did the Miaus leave their seats, for they never lost a single note or departed till the curtain had come down for the last time. During the painful descent of the broad staircase, which was packed with people, various of their intimates came up to them, including the lame Guillén, also a few of those women friends who had laughed so unkindly at their appearing in the front.

When they got home they found Villaamil waiting up. Victor had not yet got in and did not do so until very late, when they were all asleep except for Abelarda who, hearing the noise of the latchkey, jumped out of bed and, looking through the door-crack, saw him enter the dining-room and shut himself in his bedroom, having first drunk a glass of water. He had come in cheerfully humming a tune, with his overcoat collar up, and a silk scarf negligently knotted round his neck. But the nap of his hat was crushed and thin in places. He was the complete picture of a rakish man-about-town.

Next day he caused the family considerable trouble by asking for first this and then that bit of sewing: a button to be put on, or a ticklish bit of darning, or something to be done to a shirt. But Abelarda attended to all his wants with great care. At lunchtime Doña Pura came in and said that the little boy at the pawnshop had died; a fact that was afterwards confirmed by Luis, merely as a piece of news. For, as was natural at his fortunate and heartless age, there was no sorrow in his voice. Villaamil treated the dead child to a triumphant funeral oration, proclaiming that it is lucky to die in infancy and so be free from the sufferings of this confounded life. Compassion should be reserved for the parents who remain on earth and suffer appalling hardships while the child flies to heaven to take his place in the glorious company of the angels. All agreed with these thoughts except Victor, who received them with a mocking smile. When his father-in-law had departed and Milagros had gone to the kitchen and Doña Pura was dodging in and out of the room, he turned to Abelarda, who was still at table, and said: 'Happy are they that believe! I don't know what I should give to be like you, who go to church and stay there hour after hour entranced by all the scenic effects they use to cloak the eternal lie. Religion, as I see it, is the gaudy dress with which they cover the void, to prevent it from frightening us. Don't you agree?'

'How could I agree?' cried Abelarda, offended by the sly persistence with which Victor wounded her religious feelings every time he found an opportunity. 'If I believed that I shouldn't go to church, or I should be a play-acting hypocrite if I did. You oughtn't to say things like that to me. If you don't believe that's your own concern.'

'But it gives me no pleasure to be without faith. It grieves me, I assure you, and you would be doing me a kindness if you could convince me that I'm wrong.'

'Me? But I'm not a professor or a preacher. Belief comes from within. Doesn't the thought ever strike you that there may be a God?'

'It did once. But ideas like that departed long ago.'

'Well then . . . What do you want me to say?' (taking him seriously). 'Do you think that when we die we don't have to give any account of our actions?'

'Who can ask us to? The worms? When the moment comes for our exit, the lady earth receives us into her arms. She is a very worthy person but she's got no face or thoughts or plans or conscience or anything. Into her we vanish and are dissolved completely. If I believed as you do, I mean that somewhere or other in the sky there exists a judge with a white beard who pardons or condemns, and confers passports for heaven or hell, I should go into a monastery and spend all the rest of my life praying.'

'And that's the best thing you could do, stupid!' (taking the napkin from Luis' neck. The boy was staring at his father with astonished eyes).

'Why don't you do it yourself?'

'And how do you know what I shall do today or tomorrow? You look out or God will punish you for not believing in him! He'll strike you with his hand, and his hand is heavy, as you'll see.'

At this moment, much upset by his father's crude language, Luis could contain himself no longer. With childish audacity he picked up a crust of bread and threw it in his progenitor's face, crying: 'You're a beast.'

Everyone laughed at this sally, and Doña Pura covered her grandson with kisses, egging him on in these terms: 'Go on, give it to him, darling! He's a villain. He only says he doesn't believe to make us angry. That's a fine boy! He's worth his weight in gold. He knows more than a hundred doctors. My boy's going to be a priest when he grows up, isn't he? So that he can get up in the pulpit and read us his sermons, the darling, and sing the mass. We'll be old bags of bones then, but we'll go down on our knees and let our darling new priest give us his blessing. And who'll be the humblest of us all, with his mouth watering for joy? Why, this scoundrel, I promise you. And you'll say to him: "Papa, you've come to believe in the end, haven't you?" '

'He's a fine boy and he's got brains,' said Victor, getting up joyfully to give the child an encouraging kiss. But Luis hid his face to avoid it. 'I love him for it too, really I do! . . . I'm going to buy you a bicycle, so that you can ride about the square opposite. Your school-friends'll envy you, you see.'

The promise of a bicycle momentarily turned all his ideas upside down. He reckoned with crude egotism that his wish to be a priest and serve God, and even to end up as a saint, need not prevent him from having a marvellous bicycle, and riding it under the noses of all his school-friends who would be green with envy.

28

NEXT morning Villaamil had an interesting conversation with his better half. On hearing her come in from shopping, he hissed to her mysteriously from the study where he was writing letters, shut himself in with her and said : 'Not a word about this to Victor. He's a scoundrel and he might spike my guns. Although I've got no hopes I've made one or two moves. A deputy with a lot of influence is backing me. We had a long talk about things last night. I'll tell you, so that you're in the know, that my friend La Caña introduced me to him. I gave him my record and he was amazed that they had kept me out of a post. So, as if I had nothing to gain from it, I told him my ideas about the Treasury, and by an amazing coincidence they coincided with his own. He thinks exactly as I do. That they ought to try new ways of raising revenue, and attempt to simplify things, by relying on the tax-payer's honesty and going out for cheapness of collection. He promised to give me his complete support. He's a very important man, and it seems they never refuse him anything.'

'Is he in the opposition?'

'No, on the ministerial side, but in disagreement. That's the joke. He's always upsetting the government. He's an important man, very important. The sort of man who cares about nothing except the good of his country. The ministerial benches tremble when he gets up to speak, because he proves to them point by point that the country will go to the devil if things continue as they are, and that agriculture's ruined, and industry's dead and the whole nation's in the most appalling plight. Anyone can see that. Well, the government look on him as their prosecutor, they're frightened of him, my dear, in fact they're so petrified that whenever he asks for anything he gets it. He collects appointments by the basketful. So we came to an arrangement that I should inform him if there's any vacancy today, as soon as I've found out from Pantoja and Sevillano. I shall go to the Ministry directly after lunch, find out if there's a vacancy or not, and if there is write to him at his home or in the Congreso according to the time. He has promised to speak to the Minister this evening. The Minister is very grateful to him for refraining from making an interpellation about a certain contract, which could lead to an awful stink. So naturally he'd give him David's harp today if he asked for it.'

'Yes, my dear, yes' (beaming with satisfaction). 'I don't think anyone will snatch the cake from us now if things are like that.'

'Oh, I wouldn't be confident. I don't feel what they call confident. You know I always expect the worst. But let's make our plans. I'll go to the Ministry, and you keep Luis back from school this afternoon, because I count on him to take the letter. I shan't see him myself because Victor insists that he and I shall go to see the Chief of Personnel this evening. I shall go with him, to put him off the scent. Understand? Be careful not to let that scoundrel guess which way the wind's blowing from at present.'

He got up greatly excited and started walking up and down the little room. His wife, highly delighted, left him alone, and her sister and daughter read the good news in her face. She was one of those people who carry within them a battery of spiritual arms against the ills of life, and who possess the art of altering facts, converting and assimilating them by virtue of a sweetening power that she carried in her body, like the bee that converts everything it sucks to honey.

For young Luis this was a free day since the master had

arranged that in the morning they should all go to the unfortunate little Performer's funeral. Luis was one of the boys chosen to carry the ribbons of the coffin, because, thanks to his father, he had perhaps the best clothes. His grandmother dressed him in his communion suit, with gloves and all, and he went out in all his finery, delighted to look so smart and in no way depressed by the sad reason for it. The scribe's wife kissed him all over and congratulated him on looking so grand, and Luis made for the pawnbroker's house followed by Canelo who also wanted to poke his snout into the burial, although it was unlikely that they would give him a candle to carry. As he turned into the Calle del Acuerdo, Cadalso met his aunt Quintina, who smothered him with kisses; dilated on his smartness, smoothed the shoulders and sleeves of his jacket, and arranged his collar to make him look smarter still.

'You owe this to me, because I told your father to buy you a nice suit. Such a thing would never have occurred to him, he's so absent-minded. I'm fighting your father harder than ever to bring you to live with us, darling. Why did you do that? Why did you make that face? You'd be much better off with me than with those mincing Miaus. You ought to see what pretty things I've got at home. Oh, I do wish you could see the Infant Jesuses. They look just like you with little orbs in their hands, and beautiful cribs, really beautiful. You really ought to see them. And now we're expecting some little chalices, and some custodials – they're really sweet – and some chasubles too. So that good children can play at mass. And saints this size, look, like lead soldiers, and whole hosts of little candles and lamps to light on toy altars. You ought to see them. If you come to our house you can play with them all as much as you like, because they're all for you. Will you come, Luis my darling?'

His eyes wide with wonder at the description of all these sacramental toys, he nodded assent, though distressed by the difficulty of seeing and enjoying them all since his granny did not let him set foot in the place. Now they had arrived at the door of the house of mourning where Quintina, having first given him a big kiss and pinched his cheeks, left him to join the other boys who were already there, making more noise than was suitable to the sad circumstances. Some out of envy, and others because they were always ill-mannered, began to chaff their friend Cadalso about the brand-new suit he was wearing, and his blue stockings, and especially about his gloves, which were also blue and, let it be said in parenthesis, constricted his hands. He would not let them touch him. He was determined to defend the purity of his sleeves against all attacks by rogues or envious rascals. There was then a discussion as to whether they should go up to see Paco Ramós' body, and among those who voted in favour was Luis, who was actuated by curiosity. He should never have gone.

For Luis was so much upset by the sight of the dead boy that he almost fell in a faint. He felt a pain in the pit of his stomach as if something had been torn out. The poor little Performer looked bigger than he was. He was dressed in his best clothes, his hands were crossed and held a palm-leaf, his face was very sallow and blotched with purple, his mouth was half-open and almost black in colour, and you could see his two middle teeth, which were large and white, larger than when he was alive. Luis had to rush away from that terrifying spectacle. Poor Performer! He had been quicksilver itself and now he was still. He had never stopped creating disturbances, laughing and talking at the same time, and now he was silent. He had been the soul of mischief, and had kept the whole class in an uproar, but now he was serious. While Luis' mind was in this great state of upheaval to which he could give no name, not knowing whether it was grief or fear, he was struck by a thought that mastered all these feelings, for the voice of egoism is stronger in youth than pity. Now, he reflected, he won't call me Miau. This deduction seemed to lift a great weight from his mind; it was as if he had resolved a hard problem or had seen a danger averted. As he went down the staircase he tried to compose his feeling of disquietude by repeating to himself: Now he won't call me Miau. Let him start calling me Miau now!

It was not long before they brought down the blue coffin to be put in the hearse. On every balcony in the house, not excepting those of the pawnbrokers' apartment itself, a number of women appeared to watch the funeral start. The lame Guillén appeared, his eyes red with weeping, and with such a serious expression that he looked quite different. He was in charge of everything and apportioned the ribbons, entrusting one to Cadalso. He then got into the carriage, in which the school-master was riding also with his rattan cane and his worn silk-hat, and the shopkeeper from next door in a clean shirt with a low collar and no tie, and an old gentleman whom Cadalso did not know. A start was made. Luis thought that his suit made an impression and was not untouched by the pleasures of vanity. He was much flattered that he had been chosen as ribbon-bearer and thought that the funeral would not have been half as splen-did if he had not been. He kept an eye open for Canelo; but once Mendizábal's wise dog had discovered it was a funeral, which is not an amusing event and prompts misanthropic thoughts, he turned away and took the other direction, con-cluding that it would be better to see if there was not some smart and impressionable bitch to be found in the district.

At the cemetery, curiosity was more powerful than fear and compelled Cadalso to watch everything. They took the body down from the hearse, one of them stood on each side of it, and then they opened the coffin. Luis could not understand why, after covering his face with a handkerchief, those brutes put lime on it. But a friend explained. As he watched these opera-tions, Cadalso felt as if he were choking. He stuck his head between the legs of the older people to see, to see more. The strange thing was that the Performer was so calm and silent while they wickedly covered his face with lime. Then they closed the lid. How terrible to be shut inside! They gave the key to the lame man, and then they put the box in a hole, and shoved it right to the back, right to the back. A bricklayer began to stop the cavity with bricks and mortar. Cadalso could not take his eyes off that job. When he saw that it was finished he heaved a very great sigh. He had been holding his breath for so long that it was like an explosion. Poor little Performer! Now, Lord, everyone will call me Miau who wants to. But he'll never do it again.

As they left, his friends chaffed him again about his spick-and-span clothes. One of them mooted the malicious idea of pushing him into a ditch from which he would have emerged in a frightful state. Various filthy hands touched him for reasons easy to guess, and Cadalso did not know what to do with his hands, imprisoned in his gloves, for they were numb and incapable of movement. In the end he freed himself of this constriction by taking off his gloves and shoving them in his pocket. The boys dispersed before they came to the Calle Ancha and Luis went on with the schoolmaster, who left him at the door of his house. Canelo was already there, having returned from his lewd expedition, and they went up to lunch together, for the dog was not unaware that there had been a fresh delivery of provisions upstairs.

'Where are your gloves?' Doña Pura asked her grandson when she saw him come in with naked hands.

'Here they are. I didn't lose them.'

Villaamil came in from the street at about three, greatly preoccupied. Shutting himself in his study, he wrote a letter in his wife's presence. She was delighted to find him healthily excited, a sign that things were really going ahead.

'Right, Luis can take this letter and wait for the answer. Sevillano has told me that there is a post vacant, and I want to know whether the deputy will ask them to give it to me or not. I've got an appointment with Victor, and I'm going to keep it, so as to put him off the scent. It's a ticklish business I've embarked on and I must proceed very carefully. Give me my hat . . . and my stick, and then out I go again. May God be on our side! Don't let Luis come back without the answer. Tell him to give the letter to one of the porters, and wait in that room on the right-hand side as you come in. I have no hopes. But it's necessary, it's necessary to try every possible means, every possible means.'

Young Cadalso went out at about four with the letter and without his gloves, followed by Canelo and still wearing his funeral clothes, for his grandmother thought that there was no better occasion for looking smart than this one. She did not have to tell him how to get to the Congreso, because he had been there on a previous occasion on a similar errand. In twenty minutes he was there. The Calle de Florida Blanca was crowded with carriages that had formed a line after leaving their owners at the door. The drivers, in braided silk-hats and capes, were chatting from box to box, and the line stretched as far as the Teatro de Jovellanos. Outside the doors of the Congreso that gave on the Calle del Sordo there were queues of people, watched over by the guardians of Public Order who took care that they did not get much out of line. Having inspected all this, the observant Luis went in through the door with a glass canopy. A porter in a frock-coat pushed him gently aside in favour of some important gentlemen in fur coats, whom he let through the red screen. Young Cadalso then went up to the character in the frock-coat, and taking off his cap – because, always polite when he saw braid, he could not distinguish hierarchies – gave him the letter, saying timidly : 'I shall wait for an answer.'

The porter read the envelope and said : 'I don't know that he's come. He won't be long though.' And pushing the letter through a grille, he told Luis to go into the room on the right.

There were quite a number of people there, the majority standing near the door, men of different types, some very badly dressed with mufflers twisted round their necks who had the look of beggars, and women with veils across their faces with rolled papers in their hands that looked very much like petitions. Some watched the gentlemen coming in with anger in their faces and prepared to waylay them. Others, who looked more prosperous, had only come for tickets for the gallery, and went away without them since they were exhausted. Young Cadalso also started to watch the gentlemen who entered in groups of two and three talking heatedly. It must be a very great building, thought Luis, if it holds all these gentlemen. Finally, tired of standing up, he went inside and sat on one of the benches that ornamented the waiting-room. There he saw a table at which people were writing letters or notes, which they gave to the porters, and then waited with ill-concealed impatience. There was a man who had been there three hours and would have to wait another three. The women, motionless in their seats, sighed as they dreamt of an answer that did not come. From time to time a screen that gave on to another room was pushed aside, and a porter called 'Señor So-and-so'. Señor So-and-so got up very pleased.

An hour went by, and the boy yawned, greatly bored on that hard bench. To amuse himself he got up from time to time and went to the door to see the personages coming in. He reflected on the mysteries of this house and on what such a lot of great gentlemen came there to play at. The Congreso, as he knew very well, was a place where they talked. How many times had he heard his grandfather and his father say: 'Somebody or other spoke today, and said this, that or the other.' And what could the place be like inside? He was very curious. What could it be like, the place where they spoke? It must be enormous, as large as a church, with a huge lot of benches on which they sat down to talk, all at the same time. And what was all this talking for? Because the Ministers went in there too. And who were the Ministers? The ones who governed and gave appointments. He also remembered having heard his grandfather say in frequent moments of ill-humour that the Cortes was a farce, and that what they did there was just a waste of time. But at other moments the good old man was enthusiastic and would praise a speech excitedly. In fact, Luis could not form a clear judgement. His mind was all confused.

He returned to the bench, and from there saw someone come in who looked to him like his father, and they opened the screen for him as for the rest. He was on the point of running after him, and shouting 'Papa, papa!' but he was not quick enough, and stayed where he was. And can my father be one of the men that talk? If only Mendizábal could have come here to explain. He knew so much and said such good things. At this point he felt his vision clouding over, and a sharp chill went down his spine. The onset of his malady was so quick and violent that he had only time to say to himself, Here it is. It's come. Then, letting his head fall on his shoulder and resting his body in the corner beside him, he fell into a deep sleep.

29

FOR a moment little Luis saw nothing in front of him. All was void and darkness. After a while the Lord appeared before him, seated. But where? Behind him was something that resembled clouds, a white, luminous mass that swirled and billowed smoke. The Lord looked grave. He gazed at Luis and Luis gazed at him, hoping that he would say something. It was a long time since he had seen him, and his respect for him was greater than ever.

'The gentleman to whom you took the letter,' said the Eternal Father, 'has not answered yet. He read it and put it in his pocket. He will answer you soon. I have told him to answer with a yes, as big as a house. But I don't know whether he'll remember. Now he's doing a lot of talking.'

'Talking,' repeated Luis. 'What's he saying?'

'Lots of things, young man, lots of things that you wouldn't understand,' replied the Lord with a benevolent smile. 'Would you like to hear all that stuff?'

'I should think I should.'

'They're in a dreadful wax today. They'll end up with a first-class row.'

'And you, sir?' asked young Cadalso timidly, who still could not make up his mind to call God 'thou'. 'Don't you say anything?'

'What, here? My boy, I'll tell you something. No, perhaps I'll tell you something one day. What I do nearly always is listen.'

'And don't you get tired?'

'A bit. But it can't be helped.'

'Will the gentleman I took the letter to say yes? Will they give my grandfather a post?'

'I can't tell you for certain. I've told him to. I've told him to three times at least.'

'But things are different now' (boldly) 'because I'm doing my lessons.'

'Don't you get a swelled head. You're paying a bit more attention. But here, between us, there's no point in exaggerating. If you didn't waste so much time on that stamp-album you'd do better for yourself.'

'I knew my lesson yesterday.'

'Compared with your usual performance, you weren't bad. But that's not enough, my boy, that's not enough. What's more, if you're set on being a priest, you'll have to work hard. Just think, to say me a mass you have to learn Latin, and if you want to preach you have to study a whole heap of things.'

'When I'm older I'll learn absolutely everything. But my papa doesn't want me to be a priest. He says he doesn't believe in you at all, and nobody could make him. Tell me, is my father a wicked man?'

'He's not much of a Christian, let's say.'

'And Aunt Quintina, is she a good woman?'

'Aunt Quintina – yes, she is. If only you could see all the pretty things she's got in her house! You ought to go and see them.'

'Granny doesn't let me' (sadly). 'It's because Aunt Quintina has got the idea of having me to live with her, and everybody in the house is against it.'

'That's natural. But what do you think about it yourself? How would you like to stay where you are and be allowed to go to your aunt and see the saints?'

'That's just what I should like. But tell me, is my papa inside there?'

'Yes, he's in there somewhere.'

'And will he be talking too?'

'Yes, he will too. It's quite ridiculous, but . . .'

'Excuse me. My father said the other day that women are very wicked. So I don't mean ever to get married.'

'That's very sensible' (restraining a laugh). 'None of these rash marriages. You're going to be a little priest.'

'And a bishop, unless you command otherwise.'

At this point the boy saw the Lord turn round, as if to drive away something that was bothering him. He craned his neck to see what it was and the Eternal Father said : 'Be off. Get away from here and leave me in peace.' Then Luis saw the faces of a lot of little urchins peeping out from under the folds of his celestial friend's robe. The Lord pulled up his skirts, to reveal three or four children stark naked and wearing wings. Young Cadalso had never seen them before, and now he could have no doubts that this was really God since he had angels. A few more began to appear from the clouds behind him, laughing and kicking up a din and cutting continuous capers. The Eternal Father told them again to go away, and swished them with the corner of his robe as if they were flies. The smallest of them fluttered up to the ceiling (because there was a ceiling there), and the bigger ones pulled the good old man by his dalmatic, to make him go with them. In the end he got up rather crossly, saying: 'All right, I'm coming, I'm coming. How tiresome you are! You're being quite unbearable.' But he said this in the most kindly and tolerant tone. Young Luis was fascinated by this beautiful scene. Then he noticed one of the winged urchins who stood out from the rest.

Blowed if it wasn't the Performer, the little Performer himself, not stiff and livid as he had seen him in that coffin but lively and happy and ever so handsome. What most surprised young Cadalso was that his school-friend came up to him and said with all the brazenness in the world: 'Miau, phoo, phoo!'

All the respect he owed to God and his train did not prevent Luis from taking offence at this sally. He even went so far as to retort: 'You're nasty and you're common . . . your pig of a mother taught you to say that and your pigs of aunts that they call the harpies.'

The Lord smiled and said: 'Quiet now, be quiet all of you! Let's go.' And he departed slowly, driving them off in front of him and shooing them with his hand like a flock of chickens. But just as the Heavenly Father was disappearing among the clouds, that confounded Performer turned back, already far away, and confronting his erstwhile schoolmate, with his legs apart, gazed at him with a broad grin. Then he made a lot of grimaces, stuck out his tongue as far as it would go, and said once more: 'Miau, Miau, phoo, phoo!'

Young Cadalso raised his head. If he had been holding a book or a glass or an inkwell he would have flung it at his head. The little Performer skipped away and, making a trumpet of his hands, emitted from the distance a 'Miau' so loud and long that the whole Congreso echoed with his mewing and seemed about to collapse.

The boy was awoken by a porter with a letter in his hand. It took him some time to come round.

'Boy, boy, are you the boy who brought the letter to that gentleman? Here's the answer, for Señor Don Ramón Villaamil.'

'Yes, that's me. I mean that's my grandfather,' Luis answered at last, and left the place rubbing his eyes.

The freshness of the street somewhat cleared his head. It was raining, and his first thought was that his clothes would get spoiled. Meanwhile Canelo had been killing time in the Carrera de San Jerónimo, strolling up and down the street to look at the pretty 'girls' who passed, some of them in carriages, and all in swell collars. But by the time that Luis came out of the Congreso he had returned from his walk and was waiting for his friend. He joined him in the hope that he would buy some cakes. But the boy had no coppers, and even if he had had he was in no mood for a blow-out after the things he had seen and with his whole body still upset and trembling. And the letter? What did the letter say? Villaamil opened it with a trembling hand, while Doña Pura took the boy into the bedroom to change his clothes. As he read it his heart sank. It was one of those routine letters of which hundreds are written every day in the Congreso and the Ministries. A number of formal politenesses, considerable play with vague promises that said nothing either way. When his wife came in to hear the news Villaamil offered a tragic spectacle. He pointed to the open letter which he had thrown down on the table.

'Oh,' said the Miau when she had read it, 'the usual rubbish. But don't get upset, man. Go and see him tomorrow, and . . .'

'But I tell you' (in profound discouragement) 'they're just playing with me, both of them. . . .'

He passed the night in black gloom, but first thing in the morning his mood changed completely. These abrupt contrasts that raise you from despair to hope are common features in the weary life of an office seeker. Villaamil received a note from the great man, asking him to visit him at his home between twelve and one. He was so eager and hurried that he could scarcely struggle into his overcoat. He's sending for me to tell me some nonsense, he thought, clinging as ever to the worst, but come on, let's go! And he went out, leaving his wife greatly excited by the expectation of approaching triumph. On the way he tried to steep himself thoroughly in his pessimistic fatalism. According to his theory what happens is always the opposite of what one thinks. When one considers why one never wins anything in the lottery everything is revealed. It's because one buys a ticket with the firm intention of winning the big prize. The expected never occurs, particularly in Spain, because by a historical law Spaniards live for the day, are surprised by events and have no control over them. According to this theory of the failure of all anticipatory endeavours what should one do to make a thing happen? Foresee the opposite, steep oneself thoroughly in the idea that it will not come off. And to prevent a thing from happening? Imagine that it will happen, finally convince oneself by dint of a sustained intellectual effort that one has grounds for this supposition. Villaamil had always practised this system with success, and remembered a great number of conclusive instances. When a wild storm was blowing, during one of his voyages to Cuba, he steeped himself completely in the idea of drowning, plucking all hope from his mind, and of course the ship remained afloat. Another time, finding himself threatened with loss of office, he thoroughly persuaded himself that the disaster would occur. He thought of nothing but the inevitable letter of dismissal. He saw it on his table day and night lying before him in all its brutal brevity. And what happened? Why, they gave him a promotion.

In fine, on his way to the house of this father of his country, Villaamil impregnated himself with the certainty of disaster. It's absolutely plain, he thought to himself, this gentleman is going to give me a knock-out blow. I'm very sorry, my friend, he'll say to me, the Minister and I are on bad terms, and I can't do anything for you.

But the words of that favoured individual were very different, and Don Ramón could never have guessed that he would begin

191

on this note: 'After I had written to you last night, I spoke to your son-in-law, and he said that it would suit you better to have an appointment in the provinces. That changes things entirely because the provinces are much easier. I'll deal with the matter today.'

In the midst of his pleasant surprise at this cheering news our friend felt somewhat angry that Victor should have interfered in this business, and he returned home uneasy because he very much disliked finding Cadalso's person and opinions mixed up with his affairs. But Doña Pura did not share these reservations and the sun of her delight shone from a cloudless sky. They certainly disliked the idea of having to pack up and go. But they were in no position to choose the best. They could only put up with what was possible and thank God for it.

From that day Villaamil haunted the churches in a shameful manner. If the Comendadoras was open when he went out, he would slip in for a while and hear mass if it was at mass time; and if it was not, he would kneel for a little, trying no doubt to harmonize his fatalism with Christian belief. Did he succeed? Who knows? Christianity says: Ask and it shall be given you. It tells us to trust in God, and to expect from his hands the remedy for our ills. But the experience of a long life suggested these thoughts to Villaamil: Do not expect and you shall receive. Have no trust in success in order that success may come. He must have reconciled the two ideas in his mind. Perhaps he renounced his diabolical theory and returned to a consoling faith. Perhaps he submitted himself with all the outpourings of his spirit to the God of mercy, putting himself in his hands and trusting him to give him what was most fitting, death or life, a post or eternal suspension, a modest livelihood or awful penury, the happy peace of a servant of the state or the hungry despair of the office-seeker. Perhaps he expressed in advance his warm gratitude for the first alternative and his resignation to the second, and decided to accept the divine decision with a stoical heart, renouncing all anticipation of events – the sinful product of man's pride.

Just about nightfall one evening, as he was on his way home he saw the Montserrat open and went in. The church was very dark. Almost groping, he made his way to a bench in the middle of the nave, knelt beside it, and gazed at the altar, which was lit by one lamp. The steps of some worshipper going out or coming in, and the thin whisper of prayers were the only sounds that broke the silence into the depths of which the suspended official cast his melancholy plea, an absurd mixture of devotion and official formality: 'However much I search my conscience I can find no great sin that should earn me this cruel punishment. I have always worked for the good of the state, and have on all occasions tried to defend the administration against fraud. I have never indulged in or condoned sharp practices, never, Lord, never. Thou knowest very well that this is true, Lord. The books are still there that I kept when I was auditor of accounts. Not one faulty entry and not one erasure. Why so much injustice in every confounded government? If it is true that thou givest us all our daily bread, why dost thou refuse it to me? I'll go further: if the state should show equal favour to all, why does it abandon me? Me, who have served it so loyally. Lord, thou must not deceive me now. I promise no longer to doubt thy mercy as I have doubted it before. I promise not to be a pessimist and to hope, to put my hope in thee. Now, O Lord, touch the heart of this overworked Minister, who is a good man. Only they're driving him out of his wits with all these letters and recommendations.'

After a while he sat on the bench, because kneeling tired him. His eyes, becoming accustomed to the half-light, began vaguely to distinguish the altars, the images, the confessionals and the people, two or three old women who crouched around the confessionals reciting prayers. He did not expect the happy encounter that befell him about half an hour after coming in. As he was sliding about the bench or shifting his backside on the hard wood his grandson appeared before him: 'I didn't see you, my boy. Whom did you come with?'

'With Aunt Abelarda. She's in the chapel over there. I was waiting for her here when I went to sleep. I didn't see you come in.'

'I came in a little while ago,' said his grandfather, clasping the boy to him. 'But tell me, do you come here to have your afternoon nap? I wish you wouldn't. You might get cold and catch a chill. Your hands are frozen. Let me have them and I'll make them warm.'

'Grandpa,' asked Luis, clasping his grandfather's face and tilting it to one side, 'were you praying for them to give you a post?'

The old man's spirits were so perturbed that his grandson's question reduced him from laughter to tears in less than a second. But Luis did not notice that the old man's eyes had grown moist, and he gave a heartfelt sigh on hearing him reply: 'Yes, my boy. You know very well that we must ask God for all that we need.'

'Well,' replied the boy, leaping in a totally unexpected direction, 'I have been telling him that every day, but he doesn't do anything.'

'You? Do you ask him too? What a treasure you are! The Lord gives us what is good for us. But we have to be good. If we're not, nothing comes of it.'

Luis heaved another very deep sigh, as much as to say: That's the blooming difficulty. You have to be good. After a long pause, putting his hands once more on his grandfather's face, to compel him to look at him, the child murmured: 'Grandpa, I knew my lesson today.'

'Did you? I'm very pleased.'

'When will they put me in the Latin class? I want to learn Latin so as to sing mass. But I say, I don't like it in this church. Do you know why? There's a Lord God in that chapel with long hair. He frightens me very much. I wouldn't go in to save my life. When I'm a priest I won't say mass in there.'

Don Ramón burst out laughing.

'Your fear will depart bit by bit, and soon you'll be saying your mass ever so nicely, just you see if you don't, and you'll say it to the Christ with the long hair too.'

'I'm learning to say it already. Murillo knows all the Latin words and when you have to ring the bell and lift the priest's train.'

'Well now,' said the old man without understanding what he had said. 'Go and tell your aunt that I'm here, and that it's time for us to go home.'

Luis went to take the message, and the tapping of his heels on the church floor sounded a happy note in that mournful silence. Abelarda, who was squatting like a Turk, looked behind her, got up and went to sit beside her father.

'Have you finished?' he asked her.

'I'm not quite ready yet,' she answered, and went on muttering with her eyes fixed on the altar.

Villaamil had great faith in his daughter's prayers, which he believed were for him. So he answered: 'Don't be in a hurry. Pray calmly and as much as you want to. There's still plenty of time. It seems to lift a great weight off the heart when we tell our troubles to the only being who can relieve them, doesn't it?'

This remark sprang spontaneously from the depths of his heart. The place and the time were propitious for the gentle act of opening the gates of the spirit and revealing all secrets. Abelarda was in the same psychological situation, and felt even more strongly than her father the need for some relief. At that moment she could not keep silent. Almost inevitably confidences spilled from her lips that at another time or place she would not have allowed to escape for anything in the world.

'Oh, Papa,' the words poured out, 'I'm very unhappy. You couldn't know how unhappy I am.'

Villaamil was astonished by this outburst, since for him there was only one misfortune in the family, his lack of a post and the painful delay in his reappointment.

'That's true,' he said gloomily, 'but now we must have trust in God. He will not abandon us.'

'In my case,' Abelarda continued, 'he's certainly abandoned me. Such terrible things can happen to one. Sometimes God does such crazy things.'

'What do you mean, girl?' (in great alarm). 'God does crazy things!'

'I mean sometimes he gives us feelings that just make us unhappy. What's the good of loving, I mean, if things don't go right?'

Villaamil did not understand. He looked at her to see if her expression explained the enigma of her words. But the dimness prevented the old man from reading his daughter's face. And Luis, standing in front of them both, did not understand a word of their conversation.

'To tell you the truth,' Villaamil added, seeking for light in this confusion, 'I don't understand you at all. What's your trouble? Have you quarrelled with Ponce? I imagine not. The poor lad was talking to me so naturally in the café last night about being in such a hurry to get married. He doesn't want to wait for his uncle to die, though, by the way, the man's on his last legs.'

'It's not that, it's not that,' said the Miau with a weight on her heart. 'Ponce hasn't done anything to upset me.'

'Well then . . .'

They were both silent, and after a little Abelarda looked at her father. A malicious feeling bubbled in her heart, a wish to wound the kind old man by saying something very disagreeable to him. What was the explanation of this? Her unhappy mind was overflowing with a pity that she could not express. Her spirit, vainly seeking the good, rebounded into evil and was momentarily charmed by it. That was all. She was slightly influenced by that state of mind (related to those nervous disorders common in the female make-up) which prompts infanticide; and in this case the mysterious burst of anger was discharged over her miserable father whom she loved so dearly.

'Haven't you heard?' she asked him. 'Victor has got his post. At midday today, just after you went out, there was a knock at the door. It was his appointment. He was in the house. They've given him promotion and appointed him . . . something or other in the Financial Administration of Madrid.'

Villaamil was stunned. It was as if he had received a sharp hammer-blow on the head. There was singing in his ears. He thought he was out of his senses, and made her repeat the news. Abelarda repeated it in a voice ringing with the fury of a parricide.

'A fine position,' she added. 'He's very pleased with it. He said that if they don't give you anything, temporarily and so that you have something to do he can give you a subordinate position in his office.'

The unfortunate man thought for a moment that the church was falling on his head. And indeed a huge weight did descend on his heart, which stopped his breath. At that same moment Abelarda recovered from the mental disturbance which had obscured her reason and filial feelings, and regretted the knife-blow that she had just dealt her father. She wished to pour balm on his wounds without loss of time.

'They will be giving you a post too very soon. I have prayed God for it.'

'Me! Give me a post!' (in a fury of pessimism). 'God only looks after the rogues now. Do you imagine I expect anything from the Minister or from God himself? Everywhere it's the same thing. At the top and at the bottom, play-acting, favourit-ism, corruption! You see what we get with all our prostrations and prayers. Here am I always passed over and neglected by everyone, while that spell-binder, that liar and cheat ...'

He hit his head so hard with the palm of his hand that Luis was quite frightened and looked at his grandfather in conster-nation. Then Abelarda again felt a parricidal fury to which was joined a certain instinct to defend the passion which filled her thoughts. Life's great mistakes, like its deepest feelings, wild though they may be, tend to protect themselves and are most reluctant to die. Abelarda rushed to her own defence as she defended another: 'No, Papa, he's not' (most heatedly) 'wicked, no, he's not. You and Mamma are absolutely wrong about him. It's all because you judge him superficially, because you don't understand him.'

'How can you know about him, silly?'

'How can I not know? Other people don't understand him, but I do.'

'You, my girl!' and as he spoke a terrible suspicion crossed his mind, making him even more confused.

He quickly pulled himself together, saying to himself: 'But it's impossible. It's quite absurd.' As he noticed his daughter's excitement, however, and the wildness of her gaze, he found himself once more attacked by a cruel suspicion.

'You! You say that you understand him.'

He refused to explore this mystery which set his head crazily spinning. Yet it attracted him like some black abyss that grows deeper and more fearful the longer one looks into it. He rapidly connected some hitherto inexplicable actions of his daughter with what he had just heard; he tied loose ends, rememberd words, gestures, incidents and finally admitted to himself that he was in the presence of something very serious. So serious was it and so repulsive to his feelings that he was terrified of approaching it. He preferred to forget it or to pretend that it was an idle imagination with no foundation in reason.

'Let's go,' he muttered. 'It's late and I have some things to do before I go home.'

Abelarda knelt to say her final prayers, and the old man, taking young Luis by the hand, moved slowly towards the door, making no genuflexion and not glancing towards the altar or remembering that he was in a holy place. They went past the chapel with the long-haired Christ, and when the boy pulled at his grandfather's arm to drag him as far away as possible from the image that so frightened him, Villaamil in annoyance said to him sharply : 'He won't eat you, stupid!'

All three went out, and at the corner of the Calle de Quiñones they met Pantoja, who took Don Ramón aside to tell him of Cadalso's astonishing promotion. Abelarda continued on her way home. As she climbed the ill-lit staircase she heard someone coming down. It was he. His step was unmistakable. A mysterious presentiment filled her with shame and alarm. She would have liked to hide, so that he should not see her. Her heart warned her that something strange would happen, as a natural outcome of previous events, and this meeting made her tremble.

'Have you been to church?' he asked her. 'I'm not eating at home tonight. I've been invited out.'

'I see,' she answered, unable to think of any brighter or more opportune remark.

Victor leapt down four stairs and without a word caught the little nobody by the waist, and pressed her against him, himself leaning against the wall. Abelarda did not offer the least resistance, and when he kissed her with a pretence of passion on the forehead and both cheeks she closed her eyes, resting her head on the handsome monster's breast, like one who after great efforts enjoys a long-desired rest.

'It had to be,' said Victor in the emotional tone that he simulated so well. 'We have never spoken out, but at last we understand one another. I will sacrifice everything for you, my darling. Are you ready to do the same for this unhappy creature?'

Abelarda breathed 'Yes' through scarcely opened lips.

'Would you leave home, parents, everything to follow me?' he asked in a burst of devilish inspiration.

The little goose once more agreed, but in a more audible voice and with a brisk nod of the head.

'To follow me and nevermore to part?'

'I would follow you blindly, without hesitation.'

'And soon?'

'Whenever you like. Now even.'

Victor reflected for a moment.

'It can all be done without scandal, my darling. Let's part now. I think someone's coming. It's your father. Go upstairs. We'll talk later.'

On hearing her father's steps Abelarda woke from that short dream. Trembling with alarm, she climbed the stairs without looking back. Victor continued slowly down, and when he met his father-in-law and the boy he said nothing to them. They did not speak to him either. When Villaamil reached the second floor, his daughter had already knocked, since she wanted to hurry in before her father could detect the criminal confusion that flushed her cheeks.

30

ALL that night the little nobody was in a state bordering on dementia. Her mind was divided between wild joy and funereal sadness. At times she felt herself attacked by a stabbing mistrust. She had surrendered without conditions, without exacting in return that he should surrender his free will and end his affair with this unknown woman, a dangerous entanglement no doubt and difficult to break. Was he breaking it, though? Dissolving all his past love-affairs? He would have to. And frankly, it would not have been wrong to have said so. But there had not been time enough for anything. They had not been able to give or ask the proper explanations. It had been like a thunderbolt, this mutual exchange and abandonment of wills. It would be right, then, on the first possible occasion to clarify the situation, to remove all fear of duplicity and be done once and for all with this lady of the love-letters. After this, Abelarda would entrust herself without more ado to this man who had entranced her soul. She renounced all liberty, she belonged to him, was his in whatever form or under whatever conditions he wished, with or without scandal, with or without honour.

During dinner, Villaamil observed his daughter, and his face once again assumed his most characteristic and fiercest tigerish expression. He ate without appetite. The meat as he devoured it might have been palpitating flesh that was half alive. It seemed to groan and quiver with horrible anguish as he pierced it with his fork. Doña Pura and Milagros did not dare to speak to him about Victor's appointment. They were both gloomy and cross, and wore funereal expressions. Abelarda too seemed to belong to this silent circle of graveyard mourners. There was no performance at the Real that night. The suspended official retired to his study and the three Miaus went to the drawing-room, where they were joined by the excellent Ponce and the Cuevas girls. Abelarda had moments of feverish loquacity, and others of silent brooding.

At midnight the party ended, and it was bedtime. The house was in silence and Abelarda waited up for Victor, in order that they might say what had to be said and empty their minds one to another in a complete exchange of thoughts. But one o'clock struck and half-past and still the roisterer did not appear. Between two and three, the poor girl found herself in a state of fever which kindled the wildest thoughts in her brain. He had been killed. Perhaps the embrace, the kisses, the declaration on the stairs were just a wicked joke. She rejected this last idea as too ridiculous and, as she thought, beyond the bounds of human wickedness. Then she reflected (and by now it was half-past three) that when the fashionable lady with the coronet on her letter paper had heard, only that night, that her lover was leaving her, or had received from his own lips the sad news that he was breaking with her, she had plotted a terrible vengeance upon him. She had invited him to supper and poisoned him, by pouring some concoction of the Borgias into his sherry. The silly goose mingled in her strange fictions a hundred incidents that she had seen in operas : the plots that the mezzo-soprano works against the tenor because he scorns her for the soprano; the scoundrelly trick by which the baritone rids himself of his hated rival; the sublime constancy of the tenor (and by now it was four o'clock) who, succumbing to the joint villainies of the bass and the contralto, perishes in the arms of the soprano, whereupon both end up by swearing they will love one another in the next world.

It was five, and still Victor had not appeared. Abelarda's brain was like a volcano that emitted flashes of scorching flame through her eyes, and words of despair, love and anger through her lips. Only twice during his stay had the 'great man' spent all night out. The first time that this had happened he had come in at ten in the morning in a lamentable condition, revealing in his bearing, his words and even his clothes the excesses of a festive night spent with persons of far from sober habits. Supposing the same thing had occurred on this second occasion! But no, something must have happened to him. There was some puzzling, some mysterious connexion between their tender meeting on the stairs and this inexplicable absence. There must have been some accident, something hideous that the poor girl's clouded intellect was powerless to guess at. Six o'clock, and still nothing. She burst into tears, and laid her head on the pillow. But a moment later she was sitting on a trunk, or wandering about the room, like a bird jumping from perch to perch in its cage.

Day came, and still nothing. The first person to get up was her father. Abelarda heard him go to the kitchen and from there to his study. Eight o'clock. Doña Pura would soon be leaving her idle couch. Even if Victor were to come in now, it would not be possible to talk to him alone. The anguished girl went to bed, not to sleep or to rest, but so that her mother should not notice that she had been up all night. It was after nine when the night-wanderer returned with a very ugly look. Doña Pura opened the door to him without a word, and he shut himself in his room. Abelarda, who had come out of hers, heard him walking up and down that confined space that hardly contained the bed, the chair and the trunk.

'If you're going to church,' said Doña Pura to her, picking some coppers out of her purse, 'will you bring in four eggs? Take Luis with you. I'm not going out. I have a headache. Your father is most upset, and I can understand it. Fancy their giving a post to that wicked good-for-nothing and passing him over, an honourable man who knows more about administration than the whole Ministry put together, passing him over and leaving him in the street! What a government, my Lord what a government! And then they're surprised when there's a revolution. Don't forget the four eggs. I don't know how we shall get through the day! Oh yes, and bring back the black cord for my dress, and the hooks and eyes.'

Abelarda went to church and when she came back with the purchases for her mother, found her, her aunt and Victor in the dining-room engaged in a furious argument. Cadalso's voice was loudest as he said: 'But, my dear ladies, what fault is it of mine if they have given me a post before Papa? Is that a reason why everyone in this house should make ugly faces at me? I've half a mind, so help me God, to throw my letter of appointment into the street. Peace in the family comes first. Here have I been struggling to make you love me, trying to make you forget the troubles I've caused you, and now, for heaven's sake, because they choose to appoint me at the Ministry, my mother-in-law and my mother-in-law's sister are almost tearing my eyes out. Very well, ladies, scratch me and punch me as much as you like. I shan't complain. The more names you call me the more dearly I shall love you.'

'As if we didn't know,' objected Doña Pura in viperish tones, 'that you've got a big influence at the Ministry, and that Ramón would have had a post by now if you'd wanted him to!'

'For goodness' sake, Mamma, for goodness' sake,' replied Victor, showing true consternation, 'this is really very naïve of you. I can't believe you're speaking in earnest. A big influence, me? Come now, I've quite a little reputation in the family! And if I were to swear that I've made more efforts for Papa than for myself – what if I were to swear that? You wouldn't believe me, of course. But I say it's true and I repeat it, whether you do or not.'

Abelarda did not intervene in the dispute, but mentally took her brother-in-law's side. At this point Villaamil entered, and Victor turned resolutely to him: 'Now, sir, you're a reasonable man. Tell me if you believe, as these ladies do, that I've been working and scheming and intriguing to make them appoint me and not you. Because they're blasting my ears with this story, and, frankly, it hurts me to hear myself treated like a conscienceless Judas' (in noble tones). 'Señor Ramón, sir, I have acted honourably. It is not my fault if I have been so unfortunate as to have been preferred before others. Do you know what I should like to do? May I fall dead if I'm telling a lie. I should like to give my post to you.'

'But that's out of the question,' answered Villaamil with a serenity that cost him a cruel effort. 'A post for me! Do you imagine anyone is thinking of such a thing? The logical and natural thing has occurred. You have good patrons there, somewhere or other, whether male or female I don't know, and I have no one. Good luck to you.'

He closed his study door, leaving Victor in the passage, somewhat confused and with an answer on his tongue which he did not dare to give. He then tried to get round Doña Pura in the dining-room, endeavouring to change her mood with expressions of servile affection.

'How very unfortunate it is, my God, to be misunderstood! I wear myself out for the family, I sacrifice myself for them, I make their troubles my own and put my small means at their service, but all in vain. I am and always shall be an unwelcome guest and burdensome relation. Patience, patience!'

He spoke with subtle dissimulation, meanwhile taking some paper and preparing to write at the dining-room table. As he sat down he saw his sister-in-law standing before him and looking at him with the fingers of her right hand clasped to her chin.

Her attitude was alert, thoughtful and affectionate. In fact she resembled, except in beauty, the celebrated statue of Polihymnia in the ancient assembly of the Muses. It was not necessary to be a lynx to read in the eyes and expression of the little nobody something in the nature of this accusation: 'What do you mean by ignoring me? Don't you know that I'm the only person who has understood you? Come to me and don't worry about the others. I have been waiting for you since last night. But you, thankless wretch, had your mind on other things. What has become of your plans for elopement? I'm ready. I'll go just as I am.'

Seeing her in this attitude and reading the reproach in her eyes, it struck Victor that he had an account to settle with her. Damned if that encounter on the stairs had come into his mind once during the night. If he remembered it, it was as a trivial occurrence, a student's joke without any serious importance. His first feeling when the memory arose was one of disgust, as if he had just recalled the tiresome necessity of paying a formal visit. But he quickly composed his features. For he had a handsome mask to fit every situation in the varied repertory of his actor's nature. So after making certain that his mother-in-law was nowhere near, he put on a tender expression, looked up at the ceiling, and down at his sister-in-law. Then these brief phrases were exchanged between them: 'I must talk to you, my darling. Where and when?'

'This evening. In the Comendadoras. At six.'

That was all. Abelarda ran off to tidy the drawing-room, and Victor sat down to write, scornfully casting away his mask and thinking: The crazy creature wants to know when the sinning's to begin. Oh, wouldn't you like it to? But it never will.

31

Punctual as the clock itself, Abelarda entered the Comendadoras at the hour of the appointment. The church was silent and dark; it might have been made for the mysterious purpose of an assignation. If anyone had seen the Villaamil girl come in, he would have observed with surprise that she was wearing her best clothes, her real communion finery. Since she had gone out at five her mother had not noticed that she had put them on. The girl sat down on a bench, and prayed feverishly and distractedly. At quarter past Victor appeared. At first he could not see a thing, and wondered what part of the church to go to. She got up to lead him and touched his arm. They clasped hands and sat down near the door, in a sufficiently secluded place, the darkest in the church. It was beside the entrance to the chapel of the Virgin of the Dolours.

Despite all his experience and the ready wit with which he usually tackled the most difficult situations, Victor did not know how to approach this matter and for a moment chewed over his opening words. Finally, resolved to get it over quickly, he mentally commended himself to his guardian devil and said: 'I'll begin by begging your pardon, my darling. Your pardon. Yes, I need your pardon for the . . . rashness of my conduct. My love for you is so deep, so compelling, that last night, without knowing what I was doing, I sought to involve you in my harsh fate. You must be very angry with me, I admit, for making the proposal I did to a woman like you. What a picture you must have formed of me! I have earned your contempt. To propose that you should leave your parents and your home to follow me, a wandering star' (remembering phrases that he had read in the past and stringing them together without the least shame) – 'to follow me who flash through space in no fixed direction, not knowing whence I have received the impulse to travel nor where my wild career will end. I shall dash myself to pieces. Undoubtedly I shall dash myself to pieces. But I should be despicable, Abelarda' (taking her hand), 'I should be the worst of monsters if I allowed you to dash yourself to pieces with me. You, who are an angel. You, who are the delight of your family. Oh, I implore your pardon, and would go down on my knees to obtain it. I have deeply outraged your self-respect, I have outraged your purity by proposing to you this atrocious action, the invention of this feverish brain. Pardon me now, and accept my honest apology. I love you, I love you, and I shall always love you, though hopelessly, for I cannot aspire to possess so . . . rich a jewel. It would be an outrage to God if I were to foster such an aspiration . . .'

The Miau was quite unable to understand this verbiage, the sense of which was so contrary to what she expected to hear. She gazed at him, then at the nearest image, a St John with lamb and flag, and asked the saint whether this was truth or dream.

'You are forgiven, forgiven,' she murmured and heaved a deep sigh.

'Do not be surprised, my love,' he proceeded, now master of the situation, 'that in your presence I become shy and do not know what to say. You bewitch me, you annihilate me, you make me conscious of my own littleness. Pardon my boldness of last night. Now I wish to be worthy of myself, to imitate your divine serenity. You show me the road that I must follow, the road of the ideal, of actions in perfect conformity with the divine law. I will imitate you, I will strive to imitate you. You are peerless, and it is imperative that we part. If we were to join, your life would be in danger and mine also. We are surrounded by enemies who lie in wait for us, who watch us closely. What must we do? Separate on earth, and unite in the realm of thoughts. Think of me, and never for an instant shall I cease to think of you.'

Much disturbed, Abelarda shifted on her bench as if sitting on thorns.

'How can I forget that when all the family despised me you alone understood and comforted me? Oh, I shall never forget that, not in a thousand years! You were absolutely sublime. I'm a wretch. Leave me, abandon me to my sad fate. I know that you will pray to God for me, and this consoles me. If I could believe, if I could bow down before this or some other altar, if I could pray, I would pray for you . . . Good-bye, my love.'

He tried to take her hand. But Abelarda withdrew it, and turned her face away from him.

'Your disdain destroys me. I know very well that I deserve it. Last night I treated you disrespectfully, brutally, coarsely. But you told me that you have forgiven me. Why did you turn away? Oh, I know, I know. I pain you, I am hateful to you. I deserve it, I know I deserve it. Good-bye. I am expiating my sins, for now though I wish to part from you, as you see I cannot. Nailed to this bench!' (impatient and falling over himself to finish quickly). 'Will you remember me in your future life? Let me give you one piece of advice. Marry Ponce, or, if you don't, go into a nunnery and pray for him and me, for this sinner. You were born for the spiritual life. You are very great, and will not fit into the narrow world of matrimony, or into . . . prosaic family life. I cannot go on, my dearest, for I cannot think. My mind wanders and . . . courage! . . . One supreme effort . . . Good-bye, good-bye.'

And like a soul borne off by Satan, he left the church muttering. He was in a hurry, and congratulated himself on having concluded a tiresome business.

'Damn it all,' he said, looking at his watch and hastening his pace. 'I meant to finish it off in ten minutes and it's taken me twenty. And that woman's been waiting for me since six o'clock. But I can't help being sorry for the precious little idiot. They'll end by putting a strait-jacket on her – or a strait-corset!'

And what was Abelarda doing or thinking? If she had seen the devil in person mount the pulpit of that church and deliver a sermon reproaching the faithful for not sinning enough – if this had taken place there before her eyes she could not have been more stupefied. The monster's speech and his hurried departure left her rigid, unable to move. Thoughts and impressions from their conversation filled her brain like a substance poured into a cold mould and about to set. It did not occur to her to pray. For what? Or to go. Where? She was better there, quiet and silent, and as motionless as the St John with his flag or the

Mater Dolorosa who stood at the foot of the cross, stiff in her austere black dress and her widow's weeds, her breast pierced by little silver swords, and her hands so tightly clasped together that her fingers were inseparable. The Christ, much taller than the image of his mother, towered up the wall, touching the chapel roof with his crown of thorns and stretching his arms to an incredible distance. Below were candles, the instruments of the Passion, wax ex-votos, an offertory box with dirty edges to its chink and its padlock caked with rust. The altar-cloth was spotted with wax, and the top was painted to imitate jasper. Señorita de Villaamil looked at all this, not seeing it as a whole but picking out the smallest details. She darted her eyes here and there like a needle that pricks without piercing, while her mind sucked at the full and bitter sponge, swallowing all its wormwood. Two most serious events had coincided, each alone capable of deciding the future life of this insignificant and bewildered young woman. Within two and a half hours of the happening just described occurred another no less important. Ponce, conversing with Doña Pura in her drawing-room and without witnesses, showed some annoyance that his fiancée's parents had not yet settled the day of the wedding.

'But it is settled, my boy, it's as good as settled. Ramón and I have no other wish. What do you think about the beginning of May? On the feast of the Discovery of the Cross?'

Some minutes before Doña Pura had explained her daughter's absence from the party by saying that she had caught a dreadful chill that evening at the Comendadoras. She had come in with her teeth chattering, and in such a high fever that her mother had ordered her to bed that instant. This was the truth, but not the whole truth. The lady did not mention her surprise at seeing her come in at such an unusual hour and in a dress that she did not generally wear to pay an evening visit to this near-by church. 'Those are the best clothes you've got. What do you mean by wearing them out where no one can see you? What is the purpose of polishing the church benches, that are caked with muck and dust and all sorts of filth, with fine cashmere at three and a half pesetas a yard?' She did not mention either that her daughter had not given a rational answer to anything she had said. This, combined with the chattering of her teeth and her refusal to eat, had impelled Doña Pura to put her to bed. The lady was extremely worried, and was anxiously seeking the meaning of certain peculiarities that she had recently noticed in Abelarda. Well, whatever it is, she thought, the sooner we get her married the better. She had said something on this subject to her husband, but Villaamil had not deigned to answer a syllable, he was so gloomy and depressed.

Abelarda, who pretended to be asleep so that no one should worry her, saw Milagros put Luis to bed. The boy did not go to sleep quickly that night but went on tossing and turning. When they were left alone together, Abelarda told him to lie quiet. She was in no mood to be disturbed; it was late and she needed rest.

'Aunty, I can't go to sleep. Tell me a story.'

'No, I'm in no mood for stories. Don't bother me, or you'll see . . .'

At other times when she found her nephew wakeful, the little nobody, who loved him with all her heart, tried to soothe him with endearments; and if this was not enough, she would go to his bed, and fondle and lull him till he went off to sleep. But that night, being disturbed and overwrought, she felt a tremendous hatred for the poor boy. His voice hurt and upset her, and for the first time in her life she thought: What do I care whether you go to sleep or not, or whether you're well or ill, or if the devil runs off with you?

Being used to finding his aunt very affectionate, little Luis could not resign himself to silence. He wanted a chat at any price, and said to his room-mate in a winning voice: 'Aunty, have you ever seen God?'

'What are you talking about, silly? If you aren't quiet I'll get up and . . .'

'Don't be angry. What have I done wrong? I see God, I see him whenever I want to, if you'd like to know. But tonight I can only see his feet. They're all covered with blood and nailed and tied with a white rope, like the feet of the Christ with long hair that's in the Montserrat . . . and they make me very frightened. I don't like to close my eyes because . . . I'll tell you . . . I've never seen his feet before, always his face and his hands . . . and the reason is . . . do you know why this has happened? Because I did a big sin. Because I told my Papa a lie, I told him that I wanted to go with my Aunt Quintina to her house. And it was a lie. I only want to go every now and then to see the saints. I don't want to live with her. Because to go with her and leave all of you would be a sin, wouldn't it?'

'Be quiet, be quiet. I'm not in any mood to listen to your rubbish. What is it you say about seeing God, you little idiot? Here he is on the wall, and you can look at him as much as you like.'

A little later Abelarda heard young Cadalso sobbing. But instead of pity, she felt, strange to say, such a dislike for her nephew that it might have been called furious hatred. The wretched child was an idiot, a little play-actor who took the family in with his nonsense about seeing God and wanting to be a priest. He was a hypocrite, a liar, a slyboots . . . and ugly and sickly and spoiled into the bargain.

This hatred for the poor child was like the feeling that had arisen in Abelarda's heart the night before against her own father, an unnatural hatred, the product, no doubt, of one of those seizures related to epilepsy that destroy the primary emotions of a woman's soul. She could not explain to herself how this monstrous condition could have arisen in her mind, and she watched it grow stronger and stronger every moment, taking a certain insane satisfaction in its huge proportions. She loathed Luis, she loathed him with all her heart. The little boy's voice got on her nerves and drove her frantic.

Cadalso went on through his tears: 'I can see his legs. They're black with stains of blood. I can see his knees with very black weals on them. Aunty, I'm frightened . . . I'm awfully frightened. Come over here, do!'

The Miau clenched her fists, and bit the sheet. That complaining voice shook her very being, stirring up a red wave within her that rose till it clouded her eyes. The child was a play-actor, a babbling little liar who had only been born to torture her and the rest of the household. But there still remained in Abelarda enough of her habitual tenderness to restrain the further growth of her fury. She felt prompted to jump out of bed and run to Luis, to give him a good slap, but she quickly stopped herself. Oh, if she were to lay hands on him she would not be content with just slapping him. She would throttle him – yes, she would. There was such a fury in her soul, such a thirst for destruction in her burning hands!

'Aunty, I can see his loincloth. It's all soaking in blood, lots of blood. Please light the lamp, or I shall die of fright. Send him away, tell him to go away. It's the other God that I like, the handsome old gentleman. He hasn't got blood on him, but a beautiful cloak and a very white beard . . .'

Now she could no longer control herself and leapt out of her bed. She stayed beside it, however, motionless – not out of pity but because of a memory that stabbed her like a fierce light. The very thing she was doing at that moment, her dead sister had done on a certain unhappy night. Yes, Luisa too had suffered from these terrible impulses of hatred for him, her own child, and on a certain night when she had heard him crying had jumped out of bed and attacked him with menacing hands, no longer a woman but a wild beast. And Abelarda was repeating the dead woman's own words, saying that the child was a monster, a hellish monstrosity who had come into the world to punish and destroy the family.

This memory caused her to attribute like conclusions to like causes, and in deep anguish she thought : Can I be mad too, like my sister? My God, is this madness?

She got back under the sheets, and listened attentively to Luis' sobs, which seemed to be getting weaker as if sleep were finally overcoming him. A long time went by during which his aunt grew drowsy also. But suddenly she woke with a feeling of the same furious loathing in its most intense form. Now the memory of her sister did not stop her; there was nothing in her mind to counteract the idea, or rather the delusion, that Luis was a wicked being, a horrible monstrosity, a loathsome creature that ought to be destroyed. He was to blame for all the evils that were oppressing her, and once he had disappeared from the world the sun would shine brighter and life would be happy. That child represented the whole of human perfidy, treason, lying, dishonour and perjury.

A deep darkness reigned in the bedroom. Abelarda, barefoot and in her nightdress, threw a shawl over her shoulders and groped her way forward. Then she retreated, to look for the matches. The idea had just come into her head to go to the kitchen and look for a knife with a good cutting edge. For this she needed a light. As she lit it she looked at Luis, who was at last sleeping soundly. 'What a good opportunity,' she said to herself, 'he won't shout out or struggle. You liar, you conceited young buffoon, now I'll pay you out. Just you begin telling me that nonsense now about seeing God. As if there were such a thing as God anyhow!' After gazing at her little nephew for a while she went out, resolute. The quicker the better. The memory of the child's sobs when he had talked that rubbish about seeing the feet stirred her anger. She reached the kitchen but could not find a knife. But she noticed the axe for splitting firewood, which had been thrown into a corner, and thought that this instrument was more suitable for the purpose, surer, more practical and sharper. She picked up the axe, made the gesture of swinging it and, satisfied with her attempt, returned to the bedroom with the light in one hand, the axe in the other and her shawl over her head. Such a strange and fearful figure had never been seen before in that house. But just as she was opening the glass door of the bedroom she heard a noise and started. It was Victor's key turning in the lock. Like a thief surprised, Abelarda blew out the light with one breath, entered the room and crouched behind the door, hastily concealing the axe. Although she was in darkness, she was afraid that Victor might see her as he crossed the dining-room, and made herself small, for the fury that had led her to her last action had now suddenly changed to fright mixed with some feminine shame. He passed, lighting his way with a match, went into his room and immediately closed the door. The beams of the candle that Victor had lit to go to bed reached Abelarda weakly across the dining-room and through the two glass doors. It was shining for about ten minutes, then it went out, and all was left in darkness. But the wretched girl did not yet dare to light her light. Feeling her way to the bed, she hid the axe under the night-commode beside it, and reflected as she slipped under the sheets: 'Now isn't the

moment. He would cry out, and the other . . . I'd like to give
him such a blow with this axe as . . . But one blow wouldn't be
enough, or two, or a hundred, or a thousand. If I were to go on
hitting him all night still I shouldn't manage to kill him.'

32

THE unfortunate Villaamil was prostrated from the moment
when he learnt of his son-in-law's appointment, and to increase
his misfortune his own ministerial sponsor did nothing about
him. Immediately after breakfast he left the house, and spent
the day going from office to office. He recounted his bad luck to
everyone he met, speaking of it as an atrocious injustice which
– be it said in passing – had not surprised him, for you could
take his word for it . . . he had never expected anything else.
However, under the pressure of harsh necessity, he began to find
his self-imposed pessimism a hindrance. Therefore at moments
he threw it off like a mask and, revealing his naked heart, spoke
in imploring tones: 'My dear Cucúrbitas, I would accept
anything. My rank is administrative chief, third class. But
if they would give me a clerkship in the first division, or – very
well – in the second, I would take it even if it were in the
provinces.'

He recited the same wearisome dirge to the Chief of Personnel, and to every influential friend he had in the house, and he
wrote it in letters to the Minister and to Pez. To Pantoja he said
in great confidence: 'Although it would be a humiliation to me,
I would even accept a third-class clerkship to get out of this
misery. Afterwards, let it be as God wills.'

Then he rushed off to Sevillano, a clerk in Personnel of whom
we shall speak later, and Sevillano said to him with pity:

'Yes, my dear fellow, yes. But calm yourself. We have a
special note. You really must quieten down,' and turned his back
on him.

Little by little this simple man was belying his character,
learning to pester everybody and losing all sense of decency.

After seeing him go through the offices and plaguing his various friends, not excluding the porters, Pantoja said to him in confidence: 'Do you know what your scoundrel of a son-in-law said to this deputy of yours? He said you were off your head and incapable of filling any post in the administration. That's what he said. And the deputy repeated it in Personnel, in front of Sevillano and that brother of Espinosa's, who came to tell me.'

'Did he say that?' (stupefied). 'Oh, I can believe it. He's capable of anything.'

This drove him completely off his head. Now his tireless and insistent importunity and the growing expression of anxiety in his eyes shocked his friends. In some offices they took the precaution of not answering him, or of replying to him only briefly in the hope that he would get tired and take his tune elsewhere. But he was proof against slights, the skin of his pride had thickened. Once when Pantoja was out of the room Espinosa and Guillén made real fun of him: 'Have you heard the latest rumour, my dear Villaamil? They say the Minister's going to present a bill to the Cortes for the introduction of an income tax. La Caña's working it out.'

'Then he's stolen my ideas. My four memoranda were in his possession for more than a year. Now you can see the reward one gets for wearing oneself out, working on a project that will do something to restore this failing Treasury. This is a thieves' country, and a government of nincompoops. When they can't get together a single peseta, then they steal someone else's brains. God help them!'

And he shot out of the office, rushing down the stairs towards Indirect Taxation (in the courtyard on the left) with the intention of blowing up his friend La Caña. Half an hour later he was to be seen once more panting up the weary stairs to spend some time in the Treasury or Customs. Sometimes before he went in he would harangue the porters, telling them the whole of his administrative record: 'I entered the service when Espartero was Regent. Señor Surrá y Rull was Minister, an excellent person and a very careful man. It seems only yesterday that I first climbed this staircase. I was wearing check trousers, which were in fashion at the time, and my silk hat, which was new for the occasion. There's nobody left in the house from those days, since poor Cruz, whom I saw in this very place when I first came, left for a better world two months ago. Oh, what a life it is! Don Alejandro Mon gave me my first promotion. A fine man with incredible determination. He'd plant himself here at eight in the morning and make the whole troop work. That's how he did what he did. But there was no one who got up so early as Don Juan Bravo Murillo, and the biggest night-worker was Don José Salamanca who kept us of the Secretariat here till two or three in the morning. But tell me, do any of you remember Don Juan Bruil, who by the way promoted me to a third-class clerk-ship? Oh, what a man! He had a temper! But our friend Madoz would go off the deep end too. He was a fiery one. We had a Director-General here in '57 who never did a favour to anybody, and never settled any business either unless some woman came to beg him to. . . . Petticoat influence is the bane of this country, believe me.'

The porters humoured him for so long as they could. But they too began in the end to tire of him, and slipped away on the excuse that they had things to attend to. Having poured out his heart in the porters' lodge, the sainted man went in, and there was always somebody in Customs or in Estates, like Urbanito, Cucúrbitas' son, who would invite him to a coffee in order to start him talking and laugh at his excited complaints.

'I'm suffering all this, mark you, because I'm a decent man. If I'd chosen to disclose certain things I know about some high-up persons, if you understand me . . . I mean if I'd been like the rest and gone to the newspaper offices with stories about a bit of dirty business A, or scheme B . . . things would have been very different. But what happens? Even if one decides not to be decent and scrupulous, it's beyond one's powers. One can learn to be an orator, one has to be born a rogue. To be brief, it hasn't even helped me to have written four memoranda that amount to a complete budgetary plan, for a wicked friend to whom I showed them has stolen my idea and given it out as his own. You'd never believe it, but this confounded income tax that they're going to introduce, somewhat late in the day, was my idea. Ten years sweating my brains out over it, and to what purpose? So that a crow can adorn himself with my feathers, or with the work of my quill. I mean, if the Minister were to know this, if the country were to know it, what would happen? Perhaps nothing would happen, because the country and the Minister are going to the dogs and there's no gratitude. I wash my hands of it. I've been dismissed, and if revolutions come let them come. If the country falls into chaos, let it fall. It can go to hell! Afterwards they'll say, "What a pity we didn't introduce those four principles of that good man Villaamil: Morality, Income Tax, Additional Customs, Unification of the Debt." But I shall say, "Too late, too late! You ought to have thought of that before." Then they'll say, "Let Villaamil be Minister", and I shall answer, "When I was willing you were not, and now what's done can't be undone." '

'But, gentlemen, I must go now and leave you to work. In my time we didn't have these breaks. You smoked a cigarette, you drank coffee, then back to work. But now there are clerks who come here to write charades, to concoct farces and accounts of bullfights and write little magazines. That's what the Public Administration has come to; to put it briefly and brutally, it's like a public woman. All this really makes one sick; I don't know why you don't give in your resignations, the whole lot of you, and leave the Minister and the Chief of Personnel on their own, to see how they get along. No, I'm not joking. You're laughing, I see, but it's no laughing matter. Resignation in a body, work stops on a given day, at a given hour . . .'

Finally, tired of his incoherent chatter, they threw him out, saying: 'Don Ramón, you'd better go and get a breather. A walk in the Retiro will do you good.'

He departed muttering, and instead of taking their advice and getting some air into his lungs he went down with his cloak flung roughly about his shoulders into Mutual Exchange, where Montes worked, or into Indirect Taxation, where his friend Cucúrbitas with incredible patience put up with speeches like this: 'I tell you in confidence, between you and me, that I'd be content with a clerkship of the third class. Put it up to the

Minister. I feel very strange in the head, as if my thoughts were rambling. I feel like talking nonsense, and I suspect that sometimes I do. If they don't let me serve those two months I don't know what I shall do. I think I shall soon begin throwing stones. You know my situation. You know that I have no pension because, although I date from before '45, my first post was not a royal appointment. I didn't come on the permanent strength till '46, thanks to Don Juan Martín Carramolino. You remember that. You were under me, and I taught you how to draw up a minute. You joined the National Militia in '54, but I wouldn't because I've never liked a dust-up. That's where your good fortune and my ill fortune begin. Thanks to your helmet you were promoted at a single bound to an inspectorship of Finance, second class, while I was stuck as a first-class clerk. It's incredible, Francisco, that a head-covering could have such influence. They say that Pez owes his whole career to the big silk hat with its broad curly brim that gives him such a grave appearance. I remember very well your saying to me, "Ramón, get yourself a handsome waistcoat, it helps. Wear high collars, very high, very stiff collars because they make you carry your head high, which gives you an air of importance." I took no notice of you, and here I am. Ever since Basilio put on an English frock-coat they've begun to notice him for promotion, and I fancy that our friend Montes' squeaking shoes which lend his personality a sort of boldness or insolence or *keep your hands off me* have had some effect on his progress, which has been considerable. But above all the hat, the hat is the most essential thing, Francisco, and yours seems to me a perfect model . . . high in the crown, tapering to the top, and with a brim rather like a priest's. Then those ties that you indulge in. If they give me a post, I'll wear one like yours. You'll remember now, a third-class clerkship or anything. The point is to get on to the roll, to be something, so that I don't feel even the walls weeping for pity whenever I enter the place. Francisco, you know this house inside out. Do it for God's sake and for the sake of your sons, three of whom you've placed here as aspirants with five thousand, not counting Urbanito who draws twelve. If my wife were a Pez, if she were a fish, not a frog, I should not be high and dry. You seem to have it in your blood. When your kids are born and utter their first cry, you don't give them the teat but shove Statement A, section 8 of the budget in their mouths. Good-bye, do something for me, get me out of this morass that I've fallen into. I don't want to worry you, you've got plenty to do. I'm loaded with work myself. Good-bye, good-bye.'

It must not be supposed that our man was leaving the building. Urged on by irresistible need, he pantingly undertook another painful ascent of the staircase, and arrived breathless at the Secretariat. There on a certain day something unexpected happened. The porters, who generally let him go in, stopped him and, disguising the strict orders they had received to refuse him entry, hinted to him kindly : 'Go home, Don Ramón, and take a rest. A little sleep will calm you down. The chief has locked his door and won't receive anybody.'

This unaccustomed answer annoyed Villaamil and he even tried to override it, claiming that it couldn't apply to him. The unhappy man's cloak swept loose across the floor, and the porters had to restore his hat which had fallen from his venerable head.

'Very well, Pepito Pez, very well,' said the unhappy man breathing with difficulty. 'This is the way you repay your old chief who covered up so many of your mistakes. Ingratitude crops up where you least expect it. Just because I've done you a thousand favours you treat me like a dog. Only human logic. We understand one another now. Good-bye. Oh' (turning back at the door), 'tell the Chief of Personnel, that blown-up air-balloon, that you and he can go and pick daisies.'

33

UP the stairs again and back to Pantoja's office on the second floor. When he entered, Guillén, Espinosa and some other brainless asses were enjoying the cartoons composed by the first-named. There were a series of wretched drawings with couplets under them, coarse, vulgar rubbish with very little wit, which related the whole life of Villaamil from birth to death. Argüelles, who did not approve of Guillén's crude humour, sat away from the group, and was busy with his work. The doggerel related that Señor de Miau had been born at Coria, where the fools come from, which was actually a gross error, for he first saw the light in the province of Burgos; that he had asked for posts from the womb, and that his navel had been tied with red tape. Among other details this illustrated chronicle related in doubtful grammar: *In swaddling-clothes they don't enfold him, but in appointment-papers rolled him*, and *He cries and clamours for the breast; a budget to his lips they pressed*. Then when the worthy functionary reaches adult years: *Bursting with love beyond all measure they wed him to feline treasure*, and no sooner does he embark on matrimonial life than his hardships begin. Villaamil's dismantled home was characterized in this elegant distich: *When they're out of meat and rice they go out to hunt for mice*. But where the inspired versifier showed his genius to the full was in the description of the sublime Villaamilesque labours: *A model of hard work in fact, he invents the Income Tact.* . . . *Before the Minister he set his plans for framing a budget.* . . . *But when the Chief this nonsense read, 'To the madhouse with this man,' he said*. And then the poet threw in this jewel-like thought: *He now lives on in misery thanks to his skill in beggary*, and went on from there to prophesy the triumphal passing of his hero: *In the end he gets his ration, and expires from sheer elation.* . . . *When he dies the Pussies all intone a prayer, 'God rest his soul'*.

On catching sight of Villaamil they hid the offending papers but their ill-suppressed hilarity gave away both the joke and its object. The unhappy man had noticed before that his arrival in the office (if Pantoja was out) gave fresh life to the perpetual mirth of these idlers. Their silences, their remarks, accompanied by grimaces on seeing him come in, the comical gravity of their greetings, revealed to him that day that his person, and perhaps his misfortune, was the subject of unfeeling jokes, and this knowledge struck him to the soul. The confusion of ideas which had already begun in his mind and the exasperation caused to his spirit by all his trials were touching his pride. He was becoming embittered. His inborn meekness was yielding to angry humours, and his peaceful temperament to a quarrelsome susceptibility.

'Let's see, let's see,' he grunted, going up to the group with a very unpleasant look. 'I think you've been talking about me. What are those papers that Guillén's got in his hand? Gentlemen, let us be honest. If any of you has anything to say against me, let him say it to my face. To be frank, I have noticed that all over the house lies and calumnies are being circulated about me. It's an attempt to make me ridiculous, to put the chiefs against me, to represent me to the Minister as a grotesque figure, as a . . . And I want to know who the swine is, who! God damn his soul!' (swinging his cloak across his shoulder and thumping his fist on the nearest table).

All were cold and silent, for they had not expected this assertion of dignity. The gentleman of Philip IV's time was the first to attribute this sudden change of character to mental strain. Not only did he profoundly loathe Guillén, but he felt sorry for his friend. Throwing his arm round Villaamil's shoulder, he begged him to calm himself, and added that in his presence no one would dare to malign any honourable person. But this speech did not calm the old man, for he saw that confounded Guillén with his face flat on the desk choking back his laughter. In a burst of fury he went across to the man, and said in a stifled and trembling voice : 'Let me tell you, you confounded cripple, that no one is allowed to laugh at me. I know, I know that you've been scrawling and making stupid verses about me. They told me in Customs, something about my proposing the income tax to the Minister and being sent off to a madhouse.'

'Me, Don Ramón? What an idea?' replied Guillén, daunted and cowardly. 'I never drew those cartoons. It was Pez Cortázar in Estates, and it was Urbano Cucúrbitas who showed them round here.'

'Well, whoever made them up, the author of that stinking rubbish is a swine and ought to be in a sty. People insult me because they see I'm down. Is that the behaviour of gentlemen? Come on, give me an answer. Is that the way decent people behave?'

The good man swung round and sat down quite exhausted by the efforts this pronouncement had cost him, and went on muttering, as if speaking to himself : 'They're trying to finish me off by every possible means, to discredit me so that the Minister shall think me a crack-pot, a visionary, an idiot.'

Heaving the deepest of sighs, he buried his chin in his breast, and stayed like this for more than a quarter of an hour without speaking a word. The others were silent and looked sideways at him, gravely and perhaps pityingly. For a while nothing was heard but the scraping of Argüelles' pen. Suddenly the creaking of Pantoja's boots announced that personage's approach. Everybody pretended to be hard at work as the chief of the department came in with his hands full of papers. Villaamil did not raise his head to look at his friend, or appear to notice his presence.

'Ramón,' said Pantoja in an affectionate voice, calling from his desk. 'Ramón! But, Ramón, what's the matter?'

Finally his friend heaved a deep sigh, as if waking from sleep, got up and limped over to his table.

'But don't go on like this,' said Don Ventura, clearing a sheaf of papers from the chair beside him so that his friend could sit down. 'You're behaving like a child. They're talking about you round the offices. They say you're beginning to ramble. You really must restrain yourself, and' (becoming slightly irritated) 'in conversations about the financial proposals and the drawing-up of the new budget you must stop coming out with all this nonsense about an income tax. It's all very well as a subject for newspaper articles' (contemptuously) 'or for discussion round a café table with three or four silly idlers of the sort that arrange a country's finances by expenditure of spittle but never pay their tailor or their landlady. But you're a serious person, and you can't maintain that our taxation system, the fruit of experience . . .'

Villaamil got up as if a sharp thorn had pierced the seat of his chair, and his sudden movement interrupted a speech which would no doubt have finished in official language more proper to the *Gaceta* than to human tongue. The good departmental chief was astounded to see the expression of frenzied anger in his friend's face, the trembling of his jaw, the fire that shot from his eyes; and he was even more astounded to hear these angry words: 'But I do maintain. Yes, in God's name I do maintain that only office hacks would continue the present system. I'll go further, only cheats and swindlers. A man must have an inch of cobwebs in his brain if he doesn't see and maintain that an income tax imposed on earnings, or whatever you may call them, is the only rational and philosophical solution of the taxation question. And I'll go further. I'll say that you in this office are a pack of obstructive blockheads, and you, Pantoja, are the worst. I'll say that you're a calamity, the ruin and destruction of this house, and a blight on the country, for you're gnawing and consuming its wealth. You're a lot of complete dolts. And I'll say that to the Minister if he drives me to it, because I don't want a post or appointment or pension rights; all I want is truth first of all, and good government, and a reconciliation . . . a union . . . a harmonization' (striking his forefingers together) 'between the interests of the state and the tax-payer. And the idiot, the swine who says that I want an appointment can meet me man to man, here or in the open street, by the memorial to the Second of May, or in the field beside the canal at midnight and without witnesses' (he was now shouting so loud that the clerks in the next office were disturbed). 'They only take me for a fool because they don't know me, because they have never seen me defending right and justice against the knaves in this house who deny it. I haven't come here to beg for a confounded appointment. I would scorn one. The whole place can go to hell so far as I'm concerned, the director, the Chief of Personnel, and the Minister. All I ask for is order, morality and economy . . .'

He turned his eyes in every direction, and, seeing so many faces around him, raised his arms as if exhorting a mutinous crowd and emitted a savage cry of: 'What we want is an equitable budget.'

He tottered out of the office dragging his cloak behind him. The good Pantoja, scraping his head with his cap, followed him with a compassionate glance that expressed sincere grief.

'Gentlemen,' he said to his clerks and to some others who had been drawn in by curiosity, 'let us pray God for our poor friend. He's gone out of his mind.'

34

SHORTLY before eleven o'clock next day, which was moreover the last of the month, Villaamil toiled up the internal stairs of the Ministry, stopping at every third or fourth step to take breath. When he reached the entrance to the Secretariat, the porters who had seen him depart on the previous evening in the lamentable condition we have described were surprised to find him so peaceful, in his usual modest and kindly state of mind, as if butter would not melt in his mouth. However, they distrusted his meekness, and when the good man sat down on the bench, which was hard and narrow as that of a church, and stretched out his feet to the brazier, the youngest porter went across to him and said: 'What have you come here for, Don Ramón? You ought to look after yourself and stay at home. For you've got nothing urgent to make you wander about here.'

'You may be right, friend Ceferino. Better stay quietly at home and let these gentlemen get out of their troubles for themselves. What's it to do with me? But the state has to pay for the breakages, and one can't see all this wastage without caring. Do you know if they have taken the final budget proposals to the Minister? You don't . . . True, it doesn't concern you. You're not a tax-payer. But let me tell you the new proposals are worse than those that obtain at present. Everything they do here is one long string of stupidities and blunders. But it doesn't affect me. I can stay quietly at home watching the country fall to pieces when it could be swimming in money if they chose.'

Shortly after concluding his speech the poor man found himself alone, meditating deeply. He saw some clerks whom he knew pass by, but as they did not speak to him he said nothing. Perhaps he reflected on the solitude that was growing all round him, and on the speed with which he was forsaken by those who had been his colleagues and till recently had called themselves his friends. The cause of this, he reflected with admirable self-observation, is that my misfortunes have made me rather eccentric, and sometimes my grief is so strong that I say and do things that aren't natural to a man in his senses, things that are foreign to my character and my . . . What is that ugly word? . . . my idiosyncrasies. But let it be in God's hands!

He was distracted from his meditation by the entrance of a friend who went straight up to him. It was Argüelles, the father of a family, swathed in his black cloak or rather half-cloak, in his wide-awake hat, with his waxed moustaches and his little pointed beard jutting over his high collar. He generally dropped into Personnel for a few minutes before going down to Direct Taxation, to pour out the troubles of his heart to a friend who told him all the news and nourished his beliefs in an early promotion.

'What are you doing round here, Villaamil, my friend?' he asked in the tone in which one addresses those seriously ill. 'Shall we have some coffee? But no, perhaps coffee would disagree with you. You ought to look after yourself, and if you take my advice you had much better stay away from this resort for a day or two.'

'Where shall we go?' (getting up).

'To Personnel. We'll have a word or two with Sevillano. He'll tell us what names have been proposed today. Come on.'

And they walked down a long, rather dark corridor which first turned to the right and then to the left. As they went down this crooked and mysterious passage, the figure of Villaamil and Argüelles might have been mistaken for those of Dante and Virgil seeking by hidden signs for the entrance to or exit from the infernal regions they were visiting. It would not have been difficult to make a burlesque Dante out of Villaamil, with his plain appearance and ample cloak. But as poet, you would have had to substitute Quevedo, the parodist of the *Divina Commedia*, for the good Argüelles was more like 'The Bailiff Arrested'* than the author of that work. Neither Dante nor Quevedo dreamt in their fantastic voyages of anything like the

* One of the chapters in Quevedo's *Visions*.

224

labyrinthine offices, the discordant ringing of bells that sounds from every corner of that vast mansion, the opening and closing of screens and doors, the stampings and throat-clearings of the clerks as they hang up their hats and cloaks on the way to their tables; nothing comparable to the to-and-fro of dusty papers, glasses of water, scuttles of coal, to the tobacco-charged atmosphere, to the orders given from desk to desk, to the labour and the buzz, in fact, of those hives in which the bitter honey of the administration is made. Villaamil and his guide entered an office in which there were two tables and one person, who at that moment was changing his hat for a purple velveteen cap and his boots for slippers. It was Sevillano, an official of the Secretariat, a good lad though getting older, well liked in the house and with a reputation for astuteness. He greeted Villaamil with suspicion and looked long into his face: 'Struggling along,' said the perpetually out-of-work official in answer to his question, and took a seat beside his table.

'No news of my case?' said Argüelles, asking a question and making a statement, both together.

'None,' replied the vain Sevillano, who as he sat down at the table seemed actuated by the desire that they should see his embroidered slippers and admire his small foot. 'Nothing to speak of. They haven't proposed you yet or made any signs of doing so.'

'I'm not surprised,' grumbled the other, taking off his cloak and hat as if to counter the sight of Sevillano's slippers with a display of his own curly hair. 'That swine Pantoja has fooled me three times already, and he'll let me down a fourth time if I don't poison his meat. But I'll stand anything so long as that disgusting cripple Guillén doesn't get ahead of me. If they promote him before me; if the father of a family weighed down with children, who carries the whole weight of the office on his shoulders, is passed over in favour of that useless monstrosity who wastes his time drawing monkeys . . .' (turning to Villaamil to ask for his agreement). 'Am I right or am I not? Do you imagine that after all the years I've spent in this profession they still think it too early to give me promotion? Do you think they'll give it to that scarecrow, that grotesque instead, that bad man and worse friend who doesn't know how to draw up a minute?'

'But that's precisely why, precisely why, because he's useless,' affirmed Villaamil with profound pessimism; 'that's why he's got an assured career.'

'That's more than I can bear,' declared the gentleman of Philip IV's time, furiously stamping his foot. 'If they promote him before they promote me I shall go to the Minister and say to him . . . Well, I shall go and give him a piece of my mind. It's worse than insulting a man by spitting in his face. Yes, because this dirty business makes your blood boil, it makes you want to cast morality to the winds and join forces with Judas. That cripple Guillén with his buffoonery and his little verses and all his swinery has made himself popular hereabouts. They laugh at his stupid jokes. We must all share the blame, I admit, for encouraging him in the first place. But I promise you, my dear Don Ramón, that he'll never show his scribblings in front of me again. I'll tell him what's what, I'll tell him . . .'

Argüelles paused, thinking that he saw signs of excitement in Villaamil's face. But contrary to his fears the old man was listening quietly and showed no distress on being reminded of those coarse jokes.

'Let him be, let him be,' he answered. 'For my part, I know how to rise superior to these buffooneries. When I found them making fun of me yesterday, you remember, I didn't say so much as a word, did I? These things aren't worth noticing, one just scorns them. I met young Cucúrbitas in the street afterwards, Urbanito, the lad in Customs, and he told me that Guillén had been here with his cartoons. He said they're just idiotic, there's nothing funny in them. All about how when I was a child they wrapped me in documents instead of swaddling clothes, and about my proposing an income tax to the Minister. And I ask him now, what does it matter to him, the great idiot, whether I proposed an income tax or not? What does he understand about such subjects? They're far beyond the understanding of a seven-months frog like him. Then he says that I go round begging. A horrible calumny. Because if my need does compel me in the terrible straits I'm in to ask a friend for help that doesn't mean that I'm not going to pay him back. It doesn't make me a swindler. But one has to bear these insults with great patience. One mustn't give that infamous libeller even the pleasure of hearing one complain because it flatters his vanity to know that he can hurt. Scorn and indifference, that's what he deserves, and let him vomit poison till his soul runs dry. No, I shall never favour those reptiles even with so much as a glance. But this one I've received into my bosom, gentlemen. He visits my house, pays compliments to my family and drinks my wine. When he's there he seems to love us all like a brother, the repulsive beast! But I'll go further, I'll say that Pantoja is partly to blame too for letting him waste time making up these obscenities. I know all his scrawlings as well as if I'd seen them because Urbanito described them to me to the last detail. That boy's considered a fool, but I believe he has plenty of talent, and as for his memory there's no one to beat him. He told me also that Guillén has taken the four initial letters of my memoranda and made them into the nickname of Miau that he gives me in these cartoons of his. That M.I.A.U. is like the I.N.R.I., the infamous letters they put above Christ on the cross. Now that they've crucified me between thieves, let the rest be fulfilled. Let them put those four letters above my head and so call my great mission into scorn and contempt.'

35

SEVILLANO and Argüelles had begun by listening to him with some respect, but they hesitated between pity and laughter when they heard this conclusion. In the end pity prevailed, and Sevillano expressed it in this form: 'You are right to despise your misfortunes. There's nothing more disgusting than to make a mock of a good man who's in trouble. Those idiots brought me the cartoons too, but I refused to look at them. . . . Now, if you gentlemen would like, we'll take some coffee.'

The boy came in with the tray. Villamil politely refused the offer, and the other two sat down to enjoy their brimming cups of that aromatic beverage which is the joy and consolation of office life.

'I must admit,' stated the official without a post with all the serenity of a man who is master of his faculties, 'that you begin to get used to injustices, that you come to expect blows, and that you accustom yourself to the thought of seeing this louse get ahead of you. Spanish logic can never fail. The rogue before the honest man; the ignorant above those with knowledge, and the upright official comes at the bottom, always at the bottom. And he can be grateful if they don't reward his services by taking away his livelihood. But I don't know, I don't know that this isn't the logical consequence of faithful services.'

'I shall kick up a fuss, believe me I shall, a hell of a fuss,' said the father of a family between sips, 'if they promote him before me, I'll make such a noise that the whole deaf and dumb school will hear me, you take my word for it.'

'They'll hear you and say nothing, and you'll just have to put up with it. Now follow my reasoning' (drawing his chair up to the coffee drinkers). 'Who have you got to back you? Nobody. I say nobody because you've got no woman behind you.'

'That's true.'

'Good. Now when I see a ridiculous appointment, I ask: Who's the woman? It's proved again and again. Every time a nobody is raised above a useful official, you've only to lend an ear and you'll hear the rustle of skirts. Will you bet me I don't know who asked for the cripple's promotion? Why, his female cousin, the widow of that major fellow – she's in the Philippines – that woman Enriqueta. She's a shameless one. She has the morals of the farmyard, and the story goes that she had some sort of affair with our excellent Director. Now that you know at what doors this scoundrel Guillén knocks, you can help me see this thing straight. It'll be no use. Our friend Argüelles with all his children at his back will get nothing. He'll be left barking in the street, and the cripple will get his promotion, and on with the dance.'

Sevillano confirmed the disturbed Villaamil's observations with a smile, for he did not seem so unbalanced when he said things so close to the mark; and the gentleman of Philip IV's time stroked his pomaded hair and twisted his moustache, pulling so often at the ends that he almost tugged it out by the roots.

'Gracious me, I've been saying this for a long time. You've got to be pretty shameless to serve this devil of a state. But seeing that our friend Villaamil's in a good mood today we'll tell him something he doesn't know. Who backed Victor Cadalso and made them bury that complaint against him and give him promotion into the bargain?'

'There must have been a woman behind that, some impressionable young lady hereabouts, because Victor is clever at catching them.'

'Two deputies backed him,' said Sevillano, 'but all the wind they blew into his sails achieved nothing, until some pressure came from above.'

'Yes, Ildefonso Cabrera told me that,' observed the old man, getting angry; 'he said that scamp has connexions with marquesas, duchesses and all the big ladies in high society.'

'But take no notice of that, Don Ramón,' put in Argüelles. 'After all, that son-in-law of yours is just a vulgarian . . . nothing but a pretentious vulgarian. You don't see really well turned out young men any more, as you did when I was young. You can laugh at these conquests of Victor's. All the support he's got is from a neighbour of mine. On the first floor of my house there's a marquis living, I forgot his title. He's a Valencian. It's something like Benengeli, something with a Moorish sound. This marquis has an aunt who's been widowed twice . . . quite a youngster as you might say. My wife, who's over fifty, assures me that when she was in short clothes (my wife, you understand) she knew this lady in Valencia and she was married already. She'll be well on into her sixties, and although she was once a handsome woman no paint will restore her now, no remedies will give her back her good looks.'

'But my dear son-in-law seduced the blameless innocent for all that.'

'Wait a moment. It's public property in Valencia that this old shark fell madly in love with Cadalso, and that he . . . fell for her also, I suppose, neither more nor less. They came to Madrid together; lovers there, lovers here. I don't need telling because I see him in the street waiting for the old woman since the marquis and marquesa won't have him in the house. She comes out in her carriage, all dolled up, all soft and tender, with curls on her cheeks, false ones of course, and her face thicker in paint than the Raphael in the Prado. She stops on the corner of Relatores, and there the terror of the maidens gets in and they go off I don't know where. And I've heard from the footman who is my neighbour in an attic on the left that the old fright receives a letter every day, and sends her young man three sheets straight off in return. The footman takes her letters to the post-office, and tells me the name and address on the envelope . . . Quiñones 13, second floor.'

'If that surprised me,' declared Villaamil, half-smiling, half-scornful, 'I should be an infant at the breast. And the old spectre came here, to the sacred temple of the administration' (growing heated) 'to contaminate the state with her disgraceful recommendations in favour of that idler!'

'No, she never appeared here, there was no need,' Sevillano pointed out. 'She has wires she can pull. Women like that can play on the whole Ministry without ever setting a foot inside.'

'They only have to say a word to some big nob, and a note's delivered here immediately.'

'One of those that don't ask but command.'

'Look sharp now and get it done. And it's done in a flash. What we need here is a good lightning-conductor to catch these sparks – a Minister with character. But where is this Messiah to be found?' (striking himself hard on the knee). 'The confounded administration is a dirty whore; you can't have dealings with her without losing your honour. But if you've got children, my dear Argüelles, you can't help prostituting yourself, can you? Very well then, look somewhere around for a plushy coat to cover you, and then you're all right. Once you've got that to cover you your conquests come. . . . Soon you've got a lamprey covered with oysters on the end of your hook. Courage, young man. If I were twenty years younger!'

Sevillano laughed, and Argüelles preened himself, bursting

with fatuity and twirling his ridiculous dyed moustache. He did not seem to have taken this exhortation to himself, for age had not cured him of the vanity of a Don Juan.

'Frankly, gentlemen,' he said in the voice of a very experienced man, 'I have never cared for love as a business. Love for love's sake. I wouldn't take on a creature like this one of Victor's if I were paid for it. She's as old as Methuselah, and everything she has is false, absolutely everything, believe me.'

'No squeamishness, but up and at them!' said Villaamil, who had been seized with a nervous giggle. 'These aren't the times for making a face at anything. This father of a family is a terrible fellow. Nothing pleases him except tender young maidens.'

'You mean it as a joke but you've spoken the truth. From fifteen to twenty. Fools can have the rest.'

'Come now, if you were to chance on a rosebud like Victor's. . . . Because she must have the rhino, and with her there would be no empty purses. . . . Now things are becoming clear to me: when my son-in-law finished up the money he got from that swindle in Excise, he dipped into this old baggage's war-treasure. Well' (slapping his knee once more) 'we live in a confounded age in which we can't even blush for shame because the dung, the confounded crust of dung that cakes our faces won't let us.'

He got up to go. Argüelles gave a sigh and with a gesture took his leave of Sevillano, who got down to his work before they went out.

'Let's go to the office,' said the Bailiff Arrested, throwing his cloak across his chin, taking his friend by the arm and plunging into the passages. 'That beast Pantoja will scold at me if I'm late. What a life, Don Ramón, what a life! And by the way, did you notice that all the time we were talking about the lady who protects Victor, Sevillano didn't utter a word? He's raked up an old mummy himself, that's why. Yes, he has. Didn't you know? The widow of that man Pez y Pizarro who was director of lotteries in Havana, the cousin of our friend Don Manuel. Everybody in the place knows it. She looks after him, and gets him his spot of promotion every two years.'

'What are you saying there?' (stopping and gazing into his

face in a truly Dantesque attitude). 'So Sevillano too. Yes, I always used to say that young man was going ahead too fast. I was Inspector of Finances when he came in as an aspirant with five thousand.'

He crossed himself and they continued towards Direct Taxation. Pantoja and the rest received the poor suspended official with alarm, fearing a scene like that of the day before. But the old man reassured them by his peaceful tone and the relative serenity of his expression. Without deigning to glance at Guillén, he went and sat beside the chief to whom he said behind his hand: 'I'm feeling very well today, Ventura. I slept well last night, and woke up fresh, and now I'm contented, believe me, I'm shining with contentment.'

'It's better so, old man, better so,' replied his friend, looking into his eyes. 'What brings you here?'

'Nothing. Affection for the place. I'm cheerful today. See now, I'm laughing' (he laughs). 'Maybe I've come today for the last time, though. It amuses me, I assure you. This house amuses me. You see things here that almost make you die of laughing.'

Work ended earlier than usual that day because it was pay-day, the happy date which terminates the anguish of the end of the month and opens a new era of hope. On pay-day there is more light in the halls of that workshop, a purer air, and an indefinable transparency and joy that finds its way into the hearts of those unhappy labourers at the public finances.

'They give you your pay today,' said Villaamil to his bosom friend. The easy, good-humoured smile he had been assuming vanished from his face.

It was already obvious from the noise of footsteps, the ringing of bells and the stir in the offices that the operation had begun. Work stopped, documents were tied into their bundles, desks were closed, and pens lay on tables amidst a confusion of papers and drying sand, which stuck to sweaty hands. In some departments the officials were entering the cashiers' office as their names were called, where they had to sign the receipt and received their money. Into others the cashiers sent a messenger who carried the blessed cash on a tray, in silver and small notes, together with the receipt. The chief of the department under-

took the distribution of these metallic rations, and made each
man sign for what he was given.

36

ONE thing is certain. When Villaamil saw the porter enter with
the welcome tray, he got very excited. His incredible cheerful-
ness increased, and he expressed it in the crudest way.

'Come, come, what faces you're all making. Here is the Holy
Visitation at last, the joy of the month, the blessed St Gold-
bags. You're hardly going to fall into a decline with all this
treasure.'

Pantoja began the distribution. They all received their full
salaries except one of the junior clerks to whom the chief
handed an IOU he had given to a money-lender saying : 'This is
cancelled.'

And Argüelles received only a third, the rest being held back.
He made a grimace as he accepted the money and signed the
receipt with a flourish which proclaimed his fury. The great
Pantoja then took his share with ceremonious deliberation,
putting the notes in his wallet and the money in his waistcoat
pocket, tucking it well down so that it should not fall out.
Villaamil did not take his eyes off him while the operation
lasted, and did not cease to watch him till the last coin had
disappeared. His jaw trembled and his hands danced.

'Are you going?' he asked his friend as he got up. 'We can
take a stroll. I'm in a very good mood . . . today. Have you
noticed it? It's been very amusing.'

'I shall stay a little longer,' replied the upright official, who
wanted to rid himself of this encumbrance. 'I've got to go into
the Secretariat for a minute or two.'

'Good-bye then. I'm strolling off. I'm very happy. I shall buy
myself some pills on the way home.'

'Some pills? Yes, they'll do you good.'

'I expect so. Good-bye, till we meet again. Long life to you,
gentlemen, and a good digestion. I'm very well, thank you.'

On the broad staircase the multitudes all pouring out of the offices at the same time met like tributaries that swell a great river. Direct Taxation and Estates together disgorged their personnel on the second floor; and the current continued downward swelled by the numerous herd of Secretariat, Treasury and Customs. The human torrent, kicking up the deuce of a noise on every step, was scarcely contained by the staircase, and the noise of their steps mingled with the cheerful and sparkling pay-day conversation. To Villaamil's ears the chink of coins recently shoved into so many pockets was an additional element in this immense din. He reflected that the metal of these coins must still be cold but that it would soon warm up with bodily contact, and melt away under the fire of need. When they reached the great hall that lay between the staircase and the entrance, the crowds from Indirect Taxation, the Treasury and Mutual Exchange flowed in, and before reaching the street all currents were confused. Shabby cloaks were in greater numbers than worn overcoats; but there were also brand-new ones and shining silk-hats which stood out among the quantity of rubbed bowlers, green with age. The sound of heels deafened the whole house. But Villaamil continued to hear above the clatter of footsteps that persistent clink of five-peseta pieces. Today, he reflected, casting his whole soul into a sigh, they've issued almost all the pay in newish five-peseta pieces, and some of it in two-peseta coins minted under Alfonso.

As the current flowed into the street, the noise died down, and the building remained almost empty and deserted, and full of the thick dust raised by their footsteps. But detachments of stragglers were still emerging from the offices. The whole population of these crowded offices amounted to three thousand, three thousand salaries of different amounts that the state threw back into circulation, returning indirectly to the tax-payer some portion of what it had pitilessly extracted from him. The crowd had received its pay and was happy; and this happiness, a characteristic common to humanity, gave it a pleasing and comforting look. It was no doubt an honourable and harmless crowd, cured of the fear of revolutions, on the side of order and stability, a population with overcoats and no other political ideas except to secure and defend the stew on their stoves; the bureaucratic proletariat, the ballast of the famous ship of state; a mass bred from the crossing of the people with the ruling bourgeoisie, which formed the cement that binds and solidifies the structure of government.

Villaamil was swathing himself in his cloak to guard himself from the cold of the street when someone tapped him on the shoulder. He turned round and saw Cadalso, who helped him to get it on and secure it round his neck.

'What is it? What's making you laugh?'

'It's . . . because I'm so happy this afternoon. But it's got nothing to do with you. Can't a man feel happy when he has a fancy to?'

'Of course . . . but . . . are you going home?'

'That's another thing that's no business of yours. Where are you going?'

'Upstairs to fetch my deed of appointment. I'm in a very good mood today too.'

'Have they given you another promotion? It wouldn't surprise me. You've got all the cards up your sleeve. They'll be making you Minister next, over everybody's head. But reap your harvest now before the supply of old harridans runs out.'

'Don't be witty. I'm in a good mood because I've made it up with my sister Quintina and her barbarian of a husband. He's to keep that confounded house at Vélez Málaga, which isn't worth a fig, and to pay the costs, and I . . .'

'Dot and carry three. . . . Another thing that doesn't affect me any more than if there are fleas on the moon. What do I care about your sister Quintina, or Ildefonso, or whether you choose to make your damned peace with them or not?'

'I was . . .'

'Go on, up the stairs. Run up the stairs and leave me alone. In what low-down inn have we ever met over a meal, I should like to know? You follow your flower-strewn path and I'll follow mine. But I'll tell you one thing : with all your good luck I don't envy you in the very least. I prefer honour without ships to ships without honour. Good-bye.'

He gave Cadalso no further time for explanations, but again

tightening his collar went out into the street. But before he left the door, his cloak was plucked once more, to the accompaniment of these friendly words: 'Oh, my dear Villaamil . . . but perhaps you'd rather be alone.' Urbanito Cucúrbitas, a fair, overgrown youth, with thin hair, long legs, a large Adam's apple and an affectation of dignity, resembled the precocious offspring of that breed of hen known as Cochin China. He wore an elegant check suit, a very high collar like a paper cornet and a buff bowler. His hands and feet were enormous, he was spotlessly clean and his laughing mouth displayed all his molars, including those that might have been called wisdom-teeth if he had had any wisdom.

'Hullo, Urbanito! Have you drawn your pay?'

'Yes, I've got it here' (tapping his purse and making the money clink). 'Almost all in pesetas. I'm going to take a walk in the Castellana.'

'To look out for some little conquest, eh? Lucky man! The world's at your feet. And what a smile! But see, I'm in a good mood today. And tell me, have your young brothers drawn their salaries too? Blessed are the children into whose mouths the state puts a nipple or feeding-bottle. You'll make your way, Urbanito. I maintain that you're a clever fellow, though the general opinion is that you're a fool. It's I that am the fool here. Do you know what I deserve? To be called into the Minister's office, and made to kneel there for three hours in a dunce's cap crowned with ass's ears . . . because I've been an imbecile and spent my life believing in morality and justice and an equitable budget. I deserve to be made to run the gauntlet, and to be called insulting nicknames, to be called El Señor de Miau, and to have caricatures made of me and vulgar doggerel to raise laughter even from the walls of this house. But I'm not saying this in a complaining way. I'm laughing and happy, as you can see. I find my own imbecility a frightfully good joke.'

'Now look, my dear Don Ramón' (putting both hands on his shoulders). 'I never had anything to do with those scribblings. I admit that I laughed a bit when Guillén brought them into the office. I don't deny that I felt tempted to show them to my papa and I did show them to him. . . .'

'But I'm not asking you for explanations, my dear boy.'

'Let me finish. And my father got angry and almost hit me. The consequence was that when Guillén heard the things Papa said he vanished from our office like a flash and never came back. I mean the whole thing can be taken as a passing joke. But you know very well that I respect you, and I think it's idiotic to put together the initial letters of your four memoranda, which signify nothing, and make a ridiculous and senseless word out of them.'

'Gently, gently, my young friend' (looking into his eyes). 'That the word Miau is just an inanity I don't for a moment deny. But I don't agree that the four initials haven't a profound meaning. . . .'

'Oh! Have they?' (in astonishment).

'Because you'd have to be very stupid or downright dishonest not to recognize and admit that M I A and U have this meaning. My Ideas Achieve Universality.'

'Oh, now . . . as I was saying . . . you must take care of yourself, Don Ramón.'

'Although there are some who maintain . . . and I wouldn't be so bold as to contradict them flatly . . . some who maintain, perhaps with some justification, that the four mysterious letters should be read thus: Minister Imperial Administrator Universal.'

'Well, you know, that interpretation seems very clever and very well concealed, I think.'

'What I say is that you have to examine each version impartially, for one says one thing, another says another, and it's not easy to decide. I advise you to look at them quietly, and study them, for that's what the government gives you a salary for. Just go into the office for an hour or two in the afternoons for a little while, and not every day either. And let your young brothers study them too with the feeding-bottle of their appointments in their mouths. Remember me to Papa. Tell him that I've been crucified as an imbecile on the shameful beams of my stupidity, and that it's fallen to him to thrust a lance into my side, and to Montes to give me the sponge with gall and wormwood at the moment when I pronounce my Four Last Words, which will be "A foul death to the unclean".* The word unclean means, I wish you to understand, covered with filth or smeared with fetid and disgusting stuff, which is the symbol for hanging around without a job, or let us say for having principles.'

'Aren't you going home, Don Ramón? Would you like me to go with you? I'll get a cab.'

'No, my dear boy. Go and take your stroll. I'm going home slowly. But I've got to buy some pills first . . . just here at the chemist's.'

'Then I'll come with you . . . and if you'd like us to go to the doctor first.'

'The doctor?' (with an outrageous laugh). 'I've never felt better in my life, never felt stronger. Don't talk to me about doctors. With these little pills . . .'

'Wouldn't you really like me to come with you?'

'No, and what's more I beg you not to. A man has his little secrets, and the seemingly unimportant act of buying this or that medicine may make him feel shy. Shyness turns up, my boy, where you least expect it. How do you know that I'm not a young, I mean an old rake? So you take your way, and I'll take my way to the chemist's. Good-bye, my clever boy, spoilt darling of the Ministry, get all the amusement you can. Don't go to the office except to draw your pay. Make plenty of conquests. Always aim very high. Cling on to the well-placed ones, and when they file a complaint against you, then play the dirtiest game you know. Good-bye, good-bye. You know how fond I am of you.'

The overgrown youth turned down the Calle de Alcalá, and Villaamil, after making certain that no one was following him, took the direction of the Puerta del Sol. But before reaching it, he entered what he had called the chemist's, which was the gunsmith's shop at Number 3.

* The initial letters of this too are MIAU in Spanish.

In those few days Doña Pura and her sister noticed something strange about the good Villaamil's bearing, conversation and behaviour. Though in matters of relative importance he appeared excessively sluggish and apathetic, in others of no gravity or significance he displayed a brutal energy. On the subject of Abelarda's wedding, of fixing a date and settling certain details proper to that great event, the man did not open his mouth. Nor did his future son-in-law's handsome inheritance (for God had now called his uncle the lawyer to his bosom) draw from him even one of those hyperboles of enthusiasm that bubbled from Doña Pura's lips. On the other hand, Villaamil conferred on any trifle the importance of a decisive event, and if his wife shut the door rather noisily (because her nerves were strained) or if she had taken a number of *La Correspondencia* to make curl-papers, he would kick up a fuss that would last for half the morning.

It must also be observed that Abelarda treated the arrangements for her wedding with a supreme indifference which, in the eyes of the senior Miau, was merely the proper modesty of a well-brought-up girl, who had no will apart from her parents. On account of the family's straits, the preparations had to be very small, almost nothing. They were limited to the making of a few new underclothes, the material for which was bought with a gift from Victor, about which nothing was said to Villaamil to spare his feelings. It must be noted that since that scene in the Comendadoras Victor scarcely spent a moment in the house. He very occasionally came in to sleep, but lunched and dined out every day. The family's evening parties were unchanged, except for Pantoja and his family who came more rarely, for reasons which Doña Pura could not fathom, and for Guillén who definitely went into eclipse, very much to the pleasure of the three Miaus. The repeated absences of Virginia Pantoja caused great delays in the rehearsals for the play. The young lady of the house completely forgot her part, and for this reason and because Pura felt a distaste for entertaining until the problem of her husband's appointment was solved, the plan for a theatrical production was abandoned.

Federico Ruiz, always consistent, came sometimes in the afternoons, apologizing a thousand times to the Miaus for taking up their time since he knew that they must have their hands full with the wedding preparations. O happy preparations! How many towers and castles did the fertile imagination of Villaamil's spouse erect on these fragile foundations! One morning Ruiz came in much out of breath, followed by his wife, both darting glances of joy, drunk with jubilation and longing for their friends to share their good news.

'I've come,' said the almost breathless Federico, 'to ask you to congratulate us. I know you're very fond of us and that you'll be glad to know I've got an appointment.'

Federico and Pepita were embraced successively by all three Miaus. At this point the good Villaamil came out of his study scenting happiness and, before Ruiz had time to divulge his good news, threw his arms round him and said: 'A thousand, thousand congratulations, my dear, dear fellow. You richly deserve it, you more than deserve it.'

'Thank you, thank you very much,' said Ruiz, tightly clasped in Villaamil's huge arms which pressed him in a nervous spasm. 'But for heaven's sake don't hug me so tight or I shall choke. Don Ramón . . . Oh, oh, you're squeezing me to death.'

'But, man,' said Doña Pura in surprise and alarm, 'what a way of embracing!'

'I only,' stammered the man without a post, 'I only want to give him a hearty congratulation, a whale of a congratulation to make him remember me and how pleased I am at his triumph. And what is the appointment?'

'A little commission here in Madrid . . . that's what's so lucky . . . to consider and propose improvements in the teaching of the natural sciences . . . to see that it gets practical results.'

'Oh, what a splendid idea! I can't imagine why they've never thought of that before. And this miserable country has gone on all these years without knowing how the natural sciences are taught. Fortunately, my friend Ruiz, our uncertainties will all be resolved now. Our wise government has a real talent for choosing personnel. That's why the nation's overflowing with prosperity. Yes, your little appointment will produce results, I'm sure of it. A few more brainwaves like that and our oppressed country will be saved. I congratulate you heartily, indeed I do. And I'll say more, Señor de Ruiz; if you're to be congratulated, the country is to be congratulated too. They should be sounding the castanets with joy at the thought that there'll be someone studying this subject. Don't you agree? But with your permission I must go back to work. A thousand million congratulations.'

Without waiting to hear how Federico would reply to his expansive enthusiasm, the good man quickly shut himself in his study. The Ruizes, also the Miaus, were somewhat put out by the voluble and excited way in which he offered his congratulations, but they disguised their surprise. The happy couple departed to continue their visits of apprisal, and to harvest congratulations in sheaves. And this little commission was not the only cause of contentment that Federico had that morning, for the post had brought him another unexpected gratification. It was nothing less than the diploma of a Portuguese society devoted to the purpose of honouring acts of heroism at fires, and also those who in their writings propagate the best theories concerning this useful service. Every member of this association had the right, according to the diploma, of using the title *Bombeiro, salvador da humanidade*,* and to wear a most handsome uniform with glistening braid. The design of this dazzling tunic accompanied the nomination. The man was bursting with pride at his commission (on which the scientific future of Spain depended), at the honours of *bombeiro*, and at the shining uniform in which he would appear on the first solemn and public occasion that offered.

Young Luis went out for a walk with Paca that afternoon, and when he came back sat down to do his lessons at the dining-room table. After her extraordinary and incredible outburst on the famous night about which we have spoken, Abelarda's mind

* Fireman, saviour of humanity.

was apparently so well restored that a beneficent and healing oblivion expunged all trace of those events from her thoughts. She could remember them only with the clouded uncertainty of a dream, like a stupid nightmare the image of which vanished with the light and the realities of day. The little nobody was busy sewing her trousseau, and Luis, bored with his lessons, was amusing himself by taking and hiding her cotton reels.

'Child,' his aunt said to him, not in the least put out, 'don't make me angry or I'll give you a smack.'

Instead of smacking him she gave him a kiss, and her little nephew, growing more enterprising, invented some more of his tricks, which as usual were not very harmful. Pura was helping her daughter with the cutting-out, and Milagros was functioning in the kitchen, all over smuts and with her overall down to her feet. Villaamil was still shut in his den. Such were the dispositions of each member of the family when the bell rang and Victor appeared. They were all surprised, for he did not usually come in at such an hour. He went to his room without a word, and could be heard washing and taking clothes out of his trunk. No doubt he had been invited to a grand supper. So Abelarda thought, as she made a special point of neither looking nor so much as glancing at the door of that miserable apartment.

But the strange thing was that no sooner did the monster enter than she felt, suddenly and in terrifying strength, the same perturbation as on that distant night. Her mental disturbance burst on her like a bomb, and at the same instant all her blood froze. Her lips contracted in bitter hatred, her nerves tingled, and in the tendons of her arms and hands she began to feel a brutal itch to seize, to crush, to tear something to pieces; something that was very dear, very tender and moreover absolutely defenceless. Little Luis, at this critical moment, had the bad idea of pulling the thread of her tacking so that the cloth puckered. . . .

'Child, if you don't stop that, you'll see!' shouted Abelarda, an electric charge shooting through her body and her eyes glowing like coals.

Perhaps nothing worse would have happened. But the silly boy, deciding to be very bold, gave the thread another pull and the fat was in the fire! Without thinking what she was doing, acting like an unconscious mechanism that receives an impulse from a hidden source, Abelarda stretched out her arm which seemed hard as iron, and with her first slap caught Luis full in the face. The smack could have been heard in the street. As he recoiled, the chair on which he was sitting tottered and fell over with a crash.

Doña Pura gave a scream: 'Oh, darling, darling! Abelarda!'

And Abelarda in blind savagery pounced on her victim, digging her furious fingers into his chest and throat. As caged and torpid wild beasts recover all their ferocity at the first scratch they give their tamer, and with the sight and smell of first blood lose the sluggish apathy of captivity, so as she knocked Luis over and dug her nails into him Abelarda was no longer a woman but a monstrous being created in a trice by the insane perversion of her womanly nature.

'You damned little beast! I'll throttle you! You liar, you hypocrite, I'll kill you,' she muttered, grinding her teeth, and then began blindly groping for the scissors to plunge them into him. Fortunately they were out of her reach.

This act struck such terror into Doña Pura that she was quite paralysed and unable to step in and stop the disaster. She could do nothing but emit shouts of anguish and despair. Milagros rushed in, also Victor in his shirt-sleeves. The first thing they did was to drag young Cadalso from his aunt's claws — no difficult operation because, once the initial attack was over, Abelarda's strength ebbed quickly. Her mother pulled her away and helped her to get up. But while she was still on her knees, convulsed and quite overwrought, the girl babbled on in a staccato and trembling voice: 'This horror! This useless creature! He wants to destroy me and all the family with me.'

'But, Abelarda, what's the matter?' cried her mamma, taking no account of the brutal assault. Victor and Milagros meanwhile examined little Luis, to see if he had any broken bones.

The child, with a flushed face and breathing heavily, burst into tears. 'My God, what a horrible thing to do!' muttered Victor with a grim look. At that moment a new phase of the crisis set in for Abelarda. She gave a terrible roar, clenched and ground her teeth, turned up the whites of her eyes, and fell down like a corpse, contracting her arms and legs and snoring loudly. Villaamil then appeared and was alarmed by the spectacle: his daughter in a faint; Luis crying and with a scratched face; Doña Pura not knowing whom to help first; and the others speechless and stupefied.

'It's nothing,' said Milagros at last, running to fetch a glass of water to splash on her niece's face.

'Isn't there any ether in the place?' asked Victor.

'Darling, my darling!' exclaimed her father. 'What's the matter with you? Come to your senses.'

They had to hold her to prevent her from hurting herself, for she was still kicking convulsively and wildly swinging her arms. Finally a stupor set in which was as violent as the attack. The girl began to sob, and to pant heavily as if she were choking, and a flood of tears marked the final stage of this fierce attack. However hard they tried to comfort her, her flow of tears would not stop. They took her to bed, and there she went on crying, pressing her hands to her heart. She did not seem to remember what she had done. Villaamil and Cadalso together had succeeded in quietening little Luis by persuading him that it had all been a somewhat clumsy joke.

Suddenly the head of the household faced up to his son-in-law and with trembling jaw, intensely sallow cheeks and a look of fury in his eyes shouted: 'You're to blame for all this, you rogue. Clear out of my house at once. I wish to heaven you'd never entered it.'

'So I'm to blame, am I? He says I'm to blame,' replied Cadalso brazenly. 'It's been clear to me for some time that you're not quite right in the head.'

'One thing's certain,' observed Pura, emerging from the next room, 'before you came we didn't have this sort of thing happening here, that nobody can understand.'

'Oh, you too! So it seems you've been doing me a favour by letting me live here. And I thought I was helping you to keep yourselves from starving. Where will you get a better lodger if I go?'

Villaamil could not find words to express his indignation a

this insolence. His hand brushed the back of a chair, and he felt an itch to lift it in the air and bring it down on his son-in-law's head. He was able to restrain himself, however, and repressing his rage with the utmost effort said to him in the hollow voice of a precentor: 'Your kind offices are at an end. From now on you are not wanted here. Pack your things and clear out, with no more excuses and no more delay.'

'Don't get excited. Anyone would think I'd been living here in clover.'

'In clover or not in clover' (on the point of bursting) 'clear out this instant. Go and live with the scarecrows who protect you. What use can you make of this poor unlucky family? There are no letters of appointment, no important positions, no influence here. Here, as you might say, there's nothing at all. But we are happy in our honest poverty. Can't you see how contented I am?' (his teeth chattering). 'You, on the other hand, even at the height of your glory, will have no peace, for it has been obtained by dishonour. Quickly now, into the street. Señor de Miau wishes never to see you again.'

Victor was livid, Doña Pura was shocked, Luis was on the point of bursting into fresh tears, and Milagros was making a wry face.

'Very well,' said Cadalso in the debonair manner that he knew so well how to assume when his intentions were malicious. 'I'm going. That's what I wanted too. I've only been staying out of charity, because I'm a support here, not a liability. But the break will be complete. I shall take my son with me.'

The two Miaus looked at him crestfallen, Villaamil clenched his teeth ferociously.

'What do you expect, then? After what has happened here today,' added Victor, 'do you expect me to leave my own flesh and blood in this place?'

The logic of this argument disconcerted all the Miaus of both sexes.

'But don't be so silly!' said Doña Pura insinuatingly, in the hope of coming to an agreement. 'Do you think this will ever happen again? And where are you going to take the boy, eh? The poor fellow doesn't want to leave us.'

She was on the point of tears, and Milagros said: 'No. The boy's not leaving this place.'

'Oh yes, he is,' affirmed Cadalso with brutal resolution. 'Come on. Bring me my son's clothes so that I can pack them with mine.'

'But where are you going to take him? Don't be so simple. What ideas you do get into your head.'

'I know what I'm doing. His Aunt Quintina will look after him and bring him up better than you.'

Doña Pura sat down, overcome by a great anguish. She broke into a cold sweat and her heart pounded. The mother was on the point of falling into a faint like her daughter. Villaamil turned round and round as if sent spinning by an inner whirlwind that blew through his brain. Then he stopped still, spread his legs, raised his enormous arms and, taking up the attitude of St Andrew nailed to the cross, roared with all the force of his lungs: 'Let him take the boy away then. Let him have him, and the devil go with him! You women are crazy, you have no courage. Don't you know that "A foul death strikes the unclean"?'*

And he ran towards his study bumping against the walls. His wife followed him, fearing that he would suddenly fling himself from the balcony into the street.

38

'I SHAN'T give in, I shan't give in,' said Victor to Milagros when they were left alone. 'I shall take my son. Don't you understand that I couldn't live in peace if I were to leave him here after what has happened today?'

'For heaven's sake, my dear fellow,' replied the modest Ophelia sweetly, hoping to convince him once and for all. 'The whole thing was crazy. It'll never happen again. Can't you see that the child is our one consolation in life? If you take him from us . . .'

* Again the initial letters of this phrase are MIAU.

Emotion cut her short. The actress was silent and tried to conceal her pain. For she knew very well that if the family showed a keen interest in keeping little Luis that alone would be sufficient reason for the monster to insist on taking him away. She thought it better, therefore, to leave this delicate matter in the diplomatic hands of Doña Pura, who had a way of handling her son-in-law with a mixture of force and suavity.

When the Miau followed her husband into his study she found him slumped in a chair with his head in his hands.

'What do you think we ought to do?' she asked him in bewilderment, for she had not yet had time to make a decision.

Doña Pura's surprise was great, was immense when her husband raised his head and spoke these incredible words:

'Let him take the boy whenever he wants to. It will be painful to see him go. But how can we help it? It's no good getting excited either, and I'll say more . . . I say that the boy will be better off with Quintina than with the three of you.'

Stupefied, the figure by Fra Angelico silently contemplated the distressed features of the unemployed official. Her suspicion that he was beginning to go out of his mind was confirmed by the crazy statement he had just made.

'Better off with Quintina than with us! You're not in your right mind, Ramón.'

'And putting aside the question of the boy's interest' (moderating his cruelty a little), 'Victor is his father and has more right to him than we have. If he wants to take him . . .'

'But he won't want to. How can he? You see how I'll deal with this scoundrel.'

'I would say nothing at all to him if I were you. I wouldn't demean myself to have any dealings with him' (falling into a deep depression, now that the force of his rage had ebbed). 'I should let him have his way. He has the right, hasn't he now? If he has, then we can do nothing but quietly put up with it.'

'So we are to be quiet and put up with it' (shocked into violence) 'when this vile creature wants to take away our one joy? You're not right in the head. Let me tell you that if Victor takes the boy he'll have to tear him away and destroy us all first. But before he does that, I'll scratch the dog's eyes out.'

'My opinion is that we shouldn't argue with a creature like him. If I ever see him again I think I shall bite him. I feel a kind of physical compulsion to put my teeth into someone. I tell you, Pura, the administration is dishonoured. One can't say now as one used to, "the honest and devoted men of the Treasury", and as for an equitable distribution of the budget, not a hope of it! With the rabble that's flooding the house today it's out of the question.'

'But why do you bring in the administration?' (furious). 'What have the two things got to do with one another? Oh, Ramón, you're not right in the head! Don't talk to me about honest men . . . May the lightning strike them! Just look at yourself. Open your eyes, man, open your eyes!'

'They're open all right. They're wide open!' (emphatically). 'And what a prospect I see before me!'

Since she could not come to an agreement with her husband, she went to take things up with Victor, who had not yet departed. Contrary to Pura's expectations, he remained inflexible, maintaining his decision with a tenacity worthy of a better cause. Either of the Miaus could have been choked with a feather, and Abelarda, conscious that she was the cause of the conflict, was weeping on her bed like a Magdalen. Between looking after her daughter and arguing with Victor, she had to split herself in two. Running from one to the other, she could not moderate her daughter's distress or overcome her son-in-law's remorseless obstinacy. She had never seen that smart young man so entrenched in any purpose, and she could not solve the mystery of his unexpected harshness and stubbornness. To do so, she would have had to be aware of the previous day's events at the Cabreras'.

Cabrera had won on appeal the famous case about the ruined house at Vélez Málaga, and Victor had been condemned to reimburse him for the value of the property and pay the costs. The remorseless Ildefonso had cast the rope round his throat and was about to draw it tight by putting an estoppage on his salary, and harassing and persecuting him without pity or consideration. But the very cunning Quintina took advantage of the lawsuit to satisfy her maternal aspirations. She wheedled Cabrera with studied flatteries and blandishments, and obtained his approval to the principles of the following arrangement. The matter should be forgotten. Ildefonso should pay the costs (retaining the house, of course). And Victor should entrust his son to them. Cadalso saw an unforeseen way out, and although it went against his grain to take the boy from the care and protection of his grandparents, he had to accept blindfold. The worst that he must now face was an awkward half-hour at the Miaus', a scratching or two from Pura and another from Milagros, and perhaps a bite from Villaamil. This was most clearly the motive that governed his determination that the famous little Cadalso should change house and family.

When Milagros and Pura were most flustered, running from the inconsolable Abelarda to the inflexible Victor with a short stop beside Luis, who had also begun to whimper, Ponce entered. He could not have come at a worse moment, and his future mother-in-law, taken aback by his visit, imprisoned him in the drawing-room, where she told him: 'That wretch Victor has played us a dirty trick. There's been a real tragedy here today. Just imagine, he's suddenly decided to take his little son away, to tear him from this home where he's been brought up and cared for. We're all terribly upset. Abelarda fell into a frightful faint, an absolutely frightful faint, when she saw that this bandit was going to take him away by main force. We've got her in bed now, crying her eyes out. Oh, Ponce, what a time we've been through!'

In the end, as Abelarda was lying on the bed fully clothed, Ponce was allowed to see her. The little nobody had stopped crying, but her eyes were swollen and she was weak in all her limbs. The excellent youth sat down beside her bed, squeezed her hand and permitted himself the rare excess of kissing her in the absence of her mamma, who repeated in front of her daughter the version of the day's events that she had already given her fiancé.

'But what a wicked man he is!' said the critic to his beloved. 'He's a beast from the apocalypse.'

'You don't know how wicked,' answered the girl, looking hard at her lover as he wiped his always moist eyes with his handkerchief. 'God never put a blacker soul into the world. It's a real crime to want to take Luis away from us when he's our one delight and treasure. He owes his whole life to us because we've looked after him as carefully as the sight of our own eyes. We've nursed him through the measles and the whooping-cough at the cost of great sacrifices. It's wicked ingratitude! You know I'm a peaceful person. More than peaceful, I'm a coward. I'm so soft-hearted, even that when I kill a flea I'm sorry for the little creature. But that man, I believe I'd run him through with a knife if I found one handy. Now I've told you.'

'Calmly, calmly, my pet,' said Ponce in honeyed tones. 'You're all excited. Stop thinking about it now. Do you love me very much?'

'Of course I love you!' replied Abelarda, fully determined to throw herself over the Viaduct – that is to say, to marry Ponce.

'Your mother will have told you that we've fixed on the third of May, the Discovery of the Cross. It seems a long time to me. The days and nights are all so slow.'

'But everything comes in the end. One day succeeds another,' said Abelarda, looking at the ceiling. 'Every day is just like the last.'

Conversations between Victor and the two Miaus continued until he went out dressed in his best; neither Pura's diplomacy nor Milagros' mournful prayers had softened Cadalso's hard heart. The most they obtained was the postponement of Luis' departure till the following day. When Villaamil was informed he came out, and said to his son-in-law coldly: 'I promise you, I give you my word that I'll take him to Quintina's myself. There's nothing more to discuss. You need not come back here again.'

The monster replied that he was coming back that night to change his shirt, and added benevolently that the fact of his taking his son away did not mean that he would be forbidden to see his grandparents, because they could go to Quintina's whenever they liked, and he would tell his sister so.

'Thank you, gracious sir,' said Doña Pura contemptuously.

And Milagros: 'Me . . . go there? You've got a nerve.'

For a proper appreciation of the subject one fact was missing;

nobody knew the attitude of the interested party, whether he would lend himself willingly to a change of family or if, on the contrary, he would resist with the unshakeable stubbornness that goes with the age of innocence. As soon as the monster had gone, his grandmother began to prepare the child's mind for resistance. She assured him that his Aunt Quintina was a very wicked woman, and would shut him up in a dark room full of huge snakes and poisonous insects. Young Cadalso heard this statement with incredulity, because it was really too tall a story for a child to swallow who was beginning to grow up and to know something of the world.

That night no one had an appetite, and Milagros took the dishes back to the kitchen in the same state in which they had come into the dining-room. Villaamil did not open his lips except to contradict the frightening pictures that his wife drew of Cabrera's house: 'Don't take any notice, my boy. Your Aunt Quintina's a very good woman, and she'll look after you and spoil you properly. There are no toads or snakes there, but the nicest things you can imagine, saints that almost look as if they could speak, and pretty prints, and lovely altars and a whole lot of other things. You'll enjoy it very much there.'

When they heard this, Pura and Milagros looked at one another in astonishment, for they could not understand why the boy's grandfather had gone over shamelessly like a coward to the enemy. What whim made him support Victor's iniquitous idea, and even defend Quintina by painting her house as a children's paradise? It was unfortunate that the family was not in funds, because if they had been the first thing they would have done would have been to call in a good specialist in mental diseases to study Villaamil's condition and say what was going on inside him.

39

Young Cadalso also had no appetite for food, and even less for doing his lessons. While they were taking him to bed, his aunt, now completely recovered from her wild attack and only dimly remembering it, kissed him and caressed him most tenderly, to the slight embarrassment of the child and also of Doña Pura. Milagros was going to sleep with him that night, in case anything should happen.

Luis went to sleep quickly, but woke up at midnight with the premonitory symptoms of a vision. His great-aunt carefully covered him up and comforted him, finally lying down beside him so that he should calm down and stop being afraid. The first thing the boy saw on dozing off was a vast space: an uncertain featureless place the horizons of which merged into the sky. It seemed almost limitless, for everything was the same, near and far. He wondered whether this was earth or cloud, and then suspected that it might be the sea, which he had never seen except in pictures. But it could not be the sea because the sea has waves that rise and fall, and the surface of this was like glass. There, far away, very far away, he could make out his friend with the white beard who was slowly coming nearer, holding up his cloak with his left hand and leaning with the other on a great stick or staff of the kind that bishops use. Although he came from far away and was walking very slowly, he soon came up to young Cadalso and when he caught sight of him gave him a smile. Then he sat down. But on what, seeing that there was not a stone or a chair? Everything was completely supernatural, because Luis saw above the celestial Father's shoulders the back of one of the chairs in the drawing-room at home. But the most astounding thing was that the good old man leaned down and stroked his face with his beautiful hand. When he felt the touch of those fingers that had made the world and everything in it, young Cadalso felt a most delightful trembling go through his body.

'Now,' said his friend, 'I have come from the other side of the world just to have a chat with you. I know that strange things are happening to you. Your aunt . . . It doesn't seem possible when she's so very fond of you! Do you understand it? No, nor do I. I assure you I was absolutely flabbergasted when I saw it. Then your papa, so determined to take you to your Aunt Quintina's. Do you understand the whys and wherefores of it all?'

'I think,' pronounced Luis timidly, astonished to have ideas of his own in the presence of the Eternal Wisdom, 'I think everything that's happening is the Minister's fault.'

'The Minister's!' (with a surprised smile).

'Yes, sir; because if that man had given my grandfather a post everyone would have been happy and then none of this would have happened.'

'I'm beginning to think you're a very clever boy.'

'My grandfather's angry because they don't give him a post, and so is my grandmother, and my Aunt Abelarda too. And my Aunt Abelarda can't bear my papa, because my papa told the Minister not to give my grandfather a post. And because she daren't smack my papa, since he's stronger than she is, she went for me. Then she started crying. Tell me, is my aunt good or is she wicked?'

'I believe she's good. You must realize that the smacking she gave you today was because she loves you.'

'A funny kind of love! It still hurts me here where she dug her nails in. She's hated me a lot ever since the day when I told her she ought to marry my papa. Didn't you know about that? My papa loves her. But she can't bear him.'

'That's really very odd.'

'But it's true. My papa told her one night that he was very much in love with her – fatally in love, you know. And that he was damned, and all sorts of other things.'

'But who told you to listen to what grown-up people say?'

'I . . . was there' (shrugging his shoulders).

'Come now. What strange things do happen in your house! I imagine you must be right though. That rogue of a Minister must be to blame. None of this would have happened if he had done as I told him. What would it have cost him to make room for this poor gentleman in that huge house full of offices? But it's no use, they don't listen to me, and that's why things go wrong. Of course they have a tremendous lot of business to see to. So whatever I tell them goes in at one ear and out at the other.'

'Well, let them give him a post now. Why not? If you go there and order them to, and bang hard with that stick on the Minister's table . . .'

'No good! They don't take any notice. If it could be done by banging with a stick I'd bang all right. I'd give it a tremendous banging, of course I would.'

'Well then, blow it!' (emboldened by so much benevolence). 'When are they going to give him a post?'

'Never,' declared the celestial Father serenely, as if that *never* was not a hopeless but a comforting word.

'Never!' (not understanding how he could say this so calmly). 'Then we're in the soup.'

'No, never. And what's more, I'll tell you that I decided this myself. For what value have the good things of this world? Absolutely none. You've heard this many times in sermons, and now I tell you so with my own lips that know everything there is to know. Your dear grandfather will never find happiness on earth.'

'Where will he then?'

'Don't be so silly! Here, at my side of course. Do you suppose I don't intend to bring him here to me?'

'Oh!' (opening his mouth to its full extent). 'Then . . . you mean that my grandfather's going to die.'

'But really and truly why should your grandfather stay in this ugly, wicked world? The poor man's useless now. Do you think it's right that he should live to be laughed at, and for this petty Minister to insult him every day?'

'But I don't want my grandfather to die.'

'Quite right that you shouldn't. But see now, he's old, and believe me he'll be better off with me than with all of you. Don't you understand that?'

'Yes' (agreeing out of politeness but not much convinced). 'Then is grandfather going to die soon?'

'It's the best thing for him. You must tell him so yourself. Tell him you've talked to me, and that he mustn't worry about an appointment, but tell the Minister to fry his face, and that he'll only be at peace when he's with me. But what's this? Why are you frowning? Don't you understand me, silly? Aren't you always saying that you're going to be a priest and devote yourself to me? If that's what you intend, then you must get used to these ideas. Don't you remember now what the Catechism says? Learn it properly. The world is a vale of tears, and the sooner you come out of it the better. You'll have to preach all these things, and a lot more that you'll learn later in my pulpit when you're grown up, so as to convert the wicked. Just you see how you'll make the women cry! They'll all say that little father Miau has a golden tongue. Tell me, you do want to be a clergyman, don't you, and to learn some gobbets of the mass and bits of Latin and all that?'

'Yes, sir. Murillo has taught me a lot of things: what *aleluya* means and *gloria patri*, and I know how to sing the bit they do when they raise the host, and how they put their hands when they read the most holy Gospels.'

'You know quite a lot then. But you'll have to apply yourself. At your Aunt Quintina's you'll see all the things they use for my worship.'

'They want to take me to my Aunt Quintina's. What do you think about it? Shall I go?'

On reaching this point, young Cadalso was so emboldened by the kindness of his friend who was stroking his cheeks with his fingers, that he ventured to respond by a similar demonstration of love. At first timidly and then quite without embarrassment he pulled the Eternal Father's beard. His friend did nothing to stop him but said, in Villaamil's words, though not in the least put out, 'In what low-down inn have we ever met over a meal?'

'About the question whether you live with the Cabreras or not I say nothing. You want to of course because it'll be new to have those sacramental toys to play with, and at the same time you're afraid of being parted from your dear grandparents. Do you know what my advice is? Do whatever comes into your head when the moment arrives.'

'But what if my father forces me, and doesn't leave me time to think?'

'I don't know . . . I don't think he will force you. If the worst comes to the worst, do as your grandfather says. If he says "Go to Quintina's", say nothing and go.'

'And if he says no?'

'Don't go. Do without the little altars. And in the meantime do you know what you ought to do? Ask your friend Murillo to run over that Latin with you again, as much as he knows, and to explain the mass to you and the priest's vestments, how to put on the cingulum and the stole, and to prepare the chalice and the host for consecration . . . Murillo's very well informed, and he can show you too how they bring Extreme Unction to the sick, and what prayers they say on the way.'

'Right. Murillo knows a lot, but his father wants him to be a lawyer. How stupid of him! He says he'll end up as a Minister and marry a very pretty girl. It's disgusting.'

'Yes, it is disgusting.'

'The Performer had some wicked ideas too. One afternoon he told us he was going to have a sweetheart and play gambling games. What do you think? He used to smoke fag-ends and use foul language.'

'You lose all those bad habits here.'

'Where is he now, because I can't see him with you?'

'They're all being punished. Do you know what they did to me this morning? That little Performer and the other rascals are always up to tricks. Well, they took the world – you know, the world I keep to carry in my hand – and started rolling it, and before I noticed what was happening it had fallen in the sea. Gracious, what a business it was to get it out. Luckily it's only an ornamental world, you know. It hasn't got any people on it, so there weren't any disasters to mourn for. I gave them a couple of boxes on the ear that they won't forget in a hurry. I've shut them up for today.'

'I'm very pleased. Serve them right. But tell me, where do you shut them up?'

The celestial personage, still allowing his beard to be pulled, looked at his friend with a smile, as if not knowing what to answer.

'Where do I shut them up? Well, you tell me . . .'

A child's curiosity is implacable, and woe betide anyone who arouses and does not satisfy it immediately! The tugs at his beard must have become too strong, for Luis' kind old friend was forced to put a stop to this great familiarity.

'Where do I shut them up now? You want to know everything. Well, I shut them up . . . wherever I choose to. What's it got to do with you?'

On pronouncing this last word, the vision suddenly disappeared, and the good child was tortured throughout his dreams till morning by the curious wish to know where he shut them up. But where the devil could he shut them up?

40

VICTOR did not appear all night. But early in the morning he came in to repeat his dreadful sentence concerning Luis, which he did not retract for all Doña Pura's threats and Milagros' tears. Moved by this afflicting spectacle, the child objected to leaving, and refused to have his clothes and shoes put on. He burst into tears, and Lord knows what a fuss he would have made but for the discreet intervention of Villaamil, who came out of his bedroom and said : 'Since we've got to say good-bye to him, don't worry and torture the poor boy.'

Victor was surprised to find his father-in-law so reasonable, and very grateful to him for this comforting intervention which allowed him to carry out his intention without resorting to force or incurring difficult scenes. Seeing that the case was lost, Milagros and Abelarda retired to cry in the study, and Pura shut herself in the kitchen, uttering curses against the Cabreras, the Cadalsos and other races hostile to her peace of mind. Meanwhile Victor put on his son's boots, anxious to take him quickly before new complications should arise.

'You'll see,' he said to him, 'you'll see what pretty things your Aunt Quintina has got for you there. Magnificent saints, as big as the ones they have in churches, and small ones too that you can play with. Virgins with gold embroidered robes and silver moons at their feet and stars round their heads, ever so lovely . . . you'll see. And other nice things too. Candlesticks and Christs and missals and monstrances and thurifers.'

'And can I light them and swing them so that they smell?'

'Yes, my darling. They're all there for you to play with and learn from. And you can take the saints' clothes off too to see what they're like underneath, and then you can put them on again.'

Villaamil was walking up and down the dining-room, listening to all this. On observing, however, that after his excitement about swinging the thurifer Luis was relapsing into gloom and whimpering: 'I want Granny to take me and stay there with me,' he was forced to intervene in the catechizing. Giving the boy a pat, therefore, he said: 'There are little altars there too with tiny candles and candelabras this size, and monstrances too, and embroidered chasubles, and a ciborium that's a real joy, and a cross-holder that you can carry when you like, and other pretty things . . . like, for example . . .'

He did not know how to continue, and Victor supplied his failing imagination by adding: 'And a silver aspergill that sprinkles holy water all round and, last of all, a paschal lamb.'

'A real one?'

'No, boy . . . Yes, I mean, it's alive.'

To cut short the painful situation and hasten the critical moment of the departure, Villaamil helped to put on his jacket. But they had not yet done up all the buttons when – Holy Virgin! – Doña Pura emerged like a panther, and threw herself on Victor, the fire shovel in hand, crying: 'Get out of my house, you murderer! You shan't steal our treasure away. Get out or I'll break your head!'

And no sooner did the other Miaus hear her angry voice than they rushed in too, shrieking in harmony. In fact, things were looking very ugly.

'If you don't let him go willingly, you'll have to do so un-willingly,' said Victor, putting himself out of reach of the three furies' nails. 'I shall get the courts to support me. He's not going to stay here on any account. Understand that . . .'

Here Villaamil intervened, saying in a conciliatory voice laboriously produced from the depths of his grieving breast : 'Calmly, calmly. We had got the whole business arranged when these women came in and upset everything. Will they please leave the room.'

'You're a dummy,' said his wife, blind with fury. 'It's all your fault. If you'd backed us up the three of us would have got our own way.'

'Be quiet, you crazy woman. I know perfectly well what I must do. Out of the room with you, all of you!'

But, seeing his aunts and his grandmother so active on his side, Luis once more showed resistance. Pura wanted at least to scratch out her son-in-law's eyes, and things looked like ending badly. It was lucky that Villaamil was so reasonable and had such control over himself and the situation that day. He seemed a different man, and imposed his authority, no one knew how.

'So long as you're here,' he said to Victor, extracting him by a clever movement from between the bull's horns, or rather from the fierce hands of Doña Pura, 'we shan't get an inch forward. Go now, and I give you my word that I'll bring my grandson to Quintina's house. Leave it to me, leave it . . . Don't you trust my word?'

'You word yes, but not your power to reduce these furies to reason.'

'I'll reduce them by argument. Don't you worry. Go and wait for me there.'

Having succeeded in pacifying his son-in-law, he began with great eloquence on the family, using all his ingenuity to make them see the impossibility of preventing the child's departure.

'Don't you realize that if we resist, the judge himself will come and take him away from us?'

His harangue lasted half an hour, and in the end the Miaus appeared resigned, though not in the least convinced.

'The first thing for you to do,' he said, anxious to have them out of the way at the critical moment of the departure, 'is to go into the drawing-room and keep quiet. I'll settle things with Luis. He won't cease to love us because he goes to Quintina's. What's more, his father has promised me that he'll bring him to see us every day and let him spend the day here on Sundays.'

Abelarda retired first weeping like one taking leave of a dying man whom he will not see on his death-bed. Then Milagros went, and finally Pura, who would not have given in if her husband had not subdued her with this final argument : 'If we hold out, the judge will come this afternoon. Just imagine the scene! We will drain the cup, and God will punish the wretch who gave it to us.'

Alone with Luis, his grandfather was on the point of losing his assumed and difficult composure and bursting into tears. He swallowed the whole of the gall, however, mentally invoking the heavens with this phrase : 'It's terrible to part with him, Lord, but there's no doubt he'll be better off there, much better off. Come on, Ramón, courage and don't lose heart.' But he had not reckoned with his grandson who grew stubborn again when he heard his aunts' wailing. As the cruel moment of their departure approached he became very sad and said : 'I won't go.'

'Don't be silly, Luis,' the old man admonished him. 'Do you imagine we would take you out of the house if it wasn't for your good? Kind obedient little boys do what they're told. And whatever I say, you can't imagine the treasures Quintina has in her house, for your special use.'

'And can I take them all for myself and do whatever I like with them?' asked the little boy with that outspoken greed that betrays the boundless egoism of those early years.

'Of course. You can even break them if you want to.'

'No, not break them. You don't break things that belong to the Church,' declared the child somewhat unctuously.

'Right. Now let's go. We must go out very quietly so that they don't hear us and get excited. Yes, you'll see. One of the things is a little font. It's ever so pretty. I've seen it myself.'

'A font . . . With a lot of holy water?'

'It'll take as much water as the jar in the kitchen. Come on' (lifting him up). 'It will be better if I carry you . . .'

'And is this font for baptizing people?'

'Naturally! You can play with it as much as you like, and all the time you'll be learning the way to baptize a baby, for the time when you're a priest.'

Villaamil crossed the corridor with cautious strides, carrying his grandson in his arms, and as throughout their perilous passage the child continued his flood of questions without lowering his voice, his grandfather stopped his mouth with his hand, whispering in his ear: 'Yes, you can baptize babies, as many babies as you like. And there are mitres too that would fit your head, and gold-embroidered copes and a staff for when you dress up as a little bishop and give us your blessing.'

At this moment they went out through the door, which Villaamil did not shut, to avoid the noise. He went down the stairs two at a time like a thief escaping with a stolen object, and he did not take breath till, safe in the doorway, he could put his load on the ground. He could do no more. He was not by any means strong, and could not carry weights, even such light weights as his little grandson. For fear that Paca and Mendizábal might say something indiscreet, he was sparing with his salutations. The fat woman wanted to say something to Luis, to condole with him on his departure. But Villaamil was very sly. 'We'll be back in a moment,' he said, and rushed into the street as quick as lightning. Fear that Luis would prove stubborn again stimulated him to renew his romancing tactics when they were in the street.

'You'll find a huge lot of artificial flowers for altars. It'll take you a whole year to look them all through. And fat candles of all colours . . . and hundreds of altar-candles. Then there's a San Fernando dressed as a warrior in armour, you'll be surprised at that, and a San Isidro with his herd of oxen that looks as if they were real. The little altar for you to say mass at is prettier than the one in the Montserrat.'

'Tell me, Grandpa, is there a confessional too?'

'Of course there is! A lovely one, with grilles for the women to tell you their sins, and they'll tell you plenty. You're going to be very happy, I can tell you, and when you grow up a little, you'll find you've grown into a priest without noticing it, and you'll be as wise as Father Bohigas at the Montserrat, or the chaplain himself at the Salesas Nuevas, who is just being made into a canon.'

'And shall I be a canon, Grandpa dear?'

'Not a doubt of it. And a bishop, and you might even come to be a Pope.'

'The Pope is the one who gives orders to all the priests, isn't he?'

'That's right. Oh yes, and you'll see an altar for Holy Week constructed of at least a thousand parts, and goodness knows how many statues all white like icing sugar. They seem as if they'd just come from the confectioner's.'

'And can you eat it, Grandpa, can you eat it?' asked young Cadalso, so deeply interested in all this that his home, his grandmother and his aunts were blotted from his mind.

'Of course you can. When you're tired of playing with it you can take a bite,' replied Villaamil, who was now quite confused again, for his imagination was drying up and he did not know which way to turn.

The old man walked rapidly along the pavement of the Calle Ancha, and for each step he took little Cadalso took three. He held, or rather hung from, his grandfather's hand. Don Ramón stopped short, turned round and made for the upper part of the street where the Hospital de la Princesa stands. It struck Luis that this was the wrong direction, and he remarked impatiently :

'But, Grandpa, aren't we going to Aunt Quintina's in the Calle de los Reyes?'

'Yes, my boy. But first we'll take a stroll here to give you a bit of sun.' The unhappy old man suffered a sudden reaction; he now rejected the vigorous thoughts that had governed all his actions in this matter of giving up his grandson and taking him to his aunt's. The boy went on chattering for all he was worth, and pulling his grandfather's arm when his answer did not follow immediately upon the question. The old man answered evasively, in monosyllables, for his whole mind was concentrated on the inner world of his thoughts. With head down and eyes fixed on the ground, as if counting the joints in the pavement, he toiled up the hill, dragging Luis, who did not notice his grandfather's anguish, nor the trembling of his lips as he mumbled the ideas passing through his head: 'It's not really a crime, what I'm going to do, or not really two crimes I should say. Hand over my grandson and then . . . Last night when I'd thought them well over, both things seemed quite right, one followed on the other. Because if I am to . . . stop living very soon, Luis will be better off with the Cabreras than with the family. I thought that my family would bring him up badly, carelessly and let him get into a lot of bad habits, not counting the danger he's in from Abelarda, who will break out again one of these days. I dislike the Cabreras; but I know they're decent, orderly people. How different from Pura and Milagros! They're quite useless, with all their music and nonsense. That's what I thought last night, and it seemed to me the sanest course that human brain could devise. Why do I go back on it now and feel like taking the boy home again? Will he be better off with the Miaus than with Quintina? No, indeed, he won't. Is there a weakening in my saving resolution to give myself liberty and peace? Are you suddenly beginning to fancy the idea of going on living, you coward? Do life's little allurements attract you now?'

Tortured by the cruellest doubt, Villaamil heaved a deep sigh. Sitting down at the base of the railings that divide the hospital from the Paseo de Areneros, he took the boy's hand and stared at him hard, as if he might read in his innocent eyes the solution of his own terrible conflict. The boy was burning with impatience. But he did not dare to hurry his grandfather, in whose features he could see grief and weariness.

'Tell me, Luis,' Villaamil began, embracing him tenderly, 'do you really want to go to your Aunt Quintina? Do you think you'll be happy with her, and that the Cabreras will bring you up and teach you better than at home? Tell me frankly.'

Now that the question was transferred to the pedagogic field, and the attraction of the sacramental toys was ruled out, Luis did not know how to answer. He sought for a way out and at last found one: 'I want to be a priest . . .'

'Agreed. You want to be a priest and I approve of that. But supposing I am not there, and that Pura and Milagros go to live with Abelarda, who marries Ponce, where do you think you'd be better off?'

'With Granny and Aunt Quintina, both together.'

'That's not possible.'

Young Cadalso shrugged his shoulders.

'And wouldn't you be frightened if you stayed where you are that my daughter would get worked up again and try to kill you?'

'She won't get worked up again,' said young Cadalso with remarkable wisdom. 'She's going to be married now. She won't beat me again.'

'So you . . . you're not afraid? And which do you prefer, us or your Aunt Quintina?'

'I prefer . . . that you should all live with Aunt.'

Villaamil was just opening his mouth to say, 'Look, all that I've told you about those toy altars is rubbish. We've been tricking you so that you shouldn't refuse to leave the house.' But he checked himself, hoping that Luis himself would throw light on this tremendous problem by some simple idea which his innocence would suggest to him. Little Cadalso put one leg on his grandfather's knee and one hand on his shoulder to steady himself, and ventured to say: 'What I want is that Granny and Aunt Milagros should come and live with Quintina.'

'And I?' asked the old man, astonished at being passed over.

'You? I'll tell you. They won't give you a post, you know. They won't give you a post now or ever.'

'How do you know that?' (with his heart in his throat).

'I do know it. Not now or ever . . . Never mind how badly you want it.'

'But how do you know? Who told you?'

'Well . . . I . . . I'll tell you, but don't you tell anybody . . . I see God . . . I sort of fall asleep, and then he appears and talks to me.'

Villaamil was so astonished that he could make no comment.

'He has a white beard, and he's as tall as you, and he has a beautiful cloak. He tells me everything that happens, and he knows everything, even what we boys do at school.'

'And when have you seen him?'

'Very often. The first time it was at the Alarconas, then somewhere near here, and in the Congreso, and at home. . . . First I

264

have a sort of faint, I feel very cold, and then he comes and we start talking. . . . What, don't you believe it?'

'Yes, my boy, I believe it' (with the deepest feeling). 'Why shouldn't I believe it?'

'And last night he told me that they won't give you a post, and that this is a very wicked world, and that there's nothing more for you here and the sooner you go to heaven the better.'

'Now that's really wonderful. He said the same thing to me.'

'But do you see him too?'

'No, I don't exactly see him. I'm not pure enough to deserve that grace. But he talks to me every now and again.'

'Well, that's what he told me. That it would be better for you to die soon, and have a rest and be happy.'

Villaamil was completely stupefied. His grandson's words were like a divine revelation of irrefragable authenticity.

'And what does the Lord say about you?'

'That I'm to be a priest, you see? Just the thing, the very thing I wanted . . . and that I must study a lot of Latin and learn about it all very soon.'

The old man's mind was overwhelmed by what one might call a positive, categorical knowledge which excluded every shadow of doubt. It firmly established the order of ideas which his will with iron resolution must transform into deeds.

'Come, my boy, let's go to your Aunt Quintina's,' he said, getting up and taking his grandson's hand.

He took him there quickly, without bothering to regale him further with hyperbolical descriptions of sacred and entertaining toys and knick-knacks. When they rang at the Cabreras' door Quintina herself came to open it. Seated on the top stair, Villaamil covered his grandson with kisses, handed him over to his paternal aunt, and fled without even saying good morning to her. On his way down he thought he heard the child's voice whimpering; and he hurried even faster, rushing into the street with all the speed his weak legs would allow.

41

IT was now nearly midday and, having had no breakfast, Villa-amil felt hungry. He made for the Plaza de San Marcial, and on reaching the rubbish tips where the gardens of Príncipe Pío had once been, stopped to survey the depression of the Campo del Moro and the distant fence of the Casa de Campo. It was a splendid day, with a bright and unbroken blue sky and a lightly burning sun : one of those premature summer days in which the heat is the more oppressive because the trees are still without their leaves. The horse-chestnuts and black poplars were beginning to sprout, but the plane trees were only just budding, and the sophoras, gleditchias and other leguminous kinds were still completely bare. The little pink flowers could be seen on some Judas trees, and the privet hedges were already showing their proud new leaves, which rivalled those of the perennial spindle tree. Villaamil observed the different times at which the various kinds of trees awake from their winter sleep, and took pleasure in breathing the warm air that rose from the Manzanares valley. He strolled on, forgetting his brisk appetite, towards La Montaña, across the little garden that had recently been planted on the levelled ground and round the barracks until he could see the Sierra, bright blue with patches of snow like a streak of water-colour spread across the paper by the natural blotching of a single drop, the work of chance rather than of the artist's brush.

'How lovely that is !' he said to himself, loosening the neck of his cloak, which was making him very hot. 'It's as if I were seeing it for the first time in my life, or as if the Sierra and those trees and this sky have only just been created. The fact is that I've been so full of work and worries all my wretched life that I've never had time to look up or in front of me. I've always kept my eyes on the ground, on this foul earth, which isn't worth a farthing, and on the confounded Administration – may the lightning strike it ! – and on the swinish faces of Ministers,

Directors and Chiefs of Personnel, and much good it's done me! One thing I know. Even the smallest patch of blue sky is more interesting than Pantoja's face, or Cucúrbitas', or the face of the Minister himself. Now, thank God, I can enjoy this pleasure of looking at nature, because my troubles and griefs are over, and I'm not worrying any more about whether they'll give me a post. I'm another man now, and now I know what independence is. I know what life is now, and now they can all go to hell. I don't envy anybody. I'm . . . I'm the happiest man in the world. Well, I'll have something to eat, that's decided, and then forward!'

He flicked the fingers of each hand repeatedly and, securing his cloak again, made for the Cuesta de San Vicente. After walking almost the whole length of the street, looking at the shop windows, he finally stopped in front of an eating-house that looked attractive, muttering: 'The cooking must be very good here. Enter, Ramón, enjoy yourself!' No sooner said than done. A few moments later Villaamil was sitting at a round, four-legged table with a plate of most savoury beef stew, a bone-handled knife and fork, a jug of wine and a hunk of bread in front of him. This is splendid, he thought, resolutely attacking the stew, to be like this, without duties and without a thought for the family . . . because, I'm happy to say, I have no family now, I'm alone in the world, alone and master of my actions. What a joy, what a very great pleasure! The slave has broken his chains, and today he hasn't a care in the world. He sees his oppressors pass by, and doesn't know them from Adam. But how good this stew is! That fool Milagros never cooked anything as good in her life. All she knows is how to make meat-balls, and to sing and miau at the top of her voice her eternal 'Moriamo, moriamo'. She is like a puppy when you pinch its tail. This beef stew is really fine. How good they are at seasoning in this place! And what a nice person the boss looks, and how well his green cuffs suit him, and his carpet-slippers and his fur cap. He looks a great deal handsomer than Cucúrbitas or Pantoja even. And, goodness, how cool and sharp this little wine is! I like it very much. Effect of the liberty I'm enjoying, of not caring a rap for anybody, and having my mind free of difficul-

267

ties and nightmares. Because I've left everything very well arranged. My daughter's marrying Ponce, who is a good lad and has enough to live on. My grandson is in Quintina's charge, and she'll bring him up better than his grandmother . . . and as for those two nasty old women, Abelarda and her husband can look after them. In short, I haven't got to provide for anyone now I'm free now, and happy and independent, and 'surrender to the Carthaginians without a thought'! What luck! Now I haven't got to wonder what Christian soul I must write to tomorrow asking for a loan. What a relief to have put an end to all that shame. My soul is expanding. I'm breathing better, the appetite of my youth has returned to me, and whoever I see I want to shake him by the hand and tell him I'm happy.

He had got so far with his soliloquy when three lads came into the eating-house who had probably just come off the train. Each had a pack on his back and a stick in his belt, and they were dressed like countrymen. All three wore cord sandals on their feet, but their headgear was different. One of them had a round hat, another a beret, and the third a linen handkerchief tied round his head.

What fine-looking lads! thought Villaamil, watching them rapt as they noisily and high-spiritedly called to the boss for something to satisfy their violent appetites. I suppose they are young farm-labourers who have left the obscure poverty of their villages to come to this Babel and look for jobs that will give them the varnish of gentility and the appearance of well-to-do people. Poor fellows! It would be doing them a great kindness if I were to disillusion them!

Without more ado, he went over to them and said: 'Young men, consider what you are doing. You have still time. Go back to your cottages and your pastures, and avoid this treacherous abyss of Madrid, which will swallow you and make you miserable for the whole of your lives. Follow the advice of a well-wisher and go back to the country.'

'What's the fellow saying?' returned the most lively of them slinging his jacket over his shoulder, from which it had fallen 'Devil take the old man. We're recruits of this year's call-up and they'll shoot us if we don't report . . .'

268

'Oh, I see, I see! If you're military men that changes things entirely. To defend the country. I defended it too. I marched in a company of volunteers when that rogue Gómez was advancing on Madrid. But I must tell you all the same, my boys, pay no attention to what your officers preach at you, and revolt at the first chance of a change. Have no respect for that whore the state. Or perhaps you don't know what the state is?'

The three lads laughed, showing their healthy white teeth; they must have been greatly amused by the old scarecrow in front of them. None of the three knew what the state was, and Villaamil had to explain in these terms: 'The state then is the greatest enemy of the human race. If it gets hold of anything it breaks it to bits. Keep your eyes open. Always be free and independent, and pay no attention to anybody.'

One of the lads took the stick from his belt and banged so hard on the table that he almost split it in two: 'Landlady, we've got a hunger. In the name of Solomon the damned, bring us our bacon.'

This genial witticism pleased Villaamil, and he admired the lads for their warm-bloodedness and their youth. The boss of the eating-house begged them to wait a minute and put bread and wine before them to kill their gnawing pangs. Villaamil then paid, and the boss, now somewhat surprised by his strange manner and concluding that he was a bit crazy, came up to offer him a glass of sweet wine. Touched by such kindness, the out-of-work official accepted the wine, and taking the glass raised it 'to the prosperity of this establishment.' The recruits bellowed: 'Madrid, five minutes stop and into the refreshment-room! Here's to Nastasia, and Bruna, and Ruperta and all the girls of Daganzo de Arriba!'

When, politely taking his leave, Villaamil praised the good service and the excellent seasoning of the stew, the boss replied: 'There's not another house to compare with it. Fix the name in your memory, La Viña del Señor.'

'No, I shan't be coming back. Tomorrow I shall be very far away, my friend. Gentlemen' (turning to the lads and saluting them, hat in hand), 'look after your health. Thank you. Enjoy your meal. And don't forget what I told you . . . to be free and independent . . . as the air. Look at me now. I don't give a damn for the state. Good-bye.'

He went out dragging his cloak, and one of the lads put his head out of the door to shout: 'Hey, old fellow, pull yourself together or you'll fall down. Hey, old fellow, you've left your wits behind. Come back here.'

But Villaamil heard nothing and went straight on looking for a road or path to climb the Montaña. He finally found one, crossed one vacant lot and then another already fenced in for building, and finally, after countless twists and turns, and jumping of ditches and climbing the shifting soil of the hillocks, he reached the terrace before the barracks and went round, not stopping till he came to the bare slopes that drop from the suburb of Argüelles to San Antonio de la Florida. He sat down on the ground and took off his cloak. The wine inside him and the sun outside made him hotter than he could stand.

'What a quiet lunch I had today! I haven't been happier than I am now since the days of my youth, when we marched out to chase Gómez. Then I wasn't free in body, but I was in spirit, just as I am at the present moment; and I wasn't worried whether they had money or not to give the orders next day in the market. This business of having to go out every day to buy the food is what makes life unbearable. Look at those pretty little birds pecking around. Do they worry about what they're going to eat tomorrow? No. That's why they're happy, and now I'm just like them, so contented that I would chirp if I knew how to, and fly from here to the Casa de Campo if I could. I should like to know why God doesn't make one a bird instead of a human being. . . . They should at least let us choose. Certainly no one would choose to be a man, to be always breaking his head about his jobs and to be compelled to wear a silk hat and a tie and all that paraphernalia, which is not only a nuisance but costs the earth. It's cheap and convenient to be a bird. Look, just look how cheerful they are, pinching whatever they find and gobbling it down so greedily. None of them can be married to a hen-bird called Pura, who doesn't know and never has known how to run a house, and has no idea of saving. . . .'

When he saw the sparrows about four yards in front of him, hopping forward stealthily yet boldly to search the ground for food, the good man took from his pocket the bread that was left over from his lunch, which he had saved in the eating-house, crumbled it and threw it to the little birds. Although the movements of his hands frightened them off they soon came back and, finding the bread, now of course fell on it like wild beasts. Villaamil smiled and mopped his brow as he watched their greed, their pretty way of shaking themselves and their funny way of hopping. At the smallest noise, the slightest approach of a shadow or sign of danger, they flew away. But their furious appetite quickly brought them back to the same place.

'Eat, eat in peace,' the old man said to them mentally. He was spellbound, and motionless from fear of frightening them away. 'Things would have been very different with us if Pura had followed your system. Can anything be more natural than to confine yourself to your possibilities? If there's nothing but potatoes, then potatoes let it be. If the situation improves and one can rise as high as partridge, then partridge. But gracious me no, she isn't content without partridge every day. Thanks to that we've suffered thirty years of embarrassment, always trembling with fear. If we had any food we swallowed it down, as if we had some pressing reason for finishing it, and when we hadn't we lived on small debts and loans. Therefore when an appointment came we were already a whole year's salary in debt. It was always the same with us, "We sigh to thee". And then we raised our eyes to the stars. . . . Thirty years like this, my God, and they call it living. "Ramón, why on earth don't you go to this friend or to that one? Ramón, what are you thinking of? Do you imagine we can live off air? Ramón, make up your mind to pawn your watch, the child needs some boots. Ramón, I have no shoes, and although I can put up with it for a day or two I can't go without gloves because we shall be going to Furranguini's benefit. Ramón, ask the cashier to advance you a hundred pesetas. It's your birthday and we must ask the Xs and the Ys . . . Ramón.' And I haven't been man enough to seize my wife and put a gag in that mouth of hers. It should have belonged to a

271

friar, it's got such a beggarly whine! . . . Fancy putting up with that for thirty years! But now, thank God, I've had the courage to cut my chain and recover my identity. Now I am I, and nobody challenges me, and at last I'm able to do what I couldn't do before: to disown Pura and all her relatives and consign them to the flames.'

Unable to contain his joy and excitement he gesticulated so wildly that the birds flew away.

42

'DON'T be absurd. No one's attacking you. Whom do you take me for? For some merciless Minister who snatches the bread from the fathers of families to give it to some vagabond? For you're fathers of families too and have little children to keep. Eat your crumbs and don't be frightened. Believe me, if someone else had been my wife, Ventura's wife for example, I should never have arrived in this situation. Ventura's wife, whom my wife makes such fun of because she says "Scuttish" haddock is worth more than a hundred of her. No money's enough for Pura, not even a Director's pay. Her confounded pretentiousness, her rags and tatters, her visiting, her theatres, her gew-gaws and her way of going about with her head in the air pretending to be a very high-up person, all together they've destroyed us. Don't be afraid, sillies. You can come close. I've still got my crumbs. As for Milagros, you'll agree with me that good and simple though she is nevertheless she's useless as a sister. That fellow was right who jumped into the water! Because if he hadn't jumped and had burdened himself with her, he would have drowned a hundred thousand times by now and still remained alive, which is the worst thing that can happen to any Christian. Those two dear sisters, between them, have held me for the greater part of my life with a noose at my throat, tightening it for all they were worth. They can't say that I've treated them badly, because ever since I married . . . But now it strikes me that when I went to ask Doctor Escobios for his daughter's hand the worthy surgeon of the Fourth Mounted ought to have given me a good box on the ears which would have sent me to the right-about. How grateful I should have been to him for it in later years. Eat, eat in peace. Here we don't take people's food away. As I was saying, from the time I married till today I've been the victim of the unreliability and mismanagement of those two gorgons, and they can't complain that I haven't been patient and submissive, or that now I'm abandoning them and leaving them in penury. Because I didn't make up my mind to recover my liberty till I knew that I was leaving them in Ponce's protection. He's a kindly simpleton, and he'll give them enough to eat. That's what his uncle the notary left him all his crumbs for. Oh, excellent Ponce, what a bad bargain you've made! You'll soon see that it's not all honey. They'll liquidate you if you don't look out, they'll evaporate you, they'll volatilize you, they'll suck you up. But that's his affair. I've done my duty. I've carried my cross for thirty years. Now let someone else carry it. It needs young shoulders . . . and the weight is tremendous, my friend Ponce. You'll see. To be honest with you, I'll say that, though she's no genius, my daughter is worth more than her mother. She has some ideas of orderliness and foresight. She's less pretentious. But handle her carefully, friend Ponce, because if I know anything of women's affections and likings my Abelarda's about as fond of you as she is of the toothache. Nobody will convince me that this rogue of a Victor hasn't turned her head. It's as well that she's marrying, and if the Miau ladies are lucky enough to learn now what they did not know in my time I shall be very glad. I shall even applaud them from the other side. I shall applaud them heartily.'

With these thoughts, which were considerably longer and more diffuse than they appear in this narrative, Villaamil spent the afternoon. Two or three times he moved his position, wickedly treading down, as he passed, some of the little trees which the City authorities had planted on that waste plot. 'The Municipality,' he said, 'is the child of the Provincial Deputation and the grandchild of the swinish state, and it's quite permissible, without scruples of conscience, to damage the whole confounded brood. Like father, like son. If I had my way I shouldn't leave a tree or a lamp-post. They made it, they can pay for it . . . and then I'd go on to the buildings, beginning with the Ministry of god-damned Finance, and I'd raze the place to the ground, I'd leave it level with the earth . . . flat as the palm of your hand. Then I'd go for the railways. I wouldn't leave a train on the lines, or a bridge, or a warship, and I'd smash up the cannon in the fortresses too.'

He wandered on over these waste-plots, with his hat in his hand, receiving the rays of the sun full on his head; and as it was now setting they shone powerfully, scorching the ground and everything on it. He carried his cloak over his arm, and had some thought of throwing it away but did not do so because it struck him that it would come in useful at night if only for a short time. He stopped on the edge of the great slope that drops from beside the Cuesta de Areneros to the new potteries of Moncloa and, looking down the sharp incline, said to himself with the utmost serenity : 'This seems to me a good spot. I should roll down here like a sheep and then they could look for me. . . . Unless some goatherd were to find me. A nice place and convenient what's more, whatever they may say.'

But afterwards the place could not have seemed to him so suitable for his dreadful purpose, for he went on, climbed down and came up again, and inspected the terrain as if about to build a house there. The sparrows now began to retire to the tileworks at the bottom, or to the trees of San Bernardino and the Florida. Suddenly this simple soul was prompted to take out the revolver that he carried in his pocket, to cock it and point at the innocent sparrows, to whom he said : 'You rogues, you villains, now that you've eaten my bread you go away without even wishing me good night. What would you say now if I were to put a bullet in your bodies? Not one of you would escape, I promise you. I'm a very fine shot. Be grateful that I don't want to leave myself short of bullets. If I had enough, though, I'd make you pay, the whole lot of you. Indeed I feel like putting an end to every living thing, as a punishment for the evil I've suffered from Humanity, from Nature and from God' (in furious excitement). 'Yes, yes, if you call it behaviour, they've behaved like swine. . . . Everybody has abandoned me, and that is why I adopt the motto that I've invented tonight, the words of which are "A foul death to the whole universe".'*

Humming this refrain he walked a considerable distance further, and when night had fallen found himself on the heights of San Bernardino that look over towards Valle-hermoso. From here he gazed back at the shapeless masses of the houses of Madrid, with their crown of towers and domes, and the swarming lights in the darkness of the buildings. His murderously destructive excitement had died down, and the poor man now resumed his topographical researches. . . . 'Now this is a first-class place. . . . But no, the excise officers who are in those huts might see me, and perhaps . . . they're very stupid . . . they would prevent me from doing what I wish to and what I must do. Let's go on to the Patriarchal cemetery. There'll be no busybodies there to poke their long noses into what doesn't concern them. Because I want the world to see one thing, that I don't care a straw any more whether they balance the budget, and that I don't give a damn for the income tax or for the whole filthy Administration. They'll realize that when they pick up my . . . remains; and it's all one to me if they put them on a dungheap or in the royal Pantheon itself. All that matters is the soul, which goes flying up to what they call the . . . empyrean, which is somewhere up there, beyond those stars that shine and seem to wink at one, as if in invitation. But it's not time yet. I shall go back into that swine of a city, and blackguard those beastly Miaus who have made my life such a misery.'

Hatred for his family, which had sprung up in his mind in recent days and was now gradually assuming the proportions of a wild frenzy or violent madness, now broke out in full strength. He clenched his fists, gnashed his teeth, and hurried on faster with his hat on the back of his head and his cloak dragging behind him. His appearance was altogether wild and sinister. The night was now black. He marched resolutely towards the Calle del Conde Duque, passed the barracks, and, as he approached the Plaza de las Comendadoras, began to walk cautiously, keeping out of sight and in the shadows and changing direction every moment. Having started down the deserted Calle de San Her-

* Again in Spanish the initial letters make MIAU.

mengildo, he turned back towards the Plazuela del Limón, walked round the block of the Comendadoras, and finally took the risk of crossing the Calle de Quiñones and looking up at the balconies of his house, not without previously making certain that Mendizábal and his wife were not in the doorway. Crouching in the corner of the dark square, which was silent and deserted, he glanced repeatedly at the house, watching to see if anyone came in or went out. Would the Miaus go to the theatre that night? Would Ponce and their other friends pay them their evening visit? In the midst of his rambling, he was able to return to reality and finally accepted the inevitable certainty that Pura would be alarmed by her husband's absence and set all the friends of the family in motion to look for him.

From the shelter of his corner, Villaamil craned his neck like a thief or an assassin to watch without being seen. In fact his body was in the Plazuela de las Comendadoras and his head in the Calle de Quiñones; his flaccid neck, endowed with prodigious elasticity, actually bent round the angle. 'Here's the excellent Ponce in all haste. They must have been to Pantoja's, to the café and to all the places I usually frequent. The one who has just arrived puffing and blowing looks to me like Federico Ruiz. No doubt he's come from the police station or from the coroner's court. He will have gone there to inquire. Poor creatures, what a lot of trouble they're taking. And what a lot of pleasure it gives me to see them so busy, and to think how perturbed the Miaus must be . . . Let them worry themselves to death; and you, Doña Pura from the pit, now you can swallow the hemlock. I've been swallowing it for thirty years without complaint . . . Oh, someone's coming out and making in this direction. Looks as if it's Ponce again. Better crouch in this doorway. Yes, it's he' (seeing the critic cross the Plazuela de las Comendadoras). 'Where will he be going? Perhaps to Cabrera's. I'm giving you some work. Was there ever a fool like him? No, you won't find me. You won't catch me, you won't rob me of this blessed liberty I'm enjoying at last. Blessed liberty! You'll never strike my trail, idiots, even if you turn the whole world upside down. What do they think?' (shaking his fist at an invisible being). 'That I shall return into the clutches of Pura and

276

Milagros so that they can make my life a misery with their perpetual begging for money, with their mismanagement, their silly talk and their pretentiousness? No, I'm fed up with them. The cup is full. If I were to go on living with them, one day I should go mad, and with this revolver . . . with this revolver' (finding the butt of his revolver inside his pocket and grasping it fiercely) 'I'd finish them all off. Better finish myself off, free myself for ever and disappear. Ah, Pura, my dear Pura, my punishment is over. Stick your claws into another victim. You've got Ponce there with his new money, gorge yourself on him. It won't hurt me. It'll make me laugh a lot. Because this Doña Pura, my dear Ponce, is a dreadful woman, and when she's got money in her pocket she spends it wholesale. Food and clothes and everything else have to be of the best and she doesn't give a thought that there won't be a note in her purse next day. Oh God, God, at those moments I've envied the humblest workman, the saddest beggar in the streets. But today, free and with the rope off my neck, I wouldn't change places with the king. No, I wouldn't change places with anybody, and I say this with all my heart.'

43

EMERGING from the doorway, he resumed his spying. 'Now young Cuevas is coming out, in a great hurry and bother. Where will he be going? Look for him, my boy, look for him and Doña Pura will reward you with a glass of muscatel. That idiotic Milagros will be on tenterhooks because the poor creature's fond of me. . . . It's natural. She's lived with us all these years and eaten my bread. And if we're to be absolutely fair Pura is fond of me too. . . . In her own way, of course. I was very fond of them also. But as things are now, I loathe the pair of them. But why did I say the pair? The three of them, for my daughter is a burden on me too. They're three dead weights that have settled themselves here in the pit of my stomach, and when I think of them my blood seems to turn to molten metal and the top of my brain to be on the point of blowing off. To hell with the three Miaus! Good luck to the man who invented that nickname for you! Not to live with crazy women any more. And what the hell came over my confounded daughter? That she should take a fancy to Victor! It was a crazy sort of fancy if I'm not much mistaken. God in heaven, what a set of women! To fall for a swindler because he's got a handsome face, without thinking . . . and he despises her, not a doubt of it. I'm very glad. . . . It serves her right. Swallow your snubs, idiot, and come back for more, and then marry Ponce. Really if one didn't put an end to oneself to get out of one's miseries one would have to do it so as not to see such things any more.'

When he saw a light in the study he grew more excited: 'Tonight, darling Pura, delight of my heart, there's nothing on at the theatre, is there? So, thank God, you have to stay at home. I can see you now contriving where to get the money for the mourning. Much I care! Get it for yourself . . . from anywhere you like. Sell my skin for a drum or my bones for buttons. Magnificent, admirable, del-i-ci-ous!'

As he spoke he saw Mendizábal in the doorway, and unfortunately Mendizábal saw him too. Great was the old man's alarm and perturbation on noticing that the scribe was watching him suspiciously. 'That creature has recognized me and will come after me,' thought Villaamil, hugging the wall of the Comendadoras as he slipped away. Before turning the corner he looked round, and in fact Mendizábal was following him step for step, like a hunter stalking his prey and taking care not to startle it. As soon as he was out of the square, Villaamil gathered up his cloak and started running in terror as fast as he could. He seemed to hear the steps of his pursuer. He expected an enormous arm to reach out for him and seize him by the back of the neck. The poor man had an unhappy moment. Luckily there was no one about in those streets. Because if anyone had been passing and it had occurred to Mendizábal to shout 'After him!' the good suspended official's precious liberty would immediately have been at an end. He fled with incredible speed across the Plazuela del Limón; and passed in front of the barracks, in fear that the guard might arrest him. As he went down the Calle del Conde-Duque, he looked back and saw that though Mendizábal was following him he had dropped far behind. Without pausing for breath he made for the deserted terrace and before his pursuer could catch sight of him hid behind a pile of paving-stones. Removing his hat and sticking his head out very cautiously through a gap in the stones, he saw that the monkey-man had lost the scent. He was looking to right and left, and particularly in the direction of the Paseo de Areneros, along which he believed his prey had got away. 'So you'd like to catch me, would you, you great obscurantist? But you won't succeed. I'm sharper than you, you ugly monster. As ugly as sin and more bigoted than Judas. I've always been a Liberal, as you know very well, and I'd rather die than support despotism. Go to the devil, you great reactionary, because you'll never get your chains round me. I spit on your absolutism and your inquisition. Go and burst with spleen, you horrible creature, you Carlist liberticide, because I'm free. I'm a Liberal and a democrat, and an anarchist and an incendiary, and I shall do what I damned well like . . .'

Although he had lost sight of the ugly gorilla he was still worried. Knowing the Herculean strength of their porter, he knew that once he laid his paws on him it wouldn't be easy to shake him off. So to avoid meeting him he crouched down, seeking the shadow and protection of the stone blocks or heaps of paving-stones which were spaced along the terrace. Protected by the thick darkness, he caught sight of the scribe once more. He was apparently going home, having lost hope of finding him. 'Goodbye, you owl, paid assassin of fanaticism and oppressor of the people. Look at it now! What a mug, what arms and what a body! It's a blessed wonder you don't go on all fours. Tire yourself out looking for me, and make yourself important with Doña Pura by telling her you've seen me. Idler, clerical, savage, may the devils carry you to hell!'

Once he thought himself safe he turned down into the streets again, always with the suspicion that Mendizábal was pursuing him, and glancing to either side at every step. He expected him to come out of every doorway or to be crouching at every dark corner waiting to fall on him with the spring of a monkey and the courage of a lion. As he turned the corner of the Callejón del Cristo to go into the Calle de Amaniel, there all of a sudden was Mendizábal talking to some women. Fortunately the scribe had his back to him and could not see him. But, finding himself cornered, Villaamil was suddenly inspired to enter the first door he came to. He found himself in a wine bar. To justify his abrupt entrance, after his first moment of surprise he went up to the counter and ordered a sweet wine. Whilst he was being served he inspected the clientèle; two sergeants, three peasants in short jackets and four very low-class tarts. 'What pretty girls!' he reflected, looking at them as he drank, over the rim of his glass, 'and smart too! Blowed if I don't feel like paying them a compliment, I who haven't so much as said one flattering word to any other woman since I led Pura to the altar. But now that I'm free I seem to be rejuvenating. My youth seems to be returning. Well now! And a feeling of happiness is dancing all over my body. Strange that a man can spend thirty years without a thought for any woman except his wife. Fancy now! And I also feel an urge to drink another glass of wine. Thirty years of virtue excuse a man's shaking a loose leg occasionally now.' (To the barkeeper) 'Give me another glass. Those little girls are very much to my taste, and if it wasn't for those loungers who are making up to them, I'd say a couple of words to them that would make them see the difference between dealing with gentlemen and going about with oafs and common soldiers . . . I should like to strike up a conversation with them, if only to give Mendizábal time to disappear. Oh God, free me from that savage Ultramontane and agitator! But, I do like those girls, especially the one with the high top-knot and the red shawl. She's looking at me too, and . . . Oho, Ramón, these adventures are dangerous! Calm down, and have another glass to spin out the time. Another, friend . . .'

The party went out, and Villaamil, making an inspired and hasty calculation, said to himself: 'I'll go out with them, and then if that scarecrow's still about I'll slip away behind those young men and their ladies.' He did so, going out close behind the girls, who seemed the real thing to him, and the soldiers. Mendizábal was no longer in the street, but Don Ramón was still afraid and followed the little crowd, keeping as close to them as he could, and reflecting: 'In the last resort, if the orang-utan attacks me these brave soldiers will probably spring to my defence. All is well, Ramón, don't be frightened. No one will take away your sacred liberty now, liberty, the daughter of heaven.'

As he came to the Capuchinas he saw the happy band disappearing up the Calle de Juan de Dios. He heard the giggling of the shameless girls and the loud-mouthed oaths of the soldiers. Looking sadly and enviously after them, he said, 'Oh happy age of freedom and devil-may-care! May God prolong it for you. Commit all the follies that come into your heads, young people, sin as much as you can, and laugh at the world and its duties before black care overtakes you and you fall into a horrible servitude to your daily bread and social status.'

With these words all his accessory and incidental ideas vanished, leaving in sole and complete possession his overriding idea, the governing factor in his unhappy psychological state. 'It must be getting late, Ramón. Hurry up and put an end to yourself. It's God's will.' He now went on to remember Luis, to whom he was very close, for the old man had come into the Calle de los Reyes. He stopped in front of Cabrera's house and, looking up at the second floor, spoke these words into the collar of his cloak: 'Little Luis, my child, you the purest and noblest of the family, worthy son of your mother whom I'm going to see very soon, how are you feeling with those people? Do you find the house strange? Don't worry, for you'll soon get used to them. They're good people and good managers. They don't spend much, they'll bring you up well and they'll make a man of you. Remember me, I love you so much, and I almost feel like praying to you, because you're on the way to being a saint, and one day they'll canonize you. I can almost see it now. Your innocent lips confirmed what had been revealed to me long ago. I still doubted, but when I heard you speak I doubted no longer. Good-bye, God's own child, your old grandfather blesses you . . . or rather he should say begs for your blessing. For you are a little saint, and the day you sing mass, you'll see, you'll see what joy there'll be in heaven . . . and on earth. Good-bye, I'm in a hurry. Sleep well; if you're unlucky and someone takes away your liberty, do you know what to do? Clear out . . . there are plenty of ways . . . and you know where you can find me . . . Yours always.'

When he spoke these last words he was strolling peaceably towards the Plaza de San Marcial like a man coming home unhurried after concluding the duties of the day. He found himself once more on the slopes of the Montaña where he was out of range of the street lamps, and where the unevenness of the ground exposed him to the danger of a premature fall. Finally he stopped on the edge of a recently piled embankment, on the shifting slopes of which no one could venture without sinking to the knees, not to mention the danger of rolling to the bottom which was out of sight. As he stopped he was struck by one of his depressing thoughts, the fruit of his habit of seeing the worst and making the most pessimistic calculations: 'Now that I'm coming near to the end of my slavery and to my entrance into Eternal Glory, my confounded fate will play me another trick, I'm sure. What'll happen is' (taking out his revolver) 'that this confounded thing will fail . . . and I shall be left alive or half dead, which is the worst thing that can happen to me, because they'll pick me up and take me back to the confounded Miaus. I'm so unlucky! This thing I'm afraid of will happen . . . I can see it now . . . I've only got to want a thing for the opposite to take place . . . I want to put an end to myself. Then my swine of a fate will arrange for me to go on living.'

But the logical method which had brought him such good results throughout his life, that system of imagining the reverse of what he wanted in order that what he wanted should occur, inspired these thoughts: 'I'll imagine that the damned shot misses, and if I imagine it thoroughly, by a persistent effort of the mind, the bullet will strike true. Always the opposite. So off we go . . . I imagine that I shan't die, but they'll take me home. Oh Lord! Pura and Milagros and my daughter again, with their stupid visits to the theatre, and penury, and constant begging . . . back to pretentiousness and pestering our friends. I can see it before my eyes. This swine of a revolver's no good. Did that wretched gunsmith in the Calle de Alcalá cheat me? . . . Let's try it, now . . . but of course it won't finish me off . . . only . . . in any case I commit myself to God and to San Luisito Cadalso, my darling little saint . . . and . . . No, no, this thing's no good . . . I bet the shot fails. Oh, horrible Miaus, how you'll laugh at me! Now, now . . . of course it won't go off.'

The shot echoed in the solitude of that dark and deserted place. Villaamil gave a terrible leap, his head plunged into the shifting earth, and he rolled straight down into the gulf. He retained consciousness only for enough time to say : 'Well . . . it did . . .'

Madrid, April 1888

*Some other books published by Penguins
are described on the
following pages*

DON QUIXOTE

Cervantes

For English readers, *Don Quixote* is by far the best-known representative of Spanish literature. Cervantes (1547–1615) originally intended his work as a skit on the traditional popular ballad, but in the many adventures of Don Quixote and his faithful squire, Sancho Panza, he also parodies the romances of chivalry. The result is a detailed picture of Spanish life on all levels, including an account of the expulsion of the Moriscos by Philip III.

J. M. Cohen, whose predecessors in this task have been, among others, Shelton, Motteux, Jarvis, and Smollett, here achieves a lively, vigorous, and contemporary translation.

THE PENGUIN CLASSICS

The Most Recent Volumes